D1602433

SURLY

BONDS

What people are saying about

Michael Byars Lewis'

Award-Winning Thriller *SURLY BONDS*:

"The Bottom Line: Guaranteed to please Brad Thor fans…"

- Bestthrillers.com

"An unforgettable debut…non-stop action
and intrigue from start to finish."

*- Gary Westfal, author of the Amazon.com
#1 Best Seller, DREAM OPERATIVE*

"If you like mysteries and thrillers akin to works by Vince Flynn
and John Grisham, read SURLY BONDS."

*- Dennis Barnett, Editor-in-Chief,
Air Commando Journal*

"A page turner to the end. Hats off Mr. Lewis for a job well done!
If you like thrillers, you will love Surly Bonds!"

- John Mese, Award-Winning Writer/Actor/Director/Producer

"…a suspenseful and well-crafted thriller that delivers…"

- Jack Mangus, Readers' Favorites

Awards won by SURLY BONDS

2014 Beverly Hills Book Awards

Winner – Military Fiction Category

2013 Next Generation Indie Book Awards

Finalist – First Novel over 80,000 Words Category

2013 Readers' Favorite Book Awards

Bronze Medal Winner – Fiction/Intrigue Category

By Michael Byars Lewis

SURLY BONDS

VEIL OF DECEPTION

SATCOM PUBLISHING

MICHAEL BYARS LEWIS

SURLY

BONDS

First Printing: December 2012

Revised: June 2015

SATCOM Publishing

John Briggs, Editor

ISBN: 978-0615663951

Cover Design by Damonza

Interior artwork by Michael Byars Lewis

Printed in the United States of America

To Scott and Scott, thanks for getting me through . . .

To my mom and dad, who always believed in me . . .

To my brother, who encouraged me . . .

To my lovely wife and children, without you, I would be lost.

SURLY BONDS

PROLOGUE

June 16, 1995

Sport coat in hand, Dr. David Edwards stepped out of The Void, grinning as he shook his head. Not a striking man, his five-feet nine inches sported a full head of hair, making him look years younger than forty-five. Slightly overweight for a man his age, his tailored clothes hid this physical imperfection. His most notable feature, and perhaps his most valuable asset, was his smile. A smile that told the world he knew something they did not.

As he passed the front window, he stopped to wave to her one last time.

"She looks kind of hot," a male voice said from behind him.

"What?" he replied, startled at the strange voice.

"Are they real?"

Edwards turned, his brow furrowed. "Can I help you?"

"Are they real? You'd know, right Dr. Edwards?"

He glared at the obnoxious young man standing next to him. Edwards had walked into the bar two hours earlier. The afternoon he spent with his lawyer lasted early into the evening, and he desperately needed a Scotch. One of Los Angeles' more prominent plastic surgeons, Edwards started frequenting establishments like The Void four years earlier following a nasty divorce.

The Void sat in the middle of Sunset Boulevard in downtown Hollywood. Like most restaurants in the area, it served a variety of customers. Tall windows trimmed with brass and a wooden bar with inlaid marble accentuated the interior. Coffee tables throughout the room and a small stage in the back catered to a counterculture living on the fringe of society. Dim lighting gave each table the illusion of privacy, but the alternative music reminded the customers in which town they were partying. Discretion was not an option at The Void.

He had sat at the end of the bar furthest from the entrance, surveying the clientele. Several others sat at the bar, none of whom he considered carrying on a conversation. Smoke wafted in his direction when an older woman sat next to him, her cigarette held loosely in her long wrinkled fingers. She and her partner were talking incessantly, chain-smoking between sentences.

Lost in his thoughts, Edwards lifted his glass to his lips, wiping the condensation from his glass off the marble bar top.

The restaurant filled up quickly. The smoke at the bar grew thicker as another couple replaced the chain-smoking pair that sat next to him earlier. One of them, apparently a struggling actor, had made his first commercial that morning and was now celebrating his new career. It was a tough town and a tougher career. For every lost soul who made his or her first commercial, there were a thousand out there who never found out where to start. Edwards decided it was time to leave.

Until he saw her.

A show-stopper. Period.

A beautiful woman no older than twenty-two, she wore a lime-green mini-dress; skintight all the way up to the spaghetti straps that disappeared under her long blond hair. The dress strained tautly across her pert breasts. They were real enough. He should know. Her long legs descended to slender feet fitted into lemon-yellow pumps that matched her hoop earrings. A little gaudy, but in Hollywood, who cares? Besides, it matched her personality. Her age, to him, was irrelevant. She represented something he no longer had. Youth.

All heads turned, following her through the restaurant. She moved around as if she knew everyone. After another five minutes of flirting throughout the restaurant, she stood at the end of the bar next to him, talking to the bartender.

"Would you care to sit down?" he said, offering her his seat.

"Thanks," she said. She climbed onto the stool and turned back to the bartender.

After several minutes the bartender moved to the other end of the bar and Edwards leaned over. "Can I get you a drink?" he said.

She glanced at him briefly. "Sure," she replied and continued looking around the bar.

Edwards waved the bartender back over and pointed to the blonde.

"Manhattan," she said.

"I'll have another scotch," Edwards said. He pulled out a roll of hundred dollar bills to pay for the drinks and her eyes grew wide as edges of her mouth curved slightly upward.

"Are you in the business?" she said. The "business" is Hollywood code for the movie industry.

"Sort of."

"What do you mean 'sort of?'"

"I'm a doctor. A plastic surgeon."

She tossed her head back and laughed. "Yeah, I guess you're sort of in the business." Her eyes narrowed as she paused and tilted her head. Her tongue wet the hot pink lipstick covering her upper lip and she stuck out her hand. "I'm Nikki."

Edwards shook her hand. "I'm David." Typical. He could spot one a mile away.

She took a sip of her drink then bit her lower lip. "Okay, if you're a plastic surgeon, let me ask you something."

"Okay," he said setting his drink on the bar and turning to face her.

Nikki turned on her stool to face him. "What would you do to make these better?" She sat upright and pulled her shoulders back, her breasts sticking out majestically.

Edwards glanced down briefly and his eyes locked on hers.

"Not a thing," he said with a confident grin. "You're absolutely perfect."

Her eyes grew wide and her cheeks flushed. She reached over and slapped his forearm.

"That's a great line," she said with a big smile.

"Trust me. I'm a professional."

They scooted closer together and Edwards was confident he knew the outcome. The later it got, the more the lights dimmed and the volume of the music increased. At some point during his chat with Nikki, the background music stopped and a guitar player took the stage in the back. A regular in The Void, he was popular with the crowd, but Edwards barely noticed. He wasn't paying attention to anything besides Nikki.

Two more drinks, followed by an exaggerated version of his life greatly embellished by Scotch, and she was hooked. He made promises of elegant dinners and weekends on his sailboat; she made promises of evenings in his hot tub. They flirted for a while longer then made plans for a rendezvous next week. Edwards collected her phone number, paid his bill, and left.

Outside, staring at her through the window, he was still captivated. But now his focus shifted from Nikki to the man who approached him outside the bar. He sized up the man. Vaguely familiar, he was young, early to mid-twenties. The man dressed in a black, oversized hockey jersey. Blue jeans, too big and too long, dragged beneath his Reeboks. He wore an Anaheim Ducks ball cap backwards on his head.

"I thought I recognized you," the young man said. "I wanted to say hello." As the young man started to walk off, he said over his shoulder, "By the way, you do good work."

Edwards' eyes followed him as he rounded the corner. He felt like he knew him from somewhere . . .

Unable to place him, however, he dismissed him for more important matters. He turned back to the window and waved to Nikki. She waved back enthusiastically, her tight frame bouncing in the formfitting dress. Customers around her looked out the window to see who caught this young vixen's attention. The doctor lingered for a moment, then walked toward the parking lot, his grin wider.

As he rounded the corner, Edwards left the bright lights of Sunset Boulevard. The street lay dark and the overcast evening sky blocked out any moonlight. Despite the mantra that it never rains in L.A., the weatherman had forecast rain showers for earlier this afternoon. He missed his mark by several hours.

Edwards noticed the lamppost overhead had been broken, the shards of glass crackling under his feet. Damn punks. You'd think this type of vandalism wouldn't exist in this section of Los Angeles. The cops must be busy elsewhere. Perhaps some producer beat up his girlfriend and every cop in L.A. is keeping the paparazzi away from his mansion.

A cool breeze started to pick up on the quiet street; the air felt moist. It's going to rain any second now. The streets were deserted. There weren't even any hookers out. He figured the ones who hadn't picked up their Johns for the night headed for shelter or more suitable working conditions. Several drops of rain hit his Italian-made sport coat, and Edwards started walking faster.

The silence broke with a loud crack. Edwards jumped, then realized he was the source of the noise. More broken glass. He looked up. The lamppost he stood next to was also broken. *Damn kids . . . Oh no, my car! If they've done anything to my car . . .* Scanning the vehicles in the immediate vicinity, none of them appeared to have been vandalized or robbed. Several BMWs, Mercedes, Saabs, Cadillacs, and a Jaguar XJ-6 convertible all untouched. Edwards increased his pace to a jog, his mind spinning between thoughts of the girl and fear for his car.

At the next intersection, Edwards saw his car across the lot through the darkness. Slowing to a walk, his breath came in large gasps. As he ran his hands through the slightly graying hair matted against his head, he grinned. The effects of the Scotch he'd had in The Void made him oblivious to the impending storm as the rain started to drizzle. He didn't care. Nikki . . .

Twenty yards from his Porsche, he pulled out his keys and triggered the alarm. Two loud blips pierced the increasing rhythm of the rain, and the parking lights flashed as his car alarm deactivated. The rain fell heavier now, and he picked up his pace to a brisk walk. He approached his car from the front, failing to see the silent figure move in behind him.

The assailant grabbed Edwards from behind, gripped his forehead with his left hand and jerked him back. Edwards' arms were free, struggling to loosen the grip holding his head. Flailing helplessly, his strong attacker had no difficulty sending Edwards off-balance. He saw a screwdriver in the attacker's right hand. He struggled in vain, franticly attempting to free himself. Unable to do so, frustration and fear rapidly took over his thought process. Edwards felt the tip of the screwdriver against his flesh where the skull joins the vertebrae. Visions of this nightmare raced through his consciousness as the dull tip pushed its way through his skin at the base of his skull. Edwards screamed as his face twisted in pain. The screams went unheard.

WITHOUT PAUSE, THE ATTACKER thrust the thin metal tool through the base of Edwards' neck into his brain. The screwdriver pierced the outside layer of brain tissue. A few quick rotations of the crude weapon and it was done. Death came quickly. Edwards' body went limp as the killer let it fall to the ground. Blood trickled out of the small but fatal wound in the back of Edwards' skull, mixing on the ground with rainwater and washing away in seconds. The killer briefly stared at the lifeless form on the ground before him. Kneeling next to his victim, he dropped the screwdriver by the body, deftly removing the wallet and watch.

"I do good work, too," he said as he stood up, turned, and walked away, his job here complete. He had a plane to catch.

CHAPTER 1

August 10, 1995

J ASON CONRAD SAT NERVOUSLY in the second row waiting for class to start. Typically, seats in the rear filled up first, forcing the latecomers to sit up front. He didn't mind. He made it a habit while attending the University of Florida, of sitting in the front of class. It showed the instructors that he was interested in what they had to say, and it exposed him to fewer distractions. The habit followed him to pilot training at Vance Air Force Base.

Vance AFB sat just south of Enid, a small town in Northwest Oklahoma with a population around 40,000. Originally named the Enid Army Flying School just prior to the Japanese bombing Pearl Harbor in 1941, the name changed to Enid AFB in 1948 with the creation of the United States Air Force. In 1949, it was renamed after Medal of Honor winner Lieutenant Colonel Leon Robert Vance, Jr. Over the next several decades, Vance AFB had become an integral part of the community, and Jason Conrad found himself following the path of thousands of pilot hopefuls before him.

The stack of books sat neatly in front of him on the edge of the desk, his notebook open. Tapping his pencil on the notebook, Jason shifted uncomfortably in his seat. The olive green flight suit fit him a bit too snuggly. He flipped open his workbook and skimmed through it. His eyes wandered from the book, darting around the room from side to side, observing his classmates. A small percentage of the Armed Forces had the opportunity to attend pilot training, and he felt fortunate. In an era of cutbacks and reduced funding, his timing was perfect.

Jason looked at the variety of people in the room. It was a strange mix of Air Force and Navy student pilots, a result of the consolidation of military training. To an outsider, they would appear as a room full of clones wearing olive drab flight suits, but to the insider, every person was unique, with his own ability, his own past, and his own secrets. At twenty-seven, he was older than the average second lieutenant student pilot, meaning he probably had more secrets than the rest of them.

The room was about twenty by thirty feet with an elevated platform at the far end. On the platform stood a wooden podium and a metal pushcart that contained a television and VCR. A four-paneled dry-erase board covered the wall beyond the platform. It was arranged so that the panels could be slid to the side and a slide projector used from behind the screen.

This class had him worried. He was not an engineer and had struggled acquiring his private pilot's license. That was the temp fix the Air Force used, having closed down their flight screening program at Hondo, Texas. The course at Hondo usually ran about two and a half weeks. It was designed to eliminate weak candidates and it did. The Air Force had altered the course over the years. Several years ago, they had brought the new T-3 online to replace the aging T-41, the Air Force version of a Cessna 172. The T-3 had its own faults. In its short time as an operational trainer aircraft, it had six more fatalities than its predecessor.

Jason found himself struggling in Undergraduate Pilot Training (UPT). Aircraft Systems class had been hard enough for him. The only hydraulics he knew about were X-rated videos he had occasionally seen in college. AC and DC weren't electrical currents—they were an old, heavy metal rock band. The course on weather was a challenge, too.

"ROOM TENCH HUT!"

A few chairs fell to the floor as the students snapped to attention. Jason, caught by surprise, bolted up in his seat. His legs hit the front edge of his desk, sending his books flying off the other side. The large black notebooks containing his flight publications fell with a dull thud to the carpeted floor.

A short, stocky captain made his way along the off-white wall adorned with pictures of various aircraft. When he reached the front, the class's Senior Ranking Officer (SRO), Captain Gus McTaggart saluted sharply. "Sir, all students present and/or accounted for," McTaggart said. A tall, lean fellow, McTaggart had flown in the backseat of the F-15 Strike Eagle as a Weapons Systems Officer. Captain McTaggart was one of the few officers allowed to crossover to pilot training.

The instructor returned the salute in a slow, methodical manner, pausing his hand at the outer edge of his black, horn-rimmed glasses that rested lazily on the bridge of his flat nose. This guy is straight out of a 1950's training film. His freshly cropped flattop haircut and menacing scowl suggested the next forty-five minutes were not going to be fun.

"Take your seats," he said. "I'm Captain Ralph Harrison. Welcome to Aerodynamics for Pilots." The instructor walked over to the chalkboard and began writing. Jason took this opportunity to quickly recover his books from the floor. Most of the students watched him for a moment, then realized they should start writing or they might not catch up with the instructor's furious pace. Jason recognized the first formula, the equation of lift, from his private pilot's license course.

Harrison broke down each segment of the formula and wrote out multiple equations explaining lift, air density, and velocity in excruciating detail. After what seemed like an eternity of writing equations on the board, Captain Harrison turned to the class.

"Are there any aero majors in here?" It was the first thing he said since he began writing more than five minutes ago. Samantha Williams, the black female student in the rear of the classroom, shyly raised her hand. A graduate of the Air Force Academy with a degree in Aeronautical Engineering, she was one of the smartest students in the class and had a great attitude about being in pilot training.

"And who are you?" Harrison asked.

"Lieutenant Williams, sir," she said.

"Well, Lieutenant Williams, are these formulas right?"

"Yes, sir, they are," she answered slowly, but deliberately. Samantha appeared uncomfortable with this question-and-answer session.

"And is it not true that in order to understand the theory of lift, one must understand each of the forces that compose the components of lift and how each of the parts affect the whole?" Captain Harrison leaned against his podium at the end of his question, looking smug, as he knew there was only one answer. It was obvious this was his specialty. He went immediately to the students' number one authority to quickly establish the fact that he was right.

"Williams?"

"It's true, sir."

"Thank you." Harrison went back to his writing.

Jesus Christ, Jason thought as he glared at the ceiling. A tough academic instructor was the last thing a student pilot needed in the high-pressure environment of pilot training; the flight-line training was hard enough. The squatty captain continued to write, and the students' frustration was starting to show. Jason's pulse beat faster, and his stomach tightened. He may have recognized the first formula explaining lift, but it had gone downhill ever since. *I'm doomed. I'm totally clueless. I have absolutely no idea what this means, nor do I think I ever will. I'll never finish this program. It's over before I ever got started.*

Laying his pencil down in disgust, he wiped his sweaty palms on his legs. He was defeated without ever having a chance to fly the jet. As he scanned the cramped classroom of twenty students, Jason gained little comfort in the fact that a few others were as lost as he was. Still, some of the hardcore students scribbled away in what appeared to be a losing cause.

Harrison stopped and glared at the class. "Are all of you getting this?" His voice deepened. "Do I need to slow down, or are you all able to keep up?" Various students nodded their heads, yes, while others shook their heads, no. It would have been a comical sight under different circumstances. To the stocky academic instructor, it seemed to add fuel to a raging fire building inside him. Jason watched in disbelief as this nightmare of an instructor seemed to grow into an ominous beast about to unleash his anger on them all. He moved closer to the class, to the edge of the platform, and placed his hands on his hips.

"Do you people think this information is important to you as a pilot?" All heads nodded yes. The students were silent as Captain Harrison's voice increased in volume and tempo. "And do you all agree that this information will be beneficial for you to memorize so well that you can recite it in your sleep?" He was almost yelling now, his face flushed crimson as if he was about to explode. The heads all nodded slowly and a look of doom overcame all of them. What had happened? What did they do to set this guy off? Jason's heart sank. *I can't believe it's going to be over so fast. I worked so damned hard to get here.*

"Take a good look at this board people . . . a good, hard look. Some of you will never see this information again," Harrison said loudly as he ripped off his glasses and threw them at the dry-erase board. The glasses crashed against the board and fell to the floor. No one uttered a sound. You could hear a pin drop. He stared at the class for a moment, letting his words sink into their psyche. The hopelessness despair was evident on everyone's face.

He singled out a man in the front row. "Lieutenant Bailey, what is the name of this course?"

Bud Bailey's glasses and flattop almost matched the instructor's. "A-Aerodynamics . . . for Pilots." He tagged on at the end after glimpsing the cover of his textbook.

"That's right." Harrison's voice was calmer now. He settled back, leaning against his podium again. "Aerodynamics for Pilots. Gentlemen and ladies, I am a pilot. I am not an engineer, nor a scientist. I am a pilot. I fly jets. Therefore, I don't give a hoot 'n' holler about these damn formulas on the board here."

A big smile came across his face. "Hell, I was a business major in college. I couldn't tell you what half this stuff means." Initially the students exchanged puzzled glances. A big sigh of relief overcame everyone as the students began exploding into laughter, realizing they had been the victims of a cruel but harmless practical joke.

"Folks, this is Aerodynamics for Pilots. Sure, we'll talk about lift a little, as well as a few other things, but the concepts in this course are simple. Push the stick forward, houses get big. Pull the stick back, houses get small. It doesn't get much tougher than that." Captain Ralph Harrison was beaming now. He had the look of someone who had just pulled off the con of the century, and for several minutes, he had. He gave an overview of the course, how long it would last, what the test would be like, and what they would be covering for the rest of the day.

Jason's nervousness slipped away. He felt like an inmate reprieved on his walk to the chair. With a quick glance at the ceiling again, he mumbled, "Thank you, God."

THE CLASS HAD GONE SMOOTHLY, and returning to his room, Jason placed his books on his desk and collapsed on his sofa. Pilot training was taking its toll on him. He had been successful at everything he'd ever done and usually made it look easy. This time was different. It was a new and unusual environment. The best description he could come up with was that this course compared to taking a sip of water from a fire hydrant.

UPT lasted fifty-two weeks. One full year of pure concentrated studying and flying. They told the students that the course was designed to pull any pedestrian off the street and turn them into a jet pilot. While this was true to some degree, the difficulty seemed to be accomplishing the task within the required timeframe.

The first part of the program was loaded heavily with the basic academics that would be used throughout the course. Then the students were quickly sent to the flight line to fly the initial jet trainer, the T-37. This phase lasted around six months. If the student successfully completed the T-37 phase, he was sent on to the T-38, the advanced jet trainer for the fighter/bomber track, or the T-1, which was a military version of the Beech-jet for that tanker/transport track.

UPT was an interesting place. The majority of student pilots came here with aspirations of being the next Tom Cruise. Joe Fighter Jock. Everyone wants a fighter, whether they admit it or not. It probably was the sense of succeeding and doing better than your peers. To get a fighter, you had to finish at the top of the class. You had to be the best, not because only the best could fly a fighter, but because only the best got first pick, and that was where the fighters are.

Jason's flying instructor told him on the first day, "UPT will give you the highest highs and the lowest lows of your life." So far, Jason had experienced primarily the low side of this spectrum. The T-37 phase was a humbling experience. He found out his goals were not going to be as easy as he thought. Everything came hard and fast. There was no room for slackers. Some students did very well in the T-37 phase—usually navigators who were fortunate enough to earn a pilot's slot. They were already exposed to military-style flying, possessed good airmanship, and were not intimidated by the instructors. Those with prior flying experience also did quite well.

The second phase of training was different. Advanced jet training for the fighter track was done in the supersonic jet trainer, the Northrop T-38 Talon. This jet was the great equalizer. All previous experience no longer mattered. It was a different realm. The T-1 was a little more forgiving. A newer jet, it contained the most current avionics and systems. Right now, Jason wondered if he would make it that far.

The clock said it was nine-thirty in the evening. Jason had been studying his Dash One, the T-37 flight manual, since five o'clock that afternoon. He had to get up in another six hours for a 0500 brief time. The early morning show times were the least desirable aspects of UPT. Everybody hated them, instructors and students alike. Jason ran his fingers through his hair as he glared at the ceiling. So much to do, so little time. Survival was the current goal. He was supposed to meet the guys in Lenny Banks' room for a quick study session. Lenny seemed to be a pretty sharp guy, who, more importantly, had some previous flying experience. As Jason contemplated whether to study with his classmates that night, the phone rang.

"Hello?"

"Jason? It's me," a woman's voice said. His skin went cold and his muscles tightened. He glanced at the gold band resting on a small wooden box on top of his dresser. His heart sank, as a wave of depression fell over him.

CHAPTER 2

August 10, 1995

GRITTING HIS TEETH, Jason took a deep breath. "Bethany," he paused, "why are you calling me?" Bethany was Jason's ex-wife. The divorce was six months ago, but he still had feelings for her. It wouldn't bother him as much as it did if she would just leave him alone . . .

"I-I've just been wondering how you're doing," she replied. "I've been thinking about us a lot lately. Wondering where things went wrong."

Things went wrong when she decided to screw some jerk on her parents' couch in the middle of the day.

"And?"

"And . . . and I just feel that maybe if we communicated more in the beginning that this whole thing could have been avoided."

Jason couldn't believe he was having this conversation.

"I just feel so bad. I know I let you down. I just miss you so much, and I've thought about calling you so many times."

"So why didn't you?"

"I was just afraid, I guess. Afraid that you wouldn't want to talk to me. Afraid that I didn't deserve to talk to you. I know I hurt you, and if there was any way to change it, I would. But it's done, and I can't change it. I know I did some things wrong . . . *we* did some things wrong, but if we both tried harder, I think we could make it work."

"Make what work?"

"Us, Jason . . . you, me, our relationship. We could still make it work."

Jason considered this comment for a moment. She was the last person he needed to talk to at this time of night. The phone call stirred unsettled emotions that caused his heart to race. He was not sure if he was angry or sad, and that confusion bothered him.

"Bethany, I thought you remarried."

There was silence on the other end of the phone. A curveball she did not expect.

"I don't love him. I'm going to leave him. I want you, Jason. If we . . ."

"Look, it's late, I've got a study group that I'm already late for, and I've got to get up in six hours. It's been nice talking to you," he lied, "but I must go. Good night." Jason slammed the receiver down, his mind spinning in circles. There was no way he could get anything done here. He gathered his books and headed to Lenny Banks' room.

LENNY BANKS HATED TO STUDY. Even more, he hated to study things he already understood. Lenny sat sprawled at his desk, his feet propped up on his bookcase, clicking his mouse through pages on the internet. Lenny had more flying experience than anyone else in the class. His father had a private pilot's license, but wanted his son to be the fabled military aviator he never had the chance to be. Papa Banks made sure his boy took to flying at an early age. Most kids would have died for an opportunity like that, but Lenny's interests lay elsewhere. Yes, he enjoyed flying, but he was much more at home behind a computer.

It was late. The four of them—Jason, Lenny, Vince Andrews, and Matt Carswell— crowded into Lenny's small dorm room. Jason sat on the floor in front of the window, tapping his pencil on his forehead. Matt made his temporary home on Lenny's bed, his notes and flight publications spread out all over it. Vince took up residence in the middle of the floor, stretched out, flipping through the current copy of *Air Force Magazine*.

"Call me crazy, but what the hell do they want for an answer on this hea' question fourteen?" Matt asked. He was a slightly pudgy Georgia cracker, raised in Marietta on the outskirts of Atlanta. A proud Georgia man, he refused to admit publicly that his family had lived at one time across the border in Brewton, Alabama. Matt's dark brown hair was cut into a modified wedge style that resembled the high-and-tight favored by a Marine.

"What is it?" Jason asked.

"They're asking what causes the aircraft to spin."

"Stall and yaw," Jason said. "Remember when Captain Harrison was talking about how we'll spin the jet when we hit the flight line? You raise the nose to bleed off airspeed, then as you start to feel the aircraft buffett and shake—"

"—at the critical angle of attack," Lenny added.

"Yeah, at the critical angle of attack, you feed in some rudder to yaw the aircraft, and off you go."

"Okay then, tell me this—if we use rudder to induce the spin, why do we use the rudder to recover from it?"

"Uh, good question, Matt," Jason said. "Why do we use the rudder on the spin recovery, Vince?"

"Ask Lenny, he knows everything," Vince said, neglecting to look up from his magazine. Vince's dark hair was carefully combed back across his forehead, obviously held in place by mousse or hairspray. His deep gray eyes showed little patience for those around him.

"What's the matter, Mister max-every-test-so-far?" Lenny asked. "Afraid you don't know the answer?"

"I'll know by test time, you computer nerd, and you know it. Isn't that when it counts?" Vince glared at Lenny with contempt, as if the tall skinny one had disturbed his concentration during a complicated task.

"Yeah, in your dreams."

"Gee, boys, thanks for the entertainment, but why don't one of y'all just gimme the answer," Matt said.

"By putting the rudder in," Lenny started to explain, ignoring his angry classmate, "you're throwing the rudder out into the slipstream creating more drag. Remember, Harrison called it the 'barn door effect' because it's like sticking a barn door out into the wind. That, in conjunction with pushing the stick forward, gets more air flowing over the wings to break the stall and get the airplane flying again."

"Hoo-rah," Vince said flipping through the pages of his magazine. "Give that man a beer."

"Speaking of beer," Matt said, "Gus says we might buy a keg over at Chicaros next week for a flight party."

"As long as we finish this test first," added Jason. He was worried about this test, just as he had been about the others.

Lenny turned from his computer. "Hey, I hear there's a waitress working there that is pretty hot!"

"Whoa, man," Matt said. "Her name is Kathy. Major babe, major babe." His slight hint of a Southern accent all but disappeared when he got excited. "I met her when I first got here. I think I'm in love."

"Well, don't get to attached, pal," Lenny said, "'cause once she meets this flyboy, she'll be hooked."

"Yeah, right, you pencil-neck geek. Like she's gonna fall all over your sorry ass," Vince said. "No chance for you. She's more like Comrade

Conradski's type here."

"No thanks," Jason replied, shaking his head at the floor. "A woman is definitely not what I need right now."

"What are you, gay?" Matt asked.

"No, divorced. Six months now."

"Ouch, partner. What happened?"

Jason quickly reviewed his marriage with Bethany. The two of them had met while they were in college. She was a lovely creature with strawberry blond hair and the figure of a model. Bethany quit college to pursue a career making television commercials in Central Florida shortly after they began dating. Like many others, she had hoped to become a film actress somewhere in Florida's ever-increasing film industry. Jason and Bethany continued dating while he went on to graduate with a degree in business. The relationship had been a steamy one, based primarily on heavy physical attraction and plenty of sex. After graduation, she seemed very much at ease with the idea of marriage. After all, it did not appear that her career was going anywhere. Jason had to wait just a little over a year to enter pilot training, so married life didn't seem like such a bad idea. After all, they were in love.

They were married in a small church in South Florida, and Jason got a job working in his uncle's bank in Miami while he waited to be called to active duty. He had considered contacting his father for a job, but thought it best to avoid that situation since they had not seen each other since he was a small child. Perhaps that is where Bethany started to turn. He should have seen the signs from the beginning—her wanting to get a job in a nightclub, and not wanting him to bother her at work. Bethany's drinking increased, and she appeared to become more secretive. Next came the ultimate cop-out: complaining about his future in the Air Force. She said she did not want to compete with his airplanes. *Wonderful,* Jason had thought. *I'm not even at pilot training yet, and the lifestyle is already annoying her.* The affair was inevitable, yet he failed to see it coming.

"Well, she was going to take a couple weeks to drive up to stay at her folks' place in Sarasota, but I had to stay in Miami and work." Jason hated telling this story, but somehow whenever someone asked, he had to let it all out. He figured it was some kind of therapy because it became less painful every time he told it. "Anyway, my boss decides to give me the week off to go up and surprise her, but she ends up surprising me. Caught her screwing some guy on her parents' couch in the middle of the afternoon."

"Man that sucks . Y'all see the crap that guys catch all the time, and the damn chicks act like they never do that stuff." Matt sat back, arms folded and nostrils flaring.

"The worst thing was, she acted as if it was no big deal, like I caught her going through my mail or something. She seemed to think I was supposed to expect something like that. I thought I knew her, but I guess I didn't."

"Do we ever really know the women we fall in love with?" Lenny said. "Do we even know our friends? Everybody has a past, and everybody has his vision of the future and how it should be."

"Ah, this is getting a little deep here, guys. Let's talk about airplanes," Matt said.

"Don't worry, Jason, it'll pass," Lenny said. "You've just got to keep pressing forward, putting one foot in front of the other. Jet training should take your mind off some of this stuff. Take some time, refocus, and then get out there and start dating again. You've got to walk before you can run."

"You're right, Lenny. Thanks."

"Of course, this school is so hard, you might want to start off with baby steps," Matt added. The four future aviators laughed.

"So, where's the wench . . . I mean your ex-wife now?" Lenny said.

"I don't really know. I heard through the grapevine that she married some guy, but I try not to keep track. She keeps calling me here, leaving messages on my machine. She just called before I came over here." Jason closed his book. He knew his work here was done for the night.

"I had a girlfriend do that to me when I was in high school in West Virginia," Vince said.

"I thought you were from Pennsylvania," Lenny said.

"Well, I was. I mean we moved to Pennsylvania from West Virginia."

"Didn't you two go to school together?" Matt asked Lenny and Vince.

"Yeah, at Iowa State. I was a four-year ROTC geek, and Vince came under, the two-year plan."

"Well, at least you admit you're a geek," Vince chimed in. "Lenny never went his last two years anyway. He was always at the ballpark."

"Hey, what's wrong with baseball? It's America's pastime. The greatest game in the history of the world. And if you were a true American, you'd love the game, too."

"Hey, guys," Jason said, "it's late, we've got to get up soon, and I'm beat. I think I'll call it a night. See you tomorrow." Picking up his things, Jason stretched slowly and made a feeble attempt to crack his back.

"Later, dude," Lenny said.

"See you," Matt echoed as Jason left the room.

Vince said nothing. He just continued flipping through his magazine as if he were just passing time. One might wonder how he managed to do so well if he studied like this every day. It was obvious he spent plenty of time at the gym. His five-foot eleven-inch frame held his one hundred eighty-five pounds as solid as a rock. Vince flipped the magazine against the bookcase and sat up. "Well if it's such a great game, why is it making you go broke?"

"I'm not going broke, you jerk. I gamble once in a while, but I've got all my bets covered. There's nothing wrong with that. Like you never bet on anything in your life. You're such a fricking hypocrite, Vince," Lenny said, the tension in his voice obvious.

"Kind of edgy there, aren't you, scarecrow?"

"I'm not edgy . . . and don't call me scarecrow! You asshole, you think you're so damn superior to everyone else. Let's just see how damn well you do on this next test. We'll see what a big shot you are."

Matt closed his books and gathered his papers. "I think I'll call it a night, too," he said. He picked up his things and headed for the door. "And gentlemen, try not to kill each other."

Lenny watched Matt walk out the door, then looked back at Vince, who was staring at him, the anger obvious. Lenny took a deep breath and ran his hands across his short-cut hair. Vince got up from the floor as Lenny left his computer and walked over to the refrigerator. "Y-you want a beer?" he asked.

"What are you doing?" Vince replied, ignoring the question. "What was that all about? Who the hell do you think you are? I don't give a damn about you and your problems, but you'd better watch what you say to people, mister. I mean it."

Vince was starting to get to him. Perspiration formed on his forehead, and he felt himself shaking.

"I-I'm sorry," Lenny said, "I wasn't thinking. I-I'm just having a rough time right now. I'm a . . . a little pre-occupied with other things."

"Well, you had better straighten out, mister. Don't drag me in on your little problems."

"It's just that I'm a little short right now."

"Did you get the test?" Vince asked.

"Yeah, but I'm gonna need more this time."

"How much is more?"

"Two thousand."

CHAPTER 3

August 11, 1995

THE WIND BLEW A STEADY ten knots from the north at a quarter to five in the morning. It would increase to fifteen knots by noon, as the cool mid-seventy-degree temperature would be well into the nineties by then. Vance Air Force Base was known for its rough crosswinds, making landing an aircraft difficult. Trees across the Oklahoma plains leaned to the south due to the constant wind blowing from the north. Darkness enveloped the base as several olive-drab-clothed figures moved hurriedly from the dormitories to the squadron building. The long brick building sat between two hangars on the east side of the flight line. Home to over one hundred instructor pilots and three times as many students. The five-hundred yard walk to the flight line was a daily ritual for most students. There were not many parking spaces since the instructors and married students used those. Most of the students saw it as an inconvenience to drive unless it rained.

Jason Conrad walked out of his room and began his journey to the squadron. He wore the standard-issue flight suit with his boots neatly polished. He carried the brown flight pubs bag issued to all students. In it, he carried the Dash One technical manual for the T-37, local area procedures, flight checklists, jet maneuvers manual, and academic publications. Jason had a busy day ahead of him. He had his second simulator sortie, another class in aerodynamics, and Computer Based Training (CBT) modules to complete. The diverse UPT schedule proved to be one of the biggest challenges for most students. Each student's schedule was different from day to day.

Jason reached the rectangular-shaped building in five minutes. All of the flight instructors were standing closest to the door, angry that the building was still locked. Most of the students stood close, greeting the stragglers walking from the dorm and parking lot. The building custodian unlocked the door as Jason walked up, and the instructors and students who had been waiting piled inside.

The Eighth Flying Training Squadron entrance led to a long hallway flanked by gray lockers, flight rooms, and offices on either side. The hallways were barren. A safety board placed in the middle of the hallway near the snack bar displayed a variety of safety issues. The students quickly removed whatever publications they thought they might need for the morning brief. Placing the rest of their pubs in their lockers, they filed into the flight room.

The instructors didn't waste any time in the hallway and filed into the flight commander's office. They normally showed up twenty minutes before the students did to discuss training procedures and review the morning briefing and administrative items. There were days like today when they wouldn't have enough time to cover everything they needed to. In less than ten minutes, the briefing would start.

Flight rooms reflected the personalities of the instructor pilots. The front of the room consisted of a podium placed in the middle with a dry-erase board on the wall behind it. Walls were covered with pictures and plaques, and one wall had a large picture of the flight patch painted on it. On either side of the room were desks running along the wall where the instructors and students sat. These desks were the most interesting sights in the building. It was a contest among instructors to create the coolest montage for his desk. Each one was different, usually consisting of pictures of various airplanes, patches of different classes and operational units, and photographs of wives or girlfriends. In the back of the room, another large board covered the wall with a large desk in front of it. The flight schedulers worked here. Their task was to coordinate the students' training, ensuring they received timely and consistent training.

Jason sat at his instructor's desk with his in-flight guide, checklist, and a small notebook, watching some of his classmates prepare for the brief. Each one was assigned a specific task to carry out before the briefing started. One looked for the daily operations notes. Another secured the weather briefing. Two more drew a small picture of the traffic pattern, depicting what the winds would do to the aircraft upon landing. As the SRO, Gus acted like a conductor, ensuring all the other students got their morning tasks accomplished.

The duty officer, who was also a student, sat by the door. He answered phones, filed papers, and did whatever else needed doing in the flight room. About two minutes before five, all the instructors filed out of the flight commander's office and headed toward their desks. Each instructor had two students assigned to him. As he reached his desk, his students stood, saluted, and began the morning ritual of questions and answers. Time was short today because everyone ran late. There would be no informal question-and-answer session before the briefing this morning. Jason was relieved. Dead tired from the night before, he didn't feel up to a quiz.

Jason and Matt were both assigned to Captain Mike Rawlings. He seemed a nice enough guy. Most instructors tried to avoid being too much of a buddy. It tended to cloud their judgment in grading situations.

"Room tench-hut," spouted the duty officer as the flight commander and his assistant entered the room. The flight commander, Captain Kevin Johnson, walked up to the podium and faced Gus McTaggart.

"Sir, all students present and accounted for," Gus said, saluting sharply.

Captain Johnson returned the salute. "Take your seats." He glanced at the clock behind the scheduler's desk, then at his watch. The short, trim flight commander had a deep tan, his brown hair showing traces of gray on the sides. "Forty seconds till one minute after," he said for the time hack. Captain Johnson began reading the day's operations notes, a daily information sheet for the squadron. He stopped for a ten-second countdown for a time hack of one minute after five, and continued with the ops notes.

Next, the flight safety officer stood up and discussed flight safety. Following him, the flight standardization and evaluations officer (stan/eval) walked up front. He was the individual responsible for the quality of the training the students received. The stan/eval officer was also known as the one with the "black hat", the "bad" guy. You could see the tension in the students as they shifted uncomfortably in their seats. No one enjoyed this portion. He usually asked a series of questions followed by a situation resulting in an emergency. If the student given the situation applied the wrong procedures, he was sat down for the day to study.

Like most students, Jason hated the stand-up emergency procedures (EP's). Nothing could be more frightening than standing in front of your classmates looking stupid. Nobody wanted to do that. The result? Constant anxiety for the first thirty to forty-five minutes of every day. Once you knew you wouldn't be called, you relaxed. The stan/eval officer asked a number of students questions considered important during this phase of training. Some answered correctly; some did not. As the students sensed the question/answer period coming to an end, most tried to avoid eye contact with the "black hat".

Today was not Jason's day. Given the EP of a catastrophic engine failure right at his go-no-go speed, he thought he would handle it easily. "Go-no-go" is an airspeed calculated to determine at what point the aircraft can abort the takeoff and still stop safely on the runway.

Having defined the problem, Jason attempted to solve it. Operating under the assumption he should take off, Jason elected to do so. Any emergency occurring after this calculated speed, in most cases, would be taken care of in the air after the aircraft was safely climbing away from the ground. The instructor continued to question him about various other items during his emergency, the situation appearing to get worse. After another two minutes, the instructor failed his other engine and told him to sit down. Jason knew what that meant. Life once again sucked.

"Lieutenant Bailey, you can pick up the EP where he left off, change anything you like, or start all over again," the instructor said.

Bud Bailey stood up. "Sir, I'd like to start over."

"Go ahead, Lieutenant Bailey."

"Okay sir, I've got a catastrophic engine failure at my go-no-go speed. I scan all the engines. What do I see?"

"You scan the engines, and you see the same thing as Lieutenant Conrad. Everything is winding down on number two engine."

"Okay, sir." Bailey took a deep breath. "With a catastrophic engine failure at go-no-go speed, I elect to abort the takeoff. I'll do this by applying the procedures for abort. That is, throttles idle, brakes as required. Am I able to stop the aircraft, sir?"

Jason's chin fell toward his chest as he grimaced, staring at the ground, realizing at once the mistake he'd made.

"Yes, you are."

"Okay, sir, once I do that, I'll shut down the engines and emergency ground egress. I'll make sure I get my seat pins in and exit the aircraft on my side. I take my chute and head off at a forty-five degree angle, three hundred feet away, trying to avoid any firetrucks."

"Okay, good job. Have a seat." The instructor went on to explain the emergency in greater detail. Jason tried to pay attention, but he was drained. It was only five-thirty in the morning, and he already wanted to go home. The highest highs and the lowest lows, Rawlings had told him. Why did the lows seem to come more often than the highs?

CHAPTER 4

August 11, 1995

IT HAD BEEN A LONG DAY, but Jason struggled through it, reviewing his Dash One and listening to other students brief and debrief their first ride in the aircraft known as "the dollar ride". Jason decided to take up Matt's offer to go to Chicaros instead of the Officers Club that night. Chicaros sat on the northern outskirts of Enid, on the northwest corner of a T-intersection facing an empty lot and the Enid Speedway. The outside of the building had a dilapidated appearance, a no-frills white structure with a gravel parking lot. Chicaros was a bar for pilots. The walls were lined with pictures of T-37s and T-38s flying in formation, plus snapshots of other kinds of aircraft, all sent to the bar from previous clientele. Plaques from several places hung on the walls amid pictures from Desert Storm and other hotspots.

Lenny, Vince, Jason, and Matt arrived at quarter to six. They drove in Matt's car since he had become a Chicaros regular during his short stay in Enid. Matt pulled into the back where the regulars parked. The four of them struggled to make the transition from bright daylight to the dark interior bar, squinting as they pushed through the small crowd.

"Hey, guys! Matt, the usual?" asked the fellow behind the bar as he placed mugs in the large freezer.

"Hey, bud! Four big beers," Matt said as the he sidled up to the bar.

"Run a tab?"

"Always, buddy," Matt said. "Hey, these are some friends of mine. This is Jason, Vince, and the pale-looking one is Lenny."

"Nice to meet you guys," the bartender said as he disappeared around the L-shaped bar to get their beers.

Jason surveyed the interior. He'd heard stories about Chicaros, but had never been here before now. The bartender brought out four large, thirty-two ounce frosted mugs filled with beer. "Here you go," he said as he lined them up neatly, four in a row, and moved to the other end of the bar to serve someone else.

Matt raised his frosty mug and said, "A toast."

"To what?" Vince said, as the other three raised their glasses.

"To survival," answered Jason, each tapping the others mug with his own.

"I'll second that," Lenny said. Those were the first words he had said since they had entered the bar. He started chugging his beer 'til it started pouring out the sides of his mouth. "Jason, I wouldn't worry about today. It's gonna happen to all of us sooner or later."

"Well, it happened to me today, and I didn't like it," Jason said, taking another drink. "I must be trying too hard . . . I feel like I'm putting too much pressure on myself."

"If that's what you think," Vince said, "then you probably are."

"What I think is, it's time for me to get ripped." Jason took a big swig from his mug.

"Amen, brother," Matt said, and followed suit.

Someone in the bar cranked up the music as Jimmy Buffett's *Changes in Latitudes* blared out of the speakers. Several more customers not belonging to their flight school filtered into the bar and headed for a table in the corner, far away from the pilots.

"I think I'm gonna get homesick," Jason said, "I love Buffett. He reminds me of long walks on the Florida coast as the sun went down—"

Jason's comment was cut short as someone came up behind him and grabbed him in a bear hug, spilling half his beer on the floor. The other three laughed at their helpless friend.

"No homesick momma's boys in my flight, Conrad." Jason recognized the voice of Gus McTaggart. "But if you're dying to get sick," he eased the vise-like grip, "we've got a keg of beer out back that is sure to get you bent over a toilet in no time."

Gus released Jason, setting him on the floor. "Well, I guess I'll go refill my glass since you decided to help me empty it sooner than I anticipated. But just a tad."

"Blow me," Gus said.

"Thanks, but the beer tastes better," Jason said. "Very professional of you to offer, though. Set a fine example for us young troops."

Gus took a draught of his own beer. "Go fill up your mug, you gomer."

Jason saluted mockingly, turned, and made his way through the bar to the back door. The keg sat in the far corner of the patio. Jason eagerly filled up his mug. He was tempted to grab a second and spend the night as a two-fisted drinker. *I need to get a good buzz tonight after the day I had. I've been putting too much stress on myself.* As he turned around, he bumped into someone, spilling some of his beer on his pants.

"AAHHH, this is not my day. God must not want me to drink tonight," he said, wiping the beer off his pants.

"I don't think God had anything to do with this—it was all me. I'm sorry, let me help you with that."

The first thing he noticed after her soft but confident voice was the enticing fragrance of her perfume. It had a sweet, rosy smell with an edge to it, strong but not overpowering, like her voice. But when he looked up at her, he couldn't believe his eyes. She stood about five-foot four, with jet black hair closely cropped in a wedge style and blue eyes that made his knees weak. Her olive skin was enhanced by a black tank top and khaki shorts. She reached forward, wiping his upper thigh with her towel. Jason stood speechless.

"I didn't realize you were behind me. I tend to get in a bit of a hurry when I work." She continued wiping along his thigh never breaking eye contact. "You don't mind if I do this, do you?" she said tongue in cheek.

Jason nodded his head. It should have been immensely uncomfortable, but strangely, it was only somewhat embarrassing. If she continued, he probably would have found it perfectly acceptable, and that bothered him. He had convinced himself he wasn't looking to meet anyone, not matter how she looked. "Look, it's not your fault. Sometimes I'm careless. Please don't feel like it was your fault."

"Oh, okay. Bye."

Somewhat surprised at her response, Jason watched her walk off without another word as he refilled his beer. *She certainly is quick to relinquish blame*, he thought. *I guess chivalry isn't dead, but it is easily ignored.* As he pulled his mug from under the tap, ready to walk away, he felt a tap on his shoulder. He turned around carefully to find two beautiful blue eyes staring at him again.

"That was sweet of you."

"Sweet?"

"Yes, sweet. It was clearly my fault and you did your best not to make me feel guilty. That's pretty rare for a guy these days. Especially a pilot."

"Student pilot. We're not allowed to be arrogant until we actually graduate."

"Well, if it makes you feel any better, you don't appear stressed out."

"Looks can be deceiving, but thanks. My name is Jason Conrad."

"Hi, Jason," said, putting out her hand. "I'm Kathy. Kathy Delgato."

"Hello, Kathy. It's my pleasure." He shook her hand, and for the first time all night, touched someone without spilling a drop of beer.

KATHY LOOKED HIM OVER. This man standing before her was handsome enough. He was a little better than average looking, standing about six feet tall with sandy blond hair. He looked older than most students, which was a red flag for her. *He's probably married, or has a girl back home. Same story every time. Most of them are jerks, but this guy, he's different.*

"Look, I need to get back to work," she said. "Are you going to be here all night?"

"No, if I stay too long, I'll probably do something to embarrass myself. I'm sure I'll leave a little earlier."

"Well, don't be a stranger while you're here."

"I won't. You can count on that."

Kathy turned and walked back inside, stopping to pick up empty beer bottles on the way. Glancing back in his direction, she noticed him still watching her. And he was smiling.

JASON WATCHED HER DISAPPEAR into the dark confines of the bar. He surprised himself with the interest he showed in her. It had been years since he'd noticed another woman, but he could not take his eyes off her. Sure, she was beautiful, but women like that were a dime a dozen around pilots. No, something was different about her. Something that held his attention …

Matt passed her as she walked in, his eyes following her like Jason's did.

"Man, is she a good looking gal or what?" Matt said to his dazed companion.

"She's gorgeous," Jason said, taking a sip of his beer.

"Okay, so good looking was an understatement."

"She seems nice. What do you know about her?"

"That's valuable information in these here parts, my friend. That there is a prime target for many a young buck. Come back at rutting season and you'll have to fight them off two at a time."

"Yeah, you're right. Life's too short to listen to you beat around the bush. Now, what do you know?"

"I think she's from San Antonio." He took a long swallow from his beer. "Heard something about her following some boyfriend from Randolph up here. She used to date an instructor who got an assignment and left her in Enid. Typical story. Right girl chasing wrong guy. Fella dumps her here or something like that. She didn't tell you?"

"I didn't get that far."

"You must be out of practice, partner."

"I am, bozo. Where have you been the last month?"

"I've been inside the bar here," he said. "And I've got the bar tab to prove it."

The two friends walked inside and sat back at the table. Lenny drained his beer and ordered a second before Jason and Matt were in their seats. He was too lazy to walk outside to the keg.

"Where you guys been?" said Lenny, the alcohol taking effect right away. Lenny was just entering the obnoxious state that came right before confrontational.

"Just a little recon action by my friend Conrad here. And he was quite successful, if I do say so myself," Matt said.

"If he's so successful, where's the girl?" Vince said. "Show me the money, Conrad. If you're not going home with her, you lose."

"She's not that type of girl, Vince. She's got class. Enough to avoid you," Matt said.

"Class, huh? Let me tell you something, Conradski . . . they're *all* that type of girl. It just takes the right guy to lead them down the path."

"Vince, you can be such an ass," Matt said. "Give the guy some slack. He's on the rebound."

"Only the strong survive, my friend. If you have a problem playing by the rules, you might want to take up another sport," Vince said as he stood from the table. "Now, if you toads have nothing better to do, watch a master at work."

Vince gave Lenny a sneer over his shoulder as he walked from the table to Kathy standing at the bar.

"Don't look at me for help," Lenny said, "I'm with Matt. I've always thought you were an asshole."

Unshaken, Vince continued to the bar and slid next to the well-tanned figure picking up a heavy order of beers and mixed drinks on her tray. He eyed her wantonly in a manner that would have been considered corny had it not been so rude. Slowly he studied each curved inch of her body. "You know, if I didn't know any better, I'd think I'm in love."

Kathy turned. "Nice try, soldier. That line went out in the '50s."

"Well, I watch a lot of old movies."

"Obviously."

"Look, I know you're busy. I just need to know when you're going to take me to dinner."

"Really? Don't you think I should have your children first?"

Vince smiled at her remark. He liked her. More importantly, in his mind, he wanted her. Admitting defeat, he stuck out his hand. "Hi, I'm Vince Andrews."

Kathy smiled, smug with her victory, and shook his hand. "Kathy."

"Kathy. That's a lovely name. Kathy what?"

"Oh, no, if I tell you, then I've got to tell the next guy, and he'll tell his friends. The next thing you know, all of you will be calling me day and night."

"You sound pretty confident."

"Well, you approached me, remember?"

"So what you're telling me is I shouldn't bother asking for your number?"

Kathy hoisted the tray of drinks off the bar and balanced them on her shoulder. "I think I underestimated you, Vince Andrews. You're not as dumb as I thought," she said walking off to the other side of the restaurant.

Vince smiled as she walked off. She didn't say yes, but she didn't say no either—and with an attitude like hers, she most certainly would have. They would meet again. He was sure of it.

"Everybody hits on Kathy," he heard a voice say. Vince turned to see a girl standing next to him. She stood about five-seven with more than ample breasts and bleach-blond hair. A looker, though Vince thought she could stand to lose fifteen or twenty pounds.

"Just being friendly," Vince said, "like I'm being friendly now. My name is Vince."

"I'm Gwendolyn," she said. "I'm a travel agent downtown. Are you a pilot?"

"Yes, I am," Vince said, not disturbed by his less-than-truthful answer. "Would you like a drink?"

"Sure. How about a Sex on the Beach?" she said with a smile.

Vince got the hint at once, signaling the bartender. "Can I have a Sex on the Beach for the young lady here? Put it on Jason Conrad's tab."

The bartender sifted through the tabs behind the bar. "You don't have a tab open. You want me to start one?"

"Yeah," Vince grinned slyly, pointing to the table where his friends sat.

"And send all those guys a kamikaze on me."

"You got it!" The bartender took off to mix the drinks.

"Hey," Gwendolyn said playfully, punching him in the arm, "you said your name was Vince."

"It is. I'm just playing a joke on my buddy."

"Doesn't sound like a very nice joke to play on a good friend."

Vince shrugged his shoulders at her comment as he handed her the shot glass. It wasn't a nice joke, but they weren't good friends.

CHAPTER 5

August 14, 1995

SAN ANTONIO WAS UNUSUALLY HOT, even for mid-August. By the time the sun reached its highest point in the day, it averaged an excruciating one hundred and one degrees. Because of the heat, Vicki Simpson made a habit of going to work early. Thirty-five with little social life, she could afford to be an early riser. It was worth the effort during such a stifling summer, she thought.

Vicki avoided the traffic and beat the heat, both important factors since the air conditioner in her car didn't work. She secretly hoped someone would steal her 1985 Toyota Corolla. The burnt-orange paint was chipped in several places, and the film shading installed on the windows several years ago to keep out the sun had started to peel. The seams on the seats had burst, and the car maintained the scent of stale cigarette smoke. The floors were littered with empty soda cans, hamburger wrappers, and opened junk mail. Even in this haven for car theft, the thieves still had their standards. The thieves probably thought the Corolla would never make it across the border into Mexico.

Vicki glanced at her watch as she drove through Universal City, a small town outside Randolph Air Force Base, home of Air Education and Training Command. Four minutes after six. As she reached the front gate of the base, the sun began its lazy journey above the horizon to the east. Arriving early made her feel happier. The Monday morning traffic hadn't kicked in yet, but in another hour, the traffic outside the gate would be a nightmare. Vicki waved to the guard as he passed her through the gate.

The long drive down Gate Street, flanked by flags on either side, terminated at the traffic circle in front of the Taj Mahal. The "Taj", as it was affectionately known, is an old water tower built in the early days of the Army Air Corps before World War II. Vicki followed the circular intersection to the right and took the second right turn toward her office in the Air Force Personnel Center (AFPC). Finding a parking spot proved easy and served as another reason to arrive early—it kept her walk to the building short. She wheeled the old Corolla into a front-row spot and climbed out of her car.

Signs of life were beginning to show around the entrance as she reached the door. The door flew open as an older, yet trim officer came walking out.

"Good morning, Colonel Atkinson," she said as the officer passed her. The colonel looked somewhat rushed, yet he paused to hold the door open for Vicki. He placed his flight cap on his head, the shiny silver eagle on the left side glistening in the morning light.

"Good morning, Vicki," he responded. "My, aren't you an early riser? At least this way you beat the heat."

"That's the plan, sir. You have a nice day."

Vicki plodded up the stairs to her office on the second floor. She had worked in this small room for the last two years. Earning her college degree at the age of 32, she was fortunate to land a job as a computer analyst's assistant at Randolph. Due to the continuing military drawdown, she picked up one of the positions recently vacated by someone in uniform. It had been an eye-opening experience. She, like many diehard liberals, had demanded the constant drawdown of the Armed Services in order to reduce government spending. Somehow, Congress decided it was cheaper to pay a civilian twice as much money to do the same job as someone in the military. After being hired for this job, she realized the jobs and the government spending didn't disappear with the uniform. Both were funneled into other government agencies, creating an illusion that too many people were too blind to see.

The office was empty, which she did not mind. Vicki fired up the coffee pot and walked back to her desk. Flipping on her switch at the junction plug on the floor, the room came alive with the bells and whistles of turning on the computer. As a courtesy to her boss, she always downloaded the Pentagon paper, the *Early Bird*, in case it contained any interesting articles involving the military. The computer whirled as Vicki proceeded to shuffle through the papers left on her desk from the previous workday. Too little time, too much to do. She grew accustomed to it, of course. All part of her daily ritual. The loud hiss of the coffeepot got her attention, signaling the coffee had finished brewing and she could start her day. Vicki walked over to pour herself a cup.

How odd, she thought to herself as she took her first sip of the morning.

Something must be wrong with the computer. It made a click-click-click sound indicating it was still searching the hard drive. Vicki sat behind the computer to investigate the problem. *It never takes this long to log on.* She re-booted the computer to attempt again. Click-click-click.

Vicki turned off the computer, then turned it on again. Click-click-click. When she hit the escape button, the screen momentarily came to life, then turned black. Two seconds later, the words ACCESS DENIED appeared on the screen. She re-booted the computer and went through the same process again with the same result. "Uh-oh, this is not good," she said. Vicki worked on the computer for the next forty-five minutes. Several times, she attempted to call the base computer center, but no one answered this early in the morning.

At seven-thirty, she heard the click of the door to the office—her supervisor had arrived. Vicki jumped out of her chair and rushed toward his office. She was halfway there when Major Tom Sinclair walked through the door. He started to speak, but the worried look on her face cut him off.

"Tom, we've got a problem."

THE THERMOMETER SAID NINETY DEGREES, but on the aircraft ramp it easily rose to one hundred ten. Not ideal conditions to take your first ride in the T-37, but Jason showed no signs discomfort as he walked out to the aircraft with his instructor, Captain Mike Rawlings. The T-37 engines were loud; the flight doctors determined long ago that earplugs alone would not be sufficient protection from the high decibel levels produced from the Tweet. As a result, everyone wore ear muffs, or Mickey Mouse ears as they were affectionately known, on the Tweet side of the airplane ramp. The whining of the engines stretched across the ramp of the flight line as the noxious odor of JP-8 burned Jason's nostrils. He squinted to shield his eyes from the glare as he searched for their jet. The first ride in the aircraft, known as the dollar ride, was supposed to be fun. Essentially an orientation ride, it was a no-threat situation.

The T-37 Tweet was one of the oldest aircraft in the Air Force inventory. Designed to replace the T-33 back in the 1950's, it had pushed well into its fourth decade as the primary jet trainer. It sat close to the ground with a low wing configuration. The Tweet's round nose, straight wings, and small fuselage resembled a dragonfly, the name of the combat version of the Tweet, flown in the Vietnam conflict. The wide bubble canopy housed the cockpit in which the instructor and student sat side by side. The students didn't enjoy this because the instructors could watch their every move. It was precisely for that reason that the instructors liked this seating arrangement. Instructor Pilots wanted to be aware of what the students were doing at all times. The Tweet had the distinction of being the only aircraft the Air Force had specifically designed for spin training. The T-37 also had a reputation for being an aerobatics marvel. T-37 instructors constantly ribbed their supersonic counterparts in the T-38 by saying real men didn't need G-suits. The constant G environment proved a hindrance to the students as G-LOC (gravity-induced loss of consciousness) washed many students out of the program.

His instructor didn't say anything while walking to the aircraft. Jason wouldn't have heard him anyway, the earplugs/headset combination blocked out any noise, except the high whine of the Tweet's engines already running on the ramp. When they reached the aircraft, the instructor tossed his parachute on the right seat and grabbed the aircraft's Form 781, an orange covered notebook encased in plastic.

"This is the maintenance form of the jet. You need to check this out each time before you fly," he yelled to Jason.

Jason nodded his understanding, placing his parachute in the left seat. He reviewed the aircraft's forms and started his pre-flight walk around. With his checklist out, he carefully inspected each item. Captain Rawlings let him go for a few minutes, until his frustration got the best of him.

"Okay, Lieutenant Conrad," he hollered, "we're not gonna buy it, we're just gonna borrow it for an hour or so. Let's pick up the pace a little bit or we're going to miss our takeoff time." Jason, getting the hint, started to move faster. When he finished the exterior inspection of the aircraft, he climbed inside and strapped in.

After struggling for a minute or two, he managed to put on his parachute. Rawlings tapped him on the shoulder. Jason looked over at his instructor, who was already strapped in and wearing his helmet.

"Let's hurry it up, Lieutenant. We don't have all day."

Jason had heard about the student harassment on the flight line, but didn't expect to get it on his dollar ride. Wasn't this supposed to be fun? Finished strapping in, he ran over the interior checklist. Everything was challenge and response in the beginning.

Jason signaled the crew chief he was ready to start the number one, or left engine. He held up the starter switch and flipped the ignition switch. The small J-69 engine roared to life making its trademark high-pitched squeal. *No wonder they call this jet a six-thousand pound bird whistle*, he thought. The number two engine started as easily as the first. As he continued with his engine-start checklist, the perspiration poured down his face, the sweat stinging his eyes. "The longer we sit here, the more we'll sweat," said Rawlings sarcastically.

Jason finished his checks and called for taxi clearance. "Vance Ground, Bison Seven-Four, taxi with information Echo, Dogface."

Dogface—Vance's auxiliary airfield where the T-37 students could accomplish the majority of their pattern work without terrorizing the control tower at Vance.

"Okay, I'll tell you what," Rawlings said. "I have the aircraft. I'll taxi us out on the taxiway, then I'll give it to you to taxi."

"Roger, sir. You have the aircraft," Jason responded as his instructor shook the controls.

After giving the crew chief the signal to remove the aircraft's chocks, Rawlings advanced the power and the aircraft crept forward onto the taxiway where he accomplished the taxi checklist, then gave the aircraft back to Jason.

"Don't forget to engage the nosewheel steering," he said as he noticed Jason immediately veering off to the left.

"Got it."

"It can be a little tough at first. Like everything else, it takes a little practice."

Jason taxied up to the T-37 runway, known as Eastside because, of the three runways at Vance, it is on the east side.

"Okay, Lieutenant, not too bad. I have the aircraft for the takeoff. IP demo."

"Eastside, Bison Seven-Four, number one, Dogface." Dogface was the auxiliary airfield where students from Vance practiced landings.

"Bison Seven-Four, cleared for takeoff."

"Bison Seven-Four, cleared for takeoff," Rawlings repeated.

Jason closed the canopy as Rawlings taxied out onto runway 17 and lined the aircraft up in the center of the runway. Rawlings pressed his toes down, applying the brakes, then slowly pushed the throttles all the way forward to military power. He checked the warning lights, followed by the navigation and engine instruments.

"Four green, no red, no amber. Engines look good. Let's go."

Letting go of the brakes, Rawlings used the nosewheel steering to guide the aircraft until it travelled fast enough for the rudder to become effective. The aircraft slowly accelerated due to the heat, but it managed to reach its go-no-go speed without much problem. Rawlings began to rotate at eighty knots indicated airspeed as the Tweet lifted off the ground.

"Two positive climbs, gear clear."

"Gear clear," Jason said.

Rawlings raised the gear, but waited to pass through one hundred ten knots before raising the flaps. Once they put T-37 in a clean configuration, it began to accelerate. At one hundred eighty knots, Rawlings raised the nose to hold his speed as the jet climbed lazily to five thousand feet on the departure to Dogface. The T-37 wasn't known for its speed, but Jason was thrilled regardless. This was faster than any airplane he had ever flown.

"You're going to find out in this program there's not a lot of time for sightseeing," the instructor said. "I'll go ahead and fly the departure so you can see some of the reference points."

"Roger."

"Departure Control, Bison Seven-Four, Airborne passing two thousand feet, Dogface," Rawlings said over the radio.

"Roger Bison Seven-Four, cleared northern transition."

"Bison Seven-Four."

Jason observed the terrain surrounding Vance Air Force Base. It did not offer much variety. Enid had some of the flattest land in a very flat state. Wheat fields spread across the horizon in all directions. As they leveled off at five thousand feet pointed toward the north, he could see the Salt Plains Reservoir located next to Dogface. The auxiliary airfield sat nineteen miles from Vance. Bison 74 would be there in a matter of minutes.

"Are you ready to fly?"

"You bet," Jason responded.

"Okay, you have the aircraft."

"Roger, I have the aircraft." Jason took the controls. The instructor trimmed the aircraft for straight and level flight. At first he had difficulty holding his altitude, but after a few moments, Jason had it to plus or minus a hundred feet. Not bad for his first time.

"Watch your airspeed."

"Oh, yeah, thanks."

"You need to start building an effective cross-check. Eighty percent of it should be outside at this stage. Don't stare at the instruments—they won't hit you. It's the things outside the airplane that will hit you. That's why you need to look outside."

"Gotcha."

"Use the horizon like a big attitude indicator. You should be able to tell if you are in a climb, descent, or a turn just by looking at it."

"Okay." The more Jason worked on his cross-check, the harder it became. He had to fight off the urge to stare at his instruments.

"See this black field here?" Rawlings said as they passed the blackened coal plant. "That's the town of Kremlin. We normally accomplish the approach to field check here. That will help you to keep from forgetting it."

"Thanks," Jason said as he began the checklist. At five thousand feet, the air vent now blew cool air on them, making the flight a little more comfortable, though still a long way from being an effective air conditioner. Captain Rawlings took the aircraft again for the descent at the "football", a big river bend several miles east of Dogface. He continued to point out various reference points all the way into Dogface.

The instructor flew the aircraft to the runway for a quick touch-and-go landing, then departed the traffic pattern for the Military Operating Area (MOA). The MOA's were split into two separate blocks for the T-37's: seven thousand to twelve thousand feet, and thirteen thousand to eighteen thousand feet. It was in these areas where the students practiced stalls, spins, and aerobatics.

They received an area assignment from MOA control and made their climb toward it. *This is great,* Jason thought. *This would be an awesome view if there were anything to see.* The jet climbed through seven thousand feet and they entered the working area.

"One of the most important factors you need to remember when doing your area work is to always maintain your energy level," Rawlings said. Rawlings maneuvered the aircraft around a small puffy cloud hanging alone near the middle of their area. "If you ever get slow, make sure you do it at the top of your area. That way, you can turn your potential energy into kinetic energy. Never get slow at the bottom of your area. If you do, you're screwed. You'll waste a lot of time and burn a lot of gas trying to get it back."

"Got it."

"Well, I can show you the stall and crap you're allowed to see, or we can have some fun. What'll it be?"

"Fun, I hope."

"I'm glad you said that," Rawlings said as he rolled the T-37 inverted 'til the nose tracked below the horizon twenty degrees. Rolling the aircraft upright, he let the jet accelerate to two hundred and fifty knots, then pulled the stick into his lap, flying a tight, three-G loop. Jason felt his body instantly increase to three times its normal weight as he sank into the seat. He quickly began his anti-G straining maneuver of controlled breathing and muscle contraction to keep the blood from pooling in his feet. This forced his blood to stay in the top part of his body, keeping him conscious.

Seconds after starting the maneuver, they were finished. "What do you think?" the instructor asked.

"Awesome, man. Awesome!"

"Are you ready to try one yourself?"

"Can I?"

"Well, let's say I never saw it if you did. You have the aircraft."

 "Awesome, I have the aircraft."

"That's 'roger', you have the aircraft."

"Roger."

Jason set up his parameters as the instructor talked him through the maneuver. His heart raced as he lowered the nose of the aircraft and he watched the airspeed increase to two-hundred fifty knots. Before he had a chance to pull back on the stick he felt Rawlings start to pull back. Jason increased the pressure on the stick.

"Pull it straight back into your lap and cross check your G-meter," Rawlings said with a grunt easing the pressure he exerted while shadowing Jason's control inputs.

Jason saw the G-meter read three point five G's and he relaxed the stick pressure to three G's. The jet flew up and over the top, Jason grinning as he viewed the world upside down. He flew out of the maneuver fast and off-center, with his wings cocked at thirty degrees.

"Not too bad for the first time," Rawlings said shaking the stick. "I have the aircraft."

"Roger, you have the aircraft," Jason said as he walked the rudder pedals.

They stayed in the area for another twenty minutes before heading back to Eastside, the instructor constantly talking and demonstrating various maneuvers. They returned for several overhead patterns, used to expedite takeoff and landing practice. When the flight ended, an elated Jason bounced out of the aircraft. He didn't get sick, he didn't pass out, and he had flown a military jet. Baby steps.

CHAPTER 6

August 14, 1995

LIFE STARTED TO IMPROVE. It had been a good first day in the jet, especially after his disaster on Friday. To make things better, after meeting Kathy at Chicaros, she agreed to have dinner with him tonight. She impressed him enough that he went back to Chicaros on Saturday and secured a short dinner date with her tonight. It was a daring move on his part, and one that paid off.

Jason climbed in his 1965 Ford Mustang and started the engine. The canary yellow frame shook as the engine roared to life and he backed out of his parking space. He bought the car as a freshman in college, and it had been a project of his to restore it over the years. It was one of the few items he managed to keep after his divorce.

It wasn't a long drive to the outskirts of town—it merely felt that way. Jason's emotions were spinning like the T-37 in a training exercise. The elation of his first jet ride had been overcome by first-date fears. Not that he was afraid to date—he just wasn't sure he remembered how.

Kathy said she lived with an elderly couple named Jones in a large house with a barn and horses. The Jones' enjoyed having Kathy stay with them, she said, because she took care of the horses for them. They didn't get out much to ride their horses, but kept them for sentimental value.

The long, one-story ranch house sat alone over a hundred feet from the road. Jason could see the barn behind the house and the white-pole fence that ran far behind the house, denoting the property line. Nervously, he stepped out of his car and approached the front door. As he reached up to knock, the door swung open.

"Hi there, killer!" a lovely voice said.

Jason looked at the attractive young woman in front of him. Again, she wore shorts, but the black tank top had given way to a meticulously pressed

Oxford shirt. Slight touches of make-up greatly enhanced an already beautiful face. "I wouldn't really call me a killer. I'm not a pacifist either. I just don't look for trouble."

Kathy shrugged her shoulders as she closed the door behind her. "Sorry, just a figure of speech. Don't take things so seriously." She smiled at him as they walked to his car. Kathy was a woman who spoke her mind, and he admired that. "Where are we going to eat?"

"Well, I was kind of hoping you had something in mind," he said. "I've been living on TV dinners and fast food for the past three weeks."

"I know a small café downtown where not many people go. Okay, it's more of a diner, but it would be a nice place to sit and talk," she said enthusiastically.

"Sounds great," he answered as he opened her door. "I could use a nice meal."

The trip to the center of town took about ten minutes. Jason found a parking spot in front of the café, which sat half a block from the courthouse. The two of them walked inside and found themselves among ten other customers, none of whom were from the base. They took a small booth next to the window that gave them a good view of the diner. They quickly realized everyone was watching them.

"It's obvious we're not regulars here," Jason said.

"True. Are you nervous?"

"About them? No."

"You seem a little uncomfortable. I thought all you pilots are cocky and on top of the world."

"Well, I'm still a student pilot. I imagine the real pilots are that way. I've still got a long way to go before I get to that point."

"Interesting perspective. So I take it from your earlier statement about killing that you are not going to be a fighter pilot?"

"No, not exactly. A week ago, yes. Right now, I'm not setting my goals that high. I would be happy to graduate."

"I thought all of you pilot types wanted to be fighter jocks."

"Another of those rumors we try to perpetuate in order to boost our egos."

The waitress, an older woman well into her fifties with a pleasant smile, showed up to take their order. Both ordered the house special consisting of chicken fried steak, mashed potatoes, gravy, fried okra, and carrots broiled in butter sauce. Jason took a sip of water and started to relax. He found Kathy easy to talk to. She let him know right away that she was not impressed by the flashy pilot image, and he felt relieved that he didn't have to live up to it.

"So, Miss Delgato, tell me about yourself," Jason asked.

"Direct, aren't we?"

"Thought I'd beat you to the punch."

Kathy leaned back in the booth and flashed a bright smile. "Well, I'm a service brat. My dad is a retired Air Force Master Sergeant. He's full-blooded Italian, and my mother is half-Mexican. That probably explains my feisty attitude. I'm twenty-five, went to the University of Texas in Austin, and studied philosophy. It was interesting, but when I earned my degree, I didn't know what to do with it. I was tired of school and wasn't interested in getting a master's degree. So I did what every girl does: I went home to daddy."

"So how did you end up in Enid?"

She frowned. "Not one of my more favorite subjects. I made the mistake of letting one of my girlfriends talk me into going to the Auger Inn at the Officers' Club at Randolph. I hadn't been there since my freshman year in college."

"I've heard of that place. It has quite a reputation."

"It's not as wild as it used to be, but it's fun on occasion. Anyway, while I was there, I met a smooth-talking, tall, dark, and handsome instructor pilot. He was down for the week from Vance on temporary duty for some kind of conference. Well, I was young and stupid, and he swept me off my feet. He flew down every weekend for the next two months, and the next thing I knew, I moved up here. Daddy warned me it was a mistake."

"Sorry it didn't work out."

Kathy shifted her weight in the seat, her smile gone. "I'm not. He turned out to be an asshole. Six months later, he got an assignment to Arizona flying F-16's, and that was the end of that romance. I stayed in Enid partly because I was too embarrassed to go home."

"Why else? There's not much here."

"That's the other reason. I like it here. It's quiet. It's a nice change of pace after living in Austin and San Antonio for so long. Besides, the Joneses let me stay at their house and ride their horses whenever I want. It's really not a bad deal."

"Do you ever go home to see your folks?"

She smiled again. "Oh, sure, they've gotten over my mistake. So have I. I go home often and spend time with them. I guess you could say we've all kissed and made up."

"That's great. What are your plans for the future?"

"Plans? God only knows," she said with a laugh. "I'm having fun right now riding horses when I want, and working at Chicaros is a kick. It's fun to flirt with these young horny pilots here. I think I intimidate most of them."

"I can see how that would happen."

"Well, I must not have intimidated you very much."

"I wouldn't say that," Jason said. "I'm pretty nervous."

"Well, don't be," she said, placing her hand on his arm. "I think you're very nice."

"Thanks," Jason said, goose bumps forming on his body. They sat in silence for a moment, each oblivious to their surroundings.

"So, Jason Conrad, why don't you tell me about yourself?"

"Wow, where do I start?" he asked as he propped both elbows on the table. "I grew up in South Florida, in a place called Homestead, south of Miami . . ." Jason told her the story of his ex-wife. It never seemed to get easier.

KATHY COULD TELL THE SUBJECT was something he was not interested in talking about. These pilot types clearly are not as tough as they think they are sometimes.

"So why did you want to become a pilot? Was your father a pilot?" she asked in an attempt to change the subject.

"No, he's a politician in Texas. Has been ever since I was six. I don't really know him. His life is not the route I wanted to take. I guess I didn't want to work behind a desk the rest of my life. So I decided to fly jets. It's an exciting lifestyle and opens doors to a lot of opportunities in the future."

"I could never fly in those things," Kathy said. The fact his father was a politician didn't escape her. Now may not be the time to explore that.

"Why? They're so much fun."

"Too cramped, too confined. They're just too small."

"What, are you claustrophobic?" Jason said.

"Yes," she said softly. Jason could see her mouth tighten as she glanced at the floor.

"I'm sorry-"

"It's okay. When I was a little girl, I used to play in an old refrigerator in our back yard. One day I got trapped inside. I felt helpless there in the dark, not being able to move, barely able to breathe. Luckily, my parents were home; they found me after about fifteen minutes. It was terrifying. I've hated small, confined places ever since."

"I'm sorry . . . I didn't know," Jason stopped talking as the waitress brought their food to the table. They dropped the topic as they began to eat. The two of them ate, laughed, and told stories for the next hour. They hit it off well as far as first dates go. Jason apologized for having to rush back to the base, but it was a workday, he told her, and he had a lot of studying to do. The drive back to Kathy's place was quick; the kiss goodbye even quicker. Both of them seemed pleased with the evening.

Kathy watched Jason drive away in the darkness. She liked this guy, she decided. Jason Conrad had potential. She closed the door and headed to her room. No sooner had she laid down then the phone rang.

"Hello," she said.

"Kathy?" a voice asked from the other end.

"Yes. Who is this?"

"It's Vince. Vince Andrews . . ."

CHAPTER 7

August 14, 1995

H E FELT IT WOULD BE an unusually cold winter. Here it was mid-August, and the average temperature was already fifteen degrees lower than normal. He stared out the window through the dirty glass, his small garden showing signs of decaying life, symbolic of the nation's economic status. Everyone who lived outside the city had a garden in which they grew crops to supplement their food supply. The few flowers he once grew alongside his cottage had long since died, the aesthetic quality of his garden not being a priority. The once glorious pumpkins he and his wife had grown were sparse; his potato crop half of what it used to be. On the far northern side of his modest garden, weeds had overtaken the yams. Since his wife died two years ago, he had not tended the small garden on any regular basis. The short summer months didn't allow for many opportunities to grow crops, and the thought of an early winter didn't raise his hopes.

Viktor Vasilyevich Kryuchkov did not smile as he gathered his hat, coat, and briefcase. He paused by his wife's picture near the front door. "My dear, I'm sorry," he said. "I've had enough. Our people have had enough. It is time for a change. The old ways did not work, yet the new ways seem worse. I'm sorry."

The front door clicked shut behind him. His driver waited by the car for him in the circular driveway. The large Cyprus trees on either side of the driveway blocked out any of the morning sun. Viktor surveyed the surrounding area as he walked toward the car.

"Good Morning, Comrade Kryuchkov."

"Good Morning, Palovich. It seems not so long ago I saw you." Viktor coughed as he finished his statement.

"Yes, not so long at all. The morning chill shows signs of an early winter," said Palovich as he opened the rear door of the car for Viktor. Viktor did not reply, but the comment stuck in his mind. It would again be a hard winter on his people. A shorter summer meant fewer crops, which meant less food for the long, cold winter that lay ahead.

Palovich pulled the black Mercedes out of the circular driveway onto the country dirt road. The engine roared as he accelerated to begin the thirty-minute ride into Moscow. Viktor knew he was fortunate to lead the life he did. He had a cottage in the country instead of a crowded apartment in the city. He had a car, driver, and a modest income. By Russian standards, he was wealthy. Yet Viktor Kryuchkov wanted more. Not more for himself, but more for his people. He was sure they deserved better than they were getting.

Viktor opened his tattered briefcase, pulling out a stack of papers. Economic reports, agriculture statistics, military analysis, public opinion comments—he knew his meeting with the committee would be a tough one. Viktor had easy access to such information, and it depressed him immensely. Last year, there were close to three million crimes committed throughout the nation. Murders increased by seventy-four percent as extortion cases became the norm. The status of the military had decayed to such a point that they were unable to sustain an extended operation in another country for more than six months. Most of the enlisted, and parts of the officer corps, were forced to find work outside the military just to have enough money to buy groceries. Organized crime had filtered its way throughout the economy, making it difficult to determine which police officers could be trusted. The Russian mafia was comprised of a wide variety of thugs, from the common hood on the street to government officials and members of the former KGB.

Working as a special advisor to the infant Russian Congress, he was handed such information on a daily basis for his experienced analysis. Viktor kept most of this information for use in the future. For use on a day like today. He felt a slight thrill inside himself. As he approached his seventieth birthday, he was still a driven man. He was engaging in acts better suited for younger men.

"Palovich, we will not go to the Kremlin this morning."

The comment was unusual, Palovich Merlov noted. Viktor had gone straight to the Kremlin every day for the past five years.

"Yes, Comrade Kryuchkov. Where shall we be going?"

"You shall drive me to the Dacha Complex at Yasenevo."

"Yasenevo. The Dacha Complex. Yes, comrade."

Yasenevo was the old KGB headquarters in the middle of Moscow. The Dacha Complex is a small building west of the main structure. Outsiders knew little of what went on there. In the declining months of the Communist Party, the security in the Dacha Complex had increased dramatically, just as activity in the building increased at a steady rate. Viktor had offices in both the Kremlin and the Dacha Complex. Meetings with other hardline Communists still active in the Russian government were held in the Dacha Complex at least once a week. Viktor had severely opposed the attempt at democracy, stating from the outset that it would fail.

The streets of Moscow were virtually empty this time of day. Even in the most prosperous of times, traffic was light by Western standards. Palovich drove through downtown Moscow with no specific route in mind. Viktor enjoyed the sightseeing trip every morning, a simple pleasure for an aging man. They drove through Sverdlov Square and passed the Bolshoi Theatre.

"There it is, Palovich, Bolshoi Theatre. That is where I met my Helga in 1947."

"Yes, comrade. It was a lovely place."

"She was a lovely girl."

"Yes she was comrade." Viktor was a young man then, a boy really, a soldier of the Soviet Union who had repelled the Nazi hoard at the Battle of Stalingrad. During that time, he was in Moscow with his unit for a display of Soviet power for Stalin. Viktor's commander had invited Viktor and several of his peers to an opera at the Bolshoi Theatre in Moscow. Viktor, of course, had no interest in such things. As a young warrior, he was more interested in facing off with the Americans, the emerging threat to Soviet power.

Halfway through the show, Viktor went to the lobby to smoke a cigarette. There she stood before him, a vision of beauty, leaning against one of the columns in the lobby. He was struck at once by the freshness of her skin and her cool demeanor. She was impressed with the uniform and how he filled it out. It was love at first sight. A year later, the two married.

"I miss her deeply, Palovich."

"I miss her, too, comrade."

It was the same exchange of dialogue they had every time they passed the theatre. In recent years, the Bolshoi and its environs had turned into one of Moscow's seedier districts. Drug dealers, pimps, hookers, pedophiles, and child peddling deviants inhabited the area. Moscow, it seemed, was becoming more and more Westernized every day.

PALOVICH HAD WORKED AS Viktor's driver for the past twelve years. He'd seen Viktor face many different issues, but Helga's death affected him more than anything. She had developed breast cancer that had gone undetected due to the lack of available medical care. Viktor experienced firsthand the failure of the democratic system, at the expense of his spouse. After she died, he became a man obsessed with work. He went through all the stages. First, there was the initial shock. The next two days were spent in disbelief. Then came the sorrow and the weeping. A tough one, Viktor did not afford himself the luxury of sadness for an extended period. Two weeks had passed when he entered the next stage: loneliness.

Initially, because he'd taken time off from work to make arrangements for Helga's funeral, he had not realized what it was that had him so depressed. When it finally hit him, when he searched deep inside and realized what was happening, he became a man possessed. Burying himself in projects, he worked constantly. It was not that his life had taken on new meaning. It had simply taken a new direction. His hours at the office increased, and the work he continuously brought home had more than doubled. Viktor did not speak of the work he did. It wasn't that he was trying to keep a secret. Viktor simply never made anything other than small talk on the way to and from the office. He had many meetings with unknown persons and often brought home reams of papers at night. Viktor was calculating; always planning something. What it was, Palovich had no idea, and he never dreamed of asking.

The Mercedes made a turn east onto Moscow Ring Road, toward Yasenevo. Palovich stopped the limo at the front door of the Dacha Complex, and a Russian Army colonel opened the door for the senior bureaucrat. Viktor stepped out of the car and disappeared through the front door.

The dull thump of Viktor's shoes echoed on the marble floor. He passed several offices bustling with activity. He reached the staircase in the middle of the complex and made his way upstairs. At the top of the stairs, the security guard snapped to attention, allowing Viktor to pass without delay or proof of identification.

The second floor of the Dacha Complex was much different than the first. It contained approximately the same number of offices, but it also possessed a much finer style of architecture and museum-quality artwork.

Between every office hung a portrait of little-known KGB agents and illegals who had successful careers during the Cold War.

Viktor entered his office and the darkness enveloped him immediately. He walked straight to the window, opening the shutters. The early morning light pierced the darkness, dissolving it away with each set of shutters he opened. Beams of light crossed the room, solidifying themselves on the far side of the committee's conference table.

It had been years since his last official day with the KGB. Eight years before the collapse of the Berlin Wall, he had been named the Chief Directorate for Illegals. It had been his job to supervise and coordinate the placement of "moles", Soviet agents placed illegally in a foreign country without diplomatic immunity. When the time was right, a mole was activated for a specific mission. One might go for years without being activated, the whole time, becoming more and more a part of their assigned environment. It was a job Viktor relished. It was a job he continued to do, although on a much smaller scale.

Placing his hat and coat on the rack in the corner of the room, he took his usual seat at the end of the table. A knock on the door broke the silence.

"Enter," Viktor said.

The door opened and the dull yellow light spilled in from the empty hallway, thrusting itself throughout the darkened interior of his office. A single figure stepped from the familiarity of the brightly lit hallway, casting a shadow across the front of Viktor's face.

"Good morning, Comrade Kryuchkov," the backlit figure said.

"Aleksandr, good morning, you old fool. Come in and sit."

"Fool? I think not. As for old, you perhaps should speak on your own behalf, my friend." He entered the room, shutting the door behind him slowly, allowing his eyes time to adjust to the absence of light in the room.

"Don't remind me," Viktor said.

"What, that you are old?"

"No, that we are friends," Viktor said laughing. Aleksandr Chebrikov seated himself across from Viktor and joined him in laughter. The two had been friends for several decades now. Since Aleksandr was three years younger than Viktor, age was often brought up by the two aging warriors. Aleksandr was a former general in the GRU, the Soviet Military Intelligence. Now he merely served as a general in the army, signing papers and touring various NATO bases around Europe on goodwill exchanges. The short, trim, balding general sat in a chair next to Viktor's desk. He may not have shown it, but Viktor was glad to see his old friend, Aleksandr. He helped ease the tension of the morning.

"Where are the others, Alek?"

"They will be here shortly."

"Good. We have much to discuss."

"Tell me, Viktor, do you set out to change the world this morning?" he said as he crossed his arms across his chest.

"Actually, old friend, I do."

CHAPTER 8

August 14, 1995

THE MEETING LASTED SEVERAL HOURS. Each of the principals had an opportunity to speak. Moods varied throughout the morning, from staunch dissention to mild agreement. There were moments when the screaming across the table was too much for some of the committee. The morning grew long as many of the men shared in the desire for something productive, something "good" to come out of this meeting. Gradually, they began to agree on a few specific points. Viktor studied the eight men surrounding his table.

"Comrades, I cannot tell you how pleased I am that we all see our present situation under similar circumstances. Democracy has been tried in Russia and it has failed. Our people are on the streets starving, and crime is on the rise. The economy is not creating more jobs. More and more of our universities and secondary schools are closing. We have scientists who cannot get the support or materials to advance our technology. We don't have the medical personnel or facilities to take care of our sick and dying, and preventive medication is long since a dream. The athletes of our once-proud nation now struggle to get a decent meal. Our military is in shambles. We now sell the once-mighty aircraft of our military to capitalist pigs for joyrides. We sell weapons to Third World countries for a fraction of their cost. Russia is no longer a world power, comrades. We are dependent. Dependent on our former enemies, the same capitalists we once kept at bay with the mere tip of our sword."

"Comrade Kryuchkov," spoke Vladimir Ogoltsov, a former KGB general, "it seems we are all in agreement. Capitalism has failed our once-glorious country. The attempt at fascism several years back drove our people more toward capitalism."

"True, but look at where they failed," said Viktor. "In their effort to stir the nationalist pride, they spoke of world domination. They wanted to bring the former nations that comprised our old Soviet Union back into the fold. The reunion of the Warsaw Pact would have meant dissolving NATO's current configuration. The response from NATO and the United Nations would have been swift and sure. They were fools, and Vladimir Zhirinovsky a KGB puppet. A feeble attempt by some to hold on to the past with no plan to develop the future. The fools even spoke of taking Alaska back from the United States."

"Not a bad idea, actually," said Aleksandr. A few chuckles broke out across the table.

The seriousness on Viktor's face did not change.

"In a theoretical fantasy, perhaps not. In reality, a foolish concept. All of them."

Viktor left the head of the table, walked across the room, and poured himself a cup of tea. The steam rose from the cup as Viktor brought it to his lips and blew lightly across its surface. The warm liquid calmed him. He took the tea back to his seat.

"Gentlemen, we have listened to various statements and seen many charts today showing the status of our country," Viktor said, resting his palm against his chin. "Russia is in bad shape. Before we worry about dealing with other countries, we must worry about our own. Ours is an internal problem. We must fix it from within."

"Comrade, we all agree with your comments, but please, the day grows long. What is it you propose we do?" It was Yuri Trilisser, the overweight Minister of Finance. Viktor was surprised, as Yuri had been quiet most of the day.

"Very well, comrades. I believe it is in the best interest of our nation and the Russian people for a revolution to commence, a revolution that will overthrow the current capitalist government. We will reestablish the Communist Party."

NIKOLAI GREGARIN WALKED RAPIDLY out of his office on the second floor of the Dacha Complex. His small, five-foot five-inch frame hurried past the other workers in the crowded hallway. Nikolai had the appearance of a frustrated parent more than he did a director of a major Russian spy ring. The file folder he carried was folded over as he beat it against his thigh with each step he took. His footsteps echoed throughout the massive corridor as he stopped for no one. Nikolai was well groomed, in his late thirties, with deep-set and stoic gray eyes behind round spectacles. He had a weakness for fine tailored suits, much like the dark blue suit he wore today.

When he first entered military service at age eighteen, he served in a demolition unit for three years in the Soviet Army before being selected to go to the University in Moscow for Advanced International Studies. He already spoke fluent German, broken Italian, and wanted desperately to learn English. Within four years, he had mastered English and Italian and was sent abroad to travel as a diplomatic courier. For the next two years, Nikolai made many connections throughout Western Europe. He was a young man on the move with his finger on the pulse of society.

Then Viktor came. He offered him the opportunity of a lifetime to come work for the KGB. Those were glorious times for the KGB—the devil Ronald Reagan was set to leave the White House within months and the recruiting of foreign agents had been excellent. U.S. government workers were easy targets when the rest of society was paid so much more.

For the past five years, Nikolai had been working as the chief of Section Nine in the Directorate of Illegals. They were unknown to the outside world, and he worked hard to ensure they stayed that way.

Section Nine was the special branch of illegals. They were moles trained to be assassins, waiting for years, buried in their cover, most never doing the job they were trained to do. It was more of an insurance policy against potential threats. No one, including Nikolai, was sure how long Section Nine had been in existence. There were those who hinted Section Nine might have been involved in the slayings of Anwar Sadat and several other persons of influence over the last several decades. The John F. Kennedy and Martin Luther King assassinations were rumored to have been their handiwork, as well. There were no official records of the activities of Section Nine since the files for each assignment were destroyed following its completion. Their current size and exact organization was known only to two men: Nikolai and the man he was on his way to meet.

Reaching the northern end of the hallway, Nikolai approached the older woman sitting at the desk outside the large oak door. Inga had been Viktor Kryuchkov's personal secretary for eighteen years.

"I need to speak to Viktor," he said, wringing the folder in his hands.

"If you mean Comrade Kryuchkov, he is meeting with the committee at the moment," she said. It was obvious she enjoyed this bit of power as the secretary of one of the most powerful men in Moscow.

"Please, it is most urgent. If you let him know I'm here, I am sure he will see me."

"Comrade Kryuchkov advised me he would be busy for most of the morning and is not to be disturbed. If what you have to say to him is important, you may wait over there on the sofa," she said.

Nikolai scowled. "Thank you for your assistance, comrade."

He made his way to the couch. The smooth leather was very comfortable, the likes of which Nikolai hadn't seen outside of Western Europe. His eyes wandered about the office until they fell once again upon Inga. He and Viktor's secretary had never liked each other. She took pride in always having her finger on what was going on in the Dacha Complex. She could never figure out Nikolai, or exactly what it was he did, and it annoyed her. To each his own, he thought. A small price to pay to serve one's country.

"I noticed lately, Nikolai, you have been staying long after business hours," she said from across the room. "What exciting new project are you working on now?"

The sarcasm in her voice was evident. This was the same cat-and-mouse game they had played for years.

"Just the usual bureaucratic boring paperwork, Inga. Truly nothing of any interest to anyone," he said.

"No one except Viktor, it appears."

Nikolai ignored her. Ten minutes later, the door to Viktor's office opened. Viktor walked out, shaking hands with two older gentlemen. He turned to face Nikolai sitting on the couch.

"Nikolai, how long have you been waiting? We have much to discuss."

Nikolai marched across the reception area and smiled as he shook hands with his older supervisor. It was obvious he held a great deal of respect for Viktor. They entered his office, where Nikolai forgot about his head games with the secretary.

"Tell me, Nikolai, what brings you here this morning? You have a seriousness that could make one nervous." Viktor sat behind his large desk and gestured for Nikolai to sit in one of the chairs in front of him.

"It is about Oleg again, sir. I fear he might be getting out of control. When we planted him four years ago, he seemed stable. Since then, however, we have obtained evidence he has been participating in a series of unauthorized terminations."

Viktor winced. The term placed a low value on human life. For the members of Section Nine, however, that was their job.

Nikolai continued. "We began investigating him fourteen months ago when new evidence appeared for an unsolved murder that took place ten miles from the training facility. Evidence indicting Oleg. We then studied his movement throughout the United States and noticed a series of deaths that followed him across the country."

"Are you sure Oleg is responsible for these deaths?"

"No, sir, we are not sure of all of them, though several people were terminated using methods we teach at the schoolhouse. Those we feel about quite strongly. We plotted other unsolved deaths which occurred when Oleg was in the area. We feel he is probably responsible for those, as well."

Viktor sat back in his chair, his intensity not wavering. "How many deaths are we talking about?"

"Nine using the methods taught in the schoolhouse and four which match Oleg's location at the time. These do not include the most recent evidence we have obtained."

"Explain," Viktor said, his eyes searching Nikolai's face for an answer.

"Yes, sir. When we noticed the trend, we decided to monitor Oleg's actions. Five months ago, we placed another operative in his zone to observe him."

"You realize, Nikolai, that is not standard procedure," Viktor said disapprovingly.

"Yes, comrade, I do. However, we decided it was a necessary step to ensure the integrity of our operation."

"Very well. Continue."

"Our operative observed several things. First, Oleg has been withdrawing significant amounts of currency from his expense account. Second, the lifestyle he is living draws too much attention to himself. He is not keeping the low profile we like to see in our agents."

"But Nikolai, these are common with agents we place in America. They often are tempted by the Western luxuries."

"Yes, I understand sir, but there are limits. We just received a report that our operative witnessed Oleg terminate an individual four weeks ago in Los Angeles."

"I see . . . this changes things." Viktor turned in his chair, staring outside. The overcast sky muted the sun that came through his windows. Surely, when there are only allegations or rumors, it was easy to ignore. But Nikolai had proof, a witness to a murder committed by one of his operatives. So much time and so much money to train such a specialist. "Continue. Who was this person he killed?"

"When Oleg was first placed in the United States, his identity and job placement required him to look several years younger. We placed him in this position because of his special skilled background. The position was too important to risk an individual who might not succeed.

"So in order to make Oleg appear younger, he was sent to Los Angeles to get a series of operations to change his appearance. The individual killed was the Beverly Hills plastic surgeon who did the surgery. Our operative witnessed it."

"This is a bad situation indeed, Nikolai. We cannot have a renegade murderer running around the United States killing at his discretion."

"What do you propose we do to alleviate this situation, Comrade Kryuchkov?"

Viktor stood with his hands clasped behind his back and stared out at the cold gray morning sky. "I have an idea that might solve both of our problems." He glanced over his shoulder with a quick turn and asked, "Where did you say Oleg is operating?"

"Currently, he is a lieutenant in the U.S. Air Force attending pilot training at Vance Air Force Base in Oklahoma."

PALOVICH LEFT THE HARD BENCH on the first floor lobby and walked out the front door. His pudgy hands pulled the pack of Marlboros from his pocket as he walked toward the limousine. The small gravel spread loosely in the driveway crackled under the weight of his shoes. The noise was accompanied by the wind as it whistled between the buildings.

It was unusual, he thought, for the meeting to last this long. Glancing at his watch, he saw they had been in Viktor's office for over three hours. Fresh loaves of bread, fresh cheese, and sausage had been brought in to the room. Something special was going on today. There had been many meetings in that room over the years, but somehow this one was different. Palovich reached into his pocket, pulled out his wallet, and removed a piece of paper with a phone number on it. He then lit his cigarette and leaned against the limo, still staring at the number.

A cool breeze blew as Palovich pulled his collar higher around his neck and stuffed the number back into his pocket. Across the horizon, he could see the setting sun was out of sight already. The temperature had dropped ten more degrees and the wind blew harder. Dark clouds were gathering overhead. A storm was beginning to develop.

CHAPTER 9

August 17, 1995

FOR THE THIRD TIME IN A ROW, Vince maxed a test with a one hundred percent score. Vince wasn't the only person in the class who accomplished this feat, but he made it look easy. Right now, though, he had his mind on other things. Vince's finances were a problem, no thanks to Lenny. And he could not get the waitress out of his head. Kathy had ignored him at Chicaros. It had been an easy twenty dollars to the bartender to get her number. She hung up when he called, and that made him want her more. He'd try again. He enjoyed a challenge.

Vince set his books on the counter and moved into the bathroom to wash his face. The cool water was refreshing, exciting the nerves in his cheeks, jump-starting his system. Gazing into the mirror, he spoke to the weary figure staring back at him. "How long can you keep this up?"

There was no response.

He moved into the living room and picked up the remote control to the television. Before he could turn it on, there was a knock at the door.

Vince walked across the room in his stocking feet. He opened the door to see the tall thin figure of Lenny Banks standing in the doorway.

"What do you think, buddy?" Lenny said, pushing his way past Vince into the room. "The Len-meister comes through with the goods again."

"Yeah, nice job," Vince said, his eyes following Lenny into the room.

"Was there ever any doubt?"

"Yeah, there's been doubt," Vince said, slamming the door. "I doubt you're able to keep your fricking mouth shut."

"W-what?" Lenny said, the confidence leaking out of his voice.

"Don't 'what' me, you prick. You think you're funny with your little innuendos and comments trying to make me look like an ass in front of everyone. I oughta stick my fist down your throat and rip out your liver."

"Look, Vince, I'm s-sorry. Don't take this the wrong way. I sure as hell don't want you to get busted. If you go down, I'm fried for sure. You just cheated on some tests, okay? I'm the bozo who's committing the felony here. Yeah, I'm under a little pressure, but how many other students do you know who can access Air Education and Training Command's mainframe to get copies of the tests. None. Nobody. You got zippo. So stay off my back. Being a genius can be stressful."

Vince left the doorway and moved to the chair next to the couch. "Just don't let your genius ass get us caught."

"Look, I'm tired of you pinging about this. Just give me my money, and I'll split." That had always been the deal. Half before, half after.

"I'm not pinging about this, I'm pinging about you. You need to learn to keep your mouth shut."

Lenny leaned back on the couch, his long skinny legs outstretched, his G.I. flight boots pointing to the ceiling. "Yeah, yeah, I guess you're right."

"Two thousand a test now, huh?"

"Hey, bud, supply and demand."

"There seems to be a bad precedent being set here Banks. Your prices keep going up at an excessive rate. Doubling the price is a pretty risky move."

"Hey, screw you!" Lenny said, running his hands through his thinning hair. "I'm the one taking the risks here! If you don't like it, try studying for a change."

Vince cringed at this abnormal assertiveness, but deep inside he knew Lenny was right.

LENNY HAD BEEN RUNNING THIS SCAM for years. It started back in college when they were Air Force cadets in the R.O.T.C. program. He was a computer hacker in the truest sense of the word. One day while surfing through the university's website, he stumbled across a chat column and met another hacker. This guy informed him about a program he could download enabling him to backdoor almost any computer system. Informally, it was known as a "lock pick" because it could access password protected areas. On the 'Net, it was known as a "weasel", a hacker's Shangri-La, the imaginary golden idol that didn't exist. Only it did. And Lenny Banks had it.

It was a fortunate time for Lenny because the university's various departments were beginning to put their entire testing systems on a mainframe. The university essentially put a degree in his lap. Lenny wasn't sure why Vince approached him back then, but Lenny readily accepted the offer. He desperately needed the money, and Vince had what seemed an endless supply to spend.

The two were fortunate enough to receive pilot slots to Undergraduate Pilot Training. It wasn't long before Lenny discovered he could access the Air Force's mainframes, as well. Lenny's first venture toward borderline treason was the one that placed the two of them in the same UPT class. He justified his action by telling himself it didn't matter. He didn't take anything away from anyone; he just put himself in a preferred location. Vince was his money tree, and he didn't want to be far from his secondary source of income. It was only a matter of time before Lenny figured out how to infiltrate the mainframe containing the tests for UPT. Then the payoff increases started.

Lenny always thought he wasn't intelligent. Oh, he had street smarts for sure. Lenny even said he was "athletic and charming." But book-wise, he was dumber than dirt. Vince could not maintain the fast pace of the technically oriented flight training. He needed Lenny, and Lenny knew it. Over the past several weeks, however, Lenny placed himself in a position where he needed Vince and his patronage more and more.

"You're awfully cocky today," Vince said as he moved to his closet. "Was it something you ate, or are you finally developing a backbone?"

"Screw you."

"No thanks. I'll pass." Vince reached into the bottom of his closet, pulling out a black duffel bag. He thrust his hand inside the duffel and removed a black, zippered cloth briefcase the size of a notebook. Unzipping the case, he pulled out a small stack of one hundred dollar bills, counted out ten of them, and handed them to Lenny.

Lenny stared at the crisp bills as he fanned them out in his hands. "Holy crap, Vince. Where did you get all that cash?"

"Never mind. You've got your problems, I've got mine." Vince zipped up the notebook, returned it to the duffel bag, and placed it back in its nesting place.

"I wish I had your problems. You rich kids have it made."

"I'm not a rich kid."

"Yeah, right. Either you're a rich kid, or you're one helluva better gambler than me."

"Mind your own business, Lenny Banks." Vince's face muscles grew taunt, his hands curled into tight fists. "You've got your money, now leave. You've got a job to do."

Lenny realized he'd overstayed his welcome. With nervous hesitation, he inched onto his feet, slipping the money into the left breast pocket of his green flight suit. "Yeah, see ya around." Lenny edged out the door as a weak smile started to form on his worn, thin face. Lenny placed his hand over the cash in his pocket, feeling reassured. He had his problems, but they would soon be over.

VICKI SIMPSON SHIFTED NERVOUSLY in her seat. She wasn't uncomfortable, physically anyway. Vicki felt like he watched her as if she were under a microscope, her every action monitored. Since childhood, she had always mistrusted any type of law enforcement officer. Her father was a cop who abused her mother and her sisters, but once he put on the uniform, he was the pillar of society. She knew better.

Now here was this man out of uniform from the Office of Special Investigations (OSI), standing at her desk waiting to see her boss.

"Just what type of investigations do you do?" she asked the tall heavy-set black man.

"Special ones."

"Right."

"I'm sorry," the man said, "industry joke. The OSI investigates espionage, terrorism, fraud, computer tampering . . . anything that might threaten Air Force or Department of Defense personnel and resources."

"So you're a spy."

"No, not a spy. More like an investigator." Special Agent Alonzo Jacobs towered over Vicki Simpson's desk. An intimidating figure, his deep voice carried across the room, making his presence more ominous. His dark black skin and dark gray suit made him stand out in the small, pale government office.

"Miss Simpson, I need to ask you a few questions."

"I don't think I should say anything until my boss returns," she said, focusing on her computer terminal. "He's on his lunch break. Actually, he's at the gym. Thursday is racquetball day." She pointed to the calendar as she spoke. "He should be back shortly, if you want to have a seat and wait."

"That will be fine. I'll wait." Alonzo sat in the lone chair against the wall at the entrance to Vicki's office.

"So what department do you work in?" she asked, looking briefly at him as she continued typing.

"Counterintelligence."

"I knew you were a spy."

Alonzo chuckled. "I assure you, I'm not a spy. If I were, I think my wife would beat me."

That comment put Vicki at ease as a faint smile formed on her face. Perspiration began to develop on her forehead. Vicki hated summer. It seemed like all she ever did was sweat.

I'M GETTING TOO OLD FOR THIS, he thought, as he removed a handkerchief, wiping his forehead. At fifty-five, Alonzo Jacobs looked good for his age. His six-foot-five frame was lean; his neatly trimmed hair only flecked with gray. He enjoyed his job with the OSI. Alonzo had traveled a long road to get there. After he graduated from high school, he enlisted in the Army and quickly went to Airborne school followed by Ranger school. Then came Vietnam. After two tours in the 'Nam, he decided he had experienced enough of Army life and turned in his papers. He returned home to Mobile, Alabama, found a job with a supermarket chain, got married, and promptly had two children.

Raising a family. That was the excuse he used on his wife when he said he wanted to enlist in the Air Force. The truth was he missed the camaraderie and challenge of military life. Alonzo decided on the Air Force because it offered a more family oriented lifestyle than the Army. When he reached his twenty years, he retired, and through a friend, found a civilian position with OSI. He used the excuse of having two kids in college to take the job, and again his wife agreed.

The OSI was a new world to him. They recruited, selected, and trained their own agents. He spent ten weeks at the Special Investigator Course at the Air Force Special Investigations Academy in Washington, D.C., learning the basics of law, investigation techniques, and other areas necessary to work in the field. Upon graduation, he spent one year in the field on a probationary period before returning to specialize in counterintelligence. Now he found himself in San Antonio dealing with the miserable heat.

The door opened and Major Tom Sinclair came walking in, his wet hair combed over his balding scalp, and his gym bag slung over his shoulder with the racquetball racket protruding out one end.

The two old friends exchanged greetings and caught up on what their families were up to.

"I'm here to take a peek at the little computer problem you had the other day," Alonzo said.

"I didn't realize you were the computer expert. I was expecting Curt to come by."

"Actually, Curt is the computer expert from specialized services, but he had some family problems to take care. I'm here to take notes."

"Well, we'll tell you what we can. Come on, let's go sit in my office."

Alonzo stood, towering above the shorter major. The two friends walked past Vicki's desk, and Alonzo could see her following them out of the corner of her eye. Major Sinclair dropped his bag on the floor and sat behind his desk.

"Have a seat, Alonzo. Did my assistant give you a hard time?"

"Oh, not too bad."

"Yeah, she has this thing about police officers. She's one of those who thought Rodney King should be put on the next U.S. postage stamp."

"I don't think that will happen, thank God," Alonzo said. "Besides, she thinks I'm a spy."

"Nice, nice," replied Sinclair. "So tell me, what's up?"

"Well, we're investigating all incidents with suspected computer tampering. Information Warfare is the latest thing in the DOD. Ever since they installed this new security system, we have to investigate every system breach. Is there any information you can give me?"

"Not much. Vicki came in the other day, turned on the system, and got an 'ACCESS DENIED' greeting on the screen. She tried re-booting, turning it off and on, and it was still a no-go. I came in shortly after and got the same results. We called the guys at the computer center, and they got us back online. Couldn't tell us what the problem was, though."

"Is there anything here someone would want access to?"

"I wouldn't think so. We primarily track the assignments of enlisted personnel—who's been where, when. Nothing special."

"Not exactly a major national security problem."

"No, not really. It's not like we keep anyone's actual records here. We don't keep any classified information in this office. It's all public knowledge. We just keep track of it."

The phone in the outer office rang. Vicki walked into the doorway a moment later.

"Sir, the phone is for Mister Jacobs."

"Thanks, Vicki," Sinclair replied. Sinclair handed the receiver to Alonzo as he punched the blinking light on his phone.

"This is Agent Jacobs."

"Alonzo, this is Connie. I just got a call we need you to check out."

"Okay, I'm almost done here. What's up?"

"The Twelfth Operational Support Squadron called. They tried to access their computer file that contains the tests for all of Air Education and Training Command. Somebody has apparently tampered with their computers. They were denied access."

Alonzo gave Sinclair a puzzling look. "Interesting. I'll get right over there." He handed the receiver back to Sinclair. This security system was going to be more trouble than it was worth.

"I need to check something out. I'll talk to you later, Tom. Curt may come by to check out your system later in the week. Good seeing you again." Alonzo walked out the door and headed across the base to the Twelfth Operational Support Squadron.

CHAPTER 10

August 17, 1995

JASON SAT ON THE COUCH, his books and papers sprawled across the coffee table in front of him. He spent the last hour developing a plan of attack to study for the evening. His forehead wrinkled as he stood; looking at this barely organized mess, he took a deep breath and shook his head. His growling stomach indicated it was time to take a break. No sooner had he reached the kitchen then someone knocked on the door.

"Surprise," Kathy said as he opened it. "I thought I'd bring you dinner."

Jason scratched his head with a confused but happy look on his face. He stepped to the side as she walked through the doorway of the generic dorm room carrying a pizza and a bottle of red wine. Marching into the living area, she set the pizza on the only clear spot on the coffee table. Kathy started to move the books and papers scattered across the couch. "It looks as if you need to take a break," she said with smile perfectly framed by her short dark hair.

"You are amazing," he said, dumbfounded at his luck. He grew tired of studying, was hungry, and desperately needed a break. Jason continued to gaze at her. Her light blue sundress clinging to her tight, well-proportioned body in all the right places. The sandals she wore matched her dress perfectly and her firm, shapely legs were displayed nicely.

"Can you get us paper napkins?" she asked, opening the pizza box lid. "And some glasses for the wine?"

"This is the first time I've ever seen you in a dress," he said.

"Like what you see?"

"Yes," he said before walking into the kitchen, grabbing two small glasses and a stack of paper napkins. Kathy moved more books, clearing room for him on the couch. "Pepperoni and sausage. Excellent choice. You're full of surprises today, aren't you?"

She laughed at his comment. "I missed you. And I didn't want to wait until tomorrow night when you and your buddies stumble into Chicaros drunk. It's not what turns a lady on."

"I haven't done anything like that," Jason said.

"I know," Kathy replied with a wry smile, "I was just giving you a warning." She handed the bottle of wine to Jason. "Here, you open this. That's a man-type thing to do."

Jason opened the bottle, pouring as she put a slice of pizza for each of them on a napkin. They toasted each other and began to eat.

"So, Lieutenant Conrad, what do you want to be when you grow up?"

"What do you mean?"

"I mean, are you going to be a career man? Dash for the airlines? What?"

Jason took another bite of pizza and thought for a moment. "I don't know, really. I guess it's too early for me to make any decisions. I've been working hard just trying to stay in pilot training. I've never thought about what I'd do after I'm finished. A big transport plane would be nice. See the world, you know? Flying upside-down and yanking and banking is fun, but I don't know if that's my personality."

"It's unusual you don't want to be a fighter-jock."

"Well, I guess I did when I started, but I've had a few flights and talked to a lot of the instructors about it. I think cargo is the way to go for me. Besides, I'm a lover, not a fighter," he said.

"Yeah, right," she said, elbowing him in his arm. "So I guess I interrupted some serious studying," she said, pointing to the books on the coffee table.

"Well, kind of. Yes, I'm trying to catch up. I feel as if I never will sometimes."

"Oh, so you have to study more tonight?"

"Well, yes. Normally, I come home, study, eat dinner, study, and go to bed."

"What about me?"

"Huh?" Jason said, confused, yet worried about the direction this conversation was headed.

"Never mind. Eat your pizza. It's getting cold."

They ate and drank in silence for a while. The warmth and enthusiasm she had shown earlier was waning. Kathy was angry because he had to study. He could tell. He'd seen this behavior before, mostly in Bethany when they were in college.

"I'm sorry, but I have to do this. It's what I've worked years for, and it's a once-in-a-lifetime shot."

Kathy nodded. "I know, I know. I shouldn't have put the pressure on you, but I was lonely and wanted to see you." She stood up and threw her napkin and pizza crust in the garbage. "I'm not mad, okay? I'm just going to leave and let you study. But I am taking the wine," she said, sticking the cork back in the top.

"Kathy, are you sure—"

"Cool it, Conrad, I'm not mad. You've got things to do, and my life is boring. It happens."

Jason grabbed her hand as she walked to the door. "Thank you for being so thoughtful. I really do appreciate it. I'm glad you stopped by."

She leaned forward, kissing him on the cheek. Jason could see her eyes getting glassy. *She is lonely. Why is it the pretty ones are always so lonely?* Jason watched her walk to her truck and realized that his instincts were right: she really was a special girl.

"See you around, Lieutenant Conrad," she said, looking back over her shoulder. Then she was gone.

LENNY PULLED THE CHEVROLET CAMARO onto Highway 81 and headed south. To the west, the sun sat perched above the horizon, creating a wonderful display of reds, oranges, purples, and blues across the wide Oklahoma horizon. Fifteen minutes later he reached the town of Carrier and headed east on Highway 58, straight to Stillwater.

Stillwater, home of Oklahoma State University and the popular restaurant/bar Eskimo Joe's, sat about seventy miles southeast of Enid. Eskimo Joe's served as the heart and soul of Stillwater. More than twenty years ago, a former OSU student managed to turn a local watering hold into a legendary restaurant. In a few short years, he became a millionaire in his own right. Never forgetting who helped him become successful, he was famous for throwing the famous Eskimo Joe's birthday bash every summer. Thousands of people crowded the small city block around the restaurant for an entire weekend; eating, drinking, and dancing in the street. City officials eventually grew tired of the problems associated with the annual block party and called an abrupt halt to it several years ago.

Lenny pushed the accelerator to the floor as he raced toward Stillwater. He didn't have time for this, but it was the Cubs' year. The odds were too good to pass up an opportunity to bet on the Cubs. His habit of always going for the big score placed him in debt to Big Joe McCain. Big Joe covered most of Oklahoma. Wednesdays he worked Oklahoma City and Fridays he worked Tulsa. Thursday nights were spent in Stillwater, a bit out of the way, but still located between the two major Oklahoma cities. He always chose Eskimo Joe's for dinner and beer with the boys. And business. Lots of business.

Lenny learned about Big Joe running numbers from one of the waiters at Eskimo Joe's. He had been dealing with him only a month and already Lenny owed four thousand dollars to Big Joe. But this is the Cubs' year, and the odds on the Colorado game would cover his debt when he won. He knew it. Big Joe would go for that deal; sure he would. Big Joe always did.

Exactly one hour after leaving Enid, Lenny reached the city limits of Stillwater. The town wasn't big. In fact, if you removed the university, there wouldn't be much left. He stayed on 58, passed the small house where Garth and Sandi Brooks lived when they attended school there, and took a left to Eskimo Joe's. It was early evening, but the parking lot was already full. Lenny parked down the street and hoofed the block to the restaurant. He entered the front door, working his way through the crowd at the downstairs bar to the narrow staircase leading upstairs.

At the top of the stairs, he faced a solid wall of people, smoke, alcohol, and loud music. Thursday Night was always a busy one, and the partying started early. Squirming his way through the mass of people, Lenny at last reached the restaurant section of the bar. As he approached the doorway, two large shadows, ex-football player types, stepped in front of him.

"Mistuh McCain's been 'specting ya," said the large black man.

"Monroe, don't be so nice to the boy," the smaller white man said. Bob Allen was pure cowboy. Wranglers, Ropers, and rodeo hat—he looked every bit of country that he was. "Right now he's got some business to settle with Big Joe."

"H-how's it going, Bob Allen? Monroe?" It was obvious these two characters made Lenny nervous. That was their job, after all.

"Did you bring the money?" Bob Allen asked.

"Yeah, I did, sort of. I mean, I did, but I want to cut a deal."

"Seems to me you ain't in no place to be making no deals," Monroe responded as he grabbed Lenny's arm, walking him through the crowd toward Big Joe's table.

Lenny noticed Bob Allen right behind them, just in case by some miracle he escaped Monroe's grip.

Big Joe sat at a large table in the back of the bar, surrounded by a variety of people, most of whom consisted of hard-nosed thugs and beautiful women. When Big Joe saw them approaching, he stopped smiling. When Big Joe stopped smiling, everyone at the table stopped talking. Big Joe's short stocky frame shifted in his seat as his pudgy hands tilted his cowboy hat forward on his crewcut-covered head. The short blonde sitting next to Big Joe slowly stood up to leave the table. The brunette facing him stood up to make room. Lenny couldn't help noticing her long legs in the short blue-jean miniskirt. When she turned to face them, Lenny saw the rest of her figure matched her legs. She even garnered Big Joe's attention for a moment.

"Ellen, get the hell outta here," Big Joe told the brunette. "I'm going to ream this boy a new asshole, and I can't concentrate with you standing around here looking like you do."

Monroe deposited Lenny in the brunette's chair as she left the table to join the short blonde at the bar across the room.

"Good evening, Mr. Banks. I sure hope you have come to give me something. Monroe here gets mighty upset when I don't get what I'm supposed to."

"Evening, Big Joe. Those sure are some nice-looking ladies you have there."

"Don' sit there and try and blow smoke up my ass boy," Big Joe barked from across the table. "Did you bring me what you were supposed to, or are you gonna sit there and bullshit me?"

"Yes, sir. I mean no, sir. I mean I've got the money, and I'm not trying to bullshit you. I've got it . . . all four thousand."

"Well, now you're talking. Give me my money, and get your ass outa' here."

"Well, Big Joe . . . I was wondering if maybe . . . if maybe I could try again on the Cubs' game on Saturday with Colorado."

Big Joe leaned back in his chair as his pudgy fingers caressed his chin. "You seen the spread on that game, boy?"

"Yes, sir."

"Cubs are favored, two to one odds. You put all four thousand dollars up on that and they win . . . you walk away with eight grand—after I take out what you owe me, of course."

"Yeah, that's the idea. The Cubs are hot right now. I can't lose. We both come out winners."

Big Joe smiled. He knew he would get his money regardless. He always did. "Okay, boy, I tell you what. You got balls. Big balls. I like that. Hell, I like all you Air Force boys. Y'all make me a lot of money. I'll cut you some slack this time."

"Thanks, Big Joe. I think this will make us both a little bit of money."

"Kid, you just don't get it, do you?" Big Joe said, laughing. "I make money whether you win or lose."

Lenny noticed everyone smiled or laughed at him along with Big Joe—even Monroe and Bob Allen, whose faces had been nothing but stone since they first laid eyes on him.

"Bob Allen! You and Monroe escort Mr. Banks out the front door of this fine establishment and send Ellen back over here."

"Sure thing, Big Joe," replied Bob Allen.

Monroe and Bob Allen each grabbed an arm, lifting Lenny out of his seat as the shapely brunette walked back over to the table. She ran her hand across Lenny's chest in a teasing manner as she passed him.

"Oh, and Mr. Banks," Big Joe said as he took a drag off his cigar. "If you lose . . . you owe me eight thousand dollars."

CHAPTER 11

August 19, 1995

IT HAD BEEN A LONG GAME on a warm, clear, Saturday afternoon. Not since Game One of the 1970 World Series in which the Baltimore Orioles beat the Cincinnati Reds had a game been more controversial. The Cubs trailed most of the game. Colorado had a rally in the second inning and scored a nightmare six runs. They followed with another two in the third. The Cubs awakened from their slumber and held the Rockies scoreless for the next six innings. They staged a gradual comeback by scoring one in the third and one in the fourth. But here, in the top of the ninth, the Cubs came alive. Five runs, bases loaded, and one out. Leftfielder Corky Johnson stood at the plate. On a two-and-one count, he swung at a pitch low and outside. Johnson's bat was an inch from the ground when he connected. The ball took a quick bounce and headed straight toward the first baseman. The runners, seeing the ground ball, took off to advance their position. Alfonzo Lopez, the runner on third, was twelve steps from home before the ball was caught. The first baseman caught the ball, and knowing the runner will score regardless of his actions, casually stepped on first.

In the tradition of the 1970's World Series blunder, home plate umpire Alan Peterson ruled the ball a line drive, and thus a double play. Game over, Cubs lose. The sportscasters saw it, the fans saw it, and the players saw it. Lenny Banks saw it. He cried.

The following Thursday came and went. Lenny didn't go to work that day or the next, claiming illness, which wasn't far from the truth. It wasn't every day a UPT student owed eight thousand dollars to one of Oklahoma's biggest thugs. Now here he was, eight grand owed to Big Joe and he failed to show at the usual meeting at Eskimo Joe's to pay up. He had to figure out how to get the rest of the cash. Vince wasn't an option. Lenny realized he had pushed the outside of the envelope on their last transaction. He had to think of something because they would be coming for him soon.

A knock at the door broke him out of his trance. Lenny threw the sheets off to the side, swung his legs off the bed, and stepped on the floor. He walked through the darkness and carefully placed his ear against the door. Unable to hear anything, he took another gamble: he opened the door and hoped Bob Allen and Monroe did not break his legs.

"Jesus, Lenny, you look like crap."

The voice was familiar. Squinting into the bright sunlight, Lenny realized it was Jason. He breathed a sigh of relief and released the fist he had unconsciously made.

"What time is it?" Lenny asked.

"About one-thirty."

"On Saturday?"

"Yeah, Saturday." Jason leaned against the brick wall opposite Lenny's doorway. He stared at his withering shape in the doorway. "Hey man, are you sick or what?"

"Yeah, I'm sick. I mean, I'm not sick-sick. I just haven't been feeling well."

"Did you go to the flight doc?"

"Yeah, but I told him I had the runs . . . I couldn't keep any food down."

"Do you?"

"Do I what?"

"Have the runs?"

"No, no, I just haven't been well. I guess I'm better today," Lenny said from behind the halfway open door. His eyes were starting to adjust to the light, and he looked less and less like a corpse.

"Matt and I are on our way to the mall. I thought I'd check to see if you wanted to go."

"No. Thanks, though."

"Are you up to going to the party at Chicaros tonight?"

Lenny hesitated for a moment. It might do him good. It might help him think. Chicaros was safe. No one would bother him in a bar full of people.

"Yeah, I think I will."

"Great, I'll drive. We'll leave about five-thirty."

"Sounds good. Thanks, buddy. Is Kathy gonna be there?"

"Yeah. She said she wanted me to come by when I called her last night."

"How's it going with her?" Lenny said.

"I guess it's going okay," Jason said, pulling himself from the brick wall. "She's a great girl, absolutely gorgeous. I'm not sure I want another relationship right now, especially with the trouble I'm having with the books. Women detract from study time."

"Yeah, but it's not a bad trade off," Lenny said. "Hey, I'm gonna hit the shower. I'll meet you guys later." The two bid farewell as Lenny closed the door to his room. It should be safe at Chicaros. What could happen to him surrounded by his friends?

THE TRUCK ROARED THROUGH THE STREETS of Enid. Bob Allen and Monroe tapped their fingers, bobbing their heads to the upbeat rhythms of bluegrass music. The sun set as they drove north on Van Buren past Owen K. Garriott Boulevard. That eased Bob Allen's tension. He never liked doing a job in daylight.

Then again, what could go wrong on this gig? They just had to shake up this punk, scare him a little.

"What's the name of this place we're supposed to be going to?" Monroe asked as he sipped on his Coke.

The traffic light turned yellow and Bob Allen brought the truck to a stop. He'd learned a long time ago not to bring attention to yourself when you're out on a job.

"Chicaros. It's a dive on the northern part of town by the racetrack. Used to be a biker bar in the seventies and early eighties. Now it's a hangout for jet pilots."

"Jet pilots. Those fuckas chap my ass. They walk in and think they own everything. They live here a year or so and all they do is badmouth the place. I'd like to bust some heads on their own turf."

"Easy there, Monroe. Remember what Big Joe said. We're supposed to scare this kid, maybe rough him up a little bit. But not in front of a lot of people. The last thing he wants is attention."

The light turned green and Bob Allen accelerated, making a right turn into a residential neighborhood.

"Where the hell you going?"

"Short cut."

"You been here before?"

"Yeah, when I was in high school. We used to come here and sneak in through the back. They'd have live bands sometimes. That damn owner caught us every time. Guess he knew every damn customer that came into his place. Strangers stick out like a sore thumb."

It was getting dark now, and Bob Allen turned on the headlights of the dirty Chevy S-10.

"So I guess a brother like me won't blend in too well."

"Like a CPA at a rodeo, my friend."

"That's frickin' great. What's up with this place? They don't take no brothers?"

"Oh, there's brothers there. Just ain't none of 'em six-five and a hard two-sixty."

Monroe's smile beamed. "That's right, my man. Step back, jack. Ain't nobody gonna mess with The Terminator."

The two laughed as they drove toward Chicaros. Now Bob Allen was sure nothing could go wrong.

CHAPTER 12

August 19, 1995

THROUGHOUT THE COURSE of the evening, his eyes followed her. She knew it. After all, she watched him, too. They flirted back and forth all night. Occasionally she'd bring him a shot or another beer. The effects of the alcohol were starting to get to him. When she walked by, he reached out to her arm.

"Kathy," Jason said, drowned out by the Pink Floyd tunes booming on the stereo. "I'd really like to see you again."

"What? I can't hear you," she said. "The music's too loud."

"I said I'd really like to see you again." His eyes drooped and his words slurred.

"Oh, God, I've created a monster," she laughed. "C'mon, let's get you outside for some fresh air."

She steered him out the front door and into the parking lot, where she leaned him against the Mustang convertible parked right in front of the door.

"I told you I wanted to leave before I embarrassed myself." He seemed to be in better shape than she thought, though certainly in no condition to drive a car. At least not legally.

"I guess I should have laid off giving you the shots, huh?"

"Yep," he said, flinching as the headlights of a vehicle blinded him.

Kathy turned as a truck across the street turned off its lights. She looked back at Jason.

"You poor thing. Are you going to be okay?"

"Gonna be fine." His voice had a tipsy sound to it. "Just wanted to let you know . . . you are the most remarkable woman ever I've met."

His words had a definite slur to them. She knew what he meant.

"I wanted to let you know that I would like to see you when you're not working so you couldn't give me drinks and that way I could see you and I would be able to talk an' make a little bit more sense than I'm making now."

"You sweetheart, I'd love to—"

"Hey, sweet cheeks," a voice said, "we'll give you a ride home if that weenie's too drunk."

Kathy turned as the two cowboys walked toward her. These guys were big. Bigger than the average people that came here. Definitely not pilots.

"Whatcha' say, hon? Ready to see how the west was won?" the smaller one smirked.

"Get lost," she said.

The big black guy burst out laughing. The smaller one appeared angry, then started laughing as they walked through the front door.

THERE WAS A UNIQUE CHARACTERISTIC somehow instilled in the customers at Chicaros. When someone walked through the front door, everyone stopped what they were doing to look at who entered. Perhaps it was brought about by living in a small town and needing to be informed on the gossip. Lenny Banks, however, didn't look. Bud Bailey entertained everyone with a loud drunken story of his first solo ride, and Lenny was occupied with Bud's humorous interpretation of the event. He didn't see the two cowboys move through the crowd toward the bar.

"YOU GOT HIM YET?" Monroe asked.

"Nope," Bob Allen said, leaning against the bar, his eyes scanning the crowd.

"Is he gonna be here? Hell, he might have gone to the movies, or anywhere."

"You seen this punk. Guys like him don't stay home on no Saturday night. He'll be here eventually."

Bob Allen felt a tap on his arm and turned.

"Can I get you fellas something?" the bartender asked.

"Yeah—two Buds."

The bartender reached down, pulled out two longnecks, opened them, and set them on the bar.

"Four dollars."

Bob Allen pulled out a five and placed it on the bar. "Keep it." He handed a beer to Monroe and took a long draw on his own.

Monroe leaned back up to the bar. "So what if we don't see him tonight?"

As Bob Allen pulled the bottle from his lips, he looked at his partner. "Then we come back again next week." He started to take another swig when a smile formed on his face. The fat girl sitting across the bar and her friends had stood up to leave. And there he sat, right in front of him, not thirty feet away sitting with some friends.

"Monroe, there's our boy."

"Holy shit, we hit pay dirt! It's gonna be an early night."

Bob Allen moved away from the bar with Monroe close behind him. There, at a table against the wall, sat Lenny Banks.

Monroe's forehead wrinkled. "So what do we do now? We can't just walk over there and grab him if we want to keep it quiet."

Bob Allen scanned the bar. "I've got an idea. See the back door at the end of the bar?"

"Yeah."

"He's gotta take a piss sometime. The bathroom is right by that door. When he goes in, I'll follow him and you wait for us out the back door."

"Sounds simple, man. I just hope he hurries up and takes a piss."

The two thugs hunkered down at the bar and waited. Two beers and twenty minutes later, Lenny headed for the bathroom. He walked past the two cowboys without noticing them. They followed him in cautious pursuit.

Bob Allen stood outside the door until Monroe walked out the back. The old door didn't sit right on the hinges and didn't close all the way. He entered the bathroom. Lenny stood alone at the urinal. He finished his business and turned to leave, glancing up at the cowboy blocking his way.

"Oh, shit!" he said.

"Oh, shit is right, boy. You and me is gonna take a walk."

"Look, I'm gonna get the money," he said. "Got half of it. Didn't want to show up without all of it 'cause I know Big Joe would be pissed."

"Dumb move, kid. Big Joe is already pissed. But don't worry, he knows he's gonna get his money. I'm just here to let you know we haven't forgotten about you." He grabbed Lenny, shoving him toward the door. "We're going to walk out the back door nice and quiet. Then we'll walk across the street to my truck. Understand?" He pressed Lenny's face against the wall with a vise-like grip around his neck.

Lenny tried to nod his head. "Aauugh . . . dammit. Take it easy."

"I said, do you understand, turdball?"

"Yeah, I understand. Take it easy, okay?"

The cowboy released his grip, opening the bathroom door. "Okay, let's go. And kid . . . don't piss me off." They stepped out of the bathroom and headed out the back door.

"Hello, skinny white boy. We've been looking for you."

SEEING MONROE WAS NOT A HAPPY SIGHT. Lenny knew it was business with Bob Allen, but Monroe took pleasure in a good beating. The large black man grabbed his arm, dragging him to the field across the street where they parked the truck. Bob Allen looked around to check if anyone observed them. The outside of the bar appeared deserted.

They crossed the street at a brisk walk, Lenny stumbling to keep up with Monroe's fast pace. As they approached the truck, Monroe slung Lenny's one-hundred-and-fifty pound frame against the fender. Off-balance, Lenny twisted as his back slammed against the truck. He fell to one knee and before he could stand, Monroe pounced. Jerking him to his feet, Monroe delivered two quick blows to his stomach, knocking the breath out of him. Propped against the truck, Lenny struggled to regain his breath, unable to run, unable to move. All he could do was watch as Monroe drew back, delivering a crushing blow to his right eye. Lenny never noticed the blood fly through the air, only the immense pain. Dizziness overcame him, and he slumped to the ground.

VINCE GREW TIRED OF CHICAROS. He left his beer half-full and walked around the bar. Kathy was focused on Jason and nothing here interested him much. He walked out front for some fresh air. The atmosphere outside was a pleasant change. No smoke, no loud music, no more drunken stories. He was not much of a drinker. His two beers had given him a buzz. Taking a deep breath, he savored the freshness of the cool evening air, a sign of the changing seasons. An early winter possibly. He always liked the snow. It reminded him of home.

Across the street, he saw two cowboy types trying to help their drunk buddy off the ground into their truck. The two cowboys stood him on his feet. Suddenly the black one reared back, throwing a crushing blow into the man's stomach. The drunk doubled over, stumbling between the two, falling to his knees. Gasping for air with blood dripping down his face, he tried to crawl away. The smaller white man grabbed the drunk and jerked him up by his shirt collar. Vince recognized the clothes . . . the hair . . . the scarecrow frame . . . Lenny!

Darting from the shadows and across the street, Vince walked straight toward them at a quick pace. The black man saw him first, stepping in his direction.

"Get outa here, boy. This here don't concern you."

The small white guy looked up as Vince moved toward them. Releasing his grip on Lenny, he moved next to the larger black man. "Go back inside, kid. You got no business out here."

Vince didn't slow down. His confidence and determination never ebbed. He stopped in front of them as the black man reached out to grab him. Vince grabbed his right wrist and pulled the black man's hand back toward his elbow. The black man screamed in pain. Pulling the arm like a chicken wing behind his back, Vince, standing behind him now, stepped down and out, hard at his knee joint, causing the big foe to fall to his knees. As his knees hit the ground, Vince brought his left fist around in a roundhouse, smashing him in the left temple. The figure went limp as Vince turned to face his partner.

As he turned, he felt a hand reaching his shoulder. Vince grabbed the hand, spun on his heels, twisted the arm, and flipped the guy with a judo move that put the man on his back. The smaller white cowboy quickly leaped back on his feet, moving toward Vince. Vince dropped to all fours and swung his foot wide, knocking him to the ground. Vince pounced, delivering two quick blows to the jaw, leaving him dazed and bleeding in the wet grass.

The large black man wobbled to his feet. Vince turned on him now, firing several solid blows to the stomach. He moved behind him, reaching around with his right arm, Vince grabbed the man's collar on the left, placing his fist snug against his neck. Vince made an "X" with his arms, a torturous vise-like hold, and as he applied more pressure, his grip cut off the blood flow to the man's brain. Unable to breathe, the black man could no longer resist. Blood dripping from his mouth, he fell to the ground. His six-foot five-inch, two-hundred sixty pound partner fell unconscious at the feet of his smaller attacker.

Vince walked to Lenny and helped him to his feet. He was in pretty bad shape, but there appeared to be no permanent damage. Vince carried him to the bar, only stopping once to look back at the scene of the fight. The black man was unconscious on the ground and the smaller white man couldn't stand.

After setting Lenny down outside Chicaros, he headed back across the street and told the white man, "You gather up your pal, get in your damn truck, and go back to wherever the hell you're from." Not waiting for a reply, he turned, heading back to the bar.

"Let's go around the back, Vince. I don't want to walk in looking like this," Lenny said.

"All right," he said, noticing that the white man had taken his advice and was helping his partner into the truck. "You wait by the car. I'll go inside and get everyone else."

"Roger that."

Vince knew when the alcohol wore off, Lenny would be in real pain. They stopped at the back gate to Chicaros as the two cowboys drove away.

"Who are those guys?" Vince asked.

"I'll tell you tomorrow."

"Yes, you will."

Lenny nodded his head as the taillights disappeared in the distance. Vince knew the two would be back. It was just a matter of time.

CHAPTER 13

August 28, 1995

CURT DAVIS LOVED COMPUTERS. His wife accused him of loving computers more than his family. That was not true, he would tell her over the years, but he was beginning to wonder otherwise. He had sat at a computer for the last three hours analyzing every detail of the Air Force computer system. Curt continuously placed different types of software into the computer, then logged on and off the system. It was a long, laborious process, and his eyes began to hurt. He stood, stretching his legs as he peered into the hallway. Empty. No wonder, it was lunch time. The flying squadron was always empty this time of day. Curt walked down the hall to find a soda machine to get some caffeine into his body.

This had been a tough nut to crack. He thought it was a joke when they first told him about it. Who would want to steal a bunch of tests from a test bank? Dumb question. One of the students, obviously.

Curt found the soda machine and dropped three quarters in the slot. Seventy-five cents for a Coke. Highway robbery. He popped the top, walked outside, and stood by the door. He closed his eyes as the bright sunlight struck his face, and he rubbed them gently to compensate for the abrupt change. Pulling his cigarettes out of his shirt pocket, he lit one with one hand. He contemplated kicking the habit as he inhaled the smoke deep into his lungs. The nicotine fired through his body, racing into his bloodstream to calm his nerves. *Hello, old friend. It's good to see you, and I hate you. I'm gonna die before I'm forty-five, which isn't far off.*

Curt had been outside five minutes before Alonzo Jacobs drove into the parking lot.

"You know those things will kill you," Alonzo said.

"Tell me about it. Want one?"

"No thanks. How's it going over here?"

"Slow, very slow. Whoever this guy is, he's good. Took about two hours to figure out how he accessed the databank. He broke through the firewall with no problem. The databank is encrypted, but not the software. The software is two years old, and they've just now put it on the military computers. System is already outdated, and they think they have something new here. Want to know how I did it?"

"No, it might scare me. What's a firewall?"

Curt took a drag of his cigarette. "A firewall is kind of an 'iron curtain' around the computer system. It's supposed to act like a wall to stop somebody from accessing your PC. Like anything else, they get outdated."

"Are you going to be able to track this guy?"

"Finding him will be the hard part. This guy has covered his tracks well, making it impossible to trace him from what he's done so far. I did figure out what happened with your pal over at personnel, though. That was an accident. Once he hacked into the base LAN, he took a wrong turn and ended up at personnel. But the hard drive here is his target. He wants these tests."

"That makes sense. So what's your prognosis on our hacker?"

"Well, he's very good, but not very smart. Been pulling these tests out one at a time. It's like he pulls them out as he needs them."

"And that's bad?"

"Not if he wants to get caught. If he's smart, he would have accessed this system one time and pulled out every test. I think he's the typical hacker. It's a game to him. Gets his kicks by beating the system. He takes them out one at a time to see if he's been found out, or to see if the security has been beefed up."

"Sounds like you've got this guy figured out pretty good. Any ideas on who we might be searching for?"

"Student pilot. I've talked to some of the instructors around here, and they tell me there aren't many bases where he could be. Four locations: Laughlin and Sheppard in Texas, Vance in Oklahoma, and Columbus in Mississippi. Sheppard may not be a player because they have a different syllabus, and I'd say a beginning student based on the tests he's stolen. And he keeps stealing them in order. The instructors here confirm the thefts correspond to where these kids are in the program. Could be someone else, an outsider, but that's a slim, slim chance. Everything fits together too well, especially when the tests were stolen. It's a student. I'm sure of it."

"I agree. So what have you got cooked up to get this guy? If we can't track him down, how do we get him?"

"We wait. This guy has hacked several times; he'll hack again. Unfortunately, there's not another test for three weeks, which means we could be waiting for three minutes or three weeks. I think he's using a new scrambler on the commercial market called SCRAMBLTEK. It's a program that allows you to call on a modem and make the number you are calling from untraceable."

"How the hell did something like that ever get marketed?"

"Easy. The manufacturer claimed it's targeted for those millions of internet users who are plagued by junk mail sent to them from people getting their internet address. It's a good thing, but like all good things, somebody somewhere will use it for the dark forces of evil."

Alonzo laughed. "Well, if it's not traceable, how do we catch him?"

"My dear friend, lest ye forget, he may be good, but I'm better."

"Naturally."

"Of course. Now, in layman's terms, I will simply unscramble his scrambler."

"Is that possible?"

"Yes, it just takes a long time. I've built an alarm that will activate a program to track him. Been writing the program for the last hour, but I've still got a ways to go. I'm also putting in a few commands that will help me out in case that's not the exact program he's using."

"So what you're telling me is, the odds of catching this guy are pretty good."

"Oh, we'll catch him all right. It's just a matter of time."

THE MEETINGS AT THE DACHA COMPLEX had increased to twice a week during the past month. Viktor Kryuchkov sat back in his large leather chair after the latest meeting, his feet flat on the floor. The room lay empty except for him. The meeting had been long and draining. It was obvious something must be done, and he knew what his country needed, though it would be difficult to achieve. Reaction from the international community would play a pivotal role in bringing his plan to fruition. Viktor had grown tired. Planning the overthrow of a government is no easy task. He'd have to accomplish it with the minimum amount of bloodshed, in the shortest amount of time. The loud knock on the large walnut doors brought him back to the here and now.

"Enter," he said.

Viktor looked up to see his old friend Aleksandr Chebrikov carrying two glasses and a bottle of vodka.

"Aleksandr, I thought you left with the others."

"I did originally. However, I began to worry about your welfare, so I came back. Strictly for medicinal purposes."

Viktor grinned. "I am sure. And why is it you are so concerned about my health?"

Aleksandr sat across from Viktor and filled both glasses with the vodka. He leaned forward, handing one glass to Viktor across the large oak desk.

"I've been watching you the past couple of weeks. You have been working yourself far too much. There is something else, though, troubling you. Now, I am here to find out what."

Taking a sip of the vodka, Viktor smiled, leaning back in his chair to look at the ceiling. "These are bad times, Aleksandr. Russia has no soul."

"What do you mean, comrade?"

"This evolution of capitalism that has overtaken the country the past decade has brought with it all the evils of the West. Mother Russia lost her soul when we lost Communist rule. Last month, two fourteen-year-old boys were arrested for murder. Just small boys who should be playing sports. My third cousin on my wife's side? His daughter is a prostitute. A twelve- year old. Our country is disintegrating around us. We, as a country, have no universal values. There is no foundation for the young people to grow on, to build on. We have no pride; as a result, we have nothing to rally around."

"Where are you going with this, Viktor?"

"Do you remember, Aleksandr, many years ago when we were young officers stationed on the Berlin Wall?"

"All too well, old friend."

"Where do you think we went wrong with the wall?"

"I'm not sure what you mean."

"The wall was put up for a reason. It was a show of resolve on our behalf. It also kept Western spies from gaining access to our country so easily. But it was more of a symbol than an effective means of crowd control."

"I agree, but I fail to see where you are going."

"When we first put up the wall, we failed to take into account the international reaction, particularly the reaction of the United States. They viewed it as a threat, and they responded accordingly. A few years back, the fool Zhirinovsky made all his boasting and loud comments that did nothing but attract attention from the international communities."

"He did generate much enthusiasm from the people."

"He also generated much hatred among the people. Hatred for each other; hatred for the violence of the past. That was his downfall. In a modern society, no leader will ever sustain his power if he is a hate-monger. Zhirinovsky was a strong advocate of a return to the Communist Party rule, but his methods brought too much interference from the international community. He stirred the emotions of that, how do they say, 'hippie' president in the United States," he said with a chuckle. He found it hard to believe America survived as a country the way it picked its leaders. There always seemed to be some scandal surrounding them. Actors, drug-using war protesters . . . it was amazing. Truly the luckiest country in the history of the world.

"If we are to initiate the new revolution, we must do so slowly, over a period of time, to show the people gradually that the ways of the Communist Party will work for their benefit. We must develop a strong foundation that represents a significant amount of the people without attracting too much attention to ourselves. If we can accomplish this, we will be able to avoid the involvement of outside parties, especially the United States."

"But Viktor, how can you expect such actions to go unnoticed? Surely, they will not miss such events taking place?"

Viktor leaned back in his chair, glaring at the ceiling, his hands clasped in his lap. "Perhaps they need something else to focus on."

CHAPTER 14

August 28, 1995

LENNY BANKS SHIFTED uncomfortably in his seat. It had been a long day, but fortunately he was not on the flying schedule. He could leave as soon as the second period of sorties stepped to the aircraft. Lenny sat at his desk most of the day, leafing through flight publications, pretending to study. Not feeling sociable, he'd spoken to no one.

Vince was flying both periods and had been too busy to talk. Lenny tried to find him on Sunday, but he was gone all day and well into the evening. They hadn't spoken of Lenny's rescue since Saturday night. Vince saved his life. Not that it is particularly worth saving at the moment, but he felt the need to thank him. The walls were starting to close in, and he needed to reverse that process fast. He also needed to think of a way to find another four thousand dollars.

"Lenny, you okay?"

Lenny recognized Jason's voice. Still reading his pubs, he nodded slowly. "Just a little sore. No, a lot sore."

"Who were those guys?" Jason asked.

"I'm not sure," Lenny said. "Never seen them before. I must have pissed them off somehow. I was pretty drunk."

"But you were with us the whole time. You didn't have enough time to piss anyone off."

"Hey, how's things going with you and Kathy?"

Jason acknowledged the deflection and followed along. "Good, I guess. She's pretty aggressive."

"All right, my man!"

"No, not that way. Well, maybe. It's like . . . like she needs to have somebody there. She always wants to spend time together."

"And you're saying that's bad?"

"Well, I don't know. I mean right now it is. I'm getting over the divorce, and I have to study."

"I can understand that. She is one hell of a catch, though."

"True, but that's what I thought about my ex-wife."

"Hey, Banks!" someone yelled from across the room.

Lenny looked up to see the scheduler, Captain Dave Smith, eyeing him from behind the scheduling desk. He was one of those disgruntled pilots who had received an assignment out of UPT as an instructor pilot. FAIP's (fapes), they were called—First Assignment Instructor Pilots.

"Yes, sir?" he said.

"Get over here a minute," barked the instructor.

"Excuse me," Lenny said to Jason, "reality calls out to me once more." Lenny stood and walked to the scheduling desk.

"Did you get your pre-requisite for the first instrument block done yet?" Smith said.

Lenny thought for a moment. He had done everything required to start the instrument part of training, but he had not filled out the bubble sheet that would tell the computer he had finished it.

"No, sir, not yet."

"What do you have left to do?"

"I've done the readings. Still got to go to the learning center and view the tapes," he said with a poker face.

Captain Smith turned to face the scheduling board. His eyes scanned the empty slots and the names that could fill those holes. Of those names, Lenny's was the only one close to being opted for it. Lenny knew he'd have to send someone to sit in the simulator and use it for an hour. If it went unused, that would be Captain Smith's ass. The flight simulators were owned by the Air Force, but the people who controlled and operated them were civilians under contract. They could care less if someone used it—they were paid either way.

"Okay Banks, you get your ass over to the learning center and get your prerequisites accomplished." Captain Smith scanned the flight room. "Hey Lieutenant Williams. Front and center!"

Lieutenant Samantha Williams walked over to the scheduling board. "Congratulations, you're going to get to sit in the sim for an hour and go over checklist procedures."

Lenny patted her on the back as he headed for the door. "Have fun, Samantha." Once outside the flight room, he picked up his pace. He was fortunate to dodge that bullet. The last thing he needed today was to start a new block of training. He was tired and his ribs still hurt. It had been a long day, but he realized it was almost complete.

Lenny stayed in the learning center for about fifteen minutes. The tapes he was supposed to watch lasted about an hour and a half, but he refused to sit through them again. He returned to his quarters and managed to fall asleep after a mere five minutes. He woke up to the six o'clock evening news on the television set. Same old news. Crime rate in America was up, abortion rights argued, economy in Russia sucks. The news was too predictable these days. Lenny climbed out of bed and walked to the bathroom to wash the sleep out of his eyes. The cool water woke him up quickly.

He'd been asleep over two hours. *That's good,* he thought, *I need the rest.* His stomach growled. He'd skipped lunch and now his body told him it was time to make up for it.

In the kitchen, Lenny popped a frozen pizza into the microwave. The timer went off as someone knocked at the door. Lenny pulled the dinner out of the microwave and set it on the counter. The hotplate burned his hands as steam rose to the ceiling. He shook his hands to cool them as he walked to the door.

"Hello, old friend. Do you feel like talking now?" Vince said.

"Yeah, come on in," he said, turning back to his steaming dinner. "I tried to call you yesterday. You weren't home."

Vince plopped himself on the couch and stretched out his legs. His flight suit, covered with perspiration salt stains, was unzipped to his navel; the white T-shirt underneath soaked with sweat. Vince appeared tired, but seemed to be in a good mood.

"I was away on business."

"Oh. Well, you're here now, so I guess I should thank you for the other night."

"Accepted. Besides, it was fun."

"A real blast, man. I can't wait to do it again."

"Understood. So who were those guys? Friends of yours from one of the many quality casinos throughout the Midwest?"

Lenny put his dinner aside, walked to the refrigerator, and pulled out two Coors Lights. He handed one to Vince, then plopped in his recliner facing the television.

"I'm in trouble, Vince, serious trouble. I should have listened to what you said to me a long time ago. I'm in deep."

VINCE LEANED BACK, sipping on his Coors Light, carefully studying every word Lenny spoke. The kid appeared to be sincere for once.

"The guys that jumped me . . . they work for this guy in Stillwater." Lenny stared blankly at the TV as he spoke. "Big Joe McCain. He's a big-time bookie for most of Oklahoma. Anyway, I placed this bet with him about two weeks ago, and I lost. Man, I lost big. I don't know what to do. I mean, this is big-time trouble—"

"How much money?"

"—I'm in here. I can't pay this back right now. I guess I could try and get a loan, but hell, all my credit cards are maxed out—"

"How much money?"

"—and I still owe lots on my new car. Man, I'm in deep. Big Joe sends these two gorillas to collect. I mean, I should have suspected he would, right? After all, I missed the payoff date. He's been cutting me slack."

"Lenny, how much money?"

Lenny snapped out of the trance he'd placed himself in and looked at Vince for the first time.

"Eight thousand dollars," he said calmly as he took a long swig from his beer and promptly hid his face in his hands.

"You're right—you're in deep shit." Vince downed the last of his beer and walked over to the fridge to retrieve another.

As he studied Lenny, Vince almost felt sorry for him. A fool and his money are soon parted, and here was the classic example. How this skinny geek got into this kind of trouble was a mystery. There were more factors to the equation now, though. The second he stepped in to rescue Lenny, he became involved. Whoever these guys were, they would be back, next time with more friends. No doubt they would be searching for two people instead of one. This was an aggravation he did not need right now. It did not fit into his plan to maintain a low profile while at UPT. He had only one choice.

"I'll give you the money."

Lenny didn't move.

Vince said it again, "Lenny, I said I'll give you the money."

Lenny looked up, his red eyes glazed in disbelief. He leaned back in the chair and started to ask a question, but stopped before any words came out. Running his hand through his ruffled hair, he looked at Vince, unsure of what to say.

"Keep in mind this is not a gift. It's a business deal. There is no negotiating, no more price adjustments, no more B.S."

"The tests, right? Okay, there's a couple more coming up. No problem." Lenny started to come back to life. It was as if someone had lifted a great burden from his shoulders.

"I don't think you understand. I want all the tests. T-37's, T-38's, T-1's and every stan/eval test in between."

"Holy crap, Vince, that's not fair."

"Look, you little dirt bag, I've been more than generous to you, but I'm sick and tired of your bullshit. I've sponsored your debt long enough. I saved your ass two nights ago, and now it's over. I'll get your money to you tomorrow, but I want those tests."

"Yeah, sure . . . but don't expect 'em all at once. I mean, I'm not sure how they hand out the stan/eval tests."

"Make it happen, Banks," Vince said. "And by the way, old friend, don't crash and burn on this one. I promise you, if you do, you won't walk away from it."

CHAPTER 15

August 29, 1995

THE SKY TOUCHED THE GROUND from the horizon in the east to the setting sun in the west. A beautiful sight. The sparsely populated flatlands of northwest Oklahoma always made a nice foreground for a sunset on a clear night. The stars would be out soon, spreading from the ground to the top of the sky and back again, each more distinct than the next. Jason's car raced north along the deserted street out of town toward Kathy's house. The silence broke as a T-38 screamed through the sky, heading back to Vance. The jet brought his thoughts back into perspective. It would be easy for Kathy to talk him into staying longer. He'd have to fight the urge. He needed to discuss with her how much time he used during the week socializing. He'd spent two nights a week for the last three weeks having dinner with her or hanging out. A lifetime to a UPT student.

As Jason pulled into the circular driveway of the large ranch house, he noticed the Jones' car not present once again. Kathy greeted him at the door before he could knock. "Hi, tiger," she said happily. "You look deep in thought."

"Hi," he said, hugging her. He didn't know why he hugged her. He never had before when greeting her. It just seemed like a natural reaction. "I guess I was daydreaming about the beautiful sunset. My mind was just wandering."

"Well, wander in here then. I've cooked a nice dinner for you. I think you need time to relax. How did you do on your instrument test?"

Jason shook his head. The Instrument Flight Rules test was extremely difficult. He had studied like a madman, but it still didn't make sense. These were the rules pilots followed when out in the airways with the rest of the flying world. Flying instrument approaches in the weather and flying in the airways. It was tough. He barely made it.

"I made an eighty-six," he said in a low tone, his face flushed.

"What's passing? Eighty-five?"

"Yeah," he said.

"Do you know what they call the doctor who finishes last in his class?"

Jason shook his head.

"Doctor," she said smiling. "Don't get wrapped up in your grades so much. The bottom line is you finish and do a good job. You'll get your airplane, but you can't sweat the small stuff."

Kathy's words made him smile. He appreciated her understanding; her insight impressed him. Jason reached into his pants pocket. "I picked something up for you," he said.

"Jason, you didn't have to get me anything."

"Don't worry, it's nothing special," he said, placing the object in her hand.

She opened her hand to find a small, circular key chain with a horse's head in the center. The silver coating glistened in the light. "It's lovely," she cooed. "You are so sweet." She kissed him on the cheek and walked back into the kitchen, placing her new key ring on the key chain holding her keys and mini-flashlight.

"What's for dinner?" he asked as he walked into the living room. The huge room possessed vaulted cathedral ceilings and a large fireplace. There were several stuffed animals neatly mounted and proudly displayed throughout the room. Over the fireplace hung a moose head. Jason noticed the eyes of the moose followed him as he walked around the room.

"Homemade enchiladas, Spanish rice, and fruit salad. Sorry, but I won't feed you beans. Do you want a beer?"

"No thanks. Water's okay."

"Coke?"

"Yeah, sure, Coke is fine."

"Go sit on the couch. I'll bring you your drink. Dinner will be ready in about fifteen minutes."

"No Italian tonight?"

Wiping her hands on a towel, she walked to the entrance of the living room. "No. Tonight, you get to experience the hot-blooded Mexican side of me," she said with a wry smile. "I hope you can handle it."

Jason gulped at that last comment. He'd love to handle it. He wasn't sure if tonight should be the night, though. After such a poor showing on his test, he knew he'd be a target for questions by the instructors in the morning.

"I'm going to change clothes," she said, handing him a Coke. "You can turn on the television while you wait."

Jason picked up the remote and pressed the power button. The big screen television impressed him. He wasn't interested in watching anything, but the distraction might help him relax. He leaned back in the chair and closed his eyes. Jason's mind raced with a million thoughts of flying, the Air Force, his past, and Kathy. Flying should be on his mind now. Flying was why he was here, and it should be the only thing that mattered. He had to stay focused. Bethany had called again last week and that, too, had been a distraction. Flying was his goal . . .

"Wake up, Jason."

"I'm not asleep," he said, unsure if it was a true statement.

Kathy stood in front of him, striking a pose, yet seeming casual as she did so. Around her waist hung a black sarong, conveniently falling to either side of her left thigh, protruding slightly forward. She wore a white sleeveless halter-top tied in a knot below her breasts. Her skin glistened with a freshness as Jason caught the slight fragrance of her flowery perfume.

"Wow." The word fell out of his mouth.

"Easy, tiger, it's time to eat." Kathy grabbed his hand, pulling him off the couch to the table.

"This looks great," he said, eyeing the dinner. Jason hadn't seen a meal like this outside a restaurant. Two trays of enchiladas were on the table next to a steaming bowl of Spanish rice complete with fresh red peppers. Fresh bread lay neatly in a basket, and a bottle of Sangria stood between two candles.

After starting to eat, he decided to ditch the Sangria and have a beer. An hour later, he was on his third. Jason sat on the couch sipping the cold beer as he watched Kathy clean up the kitchen. He'd wanted to help, but she insisted on his relaxing on the couch. When she finished, she sat on the couch next to him. Nestling close, she curled her legs up under her and rested her head on his chest.

"This is nice," she said without looking at him.

"Yes, it is," he replied, his mind fighting to concentrate on where it should be, as opposed to where he was. It was nice having her in his arms, so why was he so desperate to leave? His plan for not staying too late was long since a dream. The pressures of UPT were building; he could feel it coming fast. Morning standup would be a nightmare. With the low score on the test, he was the logical candidate.

Without warning, she reached up, grabbed the back of his neck, and pulled his face closer to hers. Their lips met, and she kissed him passionately. The kiss was long and wet, and Jason responded with similar feelings. They shifted their bodies, stretching out along the full length of the couch. Their legs wrapped around each other; their bodies intertwined. Kathy reached for the buckle of Jason's belt and started to unbuckle it.

RRIIINNNGG!!!

"Damn!"

"Don't answer it," Jason said as he nibbled on her ear.

"It might be the Joneses. I have to check. I'm sorry, I'll be right back."

Kathy rose from the couch, not bothering to straighten her clothes, and answered the phone in the kitchen. "Hello," she said.

"Hey, babe, it's your favorite aviator," the voice said.

"Who is this?"

"It's Vince Andrews. Who did you expect?"

"Why are you calling me?"

"Why do you think? I've got a crush on you, and I think we should do something about it."

Kathy stood silent. She knew she should hang up, but something made her hang on.

"I'm busy right now."

"Oh, I hope I didn't interrupt anything. Just how busy are you? There's not some strange man over there, is there?"

"What I'm doing is none of your business," she replied harshly.

"Kathy, I don't mean to upset you. I just think you and I need to go out."

"Sorry, I've got plans. How did you get this number?"

"I understand. I can wait. We can meet another night."

"Look, I appreciate the attention, but I've got to go."

"You have a man over there, don't you?"

"What I'm doing is none of your business."

"Is it serious?"

"Why are you calling me?"

"You know, I don't think you're really serious about this guy."

"How do you know?"

"So you *do* have a man over there."

Kathy, though perturbed, found herself not wanting to hang up the phone. She glanced toward the couch in the living room and saw no movement.

"How do you know whether I'm serious or not?" she snapped defensively.

"Sweetheart, if you were serious about this guy, you wouldn't be hanging on the phone listening to what I have to say."

"Bull."

"Yeah, right. Then explain yourself."

"I don't have to explain anything. You're the one who called me."

"And you're the one on the date talking to me."

"I'm sorry. I have to go."

"You want to go out with me, don't you?"

"Goodbye!" she said, hanging up the phone hard.

Kathy slowly walked to the living room, noticing her palms were sweaty and her heart racing. What the hell was going on? Vince Andrews was an obnoxious ass, yet she found him strangely attractive in a dangerous sort of way. She lay back on the couch with Jason and curled up once again in his arms.

"Is everything okay?"

"Yes, they're fine," she said, implying the Joneses had phoned.

They cuddled on the couch with no further physical contact. Twenty minutes later, Jason was sound asleep. Kathy lay there, staring into the darkness, wondering . . .

HE'D BEEN NERVOUS ON THE HOUR-LONG drive to Stillwater. To arrive without the money might not be a good idea, but he decided it would be a good show of faith. It was also better than being killed in a dark alley. He was sure Big Joe would want him dead after what Vince did to Monroe and Bob Allen. Parking outside Eskimo Joe's, Lenny meandered into the bar and headed upstairs. Bob Allen stood at the top of the stairs. "Hey there, boy," he said. His eyes were watery and red; his breath smelled like booze.

"I'm here to see Big Joe," Lenny said to the drunken cowboy. Bob Allen glared at him, his face bruised from the fight with Vince. Lenny assumed it was a subject not to be discussed. It was exam week, so the crowd in the bar was small. Lenny walked untouched to Big Joe's table. There was still a crowd there and the same two girls fawning at Big Joe's feet. Perspiration gathered on his forehead as he scanned the room for any sign of Monroe. Bob Allen he could stomach, but he was sure Monroe wanted to kill him.

Big Joe's eyes shot daggers at him as he approached the table. "Well, well, look what the storm blew in. I hope you're here in a delivery capacity. You owe me something, boy."

"Yes, sir," Lenny said. He eyed the other people at the table. Two of the men were in business suits, engaged in a conversation with each other. Another wore a football jersey and ordered from a waitress while his hands admired the smoothness of her legs. Another pair of cowboys sat at the opposite side of the table staring at their drinks, talking to no one. No one seemed to pay attention to what Big Joe said to Lenny except the two girls. Yet they were all aware of what transpired. It was their salary that was being discussed, after all.

"You know, you're one dumb flyboy. Them two cowboys would have killed you if I hadn't a told 'em to take it easy on you. You see, when you don't pay, you're takin' food out of my family's mouth. All these here folks," he said gesturing around the table, "this here's my family."

"I'm sorry Big Joe. I got tied up at the base with training and all. I couldn't get away because I had to work. They wouldn't let me off the base. I had a check ride and . . ."

"Look at this face, boy," Big Joe said. "Do I look dumb to you? Is there something in my genetic makeup that says to your scrawny ass that Big Joe McCain is a dumbass? I hope not. I been dealing with varmints like you for well over twenty-five years. Do you think this is the first time I've dealt with some young Air Force pup?"

"No, sir, I just—"

"At least you got manners, I'll credit you that much." The two girls giggled like teenagers. Lenny wasn't sure they were even following what was going on with his situation. Not that it mattered. "Ben, you and the rest of the boys get on outa here. Me and you, Mister Banks, have a little business to discuss. You girls, y'all just stay put. I like the way you look tonight, and I think I want you to stay right here."

Big Joe gestured to a chair for Lenny to sit at the table. Lenny moved to the seat, his eyes darting around the room. This was not a good situation. He owed the fat cowboy eight thousand dollars, was two weeks late paying up, and his best friend beat up his two henchmen. Lenny placed his sweaty palms on the tabletop and looked at Big Joe.

"You know, boy," the fat cowboy began, "you have caused me a great deal of headache and aggravation over the past two weeks. I don't know who you got helping you, but roughing up my two boys didn't help out your case none."

"I didn't do that. It—"

"I am doing the talking here, Mr. Banks. Roughing up Monroe must have spooked Bob Allen something fierce. Monroe is one big Negro. Bob Allen ain't anxious to get back to Enid real soon. But see, Mister Banks, I don't like my employees getting hassled by my customers. And when you're late with your payments . . . you see it all just makes my business look bad."

Lenny could feel his heart beat faster as his situation worsened. Monroe started to move from his position behind Big Joe toward Lenny. Big Joe reached under the table, retrieving a knife with a blade about eight inches long.

"But—"

"Don't 'but' me, boy, I ain't from West Virginia," he said as Monroe stepped behind Lenny and grabbed him behind the neck. Monroe held Lenny's left hand forward on the table, laying it flat with the fingers spread. "The way I see it, boy, is you owe me eight thousand dollars, again. Now I usually take a thousand dollars a finger as collateral. I'm even gonna let you decide which two you're gonna keep," he said, moving the large knife toward Lenny's hand.

"NNOOO!!" Lenny screamed. The noise pierced the otherwise quiet restaurant/bar as the blonde at the table jumped. Tears streamed from Lenny's eyes, and he started to scream again, Monroe clasped a hand around his mouth to muffle the noise. Through the tears, Lenny noticed Big Joe smiling, a smile that turned into a laugh; a loud laugh. As he looked around, Lenny saw everyone laughing with Big Joe, even Monroe, who relaxed his grip.

"I'm through with you, Mister Banks. Get out of here. Don't set foot in here again until you've got my money."

CHAPTER 16

September 1, 1995

IT WAS A SLOW FRIDAY at Vance Air Force Base. A commander's call cut the day short— Jason's class had only two periods during which they'd fly jets. Jason passed his "recommend" ride for his contact check ride during the first period by demonstrating his basic airplane handling skills. This included takeoffs, landings, aerobatic maneuvers, and decision-making skills. With one success under his belt, he spent most of the afternoon studying with other students and reviewing area procedure tapes in the learning center. The students were released from the flight at four o'clock, and Jason darted home to drop off his Dash One. Then, he jumped in his car, cranked the engine, and peeled out of the parking lot.

Jason had a lot get done this afternoon. The most important, catch Kathy before she went to work. He was falling for her, he could tell. Kathy treated him well and she appeared stable herself. What was the line in *Used Cars* Kurt Russell said, "I just want a woman who's got her shit halfway together"? Kathy seemed to have that. She was independent; that was a plus. Jason was aware of her past relationships with pilots and hoped their actions wouldn't be reflected upon him.

Jason drove past the rectangular-shaped headquarters building and headed for the Base Exchange. It had been a long week, and he still had his Class-A uniform to pick up at the cleaners. As he pulled into the nearest parking space, Jason noticed Gus McTaggart and Matt Carswell heading toward him, each carrying a brown grocery bag.

Jason saluted Captain McTaggart and said, "What are you two up to?"

"It's Friday, Conrad," McTaggart said. "After a long, hard week of protecting America's freedom, we decided to have a mandatory margarita call in Matt's room."

"And then we're gonna hit the club and play some crud," Matt chimed in eagerly.

"Sounds good," Jason said, "I've been ready to tie one on all week long."

McTaggart looked at Jason with concern.

"How did the flying go today?" he asked.

Jason shrugged his shoulders. "It was okay. I know I can do better, I guess I'm putting too much pressure on myself."

"Yeah, that's what usually does it. Try to relax more. The airplane won't beat you—you beat yourself."

Matt's desperation took control. "Boys, it's four-thirty right now. We best take this opportunity to go mix these here margaritas before I go into shock."

McTaggart laughed, "I guess Matt's blood-alcohol limit is getting too low. He's due for a fix. We'll see you in a few?"

"Thanks, guys, but I've got some things to take care of right now," Jason said. "But believe me, I'll be there tonight in full force."

"Sounds good, buddy. We'll see you there," McTaggart said as he trailed after Matt to the car.

Jason meandered into the cleaners, picked up his uniform, and then went into the flower shop. It took a minute for him to pick out the carnation arrangement he wanted. He sprinted out the door and climbed into his car. Glancing at his watch, he saw it read four-twenty. He had about thirty minutes before Kathy had to leave for work. Once again, the car engine roared to life, its rumblings impressive for a car over thirty years old.

He headed to Kathy's place, figuring it should take a little more than ten minutes to get there through the afternoon traffic. Pulling into the driveway, he noticed Kathy's car again sat alone. Jason realized he'd never seen the Joneses, nor had they ever been there when he was at the house. As he walked up the sidewalk, he saw the front door fly open as Kathy came running out.

"Hi, tiger!" she said as she wrapped her arms around him. Kathy squeezed him tightly and he reciprocated, holding the flowers out just far enough so he didn't crush them. At last, he managed to pull back and give her the bright carnations.

"I was thinking about you today," he said.

"You are so sweet." She took the flowers and turned toward the house.

Jason followed her inside and into the living room, the moose head still staring at him. Kathy set the flowers on the table as they both sat on the couch.

"I thought about what you said last night," Jason said. "I guess I am putting too much stress on myself. It's . . . it's just that pilot training is important to me. I sacrificed a lot to get here; I don't want to screw up. And if I do screw up, I don't want to be able to blame someone else. I want the blame to lie solely with me. If I were to spend my time with you, which by the way is a terrific idea, and I screw up, I might blame you. And I don't want to do that. Please try to understand. I like you. I want to get to know you better. But I have to graduate this program."

Kathy leaned over, kissing him softly on the cheek. "I understand," she said as she pulled back. "I'm glad you decided to come out to talk to me about it. I was beginning to think maybe you didn't think I was worth any type of conversation of substance."

"That's not it at all."

"I understand, but you can't blame me for trying to steal all of your time, now can you?"

"No, I guess not." He looked into her eyes. She seemed sincere. Maybe she was the woman for him. Life is full of strange twists and turns. Perhaps during this stressful time, she could ensure he made it through okay. The two sat chatting on the couch for the next twenty minutes. They talked politics, movies, sports, and airplanes. Jason told her about his recommend ride and his upcoming check ride on Monday.

"Oh, my God!" Kathy said glancing at the grandfather clock ringing against the wall. "It's five o'clock. I need to get ready for work. I'll walk you to the door," she said, dragging him off the couch. The two had a quick embrace at the front door. "Will I see you tonight?"

"I'll be at the club. I think I'm due a good drunk. I'm not sure whether I'll be worth seeing past nine o'clock, though."

Kathy pulled him closer, resting her head on his chest. "Well, if it's slow tonight, the boss will let me off. I'll come find you."

"Sounds good to me." They kissed one last time before Jason climbed into the canary yellow mustang to head for the club.

THE VANCE OFFICER'S CLUB was small compared to other officers' clubs around the country, but large for the number of people who actually used it. It had two dining rooms, one of which doubled as a meeting room. It also contained a large formal cocktail bar and an outdoor patio for barbecues when the weather was nice. Then there was The Cockpit. The Cockpit was a room isolated on the far side of the club. It was about thirty by sixty feet with a stage at one end and a bar at the other. On one side sat a large snooker table; on the other several small tables and chairs.

The Cockpit was where the action was on a Friday night. It gave the student pilots the opportunity to get a little stress relief without having to worry about driving home. In the old club, you could get away with anything in The Cockpit—as long as no one got hurt, it wasn't too disgusting, and you paid for whatever you broke. That philosophy went the way of the dinosaurs with the Air Force's new era of political correctness. It seemed it wasn't proper for pilots to have fun anymore.

It was five in the afternoon when The Cockpit started to fill up with flight suits and miniskirts. By the time the sun set a little after seven-thirty, the bar was packed, overflowing into the formal bar. Lenny and Gus were busy gathering team members for a game of crud.

Crud was an Air Force tradition. The exact origin of the game was unknown, but it is linked historically with Air Force fighter pilot squadrons. Almost all O clubs have a crud table, better known as a snooker table. There are two teams, consisting of any number of players, though usually six on each team. One team starts on offense and the other on defense. There are two pool balls on the table: the white cue ball and the black eight ball. The object of the game is for the offensive player to roll the white ball at the black ball and knock it in one of the pockets on the table. It is the defensive player's responsibility to prevent him from doing so. Each player on each team rotates after each shot, and each player is given three lives. The last team standing is the winner. When you combined alcohol and the players' cocky attitudes, the game gets rough. Many a fight broke out over a crud game.

Gus managed to get Matt and Bud Bailey, and finally convinced Samantha Williams to play, when Jason walked into The Cockpit.

"We got five," Gus hollered across the table. "What's your call sign gonna be, Conrad?"

"Call him Comrade," a voice butted in, "and I'll be number six."

"Thanks a lot," Jason said sarcastically, turning to face Vince as he approached the table.

"No problem," he smirked as he handed Jason a Coors Light Longneck.

"Who are you?" the captain refereeing the game asked, writing down the call signs of each player on the scoreboard.

"Loan Shark," Vince said, smiling at Lenny.

Gus gathered his team at the receiving end of the table and started his pep talk. "Okay, guys, get mean, get tough, get drunk, and make good shots. We drink for free as long as we win. If we lose, we're quiche-eaters!"

The game started slowly, but the pace increased rapidly. The other team consisted of T-38 students who had the experience of playing together longer. Gus started the game by serving to the other team. Leaning across the table, he hurled the white cue ball at the eight ball sitting at the far end of the table. The two balls hit with a loud smack as the first opponent darted around the side of the table to grab the cue ball. He scurried back to the end of the table to try to knock the eight ball in the corner pocket. No sooner had he gotten in a position to shoot, then Lenny was in his face.

The faceless opponent shot, and Lenny grabbed the cue ball in an attempt to get a shot off. Both teams had a full rotation of players before Gus claimed the first "life" from the other team. And so the battle went back and forth for the next ten minutes. The friendly match soon grew into a physical grudge match; both teams throwing elbows, stepping on feet, and hurling bodies away from the table. The remaining three on Jason's team managed to hang on to win the first game.

The following games proceeded to get rougher as the teams got drunker. Jason had taken a good solid elbow to the ribs, while Matt caught a forearm across the back of his head. Samantha was all but broken into pieces, but she continued to hang in there. Vince, on the other hand, was virtually unscathed. In fact, he seemed to be dishing out more punishment than all of his teammates combined. During one game, he started to get so out of hand, that the major who acted as referee had to step in and warn Vince to ease up. Once things settled down, the boys and girl hung on to win consecutively for the next forty-five minutes.

During their fifth game, Kathy walked into The Cockpit and worked her way to the crud table. She spotted Jason at the end and waved. Jason returned the wave with a big smile, then burst toward the table to take up a defensive position. Preventing a score, he grabbed the white ball and positioned himself for a shot. As the new defensive player positioned himself for the shot, Jason hurled the white ball with too much power and it smacked into the black ball. The white ball shot off the side rail and sailed off the table into the surrounding crowd.

"Life!" shouted the opposing players.

The referee turned to make a third X by Jason's nickname. "That's three, Comrade— you're dead."

"I'm too drunk to play anymore anyway," Jason said. He pushed his way through the crowd over to Kathy, who grabbed his hand and kissed his cheek. Jason was startled at this greeting. "Well, that was nice. What was that for?" he managed to say coherently.

"I wanted to thank you for being so sweet to me lately," she said, leading him into the formal bar. "Besides, it'll give all the gossip mongers around here something to talk about."

"Can I get you a drink?"

"I think so. I'm feeling a little wild. How about tequila?"

"Ouch. Do I have to participate?"

"Only if you don't want a woman to beat you."

Jason smiled. "I'd love for you to beat me, so I guess I'd better participate. I'll be right back."

Kathy punched him in the arm, acknowledging his wisecrack, as he moved toward the bar. She sat at one of the small round tables, and in no time, Jason returned with four tequila shots and two Coronas with lime.

"You're pretty ambitious tonight, aren't you," she said more as a statement than a question.

"I've got a feeling if I have too many more of these, I won't be able to find my way to the bar again."

"Wonderful. Well, bottoms up." Kathy licked the salt, shot the first glass of tequila, sucked the lime and took a swig of beer. Jason, somewhat amazed that a female could drink with such vigor, quickly followed suit. Kathy smiled at him and repeated the process. As she watched Jason, she had reasons to doubt he would be following her a second time.

"You don't look so good," she said with concern and a smile. She reached over to grab his hand.

"I think I forgot to mention I can't stand tequila."

Kathy laughed. "You macho flyboys. You'll do anything to try and save face. My gosh, Jason, you're turning green."

"It's good to know I look as bad as I feel," he said. "Do you mind if we go home? Real fast?"

"Under the circumstances, I think it's probably best. I'm starting to feel a little cooped up in here anyway."

THE ROOM WAS DARK when they entered Jason's quarters. Jason was able to maneuver instinctively to his bed. Kathy was not as fortunate.

"Ouch!" she exclaimed as her knee hit a solid object. "Okay, Jason, where's the light switch?"

Her only answer was mumbling as Jason turned on a lamp by the bed. Kathy looked down to see she bumped into an open desk drawer. She maneuvered around the drawer and walked over to her companion. He sat on the edge of the bed, barely. He tried to talk, but the words came out incoherently. Kathy looked at her drunken friend. Jason is a good man, she thought, but like all the rest going through this grinder of a schoolhouse, he counters the pressure with Friday night binges at the O club and Saturday night visits to Chicaros.

"Here, lie down," she said as she pulled his legs onto the bed. "Are you feeling okay? You're not going to get sick are you?"

More mumbles. He was done for the night. Disappointed and wide awake, Kathy walked across the room to the kitchen and turned on the light. Casually, she took the boxes of food left on the counter and placed them in the cabinets in a nice orderly fashion. She noticed the cabinets were essentially bare, typical of most student pilots, eating on the run or eating out. None of them really had time to cook.

Placing the last box in the cabinet, she admired the newly arranged shelves, smiling to herself for a job well done. Kathy walked to the refrigerator to examine its contents. Two six-packs of Coors Light, wheat bread, skim milk, orange juice, apples, oranges, carrots, a couple of yogurts, and a bottle of Coke. She reached in and pulled out a Coors Light. When she opened the freezer, she jumped as a frozen pizza came sliding out, crashing onto the floor. Kathy laughed at the plethora of frozen dinners, placed the pizza back in the freezer, and closed the door. This fit. Quick and easy. A man on a mission doesn't eat a real meal. Hit and run, get what you can when you can, then back to the books.

She took a sip of beer as she walked back to the bed. Jason, now unconscious, sprawled out across the mattress. Kathy set her beer on the nightstand and removed his boots. He would feel bad in the morning, and one less task might make him more comfortable. Placing his boots on the floor, she shoved him to the far side of the bed and crawled in next to him. She was in no condition to drive, and he was in no condition for seduction. Turning out the light, she laid her head down on the pillow next to him. Within ten minutes, she was asleep.

THE TEAM LOST THEIR LAST GAME, a victim of their own success. That was the way crud worked. If you won, the losers bought you drinks. As long as you won, you drank for free . . . until you were too drunk to win anymore. Vince staggered around the bar for a several minutes, searching for signs of any young women who might be roaming about looking for a good time. It wasn't long until he ran into Gwendolyn, the travel agent he'd met at Chicaros. Vince talked to her for a few minutes and bought her a drink on Jason Conrad's tab again, which she found humorous this time. They talked for several minutes until her girlfriends dragged her out of the bar, anxious to leave this rowdy scene. Gwendolyn gave him her card, which had her home and office phone numbers on it, and urged him to call her soon. Tucking the card in his breast pocket, he walked out the front door of the Officers' Club and headed toward the dorm. Normally not a drinker, he'd had too many tonight, and it was taking its toll. The physical stress of the past hour left him exhausted.

As he crossed the parking lot to the dorms, the darkness of the near-empty lot was suddenly lit up by the headlights of a truck. The truck pulled to a screeching halt right in front of Vince, its headlights blinding him. In a matter of seconds, the door on each side swung open and the familiar figures from Chicaros were upon him.

Vince braced himself for the confrontation, focusing on the larger black man, when he was suddenly knocked down from behind. Placing his right arm out to cushion his fall, his body smacked smartly on the pavement.

They were on top of him in no time. Vince quickly realized there were four of them, not two. Two of them dragged him to his feet as the first punch landed squarely on his jaw, snapping his head to the side. The blows came fast and furious, mostly body shots with an occasional head shot.

Suddenly, without warning, they stopped. Jumping in their truck, the four sped off toward the main gate, confident their warning was effective. Vince fell to his knees on the coarse cement and threw up. He collapsed on the ground, propping himself up on one elbow. Blood dripped down his face. The stench of his own vomit made him wince as he watched the truck disappear into the night.

BOOM! BOOM! BOOM!

The noise was thunderous. It throbbed throughout his head, the pain unbearable. Were these explosions? Had he been injured? Where was this nightmarish hell causing him so much pain?

BOOM! BOOM! BOOM!

There must be a way out. The noise ripped through his skull. He was lying down; he must be hurt. Otherwise, he could get up and run away. If he couldn't get away, he knew he would die . . .

Jason leaned over to glimpse the clock. Five minutes after ten. His gaze slowly scanned his surroundings. The thin ray of sunlight piercing through the curtains blinded him. He was alone in his room. Even rubbing his head tenuously felt as if someone were driving an ice pick through his skull. The stench of stale beer filled his nostrils, and he suddenly felt nauseas again. He closed his eyes again to adjust his vision. Jason hurt right now . . . really, really bad.

Knock! Knock! Knock!

The knock on the door sounded as if someone were breaking through with a sledgehammer. Jason realized it was probably a normal knock, but his throbbing head told him otherwise. He gingerly swung his feet off the bed and sat up straight, looking for a reason to open the door.

Maybe it's Kathy. After all, she was with me last night, wasn't she? How did I get home? Did she bring me?

The blood rushing from his head brought more pain. He sat there a moment and gathered himself before he tried to stand. Slowly his pulse pounded away at his head. He thought he could feel each blood cell bouncing inside his skull. He had to get to the door. If Kathy were upset with him, he had to straighten it out now. He stood on wobbly knees, realizing for the first time that he still wore his flight suit. Great, he thought, I'll make a wonderful impression this morning.

Knock! Knock! Knock!

"Just a minute," Jason said in a restrained yell. His mouth was dry, as if he'd been eating cotton balls all night. Staggering toward the door, he detoured to the fridge and poured Coke in a glass. He made it to the door, grabbing the doorknob. The bright sunlight blinded him instantly. He put his hand over his eyes to shield them from the light. In the bright haze, he made out a shapely female figure standing before him. He focused on the ground, and as his eyes adapted, he slowly scanned up the trim athletic legs to the short skirt. He paused as if thinking to himself that he should know those legs, and then quickly looked the figure in the face.

"Hello, Jason."

As the grip loosened on his drink, the glass slid out of his hand and shattered on the floor, spraying Coke and glass across the kitchen tile. Neither figure noticed. Jason continued to stare at the face for what seemed like hours, but was only seconds. Finally, when he opened his mouth, one word came out.

"Bethany?"

CHAPTER 17

September 2, 1995

THE EARLY MORNING rays of the sun shot through the open window, illuminating the room. Lenny Banks rolled over and looked at the clock. Eleven-thirty. Throwing the covers back, the large comforter fell to the floor. Without thinking, he rose and headed for the bathroom, his bladder telling him it was morning. The flush of the toilet shattered the silence that enveloped the room as he walked out of the bathroom to the kitchen. He had run this drill a thousand times. Lenny continued his march to the kitchen; more importantly, the coffee pot.

He reached the coffeemaker and pulled out the glass pot. A small remnant of the coffee sat in the bottom of the pot. It was a horrible habit he'd developed of not cleaning the pot until the next day, but he had gotten used to it. Lenny pulled out the old filter and grounds, tossing them in to the trash. After cleaning the pot, he began brewing his daily coffee.

Lenny sat on his couch, blowing the steam from his coffee. He grabbed the remote for his stereo, turned it off, and switched on the television instead. He turned on CNN, sipping his coffee as the news flashed across the screen. It was the usual happenings in the world, war in the Middle East, more Defense cuts, some Senator heading to Texas for a NAFTA convention, the dollar falling below the Yen, the Cubs lost a shot at the pennant. Nothing new. Nothing unusual.

Lenny left the television running as he refilled his cup. With his second cup of coffee, he sat at his computer. The bells and whistles the computer terminal exuded were drowned out by the noise from CNN's *Moneyweek*. The terminal screen sprang to life in full color, rapidly beginning its programming to initiate his startup software. Today was the day. No more goofing around with the tests, and definitely no more gambling.

Today, he would pay Vince for the loan and access the Master Question

File for the tests for the last time. Today, Lenny would steal every one of them for the T-37, T-38, and the T-1. Then he would be done. He could start fresh with a new outlook on life. A life he looked forward to living.

After clicking his mouse on the Netscape icon, the screen once again whirled with activity as a variety of quick messages flashed across the screen. As soon as the modem accessed the engine he needed, Lenny connected Netscape to the Internet. From there, he accessed Yahoo through which he entered a chat room requiring a private code. With the code, he could gain access to classified government web pages that could be reached via military Local Area Networks. He clicked on the line that specified AETC. Soon the screen changed to a series of questions that required the answers to be typed into a box.

Please type in your code number:
3738

Do you wish to access an on-line system or private system?
ON-LINE

Please type in the number to be called now.
812-534-3685

Do you wish to access the telephone/computer option or computer only?
COMPUTER ONLY

Do you wish to activate SCRAMBLETEK?
YES

Press ENTER now.

Lenny selected "Enter" and a new page came up. The page had a listing of every test in Undergraduate Pilot Training on file.

Once again, the bells and whistles came to life as the computer answered the modem call and started accessing the Air Force system, engaging SCRAMBLETEK. The screen filled with thousands upon thousands of symbols as they traversed the screen before settling on a page. A generic, pale blue background with official navy blue writing filled the screen:

AIR EDUCATION AND TRAINING COMMAND

SPECIALIZED UNDERGRADUATE PILOT TRAINING

TEST BANK

He scrolled down until he approached the stan/eval test icon, and then selected COPY and TRANSMIT. In a matter of three minutes, he had downloaded every T-37 stan/eval test into his own computer. He started to move to the T-38 section, then he got an idea. Moving the cursor to the bottom of the page, he went to the "Select All" icon and hit ENTER. The entire screen lit up, indicating every test in the T-38 and T-1 banks were selected. He hit COPY and TRANSMIT and sat back to admire his handiwork.

The download itself took several minutes. Lenny rose to fix himself a third cup of coffee while the computer did its work. The SCRAMBLETEK program was annoying to watch while in progress, the screen a rapidly changing mosaic of digits and symbols. As Lenny took a sip of coffee, the monitor made three loud and unexpected bleeps. A look of horror froze on his face as the computer crashed right before his eyes. As he placed his coffee cup on the counter top, the screen went blank.

"Oh, no!" he said. Lenny leaped back to his keyboard as he tried to save what he could. No sooner had he sat down then the terminal came back to life and continued downloading. "What the hell was that?" he asked himself, rubbing his chin as he watched the screen. Everything appeared normal now. Perhaps a power surge in the system. The computer might be running out of memory. No, that wasn't it. It must have been a surge somewhere in the line.

Seven minutes later, the system finished downloading the tests to his hard drive, and Lenny quickly accessed the file. He was surprised every single test downloaded successfully. The surge must not have affected the download. Feeling pleased with himself, Lenny exited the file and printed out a copy of each test. Turning the computer off, he removed the printed tests, placing them in a manila envelope underneath a second manila envelope filled with Vince's cash in the center drawer of his desk.

Lenny decided he would leak the tests to Vince one at a time as opposed to giving him all the tests at once. He liked to be in control and watch that asshole squirm. The next stan/eval test would be this Friday. Lenny decided he'd give Vince the test on Thursday night. He relished the feeling of power the tests gave him. He wouldn't let Vince push him around any longer. His new life started today.

ALMOST FIVE HUNDRED MILES south of Vance Air Force Base, in the headquarters of Air Education and Training Command at Randolph Air Force Base, a tiny computer worked feverishly. Moments before, test files had been accessed for downloading. The system that had accessed the files had a backup to confuse anyone or anything trying to trace it. It took two minutes for the computer to recognize this backup as the SCRAMBLETEK program. In forty-five seconds it began to merge with the program, tracing the general location. To find the exact location took a total of five minutes. At three minutes, the computer beeped three times indicating the tracking was complete, and the system could begin accessing the location of the source. Normally, such a process would take about fifteen seconds, but SCRAMBLETEK extended the process to two minutes.

The computer worked rapidly as hundreds of digits raced across the screen. Each number was carefully screened by the system. Four minutes down, one more to go, and the system should accurately pinpoint the exact location of the accessing source. Without emotion, the computer continued its race against the clock, methodically selecting and rejecting numbers. It seemed a never-ending process. After four minutes forty-two seconds, the system stopped. This indication meant the access had stopped. The tiny computer at Randolph fell silent again and sat in the darkness.

JASON COULDN'T BELIEVE BETHANY showed up at his place. Even worse, he couldn't believe the condition he was in when she showed up at his place. His hangover embarrassed him. She kindly gave him time to get showered and dressed, though he could tell Bethany was mad. He'd seen that look a hundred times before. Jason said he would meet her at the Garfield Grill at noon. It was on Owen K. Garriott Avenue, so she should have no trouble finding it. Why was she here now? Jason had planned to spend the weekend studying for his check ride on Monday. He guessed he could wait until tomorrow to study. Perhaps his hangover would dissolve by then.

The powerful mustang rolled out the main gate, making a left on Fox Boulevard. Jason turned the radio off. He didn't want any love songs to get Him confused. But confused about what? Why was she here? Why now?

What did she want?

As he pulled into the parking lot, he saw her sitting at a booth next to the window. Her long, strawberry-blond hair flowed down her shoulders. She was out of place in a small country restaurant. Jason felt his heartbeat increase, his palms sweaty. This beautiful creature sitting in this restaurant actually made him nervous. What was he afraid of? He placed the car in park and turned the ignition key, shutting down the engine. Grabbing a towel from the back seat, he wiped the perspiration from his forehead. Jason took a couple of deep breaths, stepped out of the car, and went inside. He never realized having lunch with his ex-wife would be so difficult.

He ignored the hostess, walking straight to Bethany's table. "Good Morning," he said as he slid into the booth.

Bethany did not appear happy as she forced a smile. "Good afternoon, Jason."

Jason glanced at his watch. Twelve-fifteen. The waitress approached the table, and Bethany ordered iced tea and a salad. Jason, his stomach still somewhat unstable, ordered French fries and a large Coke. They sat in silence for several minutes until the waitress brought their drinks. Jason wasted no time in draining his. Coca-Cola was, after all, the ultimate hangover cure.

"You look like hell," she said, breaking the silence.

"Well, it's good to see you, too, Beth."

"Aren't you glad to see me?"

"Sure I'm glad to see you. How does your new husband feel about my seeing you?"

Ouch. He could tell that one hurt. Waste no time; pull no punches. Get all the cards out on the table. That one made her uncomfortable. Good, that's what he needed to do. He knew her better than anyone else, yet he didn't know her at all. If he didn't take the offensive at some point, she would dominate him. She would make him feel guilty because she fooled around on him.

"Bethany, why are you here?"

She squirmed in her seat, stirring her tea. Obviously, she wanted to discuss something and discuss it badly.

"I needed to see you again, to talk to you."

"But why? Why here, why now?"

Bethany stared out the window. Jason could see tears welling in her eyes. He wondered if they were real tears. She started to answer when the waitress brought their food. Jason asked for another Coke, ignoring Bethany while he put ketchup and pepper on his fries.

"You always did put pepper on everything," she said, looking at him.

"Yep." He was staying deliberately tightlipped. She wanted to talk, so let her.

"I miss you, Jason. I miss the good times we had. I miss the long walks in the moonlight, the picnics in the park. We were so good together; now we're apart. I miss you."

She sounded serious. He could see the look in her eyes, that all too familiar look. She wanted him . . . and he was beginning to want her.

CHAPTER 18

September 2, 1995

KATHY PULLED HER TRUCK out of the mall parking lot onto Owen K. Garriott Boulevard. She woke up early to pick up some things before she went to check on her hungover patient. Pulling into traffic, she turned the radio volume up full blast. Kathy smiled to herself for being smart enough to come to the mall early on a Saturday. Saturday mornings at the mall were never crowded, but by noon, the lunch crowd would filter in and the place became packed. When there wasn't much else to do, everybody went to the mall. Kathy had something to do. After visiting Jason and curing his hangover, she would head back home.

She drove down the street, tapping her fingers on the steering wheel to the upbeat rhythm, reflecting on her burgeoning romance. Jason was different. He wasn't like the other student pilots who came to town. They looked for a fling while they were there, then took off for bigger and better things. He seemed to be a man of good character, a true gentleman. One who enjoyed an occasional cocktail or two. He seemed like the type of man she wanted. If she had to settle on an Air Force pilot, he would be the one.

As she passed the Garfield Grill, Kathy noticed a familiar vintage yellow Mustang. *Jason? He must be Superman if he's up and running already.* She drove past and determined that it was his car. There weren't too many of those around, especially in Enid. She made a turn at the next block and doubled back to the restaurant. He would be in bad shape, but hopefully would have enough energy to visit her at work tonight.

Kathy parked near the corner of the building, four spaces away from his car. After placing her truck in park, the first thing she noticed through the restaurant window was the strawberry blonde. The long hair and the beautiful face beneath it. Across from the stranger sat Jason. She held his hands across the table, talking and smiling, Jason nodding occasionally. Kathy watched in silence. She had never seen her pictures, but Jason had described her. She came back. The ghost from the past she couldn't compete with in any way. The faceless other woman now had a face and was in Enid talking to Jason. Kathy scowled with anger as she put the truck in reverse and pulled out of the parking lot. How could she have been so wrong? So foolish? Jason said he was finished with his ex-wife. The stories he told about her had been horrifying, yet there she was, having lunch with him. She had been fooled and fooled good. Glancing at the silver horse head dangling from her keys, she shook her head as she headed north. What a waste of time . . . she would have to start over.

"I DON'T KNOW, BETHANY. I'm not so sure it would work out," Jason said staring at his Coke. "We've got a lot of damage here, and I think it's going to take a lot of work to sort it out, if it can be sorted out at all."

Bethany smiled at him. She looked beautiful. She smelled wonderful. The softness of her hands showed her delicate nature. Not a working girl, but one who enjoyed being pampered.

"Jason, I know you may not be happy with the way things turned out. I understand that. There are parts of our relationship I'm not happy with either." Bethany withdrew her hands, laying them gently on the table. The waitress set down a fresh iced tea for her and a Coke for him. Bethany opened two packs of sugar, pouring them into her tea. She removed the lemon and placed it on the table, slowly and methodically stirring her tea, pondering what to say next.

"You know," she said, "the things that went wrong before weren't necessarily my fault. I understand what I did was not right. I'm not even sure why I did it. Sometimes I get so confused. I got angry when all you talked about was your airplanes. You never spent any time with me. Your airplanes were the only thing that mattered in your life. But what about me, Jason? I have a life, too. I wanted to be part of your life. You shut me out."

She is convincing, he thought. He wanted to believe her, but things were happening too quickly. His head began to feel as if it were split open. He was in no condition to have this discussion. Sitting here, staring at her beauty, his brain half-fogged with alcohol, it was easy to remember the good times, but the face-to-face confrontation always lets you know if you still have feelings for someone. It's easy to hate someone from a distance, but the personal confrontation was a hard bluff to beat. If any feelings are left, good or bad, they will emerge. Jason sensed a little of both.

For the first time since he left his dorm room, he thought of Kathy. His feelings for her were real enough. Now this intrusion from the past was here, clouding his judgment. He shifted in his seat as he stared out the window. The clouds overhead were starting to clear, and the sunlight pushed through. The brightness made him squint, reminding him of the headache still pounding on the inside of his skull. He gently massaged his temples. His eyes rolled up inside his head as he closed them. Slowly he opened them as he returned his gaze to the window.

"Jason."

He didn't respond. Not because he had no desire to; his mind was simply elsewhere.

"Jason, talk to me," she said as she reached across the table and shook his arm. He broke out of his reverie and reached for his Coke. Taking a long sip, he set the glass on the paper coaster.

"Look, Beth, I'm sorry, but I'm in no condition to have this conversation right now. Maybe later, but not now."

Bethany's eyebrows rose, then she scowled. "Jason Conrad, I cannot believe you. I come all this way to see you. I tell you how I feel, and you're so hungover you can't even carry on a decent conversation."

"Normally, a comment like that would make me feel bad, Bethany, but since I had no idea you were coming here and I made an effort to come here even though I think my head is about to explode, no dice."

"Well!" Stuck in her thoughts, Bethany sat back in her chair with her arms folded, staring at Jason. "Why are you being so difficult?"

"Okay, Beth," he snapped, "try this on for size. We were married once, now we are not. The fact that you cheated on me is reason enough for me not to even want to talk with you. But believe it or not, for some reason, I do want to talk. But, of course, you're married to someone else, which means I now have a beautiful married woman sitting in front of me, telling me she has feelings for me and wants to make it work between us. The Air Force frowns on that kind of behavior, and if I were to participate in such, I could find myself out on the street looking for a job."

"See, it's still the same. All you ever think about is your airplane. I'm always second."

"Bullcrap! I'm sick of hearing that excuse. You talk about my airplane as if it is some kind of mistress, or someone you could be jealous of. It's my job. I need a job to pay the bills, Beth. I'm fortunate enough to have a job that I enjoy. Not many people get up every day and look forward to going to work." Jason grinned at his last remark. He had hated work the last few weeks. Despite his struggles, though, he would rather be flying jets than working in an office somewhere.

Jason looked at her. The tears began to well up again, causing her bright blue eyes to glisten. His emotions were a muddle and his headache refused to go away.

"Beth, I feel like crap right now. I don't think we are going to accomplish anything sitting here." He paused, gathering his thoughts. "Look, why don't I just meet you tonight. We'll go to dinner and talk then. Okay?"

She didn't seem too happy with this alternative, but it was all she had to choose from. They arranged to meet at her hotel, then go to a restaurant for dinner. Jason paid the bill and left her sitting in the booth right where he found her. Exiting the restaurant, he climbed in the Mustang, fired up the engine, pulled out of the parking lot, and headed back to the base.

Jason knew he needed to let off steam. The best place to do that was the gym. He could sweat the alcohol out of his system, decreasing his hangover time. He parked the car and went inside his room. It resembled a small disaster area. He could fix that later. Right now, he needed to sweat out the booze. Changing clothes, he downed two Tylenol with a large glass of water and headed for the gym.

The short walk helped loosen him up and get the blood circulating again. He walked straight through the basketball court to the weight room. A quick glance revealed five other guys working out, including Vince. That was a workable number, he decided. Finding an empty corner, he began stretching his tired muscles.

"How's the hangover, Conrad?"

"Hey, Vince, how's it going?"

"Well, I feel like you look, buddy."

"Wonderful. Misery makes good company. You don't look so good yourself," Jason looked closer at the bruises all over his face. "Game get a little rough after I left last night?"

"Nah, fell down the stairs."

"That's impressive, considering you live on the first floor."

Vince glared at him, as if telling him not to ask any more questions. Jason could take a hint. He was too hungover to carry on much of a conversation anyway. The pair headed for the bench press.

"So, Conrad," he said as he gripped the bar, "where have you been all morning? I came by earlier . . . you weren't around."

Jason told Vince about meeting Kathy at the club the night before and her bringing him home. He talked about the early morning wake-up and how he had expected Kathy, but instead was shocked to find Bethany standing on his doorstep. He explained his history with Bethany again. Now here she was, married to someone else, wanting to reestablish a relationship.

"Wow, that's a full morning," replied Vince. "What do you think you're going to do?"

"I'm not sure. We're meeting for dinner tonight. I don't know what I'm going to tell Kathy. She's a great girl; I like her a lot. I know this is going to drive me crazy all weekend, and I need to study. I've got a check ride Monday, so I've got to study tomorrow for sure. Whatever I do, I've got to decide tonight."

"Well I could think of worse decisions to make. 'Which babe do I want to keep?' You've got a rough life, buddy."

Leaning forward on the bench, Jason placed his hands on his knees and shook his head. "I don't know. I'll have to see what tonight brings. I don't know; I just don't know."

CHAPTER 19

September 2, 1995

THE GRAVEL PARKING LOT along the front and sides of Chicaros lay empty except for two cars. Vince pulled his truck next to the front door and got out. The small rocks crackled under his boots as he walked to the door. At seven in the evening, the sun was still out, making it too early for the Saturday night drinking crowd. As Vince walked inside, the darkness enveloped him. Sitting at a table in the corner, he signaled the bartender for a beer. The bartender brought the beer to the table in a large frozen mug. "You want something to eat?" the bartender asked.

"Sure, I'll take the barbecue sandwich," Vince said, taking a sip from the frosty mug.

The bartender nodded his head and turned to go to the kitchen. As he passed the bar, Kathy walked out of the kitchen. She seemed sad. Glancing around the room, she noticed Vince and walked over to him.

"I know who you are," he said as she approached.

"What?"

"You look like someone who has a broken heart. How are you today?"

"Not the best I've been in a while," she said.

"Is there anything you want to talk about?"

Kathy shrugged her shoulders with a big sigh. "No, I don't think so. I'm probably just imagining things. Oh, my gosh . . . what happened to you? Wait right here—let me get something for that."

Vince watched her intently as she walked away, like a hunter studying his prey. She must know Jason's ex-wife is in town. Vince thought about his options. Clearly he had an opportunity to take advantage of a beautiful lady in despair. They were always the easiest kind. The question remained, how should he bring it up? The direct approach was too obvious. He decided to give it time. An opening would present itself, and then he would move in for the kill.

She returned to the table and treated his cuts with hydrogen peroxide. "Are you okay?"

"Yes, I'm fine," he said, shrugging off the attention. "I'd rather not talk about it."

Vince sipped his beer, and the two sat for a few moments in silence. Kathy broke the uncomfortable quiet. "How's the flying going?"

"It's been going pretty good. I'm flying the jet well in the contact phase. I love to spin the jet. There's nothing better than flying upside-down. I'm still kicking butt on all the tests. I've got the highest average in the class. My instructor says if I keep it up, I'll have a good chance at getting a fighter."

"It's a good thing you're not too confident," she said wryly.

"You've got to be confident to fly jets. If you doubt yourself, you're dead. You've got to know what you're doing at all times. I wouldn't want to get in an airplane with a pilot who's not confident."

She nodded in agreement. "I guess all you guys believe in yourselves. The hard part is for us outsiders to distinguish what is cockiness and what is confidence."

"You can't. We're all cocky. It's the confidence part some of us lack, myself excluded."

"You're right, I can't tell the difference," she said with a smile.

"Oh, she smiles! That's a pleasant change in disposition. Can I get you a drink?"

"No, silly, I'm working."

"I can see your working pretty hard. Can I get you a stool to prop up your feet?"

"Very funny, flyboy."

Vince could tell he was gaining Kathy's trust. It was time to start moving in for the kill. He would have to be subtle. Getting her too upset would defeat his purpose.

"Look, not everybody in the program is the same. Everybody has different strengths and weaknesses. Take Matt, for instance. He's cocky, but he's not very good. Lenny is good, but he lacks confidence. I don't think he really cares much about being here. Lenny's got the talent, but his desire to be a pilot isn't there. Then there's Jason." Vince paused to let the name sink in for a moment. He could see the despair overcome her. Pretending not to notice the change in Kathy's composure, he continued. "Jason has a lot of heart. His desire is there. He's confident he can do it—he just sucks."

"What?"

"I don't mean he sucks in a bad way. It's just he doesn't have the skill to finish the program in the time they want him to. These guys out here could teach anybody off the street to fly if they had the time. They just don't have time to teach Jason. He's slow."

Vince continued to observe her, judging how his last remarks affected her. Kathy was upset, anxious. It's time. Move in for the kill.

"I'm sorry, he's probably a bad subject to bring up right now."

"What makes you say that?" she said, sitting upright.

"Well, I thought you two had . . . parted ways, so to speak?"

"What?"

"Well, with his ex-wife in town and all . . ."

"You know about her?"

"Sure, the two of them had lunch today. They were real peachy. They're going out to dinner tonight, some kind of reconciliation thing." He paused, looking into her eyes with a blank stare, offering no information, indicating nothing unusual. Kathy's eyes became glassy as she took her rag from her lap, wiping them. Vince continued to play dumb for several more moments, letting the information sink in. "You mean you didn't know?"

"No," she said. "I saw him today at lunch. I was driving from the mall down Owen K., and I saw his car at the Garfield Grill. I couldn't believe he was up so I thought I'd turn around to check on him." A tear ran down her cheek to her chin. She didn't wipe it away. "I saw him in the window. He was sitting at the table with her. I mean, I've never seen her before, but he's described her. She used to be a model. I'm a waitress in Enid, Oklahoma. How am I supposed to compete with her?" She spoke as if talking to herself.

Vince leaned across the table, placing his hand on her knee. "Hey, I'm sorry. I thought you knew. I didn't mean to upset you," he said.

"How could he do this to me?" Kathy said, "I thought he would tell me about something like this. He seemed different. I thought he was honest."

"I'm sorry, Kathy, I don't mean to sound rude, but I don't think you know the same Jason the rest of us know. Jason is very self-centered. That's how his marriage broke up in the first place. He totally ignored his wife and did his own thing. He used her to get noticed and achieve what he wanted by having a model for a wife. I'm afraid he would have done the same to you."

She smiled through the tears. "Thank you. That's a nice thing to say."

"I'm only saying what I feel is right. I feel bad. Jason is a good friend of mine. I help him with his flying all the time, but I can't tolerate how he handles women. Kathy, if I were him, I would never let you go."

CHAPTER 20

September 2, 1995

AFTER SEVERAL HOURS, the effects of the alcohol started to fade away. The trip to the gym helped, and the nap didn't hurt. His watch said seven-twenty, ten minutes before he was supposed to pick up Bethany. Jason was late for lunch; he sure didn't want to be late for dinner. But why should he care? Was he really concerned with what she thought about him? He had decided it wasn't going to work between them. Or had he? Slipping on his Bass loafers, he walked into the bathroom and turned on the light. Jason pulled out his toothbrush and toothpaste and quickly brushed his teeth, a sign he had finally sobered up. He simply felt too ill earlier to deal with it. He finished, gargled with Listerine, then a generic mint mouthwash. Before leaving the bathroom, he added a touch of Polo cologne. He never cared much for the smelly stuff, but he had always worn it for her.

It took twelve minutes in all to apply the finishing touches. He climbed into the canary yellow Mustang at seven-thirty-two. Slowly, he backed out of the parking space and pulled into the street, still thinking about where they should go for dinner. There weren't many restaurants in Enid. At least not many elegant restaurants with the proper atmosphere.

Bethany's hotel wasn't too far away. She was staying at the Holiday Inn on Van Buren Avenue, no more than a three-minute ride from the base. He pulled into the parking lot and parked in front of her room. Jason knocked on the door and stepped back. It seemed for a moment as if no one would answer, but as he raised his hand to knock again, the door opened.

Bethany stood inside the doorway. "You're late again."

"Fashionably late. Besides, I'm off-duty. I'm always late when I'm not working."

Jason stepped into the hotel room as she closed the door behind him. Bethany, of course, was not dressed yet, still wearing a Devonshire satin robe with a floral design and terry cloth lining. Her makeup was perfect and her hair meticulously set. She also wore stockings and high heels.

"Jason, do me a favor," she said, walking back to the vanity mirror by the sink. "Open the bottle of Champagne and pour us a glass."

"Sure."

Champagne was the last thing he needed, but he'd have a sip or two with her. He lifted the bottle out of the bucket of ice. Water dripped off the sides, splashing on the table. Finding a towel, he wiped the bottle off and proceeded to remove the foil packaging around the top. Cautiously, he removed the wire device holding the cap in place. As he looked toward Bethany, he saw her watching him in the mirror. She smiled when she noticed his watching her as she brushed her hair. With the wire removed, he barely touched the cap, "POP!" the cap went flying across the room, and the cool bubbly came flowing over the sides of the bottle. Jason reached for the Champagne glasses and filled them.

"Hooray!" Bethany said as she set her brush on the counter and came bouncing over to him. He handed her a glass, and she eagerly took it in both hands. "A toast," she said, raising the glass. "To new beginnings."

Jason raised his glass with a 'hear, hear,' wondering what type of new beginnings she referred to. Bethany quickly downed the drink and grabbed the bottle for a refill. She didn't act like she was in a hurry to go to dinner. He observed her actions. Walking across the room, sipping on her Champagne, she placed a cassette in her portable tape player. The erotic sounds of *Enigma* began filled the room with its slow, rhythmic beat.

"Bethany, we should probably be going soon."

She downed the second glass of Champagne and filled a third. Her movements about the room were sporadic; she seemed to be intentionally wasting time. Jason enjoyed watching her and didn't mind the delay as much as he should. She even looked gorgeous in a bathrobe.

"Make yourself comfortable. I'll be a few more minutes," she said. In a few more minutes she'll be plastered. He knew what she was like when she drank: amorous. She continued waltzing around the room, becoming absorbed in the music, giving Jason flirtatious looks. It was a ritual dance of seduction.

She was beautiful. Desirable. Obvious. Jason shifted in his seat, his nervousness starting to show. He began perspiring despite the cool air rushing out of the air conditioner behind him. He was fixated on her now, and she knew it. It was a game to her, a game he was losing. It was obvious that right now, she was in control. He sat watching her intently, wantonly, his glass of Champagne only half-finished.

She had the attention of her audience now. Slowly she positioned herself about ten feet away, turning her back to him. Looking over her shoulder, she seductively untied the robe, letting it fall to her waist. He could see her long strawberry blond hair against the perfectly tanned back as the robe gathered around her waist. Bethany paused in this position briefly, then let the robe fall to the floor. She ran both of her hands to push back her hair, her head tilted to the ceiling as she laughed.

Jason studied the finely sculptured flesh. His eyes took in the white high heels, moving up the long, shapely legs covered in white lace stockings held in place by a garter belt attached to a white lace bustier. Jason swallowed hard as he continued to watch the private show designed for his seduction. She turned to face him, the music filling the room. Walking toward him slowly, she looked like an angel, deeply tanned with long hair falling about her shoulders. She was perfect.

The smell of her perfume announced her presence. She stood before Jason, continuing her exotic dance. All he could do was watch. Memories of the past raced through his mind—what it was like to hold her, touch her, make love to her. Bethany was the woman who stole his heart many years ago, and she was the woman who shattered it into pieces in the not-so-distant past. Those things didn't matter right now. This moment wasn't about emotions . . . it was purely physical.

She reached down, grabbed his hands, and pulled him up to her. Staring into her eyes, they stood inches apart. Her thinly veiled breasts lightly brushed his chest. Slowly he reached out, touching the base of her neck. Her soft skin quivered as he ran two fingers lightly down her chest toward her cleavage. Pursing her lips, she closed her eyes, absorbing the moment. Jason's hand continued past her breasts to her hips. Suddenly, he grabbed her by the hips and pulled her toward him.

The sudden change in tactics caused Bethany to open her eyes. They looked into each other's eyes with blank stares. Jason continued pulling her toward him and kissed her, long, hard, and wet.

Bethany wrapped her arms around his neck, pressing her body into his. He stroked the small of her back, running his fingers along the elastic band of lace surrounding her hips. She pulled him toward the bed, and together they collapsed in a wild embrace. Jason rolled over on his back, Bethany straddling him, dominating him. She slowly pulled Jason's shirt out of his pants and began unbuttoning it. The music put out a slow rhythm, her gyrations driving him wild. The straps of her lace wrappings had fallen off her shoulders, inviting him to remove them.

Again, their eyes met. Jason searched the windows to her soul. Her blank stare was not promising. It was not the look of a woman in love; it was an empty void of despair. She was an unhappy lady trying to find happiness again. He could tell his gaze made her uncomfortable as she began to close her eyes, tossing her hair from side to side.

For Jason, the spell was broken. His body tensed, and he decided it was time to go. He knew she sense this as she accelerated her aggressive behavior. No, she has lost control. It's time to end this charade.

THE PATIO HAD BEEN DESERTED for most of the evening. Cool weather preceding the first cold front of the winter kept most of the customers indoors. The Midwest's famous high winds had come to Enid, and the city's year-round ten-to-fifteen-knot wind blew constantly from the north. But the most drastic change occurred when the first cold front rolled across the plains. The locals would say if it was early, it meant a big snow for the winter.

Vince sat on the patio, alone, for most of the evening. He finished the last of his beer when Kathy sat down to join him. It had been a slow night, but it was still early. Kathy came out to talk to him whenever she had a break.

"Do you want another beer?" she said.

He pushed his glass out of the way, resting his elbow on the table, propping his chin up with one hand. "When do you get off work?" he said.

A trace of a smile crossed her lips. "Since when did you start answering a question with a question?"

"Since when did you?"

Kathy laughed softly, "This could go on all night. Tell you what—I'll get you another beer. It's slow tonight . . . maybe the boss will let me off early, and I can join you."

"I like that idea. I'll wait here." He sat staring at her as she walked inside the bar. Women hadn't been part of his plan coming to pilot training, but he was a man with desires, and right now, she was upset, weak, and vulnerable. It was simply an opportunity he couldn't pass up.

Kathy returned three minutes later with two large beers. They sat in the back, making small talk concerning the male-female relationship and the trouble it had caused in each of their lives. She was open and honest about her past relationships. Vince, on the other hand, had to struggle through the conversation. Most of the stories he told were lies, and he had to be careful not to trip himself up during his stories. The alcohol started to get to him, and he decided he had had enough beer.

"I quit. I've had too much to drink," he said, moving the beer to the other side of the table.

"Uh-oh," she said, "you're not going to pass out on me are you?"

"Oh, no, I'd never do that."

"Are you okay to drive home?"

"I'm sure I could drive home. It's getting through the front gate smelling like a brewery that might be tough."

"That's what I was afraid of. I guess I could give you a ride home . . ."

Vince cut her off. "No, you don't have to do that. It's too far out of your way to go all the way out to the base on your way home."

"This is Enid. Nothing is too far out of the way." She stared hard at him, smiling playfully.

"Right." A big smile lit up Vince's face. This would be his best chance. He knew it was her own form of revenge on Jason; her way of severing the relationship. He didn't really care. "Okay," he said, "let's go."

"JASON STOP," BETHANY CRIED.

"No, Bethany, I don't know who I was trying to fool," he said, buttoning up his shirt. He was thinking much clearer now, gaining control of his thoughts and actions once again.

"But I love you."

Jason whirled around to face her. He raised a finger as if to say something, then glimpsed at her face and stopped. She tried to smile through the tears until she saw the anger in his eyes. He moved toward her and grabbed both of her arms. He tried to look her in the eyes, but she refused to let him. She awkwardly looked at the floor over her shoulder, her body convulsed in heavy sobs.

"Bethany, does your husband know you're here?"

No reply.

"Talk to me, Beth. Does he know you're here? Does he know his wife is in a hotel room, dressed in lingerie, trying to seduce her ex-husband? How do you think it would make him feel?"

Bethany sobbed heavily. "I don't love him. I'm thinking of leaving him. I wanted to know how you felt."

"Liar! Earlier today you said you were definitely leaving him. Now you're only thinking of leaving him? Why, Beth? Why here, why now? Why not later, when you are divorced or even separated?"

No reply.

"I thought about it, you know. I said to myself, 'I should screw her. I should nail this guy's wife just like he nailed mine. I want to ruin his life like he ruined mine.' But I can't do it. As much as I hate that guy and despise what you did, I can't do it."

"Jason, don't."

"No, Beth, I want you to hear this. You would never talk to me before, and now I think it's time you listened. I don't think you have any idea how much I loved you. I would have done anything for you. What you did to me crushed me. It almost destroyed me. At first, there was this hatred that built up, but in time it went away. Time does heal the wounds, Beth. I always wondered what it would be like if we tried to get back together, to make things work again.

"I didn't know what to think this morning when you showed up. When I see you, it's easy to be captivated by the good memories and forget the bad. I don't mind that. But you are married, Bethany. You are a married woman trying to seduce another man in a hotel room. I could not live with myself if we were ever to get back together, wondering if you were faithful. I don't trust you. As much as I would love to jump your bones right now, I think it would do more harm than good."

He turned and headed for the door.

"Wait! Where are you going?" she asked. The tears had stopped rolling now. She sat on the edge of the bed, isolated . . . defeated.

"I'm going to look for someone who really cares for me." He shut the door behind him and marched straight to his car. *Don't look back—just get in the car and go. Once the car is rolling, you'll be okay.* The engine roared to life and the car ripped out of the parking lot out onto Van Buren and into the night.

The ten-minute ride to Chicaros was uneventful. Saturday-night delinquents traveled up and down the strip like they always did, hanging out of their cars, pretending to be racecar drivers. Jason pulled into the crowded parking lot, and more cars pulled in behind him. Jason walked inside and noticed the place was crowded as he worked his way to the bar. He got the attention of the bartender and ordered a large beer.

"Have you seen Kathy?" he said as the bartender handed him a beer.

"Yeah, hell, I let her go earlier because nobody was here. Now that she's gone, we get swamped, and I could use her."

Jason nodded his head. "Do you know if she went home?"

The older man thought to himself for a moment and said, "I think she left here with some fella. Maybe her boyfriend, I'm not sure. She doesn't talk much about her private life around here. Well, you know, with all the gossip and all."

Jason felt as if he were turning green. "Yeah, thanks." He headed for a deserted table in the corner and sat in the booth.

Left with her boyfriend?

CHAPTER 21

September 4, 1995

THE FOUR SAT SOLEMNLY around the large oak desk as darkness began to fall outside. At the end of the table, the older gentleman shifted in his seat uncomfortably. Staring through his bifocals, Viktor Vasilyevich Kryuchkov leafed through the papers repeatedly.

"Gentlemen, we are faced with a particular problem," Viktor said, placing the papers on his desk, leaning back in his chair. "You are here today to discuss a potential solution: the good and bad aspects of it, and the potential political and international ramifications of our actions."

"Viktor," Vladimir Ogoltsov, the former KGB general, said, "we have guaranteed the support from the remaining army divisions in Russia. This will give us the stability to enact our plan."

"Yes, I know. I don't feel we will have any difficulty overthrowing the current republic. The majority of the people are calling for it. The support of the army, however, will make it inevitable."

"Comrade Kryuchkov, it is clear we the have support of the army, but what of our air and naval forces?" Yuri Trilisser, the high-ranking Minister of Finance asked, posing a challenge others seemed to be avoiding. They all sensed the nervousness in the air. Each of them knew they must tread with caution.

"Surely, they will join the cause," said Aleksandr Chebrikov, Viktor's good friend. "They have been suffering the same difficulties over the past several years as the rest of us. It can only be for their benefit, as well as ours, that they join us."

"That is a fine picture, comrade," Yuri said, rising in his chair, "but what if they choose to side with the Republic? What are our chances for success?"

Vladimir leaned forward to speak. "They pose no immediate threat; perhaps no long-range threat either. Obviously, the naval forces will not be in a position for opposition should they decline to side with us. Theirs is a coastal defense. Even if they attempt to project at sea, it would have no effect. It is impossible for them to distinguish targets from the sea in the midst of a revolution. The same would be true for the air forces. The fighters would have no adversaries; the strategic bombers would face the same targeting problems as the naval forces. They will not strike in the cities, nor would they want to. It would do them no good.

"I thought this might bother some of you," Vladimir continued. "Could someone get the lights please?" He proceeded to turn on a slide projector as the lights dimmed. The first slide was an introduction, STATUS OF FORCES, LAND, SEA, AND AIR. Vladimir continued with his preplanned briefing, meticulously prepared and carefully structured. For the next hour, he covered every aspect of each of the services, from morale and living conditions, to the quality of their equipment and amount of experience and training. Nuclear forces that remained in Russia were currently under their control. The majority of the remaining scientists would also follow the cause. Russia's space program could be a problem because of the international crew currently on board the Mir. They would have to replace them with cosmonauts immediately and return the foreigners to their homelands.

He could tell throughout the briefing that he was winning over each member of the secret council just as he intended. Viktor smiled as he observed the reactions of his fellow committee members. When the briefing ended, he leaned forward.

"It is obvious with the support of our Russian army, the overthrow of the Republic will be a success. Comrades, I now propose to you the primary purpose of our meeting today." He again studied their faces. Viktor knew it wasn't the primary reason they were here, but he realized they needed to be carried gradually toward the real purpose of this meeting. "What will be the reaction of the international community when this event unfolds?" he finally asked.

It was the obvious question, and each man barked out ideas at once. The calm of the committee meeting rapidly deteriorated as the noise level rose in a rapid crescendo.

Taken aback, Viktor stood, sternly attempting to maintain his composure in the midst of this sudden chaos. "Comrades, please! One at a time."

The noise level subsided as quickly as it had begun.

"The Americans will be outraged!" Aleksandr said. "Their policies over the past three years have all been primarily based on the fact that Russia is now, at least for all practical purposes, a democracy."

"Yes, that problem will be discussed shortly," Viktor said. "What else?"

"Britain and France will also pose the usual problems. The French have been concentrating on the buildup and modernization of its forces for a number of years now. Still, neither will pose any type of threat to the revolution within Russia. They will interfere only if we take the conflict beyond our own borders." Yuri had been an authority on Western European tactics as a young officer prior to his diplomatic deployment and had been continually consulted on potential foreign reactions to events throughout his career.

Vladimir spoke again. "Perhaps the most immediate threat will be China, who began a serious systems upgrade for all its weaponry several years ago. In five years, they will have the capability to project their power in the Western Hemisphere. If they can do that, what do you suppose they could do to us? Again, what would they have to gain from a long, sustained war with a country who is in as bad or worse shape as they? The Japanese will certainly stop their investments in developing the electrical companies in Russia, but all of Asia will most certainly watch from the outside to see what develops in Mother Russia. This could possibly trigger another world war."

"You all are acting like fools," Aleksandr said softly, looking around the room. "It is the Americans who set international policy, and the world follows. What will be their concern? If we accomplish the coup now, we will be fine. The American president is a fool and weak on foreign affairs. He will be unable to make a decision, let alone the right decision, and unable to lead the international community to take a stand."

"Correct, Aleksandr," Viktor said, smiling from the end of the table.

Aleksandr seemed caught off-guard. "Of course I'm correct," he said. "This coup we are planning will not take place for possibly another sixteen months. By that time, the Americans will have elected a new president. They are so disgusted with the imbecile currently in office that he will surely lose. They won't engage us. That Arab fool bin Laden blew up a bomb in the World Trade Center, and they leave him alone."

"Thank you, Aleksandr," spoke Viktor, "I will continue from here. Comrades, Aleksandr Chebrikov has made a most valuable statement. The Americans have destroyed the once-powerful military built by President

Reagan. The prolonged police actions in Southwest Asia and Korea, coupled with dwindling support, has crushed the morale and backbone of the armed services. With the American elections approaching, the opposition candidate, Senator Jonathan Bowman, is almost assured victory in the Republican primary and the general election according to the American media. America is looking for a savior, someone who can lead them to the path of greatness once again. Thus, we must find a way which will ensure the reigning administration remains in office. Gentleman, I would like to introduce you to Comrade Nikolai Gregarin of Section Nine, who has devised such a plan."

Everyone turned toward the back of the room to watch the short, well-dressed man rise from his seat and walk toward them. He took his position next to Viktor, a subtle gesture that implied he spoke with Viktor's authority.

"Good day, gentlemen," Nikolai began. "The information you are about to hear is not to leave this room. As Comrade Kryuchkov said, it is imperative to the success of our mission that we ensure the re-election of the current American administration. By doing . . ."

"Just how in hell do you plan to do that, comrade?" Vladimir Ogoltsov interrupted. "Are we going to tamper with their electoral system? Stuff the ballot box?"

His outbreak drew several remarks and chuckles from those sitting around the table. Vladimir sat back with a big smile, as he appeared to enjoy putting the younger Russian in his place.

Nikolai, expressionless, responded coldly. "Gentlemen, within twenty days, we will assassinate the man favored to win the Republican nomination and ultimately the presidency, Senator Jonathan Bowman."

The room fell silent.

OUTSIDE THE OFFICE, VIKTOR'S DRIVER, Palovich Merlov, sat alone in a chair, apparently sleeping. What he had just heard, however, made him sit up abruptly in his chair. He adjusted the tiny listening device concealed in his ear as he scanned the room. He was still alone. For another five minutes, he listened as Nikolai finished his brief. These men were insane. Did they actually plan to kill a U.S. senator running for president?

Palovich carefully removed the listening device from his ear, placing it in his pocket. It was something he'd hoped to never be involved in despite being recruited. Palovich never considered himself a traitor. He was defending the best interests of Mother Russia. Yes, they'd given him money, but he would have done this without it. He rose nervously, pacing the room, wondering what he could do. Staring at the phone on the desk ten feet away, he knew he had to get word to the Americans. He had the number for a one-time emergency. This situation more than qualified, he decided. He moved to the desk, looking around as he went, ensuring he was still alone. Palovich dialed the number. He let it ring twice, hung up, waited thirty seconds, and dialed again. On the third ring, someone picked up the phone.

"Hello," a male voice said in a thick Slavic accent.

"Is my friend Uri there? This is his Comrade Palovich." His voice was monotone, without emotion. Palovich was sure he was being monitored.

Uri simply was a code word positively identifying Palovich.

"No, Palovich, Uri is not here. This is Mikeal. How are you?"

"Greetings Mikeal. I was just calling to tell Uri the rabbit is running these days. Perhaps we could go hunting tomorrow."

"I'll let him know, Good day, Palovich."

The voice at the other end of the phone hung up. Palovich's message was simple: Nikolai Gregarin was on the move.

CHAPTER 22

September 4, 1995

THE MAN NAMED MIKEAL hung up his phone and nervously scanned the office. Mikeal Tolstoy, factory worker, a short, portly man with too much free time on his hands. A thick, bushy mustache hid the tense lines around his mouth. His wife had died years ago working in the fields, and their children never came to see him. He was a man alone. Mikeal removed his spectacles, cleaning the lenses with a scarf as he contemplated the message. He had never expected to get the phone call. It had been over a year since the man from the American embassy had convinced him to act as an agent for the CIA. It had seemed an easy task. The CIA didn't ask much, mainly for him to relay phone calls, then drop off information. An unknown person calls him and leaves a message; he relays the message right away to a contact from the American embassy. It was a low-risk venture, and the thousand American dollars he had been paid was well worth the risk. He scribbled the note on a piece of paper, placed it in a cigarette pack, and stuck it in his pocket.

Mikeal enjoyed being a participant in the remnants of the Cold War spy game. He wasn't really a spy—he knew nothing of any importance. How could he hurt anyone? A list of names was all he had, and they weren't even real names. He was instructed to write down the message and who called. He'd dial a number, let the phone ring twice and hang up. He'd dial a second time and let it ring three times and hang up. On the third attempt, someone would answer the phone. That was the plan. He'd never used it until today.

The phone answered on the third call.

"This is Mikeal. It's a lovely day for a walk," he said. "I think I will take one."

"That sounds nice. Have a good walk," replied the voice.

Mikeal hung up the phone, and his hands began to tremble. He'd never carried out this type of mission before. Grabbing his coat, he locked the door to his small apartment and entered the cold streets of Moscow. Normally, he would ride his bicycle around the capital, but the heavy snows that had fallen lately made that mode of travel difficult. Today, he would walk to the drop point. It should only take forty-five minutes and would give him time to think. His heart pounded and his forehead beaded with sweat. He'd never made a dead drop before, or made contact with the CIA; naturally he was nervous. Four degrees Celsius outside, and he was sweating. Along the way, he stopped to buy a newspaper, placed it under his arm, and continued his journey. Mikeal tried to avoid looking over his shoulder. He wanted to be sure he wasn't being followed, but he didn't want to be too obvious.

He walked rapidly to his destination. Despite the cold weather, he continued to sweat profusely. Occasionally, he lost his footing on the icy sidewalk and streets, but he pressed forward. He was a man possessed, oblivious to the sights and sounds around him.

Mikeal reached the contact point easily and realized he had five minutes to initiate contact. He slowed his pace as he casually scanned the area. He was new to this spy business, but he felt he would do well. The designated light pole across the street from a grocers was isolated. He took his place on the left side of it and glanced at his watch. One minute to go. He had timed it perfectly. Opening his newspaper, he stood there for the next five minutes, waiting for his contact to show.

INSIDE THE BUILDING, ABOVE THE GROCERS, two men watched through the curtains. The man outside had shown up at the appropriate time at the designated spot, but they had been unable to get a positive I.D. on him so far. They had one minute left to make the decision as to whether or not he was a legitimate agent or a plant. Across the street, twenty yards from the Russian, was a caseworker, waiting to follow the Russian if he was confirmed legitimate.

"Good gosh, put the paper down so I can see your face," the tall American said. "Nobody reads a newspaper like that. This idiot is announcing to everyone on the street, 'Hey, look at me, I'm pretending to read a newspaper.'"

"Don't be too hard on him, Hank. These guys aren't pros," the short, stocky one said.

Boston-born Hank Fielding had four years of experience as a field man with the CIA. Looking at his younger, stockier partner, Dave Loomis, he shook his head. They had both been at the Moscow embassy for several years, six between them. It lacked the excitement of the Cold War days, but still made for interesting work. Much of their focus was now on economic issues and industrial espionage.

"If he gets paid, he's a pro," Hank said. "That's all there is to it. I remember four years ago I was working with this character in New Delhi. He was a shopkeeper who had this black market carpet business on the side. Well, he goes . . ." Hank paused for a moment, adjusting his binoculars. The man by the pole had lowered his paper, looked both ways, and began to walk. "Holy moly, we got an I.D.! It's Mikeal Tolstoy, a retired factory worker I signed on a year ago. Okay let's tag him, Dave." Stocky Dave from Nebraska walked over to the curtain, drew them closed, then open again. On the sidewalk across the street, a man in an overcoat turned to follow Mikeal Tolstoy.

HE WAITED THE FIVE MINUTES as instructed and headed to the dead drop point. The streets were not crowded as he shuffled down the block, yet the nervousness inside him was building. He noticed he sweated heavily, his undershirt matted against his chest, his breathing shallow and uncontrolled. Had he been followed? Mikeal dismissed that thought immediately. He had been careful, and his actions were not out of the ordinary. His five-minute time period had elapsed. Folding the paper under his arm, he started walking north. Although the drop point was two blocks away, he picked up his pace.

Mikeal Tolstoy was ready to end this. A thousand American dollars didn't seem to be as much money now as it did when he made the deal. His heartbeat increased, and sweat poured down his forehead as he maintained his fast pace. Sooner than expected, he reached the drop point. His hands shook as he fumbled through his pockets, pulling out the packet of cigarettes containing his note. To look inconspicuous, he removed a cigarette, lit it, and inhaled deeply. The cigarette calmed his nerves somewhat, and he began to move more naturally as he stood against the building smoking his cigarette. His actions less obvious, he continued to cautiously glance around to see if he had been followed, but saw nothing unusual. There were people milling around, but no one who could have followed him. Casually, Mikeal crumpled up the cigarette pack and dropped it by his feet. He took another drag on his cigarette, tossed it on the ground, and walked away. He could feel the beating of his heart in his ears and his fingertips. It wasn't excitement he felt, it was fear. Wiping the sweat from his brow, he removed his spectacles, which had fogged up slightly over the past two minutes. He crushed the cigarette pack beneath his heel, a symbolic gesture to say he was through with this business for good.

NOT LONG AFTER MIKEAL TOLSTOY made his transaction, a medium-sized man wearing a heavy coat and carrying a briefcase, walked the same path. The man appeared like every other man walking the streets of Moscow. When he reached the spot where Mikeal had been standing, he set his briefcase on the ground and bent down to tie his shoe. Mikeal's contact picked up the cigarette pack, placed it in his pocket, and continued his stroll along the street. Rounding the corner, a dark Mercedes Benz cranked its engine as the man climbed into the passenger's seat. No sooner had the door closed than the car bolted from the curbside and disappeared around the corner.

"WELL, KIDDO, ARE YOU READY for the big day?" McTaggart said as he approached the desk.

Jason looked up from his Dash One. "I don't know. I've had a bad weekend. I got very little studying done and even less sleep."

"I suggest you get that woman stuff out of your head and focus on the job at hand, mister," Gus said. "There's always going to be women around to chase, but you only get one crack at flying jets. Don't dork it up because your Johnson didn't know what to do over the weekend."

"Yeah, Bethany did me wrong. Then, I finally meet someone I think I could care about, and now she's with someone else. It's just one big mess."

"Jason," Gus said sternly, moving right in Jason's face, "stop this crap right now. Do you hear me? Clear your mind and concentrate on the check ride. What profile do you have?"

"Profile two. I've already been briefed by the check pilot."

"Who?"

"Anderson."

"Hmph, don't know much about him. What's he like?"

"He seems okay. He's really into playing the distance thing, though. You know, 'I'm the check pilot so I'd better not get to know you. Then I can hook you with a clear conscience'."

"Stop the negative vibes right now, mister. When do you step?"

Jason stared at the wall in front of him for several moments.

"Conrad, when do you step?"

Breaking out of his momentary trance, Jason refocused his attention on Gus, "I'm sorry, I was thinking about something else."

"It better have been the check ride," McTaggart said.

"Yeah, yeah, it was," Jason said. "I step at thirteen-fifteen for a thirteen-forty-five takeoff."

"How many times have you reviewed the profile?"

"Two or three. I even did a practice boldface. Want to check it for me?" Jason said as he handed the paper to McTaggart.

Gus scanned its contents. Boldface emergency procedures had to be memorized verbatim because they had to be taken care of immediately in the cockpit. There was no time for either the student or instructor to reference his checklist for certain critical emergencies. It didn't take McTaggart long to review the paper. He found two errors. On the check ride, one error would constitute a failure for emergency procedures.

"There's two faux pas in here mister. You want to review this again?" he said, sliding the paper back to Jason. Jason took the paper, scanned it quickly, and found the errors.

"I guess I better be more careful."

"Yes, I think you better."

Jason glanced at the big clock behind the scheduling board. "It's about that time, I'd better start heading toward the ops desk." Jason walked to his locker in the hallway and stored his Dash One.

Samantha Williams approached him as he closed the door. "Hi, Jason. Good luck on your check ride. I know you'll do just fine."

"Thanks, Samantha, I'm sure it will go okay. How did your ride go today?"

"Better, than the past two, that's for sure."

"Good for you. Hey, I've got to run. I'll see you when I get back."

"See you later."

Jason reached the TOC desk and noticed the check pilot hadn't shown up yet. He started to work on the preliminary paperwork and get their airplane assignment when he sensed an uneasy feeling. Something wasn't right. He stood at the desk when he felt a tap on his shoulder. Turning around he saw Gus McTaggart standing behind him. Gus was holding up a checklist that Jason recognized immediately.

"You may want to take this with you today," McTaggart said.

"Thanks," Jason said, his face turning red. "I felt like something was wrong."

Gus handed Jason the checklist. "Relax, you're going to do fine." Gus emphasized relax, but the advice went without notice.

"Thanks, Gus. No problem." Somehow, he knew relaxing was going to be the hard part.

IT HAD BEEN TWO HOURS since Mikeal Tolstoy dropped the message at the designated spot. Hank and Dave checked it repeatedly. It could only mean one thing. Nikolai Gregarin was leaving for the United States soon to contact someone. Palovich had a limited knowledge of what and who Nikolai worked with, but his experience told him it wasn't good. The CIA had known for the past four years about the super-secret Section Nine and its elite group of assassins placed throughout the world. If he was going to the United States, it could only be for one reason.

"This could be disastrous," Dave said.

Hank shook his head in agreement. "We've got to contact Palovich again soon. We need to find out where Nikolai is going and why."

"How can we do that? Direct contact with an agent is dangerous, not so much for us, but him. They'll just send us home, but if he's caught, he's—"

"Dead," Hank finished the sentence for his shorter companion. "We need to decide how far we are willing to take this. If we can find out who the target is, we could get the ball rolling."

"Can't we just put a tail on Gregarin and follow him to the States?"

"We will. Caldwell will insist on it. But Gregarin is good. I don't think our guys can follow him all the way across three continents and the Atlantic Ocean. The guy was a fast burner during his early days in the KGB. A 'rising star' in the twilight days of a declining empire. Viktor Kryuchkov took him under his wing years back and has groomed him to be the new spy master.

"We're not exactly sure, but we think it was Kryuchkov who developed the concept of Section Nine and trained its members in the killing arts. With the fall of the Soviet Union, their people were kept in place with the intent of being killers for hire. Hell, they still pump some of these guys out. High-priced, high-tech hitmen placed all over the world, just waiting for the phone call letting them know it is time to go to work."

Dave walked over to his desk, picked up the folder on Nikolai Gregarin, and studied his picture. He didn't appear to be the genius the file described. He had the appearance of a con man. Tailored suits and slicked-back hair made him look like a 1930s gangster in the States.

"Nikolai Gregarin, no middle name," Dave began reading from the folder. "Born in Leningrad in 1958, father Peter and mother Olga both still living. Good marks in middle school and selected to attend Moscow University two years ahead of his peers. Studied Russian History with a minor in Western History and English. Apparently did so well with his minor he was recruited to attend the state language school. After graduating, he taught for a year and a half before being recruited by the KGB. Worked in various countries, primarily Great Britain, France, Italy, and Egypt, with a few known trips to the U.S. Known for being a good thinker, fast on his feet, with the ability to get himself out of many tight spots. His actions in the field caught the attention of Viktor Vasilyevich Kryuchkov who brought young Nikolai into the inner folds of the KGB in 1988." Dave paused as he continued to scan the file.

"This guy has one hell of a résumé. How long has he been in charge of Section Nine?" Hank asked, as he poured a glass of water for himself.

"Well, that's the good news or bad, depending on how you look at it. Section Nine was either unknown or not in existence to this point. We know immediately after he went to work in the KGB, they became known to us. In his younger days, Nikolai had a penchant for vodka and women, like most young successful Russian agents. In his effort to impress one particular lady, he spilled his guts about his new position. He let her know he was in charge of a small army of trained killers no one knew existed. 'Mysterious stalkers blending in with their surroundings' and 'capable of disappearing without a trace.'"

"Wow, this guy really spilled his guts. Who was the girl?"

"An agent of ours named Ivana Wuurst. East German. Here's her picture," Dave said, handing the photo to Hank and picking up his water. The long narrative made his throat dry, and the cool water was refreshing.

Hank studied the photo approvingly. "She might make me talk, too. One beautiful creature."

"Well, this beautiful creature is now enjoying shopping malls and cable TV courtesy of Uncle Sam for her little role in the Cold War. We were able to confirm through another source that Section Nine did exist, but we still have no idea about their numbers or exact locations. They are the best kept secret the Russians have. The only good thing about this is they have no idea we are aware of Section Nine. At least we know more than they think we know."

"Yeah, but we need to find out more. I'm going to contact Caldwell. We need to use Palovich again, and in a greater capacity than before. And then we need to get him out of the country."

CHAPTER 23

September 4, 1995

J ASON AND THE CHECK PILOT "stepped" to the aircraft from the life-support shack. A cold front pushed through and the cool air whipped itself around their faces, yet Jason still managed to sweat. Looking across the ramp covered with the small T-37 trainers, no crew bus was in sight.

"We'll walk," the check pilot said over the whining noise of the Tweet's engines. "Red tails are all the way down at the end, but I don't want to wait."

Jason nodded as he put on his "Mickey Mouse ears". On the long walk to the jet, Jason kept reviewing the sequence of events he needed to accomplish to complete the sortie. From the TOC desk to takeoff and flying the profile, landing, and debrief, he couldn't think of anything he missed so far.

It was a three-minute walk to tail number five-two-one. The crew chief had the canopy up for them when they reached the jet. Jason placed his parachute on the ground, buckles down, and hung his helmet bag from the canopy lock on the inside of the cockpit. With his checklist, he began a quick walk-around inspection of the aircraft. Halfway through, he remembered he should have checked the aircraft's 781 forms for any malfunction write-ups. As he walked back to his side of the jet, Jason found the check pilot closing the orange-covered notebook. The check pilot handed him the forms and began a quick walk-around himself. Jason checked over the forms and found the jet to be in good condition. Placing the forms in his seat, he started his walk-around again. He noticed that the check pilot had pulled the pins from the landing gear during his walk-around, which may or may not be a bad sign. By the time he reached the other side of the aircraft, the check pilot had strapped in the aircraft. "I thought you did a walk-around already," he said to Jason.

"I started, but stopped to go back and review the forms," he said loudly to overcome the noise of the surrounding aircraft.

"Okay, my bad," the check pilot said. Jason finished his walk-around, checked the pin box to ensure the three pins were there, and placed the pitot tube cover in there with them. Jason pulled on his chute, climbed in, and strapping himself in the jet. The check pilot sat ready to go with his dark visor down and oxygen connected. It took several moments for Jason to get ready to start his checklist. Jason began to get nervous. The check pilot intimidated him, whether he meant to or not. This was all he needed after the weekend he had.

"Okay, Lieutenant, let's get a move on. We don't have all day," said the voice over the cockpit interphone.

"Yes, sir."

Jason began the checklist before he had a chance to strap it to his leg. He rushed himself and did things out of sequence. Not normalAs he called to get taxi clearance, he noticed the crew chief holding up two fingers in front of his face. Jason nodded and lowered his visor as he keyed the mike to call Vance Ground. Sweat stung his eyes as it poured down his face. The checklists on the taxi out were rushed; not as smooth flowing as they should have been. Jason had trouble keeping his thoughts organized. He didn't think he missed anything, but he sensed something different. The jet reached the number one position for the Eastside runway as they awaited their turn for takeoff.

In three minutes, they were cleared for takeoff. Jason completed the checks and smoothly added power while holding the brakes. When the engines checked good, he released the brakes and the aircraft began to roll down the runway.

No sooner had they begun the roll than the check pilot said over the interphone, "Abort, abort, abort."

Jason jerked the throttles back to idle and kept the aircraft tracking down the center of the runway. His eyes quickly scanned the instruments to find any malfunction he might have missed. He saw none. The check pilot informed Eastside over the radio there was no emergency, and they would taxi back for another takeoff.

"Okay, Lieutenant, I have the aircraft. Do you know why we aborted that takeoff?"

"No, sir. The engines looked good. There were no abnormal lights."

"True statement, Lieutenant, but you may want to remove your seat pin before this next takeoff."

Jason looked down. His seat pin, which locked the ejection levers into position, was still in place. If he'd tried to use the handles to eject from the aircraft, they would not extend up, meaning he could not squeeze the triggers and the seat would not eject. An immediate feeling of doom came over him like a dark thundercloud. This was not good.

"WE GOT HIM," YELLED CURT as he burst through the doorway. Alonzo looked up from his desk at his out-of-breath associate. Monday afternoon started like any man's average Monday. The boss asked questions about projects nowhere near complete, he couldn't find a good parking space, and the checkbook did not balance correctly. But none of that matter to Alonzo right now. He couldn't stop grinning as he stared wide-eyed at Curt breathing heavily in front of his desk.

"Our computer boy? We got him?" Alonzo wanted to verify they were on the same wavelength.

"You're damn straight we did. I didn't think he would try so soon, but he did. Saturday morning our boy decided to be a funny man again and logged on. He's good. Our guy traveled through several different relays before accessing the mainframe. SCRAMBLETEK smeared his tracks most of the way."

"Well, who is he? Did you get a direct trace?"

Davis sat in the vinyl chair next to Alonzo's desk, shaking his head back and forth. "No, we didn't get a direct trace," he said holding up the computer printout in his hand, "but we are close. Oklahoma. More specifically, Vance Air Force Base."

Leaning back in his chair, Alonzo placed his hands behind his head. "That would fit the profile. Anything more specific?"

"No," Davis responded with a feverish headshake. "Another thirty seconds and I would have nailed the little bugger to the specific phone outlet in whatever room. He was able to download and get offline before my program could break through."

Alonzo stared at the ceiling for a minute. "Did you talk to anyone at the squadron about what he took yet?"

"No, not yet," Davis said.

He reached into the top drawer of his desk, pulling out a piece of paper with a list of all the tests available to UPT students. It covered standard academic tests for all phases of training for the T-37, T-38, and the T-1. It also contained the Master Question File for each airplane. The Master

Question File contained hundreds of questions, allowing the stan/eval officer from each flight to develop his own quiz each week by pulling questions from the file. He took the computer printout from Davis and compared the two lists. The top of the computer printout listed the downloaded tests. The list was identical to the one Alonzo held in his hand. The next two pages told the tale of the hackers routing into the mainframe and following the electronic routing back to Vance Air Force Base. Alonzo smiled at his partner's cleverness.

"I can't believe we got this lucky," Davis said. "Sometimes these investigations can take months, even years. This one has been up for two days." He had a hard time containing his excitement. "Didn't expect to get anything today, but, boy, we hit the jackpot. It's my fault for coming in late today. I was taking care of things around the office, putting out fires, the usual Monday morning crap. I decided to drop by the squadron and check out the system, and POW! Baby, we got a location! It shouldn't be hard to track him down now."

"Is it possible this location is a decoy? Perhaps he is located at another base. Maybe even here at Randolph."

"No way," Curt said shaking his head. "This guy is at Vance. I'm sure of it. That's what my program is designed to do . . . weed out the decoys. SCRAMBLETEK employs three to four decoys, dependent upon modem speed and memory size. These decoys are input by the user and activated automatically every time the program is turned on. I've heard rumblings on the 'Net of the possibility of doubling that capacity, but I haven't seen it practiced yet. This guy just had the basic system. Damn, if I had another thirty seconds."

"Yeah, your thirty seconds would've made my life a lot easier."

"Sorry, Alonzo. You didn't want to live forever, did you?"

"You're a funny man," Alonzo said, tossing the computer printout back at Davis. "Get out of here before I tell the boss I need a second man on the road with me, and he needs to be a computer expert."

"No problem, it's all part of the job." Davis relaxed. "Well, what's next?"

Alonzo stood and grabbed his briefcase. "I go to sunny Enid."

CHAPTER 24

September 4, 1995

RAIN FELL STEADILY outside and a deep puddle began to gather under the windowsill of the dorm room. The weather had a tendency to change rapidly in the plains. There was a saying in Enid, 'If you didn't like the weather, stick around ten minutes, it'll change.' The weather had changed dramatically over the past two hours. The early morning blue skies were now a deep gray, appropriately enough.

Jason Conrad sat silently on his couch, staring at a blank television screen, tapping a pencil on his forehead. It had been two hours since he returned from his checkride debrief. He could not believe how disastrous the day had been. If something could have gone wrong, it did. Jason managed to recover from his earlier mistake of not pulling his ejection seat pins. His aerobatics in the MOA turned out sloppy and his time in the traffic pattern was rough and slow. On a check ride, however, one mistake was enough and the failure to remove his pins was a safety of flight issue. Unfortunately for Jason, that was unsatisfactory.

The debrief for the sortie lasted only an hour, the check pilot made sure that he asked the required questions to test Jason's general knowledge. When he debriefed Jason on the ride, he also downgraded Jason to a fair on his cloverleaf and his single-engine landing. The cloverleaf was an aerobatic maneuver, which was a succession of four identical over-the-top maneuvers. This maneuver is done four times in the same direction and the jet should be pointed in the original direction that it started. Jason's ended up pointing roughly thirty degrees left of his original heading. Jason's single-engine landing was rough and firm, but only five knots fast which was acceptable. The impression that Jason got from the check pilot was that he needed more meat for the write up explaining the busted check ride. Those two downgrades made the write up look more legitimate.

It was funny, Jason thought to himself, how the instructors in UPT had learned to cover themselves. He had watched how they made write-ups for unsatisfactory sorties. The experienced ones only wrote up what they needed to get the job done. This was mainly because the write-ups could take forever The inexperienced ones were different, however. They wrote-up everything that they could find. Jason later discovered that it was a learning process for them as well and a smart instructor became experienced rather quickly. He was just glad that his check pilot was experienced; it could have been a bloodier write-up.

Jason's stomach growled as he propped his feet on his government-issued coffee table. He hadn't eaten since before his briefing earlier that morning and it was approaching four in the afternoon. Unzipping his sweat-stained flight suit to his navel, he walked to the kitchen. He felt depressed about the ride but not as bad as he probably should have. *Gus was right, I wasn't focused.* Opening the cabinet, he studied its contents for a snack that might cheer him up. Jason found a half-empty bag of chips, went to the refrigerator, and pulled out the picante sauce. Breakfast of champions. He spied the Coors Light longneck that sat on the top shelf for a moment. *A beer would be nice right now, but it's also what got me in this predicament.* He opted for the Diet Coke instead and moved with his bounty back to his space in front of the television. After a few seconds of channel surfing, he settled on that afternoon's episode of Cheers and began devouring his chips. Five minutes into the show there was a knock at is door.

"It's unlocked," he yelled.

The door opened and Matt Carswell, Lenny Banks, and Gus McTaggart came barreling through the door. Tracking in traces of mud, Matt and Gus walked over to the couch, Lenny went straight to the fridge. He pulled out the beer that Jason had contemplated earlier and shook the rain from his head.

"Hey we heard the bad news buddy," Gus said, "you doing all right?"

"Yeah, I'm okay. I just didn't feel like talking to anyone when I got back. I ran into my instructor on the way back from debrief and explained the ride to him. He looked at me like I was some kind of idiot for hooking for something like that."

"What did he nail you for?" Matt asked cautiously. Sometimes students who busted a checkride didn't like to talk about it. They started with things like "it was a really good ride" or "that check pilot is full of it".

"It was a sloppy ride," Jason said. "I was downgraded from good to fair on my clover-leaf and my single-engine landing. I got an unsat for ground ops."

"Ground ops? What the hell did you do?" Gus said. It was rare for a student to bust a check ride for ground ops, but it did happen occasionally.

Jason explained the seat pin situation.

"Why'd he downgrade you for the other stuff?" Matt said, sitting next to Jason and attacking the chips and salsa.

"It wasn't a bad ride . . ." Jason started to say, attempting to justify his poor performance. Jason thought a moment and said, "It wasn't a good ride either. Now that I think about it, I guess he could have hammered me for many maneuvers that just sucked. I never busted the area boundaries or anything like that, I guess it was just a fair ride."

"Forgetting those pins will get you every time," Gus said. "You kind of tied his hands with that one. Did you talk to Captain Johnson yet?"

Jason thought about the meeting with the flight commander. He was a good guy and was always doing everything he could for the students. Jason couldn't help but feel as if he'd let him down. "Yes. I talked to him before I came home. He asked the standard questions. What did I do wrong? What was the check pilot's attitude? Were there any external factors affecting me? To which I said a big 'Yes' and gave him a brief synopsis of my weekend.

"Anyway, he said I could count on a practice ride before going on my re-check ride." If he didn't pass that ride, he knew he could find himself out of the program. It was a grim thought and all of the students knew it. The consequences of failing the re-check were something seldom talked about at pilot training.

"That's a bunch of bull, Conrad," Lenny said. All heads turned to see what their companion had to offer to the conversation. It was the first thing Lenny had said since entering the room.

"What the hell do you mean by that?" Gus demanded. As the SRO, Gus took it upon himself to act as mother hen over all his flight members and his protective nature was obvious right now.

Lenny realized that his choice of words was probably not the best, but he decided to go with his previous statement. "I mean its bullcrap. Busting someone for something like that. I mean, the guy could have let you know in some way that your pins were still in."

"That's not his job Lenny," Matt said.

Lenny looked at Matt with contempt as he moved into the room in front of the T.V. "Okay, it's not his job, but it is still bullcrap that just because he left his pins in he should bust the entire ride."

"It's a safety of flight issue," Gus said, as the others heads nodded in agreement. "If those pins were in his seat in the air and he had to eject out of the aircraft, he couldn't do it."

"Well I still say its bullcrap. I've left my pin in before and my IP just casually let me know my pin was still in my seat."

"Yeah, Lenny well that's great . . . but it doesn't happen on a check ride," Jason said, effectively ending the conversation.

"So when is the practice ride?" Gus said, trying to end the negative mood of the conversation and point Jason to a more positive direction.

Before Jason could answer there was a loud knock on the door.

"Come in," he shouted across the room.

Lenny moved toward the door to open it. Before he reached it, the door swung open. Kathy Delgato stood in the doorway peering into the room. She wore a dark brown barn jacket, a plaid shirt tucked neatly into her blue jeans, and her cowboy boots. Her hair and clothes were soaking wet from the rain.

"Did I interrupt something?" she said.

"No ma'am," Matt said, "we were all just leaving. Let's go fellas."

Kathy stepped into the kitchen and before Jason could say anything, his classmates slid past her out of the room in a hail of good-byes and farewells.

When they left, Kathy looked at Jason. The seriousness in her voice was apparent. "Do you mind if I come in? I really need to talk to you." Kathy took off her wet jacket and set it on the counter in the kitchen.

"You might as well, everything else today has gone to bad, I see no reason to stop now," he said, switching off the television.

"Why, what is the matter?" she said closing the door behind her.

"I busted my contact checkride today."

Kathy moved across the room, and sat next to him on the couch. "Are you going to be okay?" she said, brushing her wet hair back from her face.

"I'm fine. I've just had a bad weekend that is rapidly evolving into a bad week."

"I know what you mean," Kathy said, "my weekend wasn't so great either." She sat back against the sofa and folded her arms.

They sat in silence for several minutes except for the sound of the falling rain outside. Jason wasn't sure what to say to her. He was glad she was here but he wondered who she was with Saturday night. Maybe it was nothing. Maybe it was just a friend. He hated himself for letting it bother him. He was here to learn to fly.

"She was here wasn't she?" Kathy said, breaking the silence.

Jason looked over at her. "Who?" Although he knew who she meant.

"Don't 'who' me Jason Conrad. You know who. Your damn ex-wife, the gorgeous blonde model. She was here and you were with her."

Jason wondered how she knew, and then simply surrendered to the fact that Enid was a small town. "She's gone now and nothing happened."

"You were with her Saturday night."

Jason could see the tears starting to form in her eyes.

"Okay look, here's what happened. After we left the club Friday night and you carried me home, I passed out—"

"Yeah, you did," she said as a tear slid down her cheek.

"Yeah, I did," he said. Hopefully this would not be too difficult to explain. Bethany showing up wasn't his idea. He was only reacting to the situation. "Well the next morning I'm passed out on my bed and I hear someone pounding on my door."

"And it's her, right?"

"Yes, it's her. I thought it was you returning to nurse me back to health but it wasn't." He shifted his position on the couch to face her more.

"Well what did she want?"

"Me. All of me. I couldn't believe she showed up here. She actually wanted to have a serious conversation at ten in the morning, and me with a serious hangover."

"And?"

"So I told her I was too hung over to discuss it at the time. We met for lunch—"

"At the Garfield Grill," she said.

"Yes, at the Garfield Grill." His eyes squinted and his head cocked to one side. Where was she going with this? What did she know, or think she knew? "Do you want to tell this story? You seem to know as much or more about my weekend than I do."

She sat back again and folded her arms across her chest. "I'm sorry, go ahead."

"Thank you. Well, we met for lunch and she gave me a line about how sorry she is for screwing someone while we were married. And she is sorry for divorcing me and she is sorry for marrying someone else."

"She sounds like a pretty sorry person."

"Right. She's laying it on pretty thick. She starts saying that she still loves me and she's not in love with that other jerk. I don't know if she was sincere or not. If she wasn't, it was the greatest acting I've ever seen her do."

Jason stood and walked into the kitchen and returned with two Diet Cokes, offering one to Kathy who took it, but didn't open it.

"Anyway," he said, "at this point, I still was suffering a massive hangover. There was just no way I could have carried on this conversation if I had wanted to. I think that kind of disappointed her, she'd come with all of her guns loaded.

"After we left the Garfield Grill, as you so keenly noted, we went our separate ways. We were supposed to go out to dinner, but I told her I didn't think it was a good idea." That wasn't exactly how it happened but he saw no reason to upset her with the story about the hotel. His tale wasn't a lie. It just didn't contain all of the truths in it that were available. He supposed this could be determined to be withholding information in a legal case. Jason decided he would sit on that piece of information unless she showed signs of knowing what went on at the Holiday Inn. "Then I left and came to Chicaros to see you. Only when I got there," he continued, "you had already left with your boyfriend. Would you care to explain that one?"

Kathy adjusted her posture and wiped the tears from her eyes.

"He wasn't my boyfriend you know that. You are."

"I wasn't sure that was an official status but I'm glad you feel that way. I do have the same feelings for you. So tell me, who was this guy? And why are you crying so much?"

She sat staring straight ahead with her hands in her lap. "It was Vince."

Jason sat up in amazement. "Vince? My friend Vince? Of all the damn guys running around this place, you have to take off with my friend?"

"Conrad I'm sorry. I didn't sleep with him or anything," she said. "I was just so mad at you because your ex-wife was in town. I didn't know what to do, I needed someone to talk to . . . we didn't do anything."

Jason sat disgusted on the couch, his elbows propped on his knees. He shook his head and thought about his horrible weekend and how it was turning into a nightmarish week.

"I think maybe I should just be alone for a while," he told her.

"Jason, I want to talk."

"I'm sorry, I can't talk right now. You'll have to accept that. I don't want it to be over between us, I don't think anything has happened that can't be fixed. It's just right now I have a world of crap around me and I'm down to my last roll of toilet paper."

Kathy stood up to leave. She walked over to him and ran her fingers through his hair. He made no attempt at acknowledging the gesture.

"I understand you are hurting Jason. I know that I hurt you and I'm sorry," she said walking to the door, "but you hurt me too. And I know you are pre-occupied with your flying so I won't press the issue today."

She opened the door and started to walk out, "And Jason . . ."

"Yes?" Jason said as he looked up slowly.

"Kick ass on that next check ride," Kathy closed the door behind her not waiting for a response.

BOB ALLEN AND MONROE DROVE slowly through the dark streets of Stillwater. Monroe was behind the wheel because he was the soberest. The two had spent the night at a popular honky-tonk which sat on the outskirts of town and they had stayed until the bar closed. Bob Allen had been doing quite well with one of the cocktail waitresses there until her husband showed up and decided it was time for her to go home. It was one of those nights when too much alcohol and too much cocaine had infested his brain. He'd tried to start two fights earlier but because he was so well known, the bouncers were able to separate them and keep Bob Allen out of trouble. Monroe was able to keep an eye on him for the short time until the bar closed. The two stumbled to Bob Allen's truck and proceeded to head home. Alone. Victims of their own good time.

Bob Allen was slumped over in the passenger seat, his black felt cowboy hat pressed up against the window, and his dirty Wranglers streaked the truck seat with mud and grass. His new white shirt with the pearl capped buttons had been ripped in the second fight of the evening and Monroe wasn't sure if Bob Allen was even aware of the predicament he had gotten himself into an hour ago.

Monroe had the radio tuned to a rap station in Oklahoma City, surprised that it even existed here. He hated listening to all the country and western music that Bob Allen and Big Joe always played. The cowboy act was too much for him to stomach. He had considered several times to move to one of the coasts, where things were a little trendier.

Monroe pulled onto a side road to avoid driving right through the campus and headed north to the outskirts of town. Big Joe had a place north of town where Bob Allen and Monroe stayed when in this part of Oklahoma. Big Joe's place was only five minutes away when Monroe felt the car shudder. He didn't hear the initial bang but the shudder definitely got his attention. The shudder lasted for a few seconds then the car sat back on its left rear. A fierce grinding sound came from the bottom of the truck as the rim of the tire screeched along the pavement.

"Shit," Monroe said, bringing the truck to a quick stop as the rim sent sparks everywhere. The jolt slammed Bob Allen into the dashboard and out of his alcohol induced slumber and the two stumbled out of the truck.

"What the hell did you do?" slurred Bob Allen staggering on the side of the road.

"I didn't do a damn thing," Monroe said as he cautiously walked around to the rear of the truck. Slowly he shook his head in disbelief at their bad luck as he looked at the condition of the truck. The rim was ruined, flattened in two areas, and it looked like the axle was bent.

"Shit, Monroe. What did you do to my truck? Did you go drive through a ditch or something? It's ruined!" Bob Allen said weaving drunk in the middle of the dark street. The only light was supplied by the headlights of the truck that shined up toward the sky now. "Big Joe is gonna have a shit fit when he hears about this. This is the last kind of shit he—,"

BAM!

Monroe pivoted to see the top of Bob Allen's head vaporize in a crimson mist and the body collapse on the pavement.

Monroe dove for the ground instantly, crawling along the road toward the ditch on the side. Who the hell was it? Why did they want to kill Bob Allen? He reached the ditch in a matter of seconds. Monroe crawled in the ditch for another thirty yards or so before crawling up the other side into an empty field of freshly cut grass. His nostrils flared from the musty smell of the grass and he sneezed twice, shattering the silence of the darkened field.

Monroe stood and ran through the field. Panic set in as he ran with neither direction nor purpose, his arms flailing as he ran.

Running away from the road, the truck, and his dead partner, he couldn't remember when he'd ever run so fast in his life. He'd gone maybe two hundred yards before reaching a small pond about the size of a football field. Out of breath and suffering from cramps in his side, Monroe staggered to the edge of the pond. Stepping too close to the water, his feet sank past his ankles in the thick black mud at the water's edge.

Backing out of the mud, he turned around to study the area for another escape route. He wasn't far from Big Joe's place. If he could get there he'd be safe. He could get help. Monroe looked back toward the river and saw a figure, walking across the field directly toward him. The figure was fifty feet away and Monroe knew he had nowhere to go. His legs grew weak and his body started to shake. His breathing came in big gasps now. Monroe's body started telling him something his mind was slow to acknowledge. He was about to die.

"Who are you?" Monroe screamed at the figure walking towards him.

No answer came from the figure, which approached him. He was ten feet away and pointing a rifle at Monroe's chest. Monroe squinted in the dark to see his face. Small traces of starlight highlighted the face of the killer. It took a moment, but Monroe finally made the connection.

"You mother-fu—" he screamed.

It was the last thing he ever said.

CHAPTER 25

September 6, 1995

MIKEAL TOLSTOY WALKED along the street for several blocks through the freezing cold of the early Moscow winter. A cold front came sweeping down from the north the night before, dropping six centimeters of fresh new snow. The street bustled with the afternoon activity of people returning from work, traveling to the market, and those heading off to work. Mikeal noticed it was unusually cold for this time of year as he rounded the corner to his apartment building. The icy chill pierced the thin gloves covering his hands, which were wrapped around two loaves of bread. The market had not been crowded when he first arrived, though he still had to wait in line for thirty minutes to buy the fresh bread. The line when he left, however, had grown considerably longer, meaning the wait could be more than an hour.

As he reached his building, several residents scurried down the steps brushing past him.

"Is it not a cold afternoon, Mikeal?" a voice called from behind him.

Mikeal turned to his neighbor who lived two flats downstairs from him. It was the elderly gentleman from the second floor. He could not remember where and when they had first met, nor could he remember his name. He supposed it didn't matter or he would ask him.

"It certainly is, my friend," he said. The man looked at Mikeal oddly, as though he used the term "my friend" out of context. The two barely knew each other, and now Mikeal was cornered. Embarrassed by his poor memory, his reaction concealed by the windblown streaks of his already red face. His eyes darted back and forth rapidly as if searching for something. "Perhaps we should go to my apartment for a glass of vodka to warm up?"

"Mikeal, that is a wonderful idea," the man said. He seemed to enjoy the idea of conversation with a neighbor for the evening, and would enjoy it more if there were vodka involved. Truth be told, the idea of a drink suited Mikeal just fine, too. Only stiff vodka would shake the memories of his spy game and calm his nerves.

The pair headed upstairs without speaking, and for good reason. By the time the two reached Mikeal's apartment on the fourth floor, they were winded. He had long ago given up attempts to a lower floor. It proved to be an impossible task.

Walking along the darkened hallway, Mikeal noticed the surroundings were unusually quiet, except for the ever-present creaking of the floorboards. None of the normal sounds were present: the neighbors across the hall fighting, the baby next door crying, radios and televisions blaring through the thin walls of the apartments. He felt more perceptive since his adventure several days ago. The feeling reminded him of the war of Nazi aggression. As a boy, the first time shells landed around his village, it was sheer terror. But after he survived such an event, he felt strong and invincible. Now, his initial fears gone, he thought he could get used to this spy business. Upon reaching his apartment, he unlocked the door, which made the familiar squeaking sound as it opened.

THE ENORMOUS RED, ORANGE, and yellow fireball intertwined with black smoke rolled out the side of the apartment building. Debris shot out of the massive hole where a window once perched. A large woman grabbed her children, barely avoiding the cascading flow of rubble. Mikeal Tolstoy's apartment covered the street below. A crowd of bystanders joined the panicked occupants of the building.

It was unclear when the first official arrived at the scene, but it wasn't very long, perhaps a minute or two. Five minutes later, the first firefighters arrived. A quick inspection of the surrounding area didn't indicate a large fire. There were a few small fires on the fifth floor, but those were quickly extinguished.

Two men in a black sedan watched from further down the street. They were impressed with the size of the explosion, but now their eyes scanned the people on the street. It was a minor task to rig the Semtex to explode when the door opened.

"I don't see him anywhere," the bald one said.

"*Nyet,*" replied his comrade.

The two sat in silence for ten more minutes, watching the mild chaos develop. The bald one slid from behind the wheel, out into the crowd.

"Wait here. I'll go see what they know."

"Perhaps he got away. What if someone else was killed in the explosion? Did he have a wife? A girlfriend? If he's gotten away, we'll have hell to pay."

"No, I don't think so." Stuffing his hands in his pocket and pulling out his cap, the bald one walked toward the crowd. "Keep the engine running," he said over his shoulder before disappearing into the crowd.

The bald one scanned the faces around the front of the building, searching for signs of Mikeal. Seeing none, he queried the police officers on hand about the tragic accident after informing them of his status with the government. The police officer was surprised there were not more people killed. Miraculously, there was no one in the surrounding rooms, above and below, where the room exploded. There was not one dead man but two, both of whom lived in the building. That was all the information the bald one was able to obtain, but it was enough. What the police officer didn't know was that the bald one and his partner had quietly evacuated the building by telling tenants there was a gas leak caused by a terrorist group. They had to leave the building and speak to no one on the way out. They didn't know who was involved. He guessed they missed someone.

The bald one returned to his car, slid behind the wheel, and put the car in gear. The car leaped forward as it pulled away from the curb.

"He's dead," the bald one said.

His partner removed his hat, revealing his eyebrows grown so close together they appeared as one straight band of hair. "One-brow" was slightly bigger than the bald one, but it was clear who was in charge.

"Tolstoy was a traitor to his comrades and countrymen," the bald one said. "Our work here is done. I think you might have used too much explosives. They say there were two men killed. Perhaps the blast was much bigger than it should have been."

"No, it was not. The blast was sufficient to do the job as it was intended," One-brow said. "Am I to believe the bodies' identities have not been confirmed?"

"It's him. We watched him walk in the building, and minutes later the bomb is set off. Now there are two bodies. It's him, I'm sure of it."

"Let us hope so. If we were to make a mistake, he might be able to make it to the Americans before we have another chance at him."

The bald one gave One-brow a double take and said, "I don't think Tolstoy was ever that big of a problem. His file was new; several days old at most. He may not have even been a traitor, just another soul that needed to be eliminated."

"Even so, now he is dead," One-brow said as he reached into the back of the sedan and pulled out a large, black briefcase. He set the briefcase on his lap, popped the clasps, and opened the lid, which revealed an unassembled sniper's rifle. As he began transforming the many parts into one, he spoke curiously, "I cannot believe Nikolai did not inform the old man of his plan. What if he is wrong?"

"It doesn't matter if Nikolai is wrong or right," the bald one said. "All that matters is Palovich must die."

HE FLIPPED THROUGH THE FILE for the third time that day. It had been brought to him early this morning, but he already knew it well. After all, he had compiled most of the information in it. Aaron Caldwell sat in his cramped office inside the compound of the American embassy in Moscow. He never complained about the office space being small; at least it was his. He didn't share it with anyone, as the other members of the embassy staff usually left him and his people alone.

Caldwell stretched the legs of his six-foot two-inch frame under the desk. His thick, brown hair was ruffled and his deep-set brown eyes surrounded by streaks of red. He had a serious look about him despite the fact he looked like someone out of a Bud Light commercial. He'd been told before he was too good looking to work for the government. He should move over to the civilian sector. He'd make more money there.

Stationed in Moscow for the last three years, Caldwell was not particularly liked by the embassy staff. "The Cold War is over," they said. He and his kind were just a bad memory. Under the embassy's diplomatic immunity, Caldwell was free to conduct his activities as a field officer for the Central Intelligence Agency. Such activities were severely frowned upon by those outside the circle of the cult, either because of the liberal beliefs of the outsiders or because they were upset about being left out of the loop.

Tossing the folder onto his desk, Caldwell leaned back in his chair and stared out the window. The snow had continued to fall for the last week. The first time he ever saw snow was when he attended courses at the "Farm". Caldwell came from Shreveport, Louisiana, and had studied political science at Louisiana State University in Baton Rouge. After four years there, he moved to New Orleans to attend Tulane Law School, where he graduated with honors. Shortly before graduation, he had been approached by recruiters for the CIA. They wanted young men and women who were looking for a challenge to help rebuild the dwindling intelligence agency. Fascinated with the opportunity for travel and adventure, Caldwell signed on immediately. It didn't take long for him to realize the CIA was not the same world you saw in a James Bond movie. There were a lot of boring meetings and mounds of paperwork that made absolutely no sense.

Four years ago, he jumped at the opportunity to apply for service at the Moscow division. After a year in Monterey at the Defense Language Institute, Caldwell moved to Moscow. The job had been interesting, but unexciting. In the beginning, Caldwell was disappointed. As time went by and he gained experience and exposure, he came to appreciate the cat-and-mouse game that still went on between the CIA and the KGB.

"What do you think?" Hank Fielding said, poking his head in the doorway.

Caldwell leaned forward, propped both elbows on the table, and clasped his hands. "Something big is going down, but I'm not sure what it is yet. Palovich has been a reliable source, but he's never been this nervous."

"Do you think they've found out about him? Maybe this is some sort of trap, and they are trying to find out who his contacts are."

"That thought hasn't been dismissed yet," Caldwell said. "It is unusual for him to use Mikeal, though. Mikeal is our no-shit emergency backup for Palovich's own protection. Why would he use him like this?"

"No telling, boss, but one thing's for sure: his days doing our dirty work are numbered."

PALOVICH MERLOV SAT IN HIS OLD, tattered lounge chair, reading a day old *Pravda*. The Russian newspaper never published any stories worthwhile; it still acted as an instrument of propaganda. Only now it had different handlers. Outside, the early evening changed from light to dark, the dim lightbulb overhead was all that lit up the room.

At forty-five, Palovich looked sixty. He'd started driving for Viktor some fourteen years earlier after a shrapnel wound in Afghanistan forced him out of the Soviet army. That experience in the worthless war had changed his thoughts forever on the dominance of Soviet power. When he walked he had a slight limp, but he managed to move well.

He couldn't remember when he was approached by Aaron Caldwell, or how Caldwell convinced him to become an agent for the Americans. He just knew it was the right thing to do. Yes, he had received money, but Palovich had been smart enough not to flaunt it and rarely spent any of it. It had been squirreled away for a better time. A time when Russia would be strong again, or he could move to old East Berlin.

Distracted by movement, Palovich turned to see his wife enter the room. She was a large woman, and her presence swallowed the room's emptiness.

"Why do you sit there, worthless?" she said.

"Woman, I work hard all day," he said, knowing exactly where this argument would go: nowhere. She argued for the sake of arguing. The relationship had become strained, and he hardly tolerated her.

Annoyed with her presence and the growing confrontation, Palovich pushed himself up from his seat and walked to the window.

"Work! You do not work! You sit on your rear all day in a plush limousine and drive KGB agents around Moscow."

"It is not a limousine, and the KGB no longer exists," he said, walking toward her.

"I do not care what they call themselves . . ." Her voice trailed off as he stopped listening. He no longer paid attention to what she said. Out of the corner of his eye, he noticed more movement across the room. A familiar movement, yet somehow out of place. Palovich focused on the small red dot dancing on the wall behind her, then on her head, then it disappeared.

CHAPTER 26

September 6, 1995

THE TWO FIGURES WALKED out of the dorms toward the grass field leading to the squadron. The sun began its slow climb out of the east as the wind picked up in the early morning chill.

"I'm supposed to get *all* the tests," Vince said. His day had not been the most enjoyable and dealing with the "scarecrow" was a nuisance he did not want to worry about any more.

"I'm sorry," Lenny said, "they're only releasing one a week. The computer releases each test on a specific seven-day cycle. You—actually I— can only retrieve a test during that period." He tried to refrain from smiling, biting his lower lip, attempting to hide his joy with himself and his little lie.

"What about the rest of the academic tests?"

"Same thing," Lenny said. He noticed Vince looking at him skeptically. "Look, this program is very concise and predictable when a specific event is going to be accomplished. That's why it's set up the way it is: to prevent people from doing what I'm doing." Lenny continued with his story. Vince glanced at him occasionally as the two walked toward the squadron. Lenny was not sure Vince believed him, but at the time, he did not really care. The two entered the building and made their way to the flight room. When they checked the scheduling board, they noticed it had changed slightly from the day before.

"Hey, buddy," Lenny said, "looks like you are on an instrument ride first period."

"Yeah." Vince set his books on the floor beside his desk. "What are you doing today?"

"Contact solo! Second period, gonna slip the surly bonds and touch the fa—"

"Don't get so dramatic on me, Scarecrow."

"Do me a favor, Vince. Can the 'scarecrow' crap." Lenny walked over to his seat and set his books on the desk.

They sat across the room from each other, staring intently. Theirs was a friendship based on convenience, and it was a strained friendship at best. There would come a time when each of them would have to make a choice for their destiny. Lenny already knew what his choice would be.

JASON ENTERED THE FLIGHT ROOM alone. There were a few other students there, but all the instructors were still in the flight commander's office for the morning meeting. His makeup ride, called an eighty-nine ride, was scheduled for first period. He was ready and relaxed. It was the first time he'd been able to say that since arriving at Vance.

When he walked across the room to his instructor's desk, Vince turned to face him, "Good morning Conrad. Did you get plenty of studying done?"

"Plenty, thanks," Jason said, deep in thought.

Jason took his seat, then pulled out his notepad, T-37 checklist, and in-flight guide. *Gus was right—I need to stay focused. I'm not here to make friends or find a wife. I'm here to become an Air Force pilot.*

THE FACT HE COULD REACT SO FAST is what surprised him the most. Perhaps it was the American TV cop shows that gave him instant recognition and quick reaction. Regardless, he moved quickly and effectively. By falling away to his right, he had saved his own life, but ended his wife's. The bullet that shattered his living room window found its way into her chest, barely missing his shoulder.

She was killed instantly, as the .30 caliber slug struck her heart and exploded. There was nothing Palovich could do for her as he lay on the floor, out of sight of the unknown assassin. Pulling the electrical cord for the lamp out of its socket, the room became dark. His heart raced as he took a moment to assess the situation. The first sound he had heard was the shattering glass, followed instantly by the impact of the bullet. The killer was using a silencer on his weapon. That meant he was close. He had to be close for the weapon to be accurate.

If they sent an assassin after him, they knew. Somehow, they knew he had been supplying the CIA with information. Now they were after him. It left him only one choice.

Run.

Run fast and run now.

Palovich scurried across the floor and into his bedroom. Cautiously, he scanned the window from the floor, crawled to his bureau, and retrieved his wallet and all the rubles he had in the house. Then, sliding the bureau two feet to the right, he lifted up a floor panel hiding a small metal box. Opening the box, he removed fifty thousand American dollars in brand new one hundred-dollar bills with a rubber band wrapped around them.

Placing the box back in the hole, he closed the panel, and returned the bureau to its original place. He quickly put on his snow boots and warmer clothes. It was likely to be a long, cold night.

"DID YOU HIT HIM?" THE BALD ONE SAID. He sat perched on the edge of his chair in an apartment across the quadrangle from Palovich's third-floor apartment.

"I can't be sure. They both fell." One-brow continued to search through the scope of his rifle for any signs of movement.

The bald one put his binoculars down. "Damn! We have to investigate. Now. If he is not dead, he might have the opportunity to contact someone. We should have shot him at the front door."

"Don't start that again, comrade," One-brow said. He had won his argument earlier to use the high-powered rifle with a silencer. It was less risky than a face-to-face kill, but now its effectiveness proved questionable.

One-brow started to disassemble his rifle, placing it back in its case. A quick check of his Tokarev TT-33 7.62 mm automatic pistol and he was ready to go. He preferred the Tokarev over his partner's Makarov 9mm. The Tokarev was slightly heavier, and One-brow said it gave him more control.

The two entered the dusty hallway of the apartment building and raced down to the street. Snow fell on the passersby as a few individuals, who heard the breaking glass, gathered on the street three floors below the window.

Reaching the entrance to Palovich's apartment, the bald one took one last glance for individuals in the streets, in case they had missed their mark. Seeing no one resembling Palovich, the two darted upstairs.

PALOVICH OPENED HIS DOOR AND PEERED down the hallway. It was quiet for this time of night. Closing the door behind him, he crept into the empty hallway. They would take the main stairs if they came for him. He would take the outside staircase. Pulling out his key, he locked the door to buy himself some time.

BAM! A door slammed on the first floor so loudly that is echo carried up the staircase. They were coming for him. The key stuck in the door and rattled as he struggled to pull it free. Palovich could feel his heart accelerate as he pictured the torture they would impose on him if they found him alive. Killing him would be the nice thing to do, but he was certain they were in no mood to do the nice thing. Not after missing their target.

He heard their footsteps racing up the stairs as the key finally pulled free of the lock. Palovich turned quickly down the hall and around the corner to the window leading to the outside stairwell. By the time he reached the window, the voices were close. Unlatching the window, he grabbed the handles at the bottom and pulled. Nothing. He tried again. Nothing.

The window was stuck, frozen from the snow and ice outside. Palovich's face showed the terror of his situation as he turned and looked back down the hallway, realizing he was trapped.

"SHOULD WE BREAK THE DOOR DOWN?" One-brow asked as the two men approached Palovich's apartment.

"No. He might be in there alive. If we break down the door, he may open fire. We will give the appearance we are investigating the disturbance of the broken glass."

One-brow beat on the door, "Is everyone all right in there?" he yelled.

No answer.

He beat again, and this time yelled, "Open up in there!" Still no answer.

As he was beat on the door for the third time, someone down the hallway opened his door. One-brow and the bald one instantly pulled their weapons and pointed them at the short, fat man wearing wrinkled slacks and a dirty white tank top.

"*Teekheey,*" the fat man said as he rubbed his eyes. Quiet. It was clear the banging had awakened him from a vodka-induced slumber as he staggered in place. When he pulled his hands from his eyes and saw the two guns pointed at him, his eyes widened and his mouth fell open.

"Go back inside and lock your door. *Meeleetsi,*" the bald one said to the drunken slob. "Police."

Quickly the drunk ducked back into his room and slammed the door. One-brow grinned as the locks slid into place.

"Break it down," the bald one said.

One-brow stepped back and kicked the door at the base of the lock. After three strong kicks, it showed signs of giving. The fifth kick ripped the door from the lock as it swung open into the dark apartment.

PALOVICH HEARD THE BEATING on the door. When the kicking began, he knew his time was limited; they would look down this hallway and he would be caught. The window was his only option as he tugged at its base. This time he felt it give, if only slightly. Slowly he made progress, rocking the window sideways to break it loose. When he heard his apartment door explode open, he gave the window a final pull.

The window broke free, opening at least two feet. *That's enough*, Palovich thought. He crawled through the opening into the cold night air. The wind on the third-floor metal staircase was slightly brisker than on the street, but he couldn't afford to worry about the frigid temperature now.

Turning back to the window, Palovich quickly closed it. On the window ledge was the stick used in the summer to prop open the window open. He grabbed it and stuck it between the top of the windowpane and the window frame, wedging the window closed. The assassins would not be able to open it from the inside.

His heart racing faster now, he climbed down the metal stairway toward the street. Upon reaching the second floor, Palovich paused to button his coat and adjust his scarf. He had no time to grab his hat and gloves, important items if he had to stay outside too long.

Lowering the ladder to the sidewalk from the second floor, he climbed breathlessly to the ground. Glancing up and down the street, he saw no one who appeared to be searching for him. There were few people on the streets and even less traffic. He walked briskly along the snow-covered sidewalk, pulling up his collar to make it look as if here were only hurrying to escape the cold.

THE TWO SCANNED THE APARTMENT quickly. There was no sign of the intended victim. Palovich's wife lay sprawled out on the blood-stained floor with a large hole in her chest, her lifeless eyes wide open, staring at nothing. They had missed, and they were angry. Dashing into the hallway, the two glanced in each direction. There were only two directions he could have gone, and they didn't pass him coming up the staircase.

"Come on," the bald one said as they darted to the corner. Reaching the hallway intersection, they looked right and saw it was a dead end. To the left was a window. The bald one started to turn back toward the target's room when One-brow stopped him.

"Wait!" he said as he rushed to the window. "He went out here. Look, the window is unlocked and the snow has recently been disturbed."

One-brow tugged at the window and it gave an inch before stopping abruptly. Examining the window, he spotted the stick bracing the window closed.

"He went this way. I'm sure of it. The window has been wedged closed from the outside."

The bald one walked up to the window and briefly studied the situation. Drawing back his Makarov, he smashed the window, sending shards of glass cascading into the snow and the alley below. Reaching outside, he knocked the stick away, freeing the window.

As soon as the bald one's arm was clear, One-brow opened the window and the two climbed onto the metal staircase. Searching for their prey, they could not distinguish him among the pedestrians below on the street.

"Palovich!" the bald one yelled into the night air. Several people stopped and looked at the men standing on the fourth-floor stairwell.

BANG! BANG! BANG! The bald one fired into the sky. The dramatic move had its desired result. People in the street either fell to the ground or ducked for cover. All except for one. A male in a large wool overcoat who now was running down the street.

"There," One-brow said, pointing at the running man. "There he is." The two assassins leveled their weapons on the moving target sixty meters away. The bald one grinned as he stared down the sight at Palovich. They fired several rounds simultaneously, the sound of gunfire piercing the night air.

CHAPTER 27

September 7, 1995

THE DAY HAD GONE UNUSUALLY WELL for Jason. From the briefing to pre-flight, ground ops, and the flight itself, things fell into place.

Typically, a make-up evaluation was stressful for students, the pressure being too much. Not the case today. Jason had done well all day long, ever since he showed up at the check pilot's office.

As he taxied the jet back to parking, he stayed focused on his task, not allowing his mind to wander. They had raised the canopy on the taxi back to parking. The cold temperature would have allowed them to taxi with it lowered, but Jason had been sweating, and the cool autumn breeze was refreshing.

Approaching the red tail section of the ramp, Jason spotted the marshaller waving at them. Waving back, he began the turn into the parking spot, clearing each direction as he did so and not going faster than a brisk walk. He followed the marshaller's signals, pulled into the parking spot, and stopped when the man made an "X" with his arms. Jason went through the engine shutdown checklist, and the loud squealing engines came to a halt.

Stay focused. It's not over until the instructor says it's over.

Removing his helmet, he replaced it with his Mickey Mouse ears and climbed out of the cockpit. He gave the aircraft a good walk-around as the check pilot exited the aircraft.

"I've already filled out the forms," the check pilot said. "Let's get on back. This will be quick."

That was a good sign. Jason swelled with enthusiasm. He knew he had a good ride, and he couldn't think of anything he might have done incorrectly. The walk back to the life-support shack was quick. As they approached the glass double doors, they flew open and out strode Lenny

Banks.

"Hey, Jason! How did the ride go?" Lenny said.

Jason acknowledged him with a simple, "It was okay," but flashed his friend a big grin, giving him the thumbs up.

"Glad to hear it." Lenny continued out to the flight line.

Noticing something peculiar, Jason stopped. "Hey Lenny," he yelled as the check pilot entered the life-support shack.

Lenny stopped and walked back, somewhat perturbed. "What? I'm in a hurry."

Jason slung his helmet over his shoulder, "Are you going flying?"

"Yes, damn it! I'm supposed to take off in ten minutes!" barked Lenny, pointing at the airplanes as he spoke.

A big grin formed on Jason's face, "That's what I thought." Lenny appeared confused as to the line of questioning. "You might want to take a helmet with you."

Lenny looked as if he had been snapped out of a trance. He followed Jason back in to the life-support shack, cursing himself out loud along the way. Jason grinned at the mistake his friend had made. Been there, done that.

The ground evaluation ended quickly, the check pilot pleased with what he saw all day. Jason passed with a very good write-up. Walking back to the flight room, he felt as if he was walking on clouds. Baby steps.

When Jason entered the flight room, before he had a chance to speak, the scheduler asked, "How'd the ride go?"

"Very well, sir. Feel free to schedule me as normal." Jason set his pubs on the counter as he studied the scheduling board.

"Good. I'll need you to be snacko in thirty minutes so I can put Bailey in a jet. You're buddy Andrews lost an engine while in Tinker's radar pattern, and they landed there. Screwed up the entire schedule for today." Tinker Air Force Base was a large logistics base located in Oklahoma City about seventy miles from Vance. Instructors from Vance frequently flew to Tinker for instrument training to alleviate some of the traffic from Vance's traffic pattern.

"Vince? Is he okay?" Jason said, unsure if he was genuinely concerned or simply curious.

"Sure, they're fine. Some engine guys are going over there right now to fix it. They should be able to fly it out this afternoon."

LENNY HURRIEDLY WALKED TO THE JET. The T-37 ramp was

half-full, as the squadron schedulers took advantage of the good weather, sending out the solo students. The noise of the Tweet engines pierced the air as Lenny adjusted the parachute on his back, his mode: full throttle and it showed. Thankfully, the crew chief had stopped him, or he never would have checked the Form 781. The aircraft required an exceptional release, a review from a rated pilot or maintenance supervisor for a minor write-up. Lenny never noticed it. Had he taken off without this, he could have hooked for ground ops on a solo jet. That would be the ultimate embarrassment. Hooking a solo ride did not sit well with your peers.

The pre-flight walk-around had been more like a run-around. Lenny didn't glance at the checklist once, looking over the panels and wheel wells by memory. In no time, he strapped in and started the engines. The long taxi out to Eastside came quick, and Lenny smiled under his oxygen mask.

"Eastside, Scare Four-Three, number one, Contact," Lenny told the controller.

"Scare Four-Three, cleared for takeoff."

"Scare Four-Three."

Lenny pushed the power up and the jet lurched forward as he taxied into position. With the throttles to full power, all the engines looked good, and everything appeared ops normal. Lenny released the brakes, accelerated down the runway, and rotated ten knots early. He recognized his error and didn't allow the aircraft to leave the runway until he reached takeoff speed. As the aircraft started to gain airspeed, he visually confirmed the jet climbing away from the ground. Lenny checked the vertical velocity indicator (VVI) for a three-hundred-feet- per-minute climb rate and raised the gear handle.

In a manner of seconds, the landing gear came up and entered the belly of the aircraft. The warning light in the gear handle went out, telling him the gear was up and locked. Seeing that, he moved his hand from the throttles to the flap lever and pushed it to the up position.

Slowly the flaps crept up into the wing as the aircraft gained more speed. Lenny kept the nose on the horizon to aid in the acceleration to the tech-order climb of one hundred-eighty knots. Five miles south of the field, he made the left turn to head back north to the training area. Scare Four-Three climbed to five thousand feet.

"YOU'RE HERE TO INVESTIGATE what?" Colonel Jenson said, rising from behind his desk, his nostrils flaring and chest heaving. Colonel Benjamin Todd Jenson was an imposing figure. He stood six feet three inches and maintained good physical conditioning by hitting the gym at least three times a week. A former F-16 driver, Colonel Jenson was a hard worker who played by the rules. Like most pilots assigned to Air Education and Training Command, he didn't want to be there. Training Command was not his idea of career progression, but it did give him the wing commander slot which was necessary to get him his first star.

The OSI agent sitting across from Colonel Jenson spoke. "I am here to investigate the theft of academic tests."

"What is your name again?"

"Jacobs. Mister Jacobs," Alonzo loved to use that line on higher-ranking officers. It was interesting to watch how nervous people get when an OSI officer came to their office.

The colonel stood from behind his desk. The large oak desk sat in front of the vast window facing the east.

"Well, Mister Jacobs, I am not aware of any test-cheating scandal on my base," he said as he walked past his "hero wall" covered with plaques and pictures. "Would you care to explain this to me? It's the first time I've heard about it. Just how is it Mister Jacobs, you know of this activity and no one here does?"

"There is at least one person here who knows, Colonel: the one stealing the tests. You see, no one here knows about it because the tests were not stolen here. They were stolen from Randolph out of the main computer bank."

"How did you discover this?" the colonel said, sipping his coffee.

Alonzo crossed his legs and began, "It started with a computer lock-up in another area of the base, one of the offices in AFPC. A new system has been installed. Whenever someone tries to access a computer mainframe on the LAN without the right access codes, the computer shuts itself down. While investigating this shutdown, I got a call from AETC. They had discovered someone accessing their test bank. I brought in a computer expert who discovered our thief was accessing the LAN via the Internet. It also explained the shutdown of the other system on base.

"Anyway, my computer man set up a trap for our hacker. Our hacker used a program called SCRAMBLETEK that prevents modem signals from being traced. My guy designed a program to circumvent SCRAMBLETEK. The next time the hacker went to work, we tracked him here."

"Do you have any leads or ideas on how you are going to conduct this investigation?"

"Based on the tests stolen, we believe it is a T-37 student. They were stolen in order until this last transaction. The guy emptied the file on that one. I'd like to start with a list of all the students in the T-37 program, their room numbers, test scores, and flights they are assigned to. I think we can isolate it to a limited number of suspects. I'd like to propose we search each of their rooms."

The colonel rubbed his chin. "It sounds as if you've thought this situation through. You can accompany one of my officers during his "mandatory" room inspections. These are common and shouldn't raise any suspicion. The last thing I want is rumors flying around base about this."

"Understandable, Colonel," Alonzo said.

"I'll have my executive officer gather the information for you. What specifically are you looking for?"

"Clues, tests, whatever we can find."

Colonel Jensen nodded as if he understood. "When would you like to start your room search?"

Alonzo looked the colonel squarely in the eyes. "Immediately."

CHAPTER 28

September 7, 1995

SELLING COKES AND CANDY bars was the last thing Jason had in mind after his highly successful flight The daily assignment as the snacko sucked, but everyone had to work in the snack bar for a few hours a day. It was one of those rites of passage.

"Conrad, congratulations are in order. I presume," he heard a familiar voice say. Looking up, he saw Gus McTaggart standing in front of him.

"Hey, Gus. Yeah, the ride went well. Thanks for the advice. You were right—I just hadn't been focused. I had to do a little soul searching and think about why I'm here. It paid off."

"Well, good," Gus said as he grabbed a Coke and a bag of pretzels. "I guess ol' Vince lucked out."

"Why, what's up?"

"He's stuck at Tinker. They flamed out an engine on short final and had to land. The engine fix is going to take longer than they thought, and his IP doesn't have crew rest to fly back when they're done."

"Why don't they drive 'em back?"

"Too much of a hassle, I guess. Someone would still have to drive back down there tomorrow and fly the plane back. Right now, Vince and his IP are going to stay overnight and fly back tomorrow morning."

"Yeah, I guess that's a good deal." It was good news for Jason, anyway. He wasn't sure Vince was someone he wanted to see right now.

SCARE FOUR-THREE HAD ESTABLISHED himself in one of the lower areas, a block altitude between seven and twelve-thousand feet. Lenny Banks was in a dream. He was supposed to be out there practicing maneuvers, but had spent most of his time loitering around his assigned airspace. The clear blue sky enticed him, and so he decided to have fun and at least enjoy the view. Occasionally, he performed an aerobatic maneuver to break up the monotony, but he was sloppy. By not paying attention to the proper entry parameters of airspeed, altitude, and power settings, he wasn't very successful.

And he didn't really care. Lowering the nose of the jet, he passed through ten thousand feet to pick up airspeed. At two-hundred-twenty knots, he raised the nose above the horizon and moved the stick to the left while he fed in some rudder. The aircraft rolled lazily around its longitudinal axis three-hundred-sixty degrees. Aileron rolls were his favorite maneuver. They had all the thrill of going upside down without the strain of the heavy, rapid G-forces encountered on the "over the top" maneuvers.

Lenny leveled off and made a one-hundred-eighty-degree turn to keep himself in his area. He performed Lazy Eights along the north-south section lines of the grid-laid flatlands of Oklahoma. The climbing, one-hundred-eighty-degree turns of reversed direction should have been symmetrical turns, but Lenny's carelessness was pushing the outside of the flight envelope. He was getting too slow at the top and too fast at the bottom.

These sloppy parameters went unnoticed, as his mind wandered elsewhere. He thought of what he could do next to piss off Vince. Lenny had reached a point where he no longer cared for Vince. He'd gotten all he'd get from him. Even though Vince had saved his life, he could not stand the son of a bitch.

"Screw 'im," he said to no one over the cockpit interphone.

He had grown tired of the constant verbal abuse, public humiliation, and name-calling. He'd had enough.

"I'll show him. I'm gonna slowly make his life miserable."

No one answered as he continued the sloppy maneuvers.

Who the hell does that SOB think he is? For the past three years I've been helping him cheat his way through one class or another and he treats me like a dirtbag. If I could turn him in without getting caught myself I'd do it in a heartbeat. Maybe if I—

Lenny's thoughts were interrupted by the jet shuddering.

"Uh-oh."

Lenny knew stalling an aircraft was not like a stalling car. A stalled car meant the engine wouldn't work, and it sits on the side of the road. An airplane can still fly with a failed engine, not as well, or very far. When an airplane stalls, the air flow over the surface of the wing is disrupted, causing a loss of lift. Fortunately, Lenny recognized the shudder for what it was, and glanced at the airspeed as he pushed the throttles full forward. The T-37's airspeed rapidly passed through ninety knots and had an attitude of thirty degrees nose high. In an attempt to help the jet recover from this unusual attitude, Lenny tried to push the nose over, then fed in a little bit of rudder and aileron to get the nose down quicker.

Suddenly, the left wing dropped rapidly to the left and the nose quickly tracked below the horizon, then snapped back up before stabilizing about forty degrees below the horizon.

Perspiration flowed from his pores as he recognized what was happening. He had applied too much rudder and aileron in his stall recovery. He yawed the jet. Stall and yaw. He knew exactly what was happening as he saw the rapidly rising terrain below him.

Time was in a vacuum as Lenny watched the earth spin beneath him. What seemed like forever lasted a matter of seconds and two revolutions of the spin before he snapped out of his daze.

Reverting instinctively back to his spin training, he found a spot on the ground to focus on to count a full revolution. It was a simple grain elevator like thousands of others across the plains. But it was *his* right now, and he wasn't going to let it out of his sight.

With the grain elevator as a reference point, he began the spin-recovery procedure. Pulling the throttles back to idle, Lenny heard the engines wind down as he centered all of his controls to the neutral position. This done, he pulled the stick to full aft position. Visually noting the aircraft was indeed spinning to the left, he confirmed this on the turn and slip indicator by verifying the needle was displaced to the left. He pushed in the right rudder hard, creating the "barn door" effect to slow the aircraft down.

With the rudder in full deflection, Lenny slammed the stick full forward with all his might. The entire sequence took a second.

"Oh, shit."

The aircraft continued its spiral toward the earth as time stood still.

Lenny went over the procedures in his head. Idle, neutral, aft. Spinning left, needle left, right rudder. Full forward.

In a hypnotizing manner, the earth continued its steady rotation. Lenny glanced at the altimeter as he passed through nine thousand feet. He tried the recovery again. Idle, neutral, aft. Spinning left, needle left, right rudder. Full forward.

Nothing.

This was not right. Panic began to set in, and Lenny never noticed the excessive play in the fore/aft movement of the stick. Trying the procedure a third time, slowly this time, he concentrated on each specific move. The throttles were indeed in idle; the flight controls neutral. Pulling the stick aft, he again confirmed the left turn and applied right rudder. He threw the stick forward, BAM! He heard and felt it hit the front stop. This should have broken the stall, and he should be pulling out of this spin into a level dive.

"Oh, Jesus. Oh, Jesus."

Lenny glanced at the altimeter. The jet, now passing through eight thousand feet, quickly approached his personal ejection minimum of seven thousand feet. That would give his parachute time to open after ejection.

Lenny reviewed the Boldface Emergency Procedures for Ejection in his mind, Handgrips-Raise, Triggers-Squeeze. Raising the handgrips armed the seat, while squeezing the trigger fired the charge that would blow the canopy and send his chair up the rails and out the aircraft. He watched the small hand on the altimeter wind down from eight thousand feet to seven thousand.

Taking his hands off the controls for the first time, Lenny reached down to the yellow ejection handles, grabbing both firmly. Taking a deep breath and sitting straight back in the seat, he pulled hard on the handles to arm the seat.

The handles didn't move.

His first reaction was to squeeze the triggers, but without the seat armed, the triggers had no effect. The handles never seemed to stick in the simulator. After tugging a second time with the same results, he looked down at the handles.

As the aircraft passed through five thousand feet, Lenny Banks was overcome with terror. The first thing he noticed was the red ribbon draped over the edge of the seat. His eyes followed the ribbon to its end attached to the pin. The pin was in place, locking the ejection seat handgrips, not allowing them to move.

Time now accelerated and panic set in as the three-ton jet plunged toward earth. Lenny did the calculations in his head as he stopped tugging on the handles and reached for the pin. His hands flailed from the forces of the spinning jet and he struggled to arm his ejection seat.

Round and round the jet turned, accelerating close to the structural limitation of the aircraft. To eject at this airspeed would surely result in bodily harm from the windblast. It was questionable as to whether his chute could successfully open in time to give him a swing or two under a full canopy.

Fumbling to remove the pin, Lenny glimpsed outside at the rapidly rising terrain. When students flew solo in the T-37, the instructors used to joke with them that when you are solo, no one can hear you scream.

Lenny Banks screamed anyway.

CHAPTER 29

September 7, 1995

THE SPEAKER CRACKLED, shattering the silence in the building. *"Attention in the building. Attention in the building. T-37 operations are Stand-down for the day. I repeat, T-37 operations are Stand-down for the day."* Jason looked up from his duties behind the snacko desk. Stand-down meant all flying stopped. That was odd—it was clear skies with no wind. They should be launching every solo in the building.

"All personnel are instructed to return to their flight rooms for accountability."

That, too, was strange. Jason moved closer to the VHF radio set up in the snack bar for students to listen to other students talking on the radio. Intended to be a learning tool, it was frequently used for harassment by their peers. He turned up the volume for Eastside's frequency.

"Bison Four-Two, you are cleared to land."

"Bison Four-Two, Gear down, full stop, cleared to land."

"Scare Four-Zero, VFR entry."

"Eastside, Bison Five-Zero. What's the idea behind the recall? I'm full of fuel."

"Bison Five-Zero, SOF directed recall. Keep channel clear. Winds calm, altimeter three zero one two."

"Scare Three-Two, inside initial, five hundred pounds."

"Bison Four-Five, in the break, breaking out for Scare on initial."

It was a zoo out there, Jason observed. They were trying to get all the aircraft on the ground and fast. The local traffic pattern filled up rapidly and the aircraft started to interfere with one another.

"Bison Five-Zero, perch point breaking out."

"On the break out, use caution. There are two of you."

"Scare Four-Seven, Echo."

The chatter continued nonstop on the radios, and he knew something out there had gone wrong. Two students from another class entered the empty snack bar, one speaking excitedly to the other, "I'm telling you, it's a plane crash . . . it has to be. I heard the duty officer talking to the SOF asking him if they had a plane to go look for him."

Jason looked up from the radio. Dashing over to the counter where he had been working, he pulled out his in-flight guide and quickly dialed in the frequency for the MOA controller.

"That's a roger, MOA. Bison Four-Niner has a tally on the target."

"Bison Four-Niner, cleared surface to ten-thousand. Maneuver as necessary."

"Bison Four-Niner, leaving ten-thousand for one-thousand."

Search and Rescue plane, Jason thought to himself. *Holy cow, this is wild.* Two minutes passed before the next radio call came over. By this time, a small crowd had developed in the snack bar, all looking for the same thing: information.

"Bison Four-Niner, leaving one-thousand for five-hundred."

The chatter built in the room between radio calls, louder and louder each time. But each time the pilot keyed the mike, the room fell silent.

"MOA, Bison Four-Niner. I have the plane in sight. Location is the zero-two-niner radial at thirty DME."

"Copy. Zero-two-niner at three-zero DME."

"That's affirmative."

"Bison Four-Niner, do you see a chute?"

A chute, Jason thought. A chute meant one person, which at this base meant solo student.

"Negative. I see no chute or movement near the aircraft. I'm starting an expanding square. I'll be bingo in two-zero minutes."

Jason left the snack bar and headed for the ops desk. It resembled a madhouse. It appeared as if every instructor with any kind of authority stood around trying to get information on the crash. The duty officer behind the desk talked on the phone, listening to Eastside's frequency simultaneously. As aircraft entered the pattern, he placed a dot by their name. As they landed, he placed another dot.

As he scanned the board, Jason noticed all but two aircraft had either entered the pattern or landed. One was Bison Four-Niner, the aircraft searching around the wreckage. The other was Scare Four-Three, Lenny Banks.

CAPTAIN RALPH HARRISON FOCUSED his attention on the numerous planes swarming overhead. "It sure is a mess up there. I wonder what's going on." Harrison had shown up ten minutes before Alonzo. After a quick introduction and in-brief by Alonzo, the two drove to the student dormitories.

"I appreciate your coming so soon, Captain Harrison," he said as they stepped out of the car. "It's imperative we locate whoever is doing this as quickly as possible." Alonzo towered over the smaller captain. He finished scanning the remaining room numbers and names as he walked to the edge of the sidewalk where Harrison stood. Alonzo observed the swarm of aircraft overhead.

"How do you know which rooms to check?" Harrison asked.

"It's pretty simple, really. The first tests stolen were T-37 tests. Whoever took them stole them in order. So, our first assumption is the thief is a T-37 student currently in the program. The timeframe for this could actually limit itself to one class, but just to be sure, we'll spread it out wider to all of the T-37 classes."

"What if you come up empty?"

"We'll expand the search in different directions. The tests were stolen from here. We were able to trace it that far. Since it came from on base, that eliminates any of the married students except for the ones in base housing. If we have to, we can check them out also, but it will be difficult."

Harrison shrugged his shoulders as they entered the first room. The search had begun.

THE AFTERNOON DRAGGED ON as information slowly crept in about the crash. Rumors flew back and forth; no one could say for sure what happened. The 71st Flying Training Wing Safety Officers had driven to the crash site with the firetrucks as soon as the coordinates had been given over the radio.

Jason sat alone in his room reviewing his Dash One, Section Three, Emergency Procedures. News of the crash troubled him, not because he flew the same airplane, but that he had lost a classmate and friend. It would be several days before they would know what caused the crash. The rumor mill had begun already, running the spectrum from poor airmanship to suicide. Hopefully, the accident investigation board would reveal something else as the cause. Thinking to himself about the irony of the situation, Jason nodded his head. Lenny had been one of the better flyers in the class. If he had an emergency, surely he would have done the right thing to solve it. Long ago, Jason accepted the fact he might fumble up an emergency—he would either fix it, get out of the airplane, or die. It was that simple. He put his book on the desk when someone knocked on the door.

"Hi, Gus," he said as he opened the door. "Come on in."

"Hey, buddy," the class SRO grimly replied, "I need to ask you a favor."

"Go ahead." The two moved into the other room and sat down.

"I've got a million things to do tonight. The flight commander wanted me to get one of you guys to collect Lenny's personal possessions for shipment back home to his family."

Jason said nothing as his SRO continued. "I would do it myself, but I've got to help the chaplain coordinate the funeral service. Anyway, I would get Vince because they were such good friends, but he's still stuck in Oklahoma City. I figured you were the next best choice."

Jason stared at the floor for a moment, then looked up at his SRO. "Sure, I'll get over there right now."

"Great, we'll be stand-down tomorrow, as well, and I wouldn't count on flying anytime soon. If the investigation turns up a mechanical failure, they'll probably ground the entire fleet until they do an inspection on each aircraft."

"Swell," Jason said gazing at the floor.

"Hey, are you okay with all this, Conrad?"

"No, I'm not okay with it," Jason said. It was a time when those who fly look inward and contemplate their own mortality. "I-I just don't understand why . . ." His voice trailed off as he struggled to finish his sentence.

Gus simply nodded. Jason knew what he meant. The first time one of your friends died was rough. The same thing for combat. Every flier had gone through it . . . another rite of passage.

"Yeah, well, look, here's the key," Gus said, placing it on the kitchen counter. "Thanks again, I've got to blast."

Jason stared at the key as he moved slowly to retrieve it. "No problem, Gus. See you tomorrow."

He slipped the key in his pocket, robotically put on his shoes, and grabbed a jacket. It was going to be a long night.

LENNY WAS A SLOB. His room resembled a disaster area. Clothes piled in various heaps throughout the room. Study materials sporadically stacked on the floor and desk. *Unbelievable. What the hell has this guy been doing for the past three weeks?* He pulled Lenny's luggage from the closet. Jason slowly packed away the clothes of his dead friend. After about a half hour, all of Lenny's clothes were packed. The quiet in the room started to get to Jason.

RRRIIINNG!

Jason leaped at the sound that shattered the silence. RRRIIINNG! The phone rang again. Jason started to answer it, but paused. What would he say? What if it was family? How could he tell them Lenny had died today? They must not know, right? Otherwise, why would they call his room? The phone rang two more times. Another sound filled the room as the answering machine buzzed and whirled to life.

"Hello? Hello? Speak louder, I can't hear you," came the message out of the machine, an eerie voice from beyond. *"Of course, I can't hear anything because I can't come to the phone right now. Leave your name and number and maybe I'll call you back."* BEEEP!

The message ended. After a pause, the caller hung up the phone. Saved by an answering machine. Jason felt more relieved than guilty. Looking around the room, Jason began to feel uneasy as the numerous pictures of Lenny Banks stared at him. Lenny with his dad. Lenny's first solo. Lenny with a college sweetheart. Lenny's graduation. Lenny's commissioning. Jason didn't like the feeling. The pictures come down next.

He turned on the television for background noise and removed everything from the walls, stacking them into neat piles. It didn't take long. Scanning the room for his next project, Jason eyed the bookcase next to the television. It could wait until tomorrow.

Jason next conducted an inventory for an accurate box count tomorrow. Moving to the desk, he gathered all of Lenny's papers, stacking them in more neat piles. He sifted through each of the drawers, emptied them, and stacked its contents on top of the desk. The bottom drawer lay empty except for a large manila envelope, heavy with some kind of papers. As he lifted it out, the papers shifted in the package and fell to the floor. Jason's eyes went wide with shock.

Money fell everywhere. A lot of money. Everywhere. Hundred, fifty, and twenty dollar bills. Shocked, Jason collected the money and counted it. Eight thousand dollars. A significant amount of cash no matter how you sliced it, especially for a second lieutenant. What would Lenny be doing with that kind of money? Jason thought about it for a moment. He knew Lenny gambled occasionally, but if he ever won, he bragged about it for days. There had been no bragging for a month.

When he looked back in the drawer, he saw another manila envelope. Jason pulled out the package stuffed with papers. Unlatching the thin metal clasp holding the envelope closed, he pulled out the papers.

"Uh-oh," he said out loud as he read the top page. Jason recognized the paper. The first page he saw he identified as the Instrument Flight Rules test. A test they would take next week. Flipping through the next few pages, he noticed other versions of the same test. In UPT, there were four different versions of every test, and Jason had in his hands all four versions of the next test.

Jason's eyes wandered nervously around the empty room as he contemplated his next action. Locking the door to the room, he sat on the couch and began going through the stack of papers.

"Wow, this is amazing," he said after five minutes of organizing the tests. His tone wasn't one of joy, but of concern. On the floor in front of him, a copy of every version of every test in the T-37, T-38, T-1, and the stan/eval Master Question File for all three jets.

Jason began perspiring as the consequences of his discovery sank in. He had, in front of him, the secret to success in the program. With this information in his possession it would relieve him of . . .

"Wait a minute!" he said to no one. "Where the hell did these come from in the first place?"

Picking up a stack and taking a closer look, Jason noticed the ink on the paper smeared easily, indicating a computer ink jet printer. Lenny's ink jet printer. The bottom of each page had the date the tests were downloaded. It was only a few days ago. They also said Randolph Air Force Base. Lenny stole the tests using his computer! He somehow tapped into the computer mainframe and took the tests right out from under their noses. That would explain why he never studied. Jason realized that while he spent most of his spare time with his nose in the books, Lenny never studied much at all.

And neither did Vince.

That could possibly explain the money. Vince always had a lot of cash to throw around. He had the nicest clothes, and was always buying drinks and dinner for everyone.

That had to be it.

Lenny stole the tests and sold them to Vince. No wonder they always fought about something. Vince treated Lenny like dirt, then Lenny would hold some secret in front of his face and Vince would back off. It started to make sense now.

Jason wondered about his two classmates. Two classmates he considered friends. These two were not what they appeared to be. Lenny acted as if he didn't care a whole lot about being in pilot training, despite the fact he flew quite well.

Vince, however, seemed to care too much. The overzealous type, he was always trying to be the best, always trying to make friends with everyone—particularly his instructors. Vince also flew quite well. In fact, he was probably the best stick in the class, but it was obvious to anyone who paid attention, he had weak general knowledge. He was a mystery, but perhaps a mystery no longer. Jason had concluded his classmate, Vince Andrews, could not be trusted.

But what about Lenny? He's a bona-fide thief. As an officer, Jason had an obligation to turn them in. But what good would it do right now? Lenny was dead and there was nothing the Air Force could do to him. It would just be one more scar on the military services after years of embarrassments. Then there was Lenny's family. How would such news affect them? Jason reached over to the stack of pictures and grabbed the top one—Lenny and his dad standing in front of a Cessna 172 after Lenny's first solo ride. Father and son, grinning from ear to ear. Lenny was close to his dad. Jason knew he couldn't destroy such a bond.

He gathered the tests and cash from Lenny's place and returned to his own room. It was a pleasant change from the cold, somber atmosphere of his dead friend's quarters. Sitting on the edge of his bed, Jason turned on his television using his remote. He flipped over to the Discovery Channel. With nothing on television worth watching, he settled for CNN. The big story of the day, Senator Jonathan Bowman would be in San Antonio next week. *Great,* he thought, *I think I've seen enough of this guy.*

Staring at the two packages in his hands, Jason thought about his decision. It wasn't right for these two items to be found in his friend's room. Lenny Banks' family would be grieving enough. There was no reason for them to find out he was a thief and possibly an embezzler. It may not have been the best decision, but it was the right decision. Now what? He had possession of stolen tests and a whole lot of cash that most likely belonged to someone else. And he had absolutely no idea what to do with it.

Jason glimpsed the senator's picture on the television. "Dad would know what to do."

It had been a long day. Placing the money and tests in his bottom drawer, he crawled under his blankets and fell asleep.

CHAPTER 30

September 8, 1995

ARON CALDWELL STOOD in the crowded airport in Moscow. The early morning sun poked its head above the horizon, its rays penetrating the glass walls, casting a yellowish hue across the lobby. Caldwell took his position next to the ticket counter. As the chief of the CIA's Moscow division, he had a particular interest in former KGB members who traveled abroad, especially when one of them was the head of Section Nine en route to the United States. Caldwell recognized the consequences could be deadly.

The difficult part was determining which route he would take to America. Caldwell had guessed his prey would take the route to New York or Washington, via Frankfurt, Germany. The other direction, through Bangkok or Tokyo, would have caused Nikolai Gregarin to stand out too much. Caldwell observed the glass doors from his position by the ticket counter. He had men located at every possible entrance. The small radio receiver in his ear crackled and he adjusted the volume.

Taking a sip of his Russian labeled Coca-Cola, he casually scanned the crowd. He knew Nikolai's face thanks to Palovich. It had been quite a score several years back when Palovich first came to them offering his services. Caldwell, on his first assignment to the Moscow division, concluded it was some kind of test. A KGB general's chauffeur offers to act as an agent? Caldwell assumed his superiors in the Moscow division were evaluating him in the situation. As a young, motivated case officer, Caldwell played the game. He recruited Palovich; even provided a background check. It was the best you could do on a Russian national. The package he put together for his superiors was flawless. When he walked into their office to make his pitch, they started bouncing off the walls. This kind of event didn't happen often. Caldwell began to realize what he had done was no test.

It was real.

A thorough check on the young agent's work revealed no errors. Indeed, the young agent had scored a major coup for the bunch at Langley. They had feared last year, when Aldrich Ames was identified as a spy for the Russians, Palovich would be one of the names to pop up on his list. But it never happened. Ames never mentioned Palovich. Unfortunately, Palovich had known nothing of Ames either, although he had known about a mole somewhere in the higher fold of the CIA. When Ames turned up, the CIA figured they had their man. Caldwell thought different.

THE LARGE BLACK SEDAN PULLED UP in front of Moscow's Sheremetyevo Airport terminal. Nikolai Gregarin stepped out from the back seat as the driver retrieved his bags from the trunk. Nikolai took the two bags and entered the terminal through the sliding glass doors.

"Main entrance," Caldwell heard over the radio. "Dark gray, double-breasted overcoat, wing-tip collar. Two bags. Headed for the gates, not the ticket counter. Repeat, headed for the gates, not the ticket counter."

Caldwell scanned the crowd trying to spot anyone who fit that description, but saw no one. He would have to rely on his men at the gates to spot Nikolai. Caldwell remained by the ticket counter in case he needed a ticket to take a different flight. A hundred dollars American to the pudgy ticket agent had ensured him easy access to another ticket on a moment's notice.

The CIA had the advantage in this situation. As far as the Americans knew, the compromising of Section Nine was still unknown to the Russians. They believed it to be their secret society where activities continued unnoticed by the rest of the world. For the most part, they were, except for Nikolai. The CIA monitored his actions. If he made a trip to the United States, Caldwell had a good idea why.

"He's heading for the john," said a voice over the interphone. The tiny earpiece fit uncomfortably in Caldwell's ear, but it could not be seen from a distance. Picking up his carry-on bag, Caldwell walked toward the restroom. The crowd in the terminal thinned slightly as the passengers from the latest arrival left the terminal, although the noise level didn't change despite the number of people who left.

Caldwell saw the figure walk into the restroom, never getting a good look at his face. Caldwell moved back to his position, keeping his eyes on the entrance to the restroom. For the next ten minutes, several men went in and out. Businessmen, tourists, pilots, fathers and children, but no Nikolai.

Caldwell glanced at his watch. Nikolai had been in the bathroom for over fifteen minutes. He observed one of his men across the terminal. The man acknowledged Caldwell by shrugging his shoulders. Caldwell nodded his head in the direction of the bathroom, and the man stood up from his chair and walked across the marble floor to the bathroom. Still scanning the crowd, Caldwell began to worry his prey might have slipped his grasp.

Twenty seconds later, his suspicions proved correct. Nikolai was gone.

PALOVICH AWOKE SHIVERING, his clothes wet and tattered. He hadn't eaten anything for a day and a half. Glancing at his surroundings, the morning light revealed what he could not see the night before. The men who gathered around the blazing fire in the deserted lot looked like he did. Thirty to sixty years of age, tattered clothes, the look of despair . . . men without hope trying to keep warm.

He had been on the run for over two days now. Who were the two killers who approached his apartment? Could Viktor have sent them? Surely not. He had driven for Viktor for years. It had to be that little bastard, Nikolai. He always did Viktor's dirty work. Palovich found it difficult to believe Viktor would have sent them. Viktor would never believe Palovich was a traitor. They had been friends too long. Surely, when Viktor found out what had happened, he would call it off. If he found out.

His thoughts turning to food, Palovich rose to his feet, stretching away the morning stiffness confining his muscles. He must find food. Brushing at the dampness of his soiled clothes, he realized the melted snow had soaked his jacket and pants. Feeling the lump of cash on the inside of his pocket, he felt secure, confident he could buy food and new clothes.

The marketplace! Head for the marketplace! The vendors there specialized in items that could not be found in the stores. Expensive items best paid for with foreign currency. American currency.

Palovich stood by the fire until he had warmed himself sufficiently. One by one, the ragged figures left the fire and moved on to their daily routines of begging, drinking, and stealing. Now, he, too, left the comfort of the warm fire and began his trek through the streets of Moscow toward the marketplace.

The rumble in his stomach grew louder with each step, the sound echoing in his ears. Food was a must at this point. He was far too old to be evading killers through the chilly streets on an empty stomach. He felt safer now. The would-be assassins should be searching for him somewhere else. His sister's house perhaps, or the homes of friends. All of these places he would avoid. It was a deadly game, but he would learn quickly. He had to, or he would die.

As he reached the marketplace, the smell of fresh-baked bread wafted toward him, causing his stomach to growl voraciously. He didn't dash for the vendor, however. He would be cautious. In order to survive, he must act smart and not draw attention to himself. He stopped thirty meters from the entrance and stood in the shadow of an apartment-house entranceway. Pulling his collar around his neck, Palovich ran his fingers through his hair, brushing off bits of ice stuck to his clothes. Now was not the time to have the appearance of a beggar. Reaching in his pocket, he pulled out several bills. He had many hundred-dollar bills, but showing this large amount of money in the marketplace would bring suspicion. Palovich separated several of the bills he had in his hand and stuffed them in his coat. The rest of the bills he placed in his pants pocket.

He was as ready to go as he would ever be. Palovich left the temporary sanctuary he had found, moving toward the entrance of the marketplace. The activity in the marketplace was incredible. The market was where the real money was made in Moscow. Hundreds of street vendors selling everything from food to passports to sex. If it could be bought or sold, you could find it here. The marketplace covered three full city blocks, with thousands of souls wandering about, attempting to find what they wanted or needed. Vehicle traffic was no longer an option through the area unless you were a vendor.

Ten American dollars got him a quarter of a loaf of bread and a sizable wedge of cheese. Palovich devoured it as he walked through the crowd. Finding a man who sold hot tea, he purchased a cup and sat on a stool. The warm liquid rushed down his throat, slowly bringing his body back to life. His joints still ached; his back sore from sleeping on the ground. After a second glass of tea, he decided he should find new clothes. The assassins, and perhaps the rest of the Russian army, would be after him now, and they would be searching for a man in a tattered gray coat.

Within five minutes, Palovich found a suitable vendor. Waiting until no other customers were around, he approached the man. The vendor, a slender man with a long, thin nose, was neatly dressed for the cold weather, Palovich thought. He stood in front of a tent next to a table holding various items of clothing. The items on the table were cheap, but they were there simply for advertising. Palovich realized the real items would be in the tent.

"Ehsty leey oo vahss shtoneeboody eez shehrsty?"

The thin man beamed with enthusiasm.

"Do I have any wool? But of course, my friend. I have wool coats, socks, pants, gloves, hats. Whatever one might need, I can get. The question then becomes can you afford it?"

The statement fell off his tongue as he scanned Palovich's ragged figure standing before him. In a normal shop, a seller of fine clothes might readily toss out such a disheveled creature, but this vendor saw something in his eyes. This man was intelligent and was once a man of means. He might still be.

"Fine, I'll take one of each. The coat, hat, socks, gloves, but not the pants. All in black. And a scarf. I'll need a scarf."

"Just one moment," the vendor said as he eyed Palovich, taking mental measurements. He turned and disappeared into the tent. Palovich took the opportunity to shift the money from his coat pocket to his pants pocket. In a matter of two minutes, the vendor returned with the items Palovich requested. Removing the old gray coat, Palovich tried on the items.

"A perfect fit for you, my friend," the vendor said.

"Yes, you've done quite well."

"So you wish to purchase the items?"

"Yes."

The vendor rested his chin in the crook of his hand as he rubbed his long, thin nose with his finger. He knew this was the difficult part of the deal. Would the man meet his price? If he did, how would he pay for it?

"How do you intend to pay for this?" the vendor said.

Palovich reached into his pocket, pulled out three American one hundred-dollar bills and handed them to the vendor. That easily covered the going rate for the clothes.

The vendor's eyes widened as his mouth fell open. He took the money and held each bill up to the morning sun, checking to make sure they were not counterfeit. The deal made, Palovich walked into the crowd with his new clothes, leaving the old gray coat with the vendor, who would sell it eventually.

Palovich stopped in front of another vendor, purchased a new pair of pants, a sweater, and a small backpack. At still another vendor's shop, he purchased more bread, cheese, and sausage. He ate a couple of bites and placed the rest in his backpack. After finding a washroom with warm water, he washed himself quickly and changed his clothes. He emerged back into the marketplace a new man. Finally feeling warm, well fed, and semi-clean, he was ready to move. Palovich had to formulate a plan, but he needed one more purchase before he left the marketplace. He needed to find a gun.

CHAPTER 31

September 8, 1995

ARON CALDWELL WAS FURIOUS. How could his men have blown such an easy tail? They remained in the airport for two more hours, randomly searching for the slippery Nikolai. Where is he? Where is he going? Who is he planning to see?

Nikolai had been known to be elusive, a hard man to follow, and Caldwell had been made a believer today. Nikolai, virtually surrounded by Caldwell's men, had slipped away, his adversaries had no way of knowing if he was still in the terminal or in the air already.

Caldwell thought Nikolai's final destination lay somewhere in the United States, regardless of where he went prior to that. All of the message traffic at the embassy indicated increased activity in Section Nine's moles stationed in America. There had also been concern about the number of kills or the priority of the targets. He wasn't sure; the messages weren't clear. Caldwell was convinced, however, that something serious was going down and Nikolai went to make sure it didn't get screwed up.

A loud bell snapped him out of his thoughts as a small cart came through carrying luggage from one of the flights. The sharp ringing bell echoed throughout the terminal. Caldwell stepped out of the way of the small vehicle driven by an elderly uniformed man. As the cart moved by, he couldn't help but stare at the old man. Was he familiar? No, but something about him was. Caldwell thought back to the tail hours earlier as he continued to stare at the old man.

The cart was past him now, moving slowly through the crowd in the terminal as Caldwell turned to follow it. Not the old man, but something about him? Something about him . . . not about him, but about his uniform. Not his uniform, but a uniform. An airline pilot's uniform! The image was clear to him now. Nikolai had entered the bathroom and disappeared.

During those fifteen minutes, several Aeroflot Airline pilots had entered and left, as well. That's where they had made the switch! Wearing the uniform of an airline pilot and perhaps some type of wig or facial disguise, he slipped past Caldwell and his men.

Hank Fielding approached Caldwell, his dark hat cocked to one side, his long overcoat opened in front. He looked more like a cop out of a 1930's gangster movie than a CIA agent.

"Take off the hat, Hank," Caldwell said, "There's nothing like being in Moscow and your clothes saying 'Look at me, I'm a spy.'"

"Sorry sir," Hank said as he removed the hat. "We've searched all over and come up empty. We've checked everything . . . twice. I don't know where to look anymore."

"Where were you positioned during the tail?" Caldwell asked as he walked toward the front entrance of the terminal. Hank turned to follow and walked alongside him, scanning the crowd, checking their faces, their movements.

"I shadowed him from the time he entered the terminal until he went into the bathroom. At that point, he was passed off, and I watched from a distance."

"Were there any back doors to that bathroom? Any way he could have gotten out other than that one entrance? An air-conditioning duct, anything?"

Hank shook his head. "No way, sir. Tom checked the inside of the place thoroughly. It's sealed tighter than a tin can."

"So he just walked right past us, just like that?" Caldwell said, snapping his fingers as they walked outside the terminal. The cold Moscow air reddened his cheeks as they walked toward the parking lot. Caldwell reached into his pocket, turning off his comm-radio.

"Not just like that. We were too alert. We knew what we were looking for."

"That's the problem—we knew what we were looking for."

Hank nodded. He understood where the senior agent was leading him.

"And since we knew what we were looking for, we overlooked the obvious. He pulled a switch on us. He had to. What are you thinking, sir?"

Caldwell walked over to the dark sedan they had driven to the terminal. As they approached, the driver jumped out, tipped his hat, and walked to the back of the car.

"What did you notice going in and out of the bathroom during the time Nikolai was supposed to be in there?"

"A bunch of passengers and several pilots."

"And you checked out the passengers thoroughly?"

"Yes, very thoroughly. He wasn't one of them."

Caldwell stood back as the driver opened the trunk of the dark sedan and pulled out two suitcases and one diplomatic pouch.

"What about the pilots?" Caldwell said, glancing at his younger companion. Hank had little experience, but he was good. No one had expected Nikolai to pull a switch on them. How would he know he was being tailed? Caldwell knew that all good spies, especially the old-timers like Nikolai, always assumed the worst.

Hank's face showed everything.

"That son of a bitch! He went in the bathroom, changed into an Aeroflot uniform, and strolled out."

"Yes," Caldwell said, "it's the only answer." He pulled the comm-radio out of his pocket, removed the miniature earpiece and tie-tack microphone, and placed them in the diplomatic pouch.

"So what are we going to do now?" Hank asked.

Caldwell placed his pistol, capped with silencer, in the diplomatic pouch. Closing the clasp and locking it, he placed the open handcuff around his left wrist.

"You and the rest of the men go back to the embassy. Stand by for contact from Palovich. Spread some men out within a few blocks of the embassy. Maybe he's trying to contact us. We know they're after him. They tried a hit and nailed his wife instead. All the traffic we've intercepted indicates he's still on the run. If we can find Palovich, maybe we can find out where Nikolai is going. Maybe even who he is contacting."

"Where are you going?"

Caldwell picked up his bags and grinned at Hank.

"To America, of course."

PALOVICH SEARCHED FOR THIRTY minutes and grew frustrated, unable to find anyone selling guns. He knew caution was paramount. He couldn't ask just anyone where he could buy a gun. Did he even need a gun? He hadn't used one since his time in Afghanistan all those years ago. The time he spent here searching for a gun could be used to escape. Was the tradeoff worthwhile? He decided yes, if for no other reason than it gave him a sense of security.

Time grew short. Palovich quickened his pace as his search became more frantic. The numerous vendors around him offered everything imaginable, but nothing he was searching for. He needed a contact; someone who could point him in the right direction. Someone who knew the dark streets. Someone who lived on the other side of the law. Someone like . . .

. . .like the man standing in front of him. Not even thirty yards away, positioned like a watchman in front of his tent. He was of medium build— not thin, not fat. He stood in front of his table with a wide selection of knives and cutlery. This type of product was surely a cover for a more aggressive clientele. Slowly, Palovich approached the vendor. He studied him carefully. The eyes said it all. They were crafty, always searching, but hollow, showing no soul. Then the eyes fell upon him. The vendor smiled as Palovich approached.

"You wish to purchase knives, do you not, my friend?"

"I wish to make a purchase, but I do not desire knives."

The crafty vendor understood, nodding his head as he walked back toward his table.

"*Zhehnshchyeenah*," he said into the opening of the tent. Come out here. A heavy-set woman of an indeterminate age came out from the back to stand in front of the table. "Follow me," he said to Palovich.

The two disappeared into the tent, where the vendor turned on a radio at a high volume. He obviously was used to being monitored by someone, probably the government or his competitors in the Russian mafia.

They sat at a small table lit by a kerosene lamp. Isolated shafts of sunlight pierced the heavy canvas tent. The vendor reached to the floor and pulled up a half-empty bottle of vodka and two glasses. After pouring, he spoke.

"So you do not wish to purchase knives today. What is it you seek?" He handed Palovich the vodka; Palovich raised the glass to his lips and took a long sip.

"I need a gun," he said. "I need a gun now. No fuss, no names. I'll pay cash."

"Rubles, francs, marks, how?"

"Dollars. American dollars."

The vendor's eyes lit up. American dollars were always good. He liked to deal in that. He downed the vodka in his glass and poured himself more.

"Just what type of gun did you have in mind?"

"Nothing too large. A pistol of some sort. Strictly for self-defense, I assure you."

The vendor waved a finger at his nervous client.

"Do not worry, my friend. You wish to purchase a gun. What you do with it is your own business. I believe I can help you."

He walked to the far side of the tent and returned with a suitcase. Placing the luggage on the table, he opened it up so Palovich couldn't see the contents.

"Revolver or automatic?"

"Preferably an automatic," Palovich said.

The crafty vendor reached into his case and came out with a German Luger in excellent shape. Palovich took it from him and studied the weapon carefully. He ejected the magazine, checked the slides, lined up the sights, tested the trigger and hammer, and re-inserted the magazine.

"This will do. How much?"

For the first time, the vendor seemed unsure of himself. He was slightly agitated.

"S-Seven hundred American dollars," he said.

Palovich could tell that was his high price, and the vender usually was talked down. That explained the nervousness. He had no time to bargain, however. He reached in his pocket and pulled out seven one hundred-dollar bills.

"I expect two extra magazines and a box of bullets to go with it," he said, as he placed the money on the table.

The crafty vendor was overjoyed. "Yes! Yes!" he exclaimed as he jumped up from the table and darted across the room. The vendor returned with the requested items. Palovich placed them all in his pocket as he rose from the table. He stopped at the entrance and glanced back at the vendor who eagerly counted his money.

"And, my friend," Palovich said, "if anyone should inquire, I've never been here."

"But of course, as I am sure I will never see you again."

Palovich eased out of the tent and out of the marketplace, back into the chilly streets of Moscow. He must make it to the train station, then to Kiev. He could lie low for a few weeks with friends, and eventually make his way over the border into Germany. He hoped to reach the American consulate there. It was now just a matter of making it to the train station. He pulled out his wallet to make sure he had enough rubles to purchase a ticket. He did. Palovich realized an attempt to pay for a train ticket in American currency would raise suspicions.

Stepping in a dark, empty alley, Palovich pulled the pistol out of his pocket. He ejected the empty magazine and quickly filled it with bullets.

Popping the magazine back into the pistol grip, he chambered a round and stuck the loaded weapon back into his pocket. Then he loaded the two spare magazines and placed them in his left coat pocket. Cautiously, he exited the alley, leaving the chaos of the marketplace behind him.

He wasn't a hundred meters out of the marketplace when he first saw them. It wasn't that he recognized any specific individual; he recognized the style. The way these "killers for the cause" carried themselves. It was an image, and these men fit it exactly. His eyes darted from face to face, verifying each potential enemy.

The first one, he noticed, stood next to a light post on the sidewalk. Cigarette smoke curled up around his face as his eyes danced back and forth, observing every passerby, the open newspaper merely a prop held in his hands.

It was too late for Palovich to turn around. That would draw suspicion to him. He continued forward, gazing at the ground, much like the rest of the people entering and exiting the marketplace. The second one he saw sat in a dark brown sedan parked at the four-way intersection up ahead. Then he saw, as he glanced across the street, another on foot. Palovich slowed his pace. He was about to be cornered. His mind racing, he needed a way out. There was no escape on his side of the street. He could either go straight ahead, past the two men in the car, return to the marketplace past the first sentinel, or enter the small alley across the street. The choice for Palovich was obvious. To go to the market, he would pass not twenty feet in front of the second sentinel. Palovich was certain they had orders to kill him.

Pulling his collar up around his neck and pushing his hat lower on his forehead, Palovich began walking to the other side of the street, directly toward the alleyway. As he moved closer, he noticed the sentinel brought Palovich into his crosscheck more and more the closer he got. The man was studying him. Approaching the entrance to the alleyway, Palovich felt relief. He could see the alley led to another street as opposed to a blank wall. A loud noise caught Palovich's attention, and he jerked his head toward the sedan. Its tires skidded in the slush as it started moving. He looked directly at the sentinel who also looked at the sedan, then back to Palovich. For one split second, their eyes locked before Palovich refocused on the ground in front of him and disappeared into the alley. He knew. The sentinel knew.

Palovich pulled the gun out of his pocket as he continued to walk at the same pace, his hands folded in front of him, tightly grasping the weapon. The garbage and slush of the alley crunched under his feet. Another twenty meters and he would be out of the alleyway.

"Palovich Merlov," a voice cried behind him. The sentinel. Palovich continued walking at the same pace, pretending not to recognize the name.

BAM! BAM! Two shots rang out, telling Palovich he needed to stop. Just another ten meters.

"Palovich Merlov, you should listen when you are spoken to."

Frozen in his tracks, Palovich could hear the sentinel walking toward him. Slowly, he turned toward him.

"Young man, I'm sorry, I have no money on me," he said as he turned. The sentinel, somewhat confused by the strange response, lowered his gun for a brief second. Palovich didn't wait for another opportunity. He whipped his weapon into view and fired three shots into the sentinel's chest. The man's eyes went wide with shock as the reports echoed through the alleyway, the bullets ripping through the sentinels' fabric and flesh. As the man fell to the ground, Palovich saw the dark brown sedan screech to a halt at the entrance to the alley. He turned and ran as one of the men leaped out of the car while the other spoke commands over a radio.

Two shots rang out as Palovich reached the end of the alley. He felt a stinging sensation in his left arm, looked down, and noticed a hole in his overcoat. He rounded the corner to his right, and then hugged the wall. Palovich counted to three silently, then dropped to a crouch and pointed his weapon back into the alley. With his new pursuer directly in his sights, Palovich quickly squeezed off two rounds, dropping him to the slushy pavement. Wasting no time, Palovich turned and bolted down the street, taking the next left, and then his next right. He ran for five minutes, changing directions, left, right, every chance he had, as he continued to get farther and farther away from the scene of the gunfight.

He slowed now, breathing heavily, his face pale with fear, his left arm almost numb. A small amount of blood trickled down his arm, highlighted on the snow-covered ground. The blood wasn't too obvious on his black overcoat and wouldn't immediately draw attention to himself. One thing was for certain, though—if he was unable to escape, he at least needed to warn the Americans.

CHAPTER 32

September 8, 1995

I T HAD BEEN A LONG TWO DAYS. Vince hung his parachute on his chute rack in the life-support building and walked to the mirror to comb his hair. His back hurt slightly from wearing the backpack-style parachute; his shoulder still sore from his being jumped in the parking lot last Saturday. The life-support shack sat empty due to the grounding of the T-37s after Lenny's crash.

Vince felt tired. The last two days had drudged on like a lifetime. It took the maintenance crew more than five hours to swap out the engine on the T-37 at Tinker. Halfway through the engine change, they realized they were missing a tool. When they finished, bad weather rolled in and brought the field to minimums. The IP didn't feel good about taking this jet off into the soup right after it had been fixed. They sat for another hour and a half until the weather cleared. At least the flight back was quick. Vince sat on his hands the entire way and responded to checklist items. Not a bad situation considering he didn't get any sleep.

Vince finished combing his hair and walked toward the squadron. Someone had painted the solo tank overnight with a tribute to Lenny. Lenny. Vince had hardly thought of him since earlier that morning. Lenny was a putz anyway. Only a fool would kill himself in an airplane. Vince entered the squadron, walking past the TOC desk toward his flight room. As he entered the sparsely populated room, one of the schedulers greeted him.

"Welcome back, Lieutenant Andrews, I hope you had a nice vacation."

Vince nodded his head with a grin.

"I talked to the flight commander. He said you're cleared to press on home for crew rest. You can make up the stan test tomorrow."

"Thanks, that's all I needed to hear," Vince said as he turned toward the exit. Stan test? Lenny's tests. The money. Vince quickened his pace to a jog, bumping into a lieutenant colonel on the way out the door. Suddenly Lenny's death created a whole new set of problems.

"Hey! Slow it down, Lieutenant!" barked the older officer. But as soon as Vince reached outside, he opened up to a full sprint, straight for the dormitories. Dozens of images flashed through his mind. He felt that Lenny had lied about getting one test at a time. Could Lenny have gotten all of the tests? If so, where did he place them? Could anybody find them? Could *he* find them? If he didn't, how the hell would he make it through the program?

By the time he reached the dorm, his lungs burned from the ice-cold air pulled in with each breath. When he reached Lenny's room, the door stood open. He approached cautiously. As he reached the opening, he peered inside.

"Jason! What the hell are you doing here?" he said as he walked through the doorway. Vince breathed heavily, the sweat pushing its way through the green Nomex flight suit despite the cold air. The room was barren, except for the government-issued furniture and the boxes stacked at various spots on the floor.

Jason looked up from the box he just finished packing.

"Vince, holy cow! When did you get back? Did you hear what happened to Lenny?"

"Yeah, I heard yesterday when I was in the city. It was all over TV and the SOF called my instructor. We almost didn't fly the plane back since they grounded them all. It was only a thirty-minute flight and the instructor was a stan/eval guy, so they let us come home. Do you know any details?"

"No more than you probably do. He was on a solo ride and crashed in the MOA."

"Did he try to eject?"

"Apparently not. Rumor has it, he was still in the aircraft. The safety guys are still up there with the FAA investigators. I guess they're flying in other safety guys from the NTSB to investigate. I'm sure they'll try to use this to get the T-6 Texan II operational as soon as possible."

Vince nodded his head in agreement. He didn't concern himself with small talk. He wanted his tests. His tests. He had paid for them, now he wanted them.

"What's with all the boxes?" he said.

"Gus asked me to box up all of Lenny's things on account of his being too busy and you being stuck at Tinker. Thanks a lot."

"So you boxed up all of this since last night?"

"Yeah, I guess Lenny's parents are coming tomorrow morning in time for the afternoon service at the chapel."

"Service?" Vince mumbled, his mind elsewhere.

"Yeah, you know, the memorial service. It's scheduled for fifteen hundred tomorrow."

"Thanks, I wasn't aware of that." Vince's mind wandered, lost in thoughts of his own. Jason continued to move boxes around, sealing them. "Hey, you didn't happen to find anything unusual in here, did you?"

Jason paused, standing in the middle of the barren room holding a box, staring at Vince. "What do you mean 'unusual'?"

"Well, you know, anything unusual. Skeletons in the closet. Smut books, women's clothing, whatever." *Stolen tests, excessive amounts of cash; things a UPT student shouldn't have.*

Jason looked at him for several seconds, as if he were studying him, searching for something.

"No. I didn't find anything unusual. Why, are those types of things you have lying around your place?"

Vince glared at him. "Up yours, Conrad." Vince walked out of the room angry. *He knows. That son of a bitch Conrad knows.* It's just a matter of time before he finishes boxing everything. When he's done, Vince would begin his search. But he knows . . .

Vince returned to his room, angry about his situation. This was not good. With Jason in the way, he couldn't reach the tests and money—if the money was still there. Lenny the loser probably lost it all gambling anyway. But he had to find the tests. He needed the tests. He'd come too far, become too dependent on having that information provided for him; now certainly was not the time to start on his own.

The shrill ringing of the telephone broke the silence in the room. Vince, initially startled, calmed himself quickly. Leaning over the couch, he snatched up the receiver before the second ring.

"Hello."

"Vincent Andrews?" a voice said. The tone serious, yet the voice unfamiliar.

"Yes."

"Have you had the chance to touch the face of God yet?" the man said.

Vince's heart raced. He began to turn pale. It wasn't fear. It was more shock.

"Who? What?" Vince squeezed out.

"You are a hard person to reach, Oleg Stolivich. You are never home."

"Who are you?" Vince stammered at the unknown voice. "What do you want?"

"It's time, Oleg. It's time to go to work."

"No, I can't. It's too soon. I have too much to accomplish right now. I- I'm not ready," he stammered.

"You are ready."

"How did you find me?"

"Don't be a fool. Do you really think there is a time when you do something we don't know about? I am disappointed in you, Oleg. I believe you have become too comfortable in your current surroundings."

Vince began to physically shake. He knew what was taking place.

"He's coming to see you, Oleg."

"Who? Who's coming to see me?"

"He who hunts. He arrives Monday at the airport. I suggest you make arrangements to meet him."

"Wait, which airport? Why is he coming? It's too soon. I'm supposed to have more time."

"You have as much time as we say you do," the man on the other end said. "Will Rogers World Airport at 5 p.m. Arriving from JFK. Don't be late, Oleg."

"Wait! I won't be able to get away for that long. Have him get a rental car and meet me in Enid at the Ramada Inn." He paused for a moment, then said, "The room will be under the name Jason Conrad."

"I'll pass the message."

Will Rogers World Airport. 5 p.m. Sweat poured down Vince's forehead, his mind racing. He who hunts . . . Nikolai was coming.

JASON FINISHED THE LAST BOX and put together a list for Lenny's parents. He hated this kind of work, but it meant a lot to the Banks family. Too much had happened in the past few days, and it was starting to take its toll on Jason. Things insidiously crept up on him until they were like another wall he had to climb before he could move on to something else.

Pilot training was his priority and should be all he worried about, but that was not the case. Now, one of his friends was dead. Jason realized his friend had been a cheat and a thief who ripped off another cheat; a cheat who was very angry. Vince could be a problem, Jason decided. A problem that needed watching.

VINCE ANDREWS. OLEG STOLOVICH. The name he had not used in years was now coming back to haunt him. Oleg Stolovich had grown up the son of a fighter pilot. His father spent many years in Hanoi during the declining years of the Vietnam War instructing the North Vietnamese in the intricacies of air-to-air combat.

At the age of two, his family moved to Moscow. His father had returned from Vietnam the year after the Americans evacuated Saigon. In Moscow, his father relished having such an adventurous and eager son. Oleg learned to fire the rifle and pistol, and by the age of thirteen became an expert marksman. Oleg never had much interest in school, but he excelled in sports, particularly wrestling. He loved to fight, on and off the mat. He started to learn karate and judo, as well. His academic skills were far from up to speed, but Oleg's father did not mind—except for his son's English classes. He always insisted the boy work hard on his English. At the age of sixteen, Oleg's father introduced him to the most influential figure in his life: Viktor Vasilyevich Kryuchkov. Viktor worked for the KGB, his father told him. His father said Viktor was a very important man. No one had to explain that to Oleg. He knew the importance of the members of KGB and had been thrilled to meet one in his own home. Viktor had been made aware of the boy's skills and his hot temper. He was also aware of his ability to master the English language. Viktor made his pitch.

Oleg went to the university and learned the English language. He learned about Americans. More importantly, he learned to be American. If he did well, he would work for the KGB and hold a high status in Soviet society. Oleg had been excited and disappointed at the same time. He wanted to be a fighter pilot like his father, but it was not to be. Oleg began to master the English language and was becoming an American. His instructors were impressed with his progress. They weren't impressed with his temper, however. He had, on several occasions, gotten into fights, and even been threatened with removal from training. His father counseled him on his actions and that straightened him out for a while.

After he graduated with degrees in American Studies and English, Nikolai Gregarin approached him about his future and quickly lined up work for him at the embassy in Washington, D.C. Nikolai was young and well-dressed, and did not represent the typical Soviet official in the KGB. Nikolai told Oleg about a potential job that was dangerous, and Oleg jumped at the opportunity. Nikolai interviewed Oleg for three days, subjecting him to lie- detector tests, asking a wide variety of questions, making notes, then asking similar questions looking for different answers. The selection had been draining, but Oleg passed. Then his indoctrination into the realm of Section Nine began.

It was at this point Oleg became Vince Andrews. Part of his training consisted of learning about this fictional Vince Andrews' past: who he was, where he was from, and why he was here now. The real Vince Andrews had been an orphan, bouncing from foster home to foster home. He had grown into a young, homeless thief who had taken refuge in one of Los Angeles' many homeless shelters. This particular homeless shelter, located two blocks north of Sunset Boulevard in downtown Hollywood, served as a Section Nine front. It was a well-run shelter, one of the better ones in the city. It was also one of the locations where Section Nine stole lost souls and turned them into real people—real people who were trained killers waiting for the call. Real people like Oleg Stolovich.

Provided with the basic paperwork—birth certificate, Social Security card, driver's license, and high-school diploma—Vince enrolled in a community college in Pennsylvania for two years. He then moved to Iowa and enrolled in Iowa State. He joined the Air Force ROTC program on a whim, to see if he could do it. His handlers at Section Nine were furious, but when his security clearance went through unscathed, they eased off the pressure. They began to appreciate the position he earned and encouraged him to earn a pilot's slot. Vince was in heaven! He would never have the opportunity in the Soviet Union to attend pilot training; therefore, he would learn from the Americans. He believed he was the only member from Section Nine to be placed in the US military. The rest were civilians and government employees. Not that it made much difference. He was a mole, an assassin to be called upon at the right moment. He might be given one kill, he might be given several—it all depended on what his handlers dictated.

While in Iowa State's ROTC program, Vince began his strange but necessary relationship with Lenny Banks. It started innocently enough. Lenny borrowed money from Vince and lost it gambling on the school baseball team. Unable to pay Vince back, Lenny offered to steal tests out of the school's mainframe for his final exams. Thus, a partnership was born, extending over the years until a few days ago. Now, Vince had to find his tests or he could potentially flunk out of pilot training. But Nikolai was coming.

CHAPTER 33

September 8, 1995

H E SIGHED AND PLACED HIS HANDS on his hips as he glanced at the young Captain.

"How many more are we going to do today?" Captain Harrison asked with a genuine curiosity. Alonzo could tell Harrison grew tired of the room-to-room search. They had covered twelve rooms and the process took far too long.

"Two more, I guess. This is taking a little longer than I anticipated," Alonzo Jacobs said. The memorial service took place this afternoon. All of the students would be done for the day, many returning to their rooms.

The two men closed all of the drawers they had been searching in and made sure they left the room as they had found it. This was getting painful. *Maybe it isn't such a good idea after all. Maybe I'm too old for this investigating stuff.* They left the room and walked downstairs to the next victim.

"107. Let's see," Harrison said, "Conrad, Jason. Second Lieutenant. He's a pretty good guy. I flew with him once."

Alonzo unbuttoned the top button of his shirt and loosened his tie. "Good. This one should go quickly. We'll knock off one more, then I'll buy you a beer."

"That sounds good to me," Harrison said, grinning at the prospects of soon acquiring a cold beer.

As they entered the room, the light from the open window lit the room effectively. Out of habit, Harrison turned on the lights anyway. Alonzo entered the room behind him and left the door open, a standard procedure. The pair wasted no time and went right to work. Harrison checked the bed stands and bookcases; Alonzo checked the desk.

"No computer," the flat-topped captain said.

"I see that. This kid's a little neater than most," Alonzo said.

Harrison fished through the bookcase. "He's not really a kid. He's about twenty-six or twenty-seven."

Alonzo flipped through the items on the desk. "I see. I always wanted to be a pilot. Wanted to fly helicopters. Must've been all those damn rides on the choppers in 'Nam. My wife kept telling me I never did have any sense."

He began opening the drawers of the desk, one by one. For the most part, he found nothing unusual—standard pilot stuff. When he reached the bottom drawer, his eyes latched on to a large manila envelope. Pulling out the contents, his heart skipped a beat. Alonzo skimmed quickly through the stack of papers.

"Must be our lucky day." Alonzo flashed the tests and cash at the instructor. Harrison's mouth fell open at the sight of the cash. Grabbing the tests, Harrison flipped through them feverishly.

"What the hell? This guy has everything! I'm going to get his ass thrown out of this program. Out of the damn Air Force!"

Harrison was furious. He couldn't stand the thought of anyone cheating. Alonzo tried to calm him. "Well, Captain Harrison, I appreciate your integrity and dedication. I'm sure the Air Force appreciates it, as well, but I'll handle the situation from here on out. I think it's time young Lieutenant Conrad and I have a little chat."

THE SKY GREW DARKER in the afternoon as the wind picked up, causing a brisk nip in the air. Figures moved toward the small white chapel that sat behind the Wing Headquarters, cutting through wind-kicked fallen leaves that crossed their paths on the sidewalks. Inside, the pews filled up quickly with the classmates, friends, and family of Lieutenant Lenny Banks. The base shut down for such an event, and personnel who didn't know Lenny Banks turned out to pay their respects for the fallen aviator. Most of the students and younger instructors wore their flight suits, but the older personnel wore their blue Class-A uniforms. Many of the wives showed up already teary-eyed, not sure why this happened, and praying to God it never happened to their husbands. The third and fourth rows were reserved for the members of Lenny's flight. They all sat in their olive green flight suits, their heads bowed out of respect. In the front of the chapel, the base chaplain sat behind the podium with the squadron commander and the flight commander. All three wore their blue Class-A uniforms and watched the small chapel fill at a rapid pace.

Vince Andrews sat in the fourth row closest to the wall. He had been asked by both the flight commander and the squadron commander to speak at the memorial service representing Lenny's classmates. Vince denied both requests. Speaking at the service was the last thing he cared to do. Lenny wasn't a friend—he was a tool, a source. And now that source was gone.

Vince scanned the chapel as his mind raced. He had to get into Lenny's room and find those tests. Could Conrad have found them? He's not very bright; if he found them, he might not have known it. He was the type who would have run to the flight commander after such a discovery, and nobody has mentioned such a thing happening.

The Color Guard marched solemnly along the aisle and posted the flags in the front of the chapel. The chaplain then began the service. The memorial service moved along at a moderate pace. All of the wives shed tears, and their sniffles were constant. Captain Johnson, the flight commander, spoke after the chaplain finished his service.

"Lenny Banks, Lieutenant, United States Air Force," he began. "Lenny was an officer, a classmate, a son. He exemplified a hardworking, honest young man taken from us at too early an age.

"No matter our relationship with Lenny, he was our teammate. All of us today, has lost a member of our team. And each of us, must do our part to fill the void left by Lenny's absence . . ."

Vince's mind drifted off as he spoke of Lenny's youth and involvement in the Air Force. *Bullshit. Lenny was a lying, stealing, little weasel who would have ended up getting himself killed either in an airplane or a bar sooner or later.*

The squadron commander, Lieutenant Colonel Skip Baker, spoke next. He talked in broader terms, about God, sacrifice, and how only the good die young. His eulogy didn't really say much about Lenny, but rather talked around him. Obviously he didn't know Lenny, but he was doing his part as the squadron commander; his words were soothing and true. The chaplain closed out the service after forty-five minutes. Just prior to the chaplain's saying "Amen," the four ship of T-37's flew over the chapel at five hundred feet. The number three aircraft peeled out of the formation into a vertical climb toward the heavens. Though unable to see the formation, those in the chapel knew the flyover took place outside. Some thought it was beautiful, and some wondered why they were inside and couldn't see it. Vince Andrews thought it was a waste of four sorties as he glared at the back of Jason Conrad's head. *The little bastard must have those tests. After tonight, I'll know for sure.*

CHAPTER 34

September 8, 1995

THE AFTER THUNDERSTORMS filled the sky. Another cold front pushed its way across the plains through Enid. The orange-red sun slipping below the horizon created a kaleidoscope of colors in the afternoon sky. A flat, gray cloud deck sat several thousand feet above the ground. A small puffy cloud could build into a towering anvil in less than an hour, only to imbed itself within the thick layers of stratus clouds. It was predictable. It happened every day. Nature had its way in the Midwest.

Kathy and Jason watched the sunset, the cool breeze blowing in their faces. Jason leaned against the rail post, still dressed in his flight suit and green nylon flight jacket. Kathy sat perched on the wooden fence, her barn jacket pulled up around her neck, not noticing the dust and grass clinging to her jeans and boots. She had been tending to the horses when Jason arrived. Although glad to see him, she wasn't ready for a big confrontation at the moment. Fortunately for her, neither was he.

"I hope you don't mind my coming over unannounced," he said. "There are a lot of things going on at the base. I needed to get away from all of that for a while."

Kathy studied him closely. It had been the first time they had been alone since last Friday after the O'Club. Something bothered him a great deal. She knew he was having problems in the aircraft program, but after Lenny died and her visit with Vince . . . Vince. What would she do about him?

"Did you take your make-up ride yet?" she said in an attempt to redirect her thoughts.

Jason nodded his head slowly, still staring at the sun setting behind the clouds on the horizon.

"Yeah, I had it two days ago. It went fine. I did good."

"I'm glad. I knew you were worried. I knew you were going to do fine, though. You always do." An uneasy silence lingered for a moment before she spoke again. "Did they ever find out what happened to Lenny's plane?"

"There are rumblings about the safety report, but the official word right now isn't out. The word on the street is the cable that controls the elevator movement, the little horizontal wing on the tail, snapped somewhere."

"What does that mean?" she said.

"It means when he moved the stick to make the airplane go up or down, nothing happened. Lenny didn't have any control over it. It also means if he went into a spin, which they are sure he did, he would not have been able to recover the aircraft."

"Why didn't he eject?"

Jason choked up. He remembered his busted check ride, and Lenny's reaction to the cause. "Lenny couldn't have ejected, although I'm sure he tried." Jason hesitated for a moment. "Lenny didn't remove his safety pin from the seat. When he went to raise the ejection handle to squeeze the triggers, the handles wouldn't raise."

"That's horrible," she said. She continued to study him, wondering what he was thinking. "Jason, are you okay? I mean, are you upset with me or something?"

For the first time, he looked at her. Jason's eyes locked onto hers before glancing at the ground. "You mean am I upset about Vince? Yes, I guess I am. It took a lot for me to become interested in dating again. It's hard for me to trust someone."

"We never had any set rules in this relationship. We never talked about dating each other exclusively."

"Yes, I realize that. That's why I can't be mad at you. I can be upset—call it jealousy or whatever—but I don't have to like the situation." His voice sounded sterner and his tempo picked up.

"Well, you don't have to live with the situation either," she said, not trying to be derogatory, but that was how it came out.

He took a deep breath as he returned his focus to the horizon. "Look, Kathy, I didn't come here to argue with you. And I didn't come here to discuss our potential future, or lack thereof."

Kathy's brow furrowed as she placed her hands on her hips. "Just what did you come here for, Jason Conrad?"

He paused, glancing at her before returning his gaze to the horizon.

"I needed a friend . . . someone to talk to. I don't want any banter back and forth about relationships. I just want someone to listen to me. I need someone to listen to me. There are a lot of issues I've got to sort out.

Someone at the base may be in trouble, and I can't figure out what to do."

Kathy felt a warm flush through her body. *This is a good man who will be going places in the Air Force.* She knew she would have to come to a decision soon. Hopping off the fence post, she stood next to him and placed her arms around his waist. He placed his arm around her as she buried her head in his shoulder. The decision would be hard. Perhaps she would have plenty of time to think about it when she went to San Antonio next week. She planned to stay there for a couple of weeks. How could she break that news to him?

JASON DROVE BACK TO THE BASE after dark. Passing the little red schoolhouse, he heard a loud roar and looked to his left in time to see the red and green lights of a T-38 go zooming to the south. Night flying again. It made it hard to study. He didn't like thinking about an airplane he might never get to fly, but it was better than thinking about Lenny and the stolen tests he found.

The parking lot of his dorm was empty. He turned off the engine of his Mustang and walked to his room. It didn't take long to notice the streak of light spilling across the cement porch, telling him his door was open.

Jason's body tensed. Who broke into his room? Had he left the door open? Slowly he approached the doorway, his fists clenched into tight balls, ready for action. Sticking his head through the opening, he noticed the lights were on and a large black man in a suit sat on his couch. Reading.

"Who the hell are you?" Jason said as he entered. "What the hell are you doing here?"

The large black man looked up from his magazine. "Oh, you caught me by surprise. Are you Jason Conrad?"

Jason grew nervous. He cautiously moved to the center of the room, his fists clenched and pulse pounding through his veins. "This is my damn room, I'll ask the questions here." *Well, that was a dumb thing to say.*

"I guess you are Jason Conrad," the black man said, rising from the couch. He was too relaxed, Jason noted. Jason started backpedaling toward the entrance. Could this guy be another one of Big Joe McCain's men who worked over Vince and Lenny? He didn't look like it, but he looked like he carried a gun . . .

"My name is Jacobs," he said, extending his hand. "Alonzo Jacobs—Office of Special Investigations. You may know that as OSI."

Jason stopped backpedaling. *OSI? What do they want? Can they just walk into people's rooms?* Gradually, he made his way over to the extended hand

and shook it. "Do you have any I.D.?" Alonzo handed him his I.D. card and badge. Jason studied both closely. "How did you get in my room?"

"I'll get to that in a moment. Do you have any idea why I'm here?"

Jason shrugged, "I don't know. Security clearance on someone? Aren't you a spy?"

The large black man studied him for a moment, chuckling at the spy comment. "What would you care to tell me about these?" Alonzo asked, pulling the manila envelope out of his briefcase.

Jason's eyes went wide. "Where did you get those?" he said.

"From your desk drawer. How about you have a seat and we discuss this?"

Jason sat on the couch where Alonzo had been earlier. Alonzo stared at the young student pilot.

"I'm gonna read you your rights now, son. You have the right to remain silent. You have the right to an attorney . . ." The OSI agent's voice trailed off into the distance as Jason's head spun in circles. *This guy thinks I stole those. I'm gonna go to jail for trying to save my dead friend some embarrassment. God must be testing me . . .*

"Do you know how much trouble you're in son? Do you want an attorney?" he said.

"No, I didn't do anything."

"You didn't do anything? Son, I've got a handful of stolen tests and several thousand dollars in cash, which is quite a bit for a second lieutenant to have lying around. Would you care to discuss what exactly you didn't do?"

Taking a deep breath, Jason thought to himself. This was not good. What in the hell was going on? Yesterday, he tried to save a dead friend's reputation and now he was being labeled a thief.

"I didn't do it."

"You've said that already. I'd like to hear something else now. I'd like you to explain where this stuff came from and who else is involved."

Jason looked up at him. "Who else is involved?"

"Okay boy, let me fill you in on where we are right now."

"Maybe I should get a lawyer or something."

"A lawyer? Boy, you are in such deep trouble right now, you'd better forget the lawyer and start thinking about a shovel."

Jason said nothing.

"It goes like this," Alonzo said. "Several weeks back, someone accessed the master computer files at Randolph. We discovered what was going on when they dialed the wrong number on the modem, and it locked up another system. That activated a warning system on everything else which shut down that unit's system. Well, whoever hacked this used a program that made the call untraceable. Now, this guy is good, but my guy is better. He designed a program to circumvent the scrambled program and tracked it to Vance. At that point, we set up a room by room search looking for clues." Alonzo held up the tests in front of Jason. "We struck paydirt with you, Jason Conrad."

Jason looked briefly at the tests in Alonzo's hand. "But I don't even own a computer," he explained, hoping for some type of proof of his innocence.

"I know," Alonzo said as he sat in the wooden chair at the desk. "That's why I'm here talking to you now as opposed to your being handcuffed in the wing commander's office explaining this to him and the security police."

"Do they know you found the tests?"

"Oh, they know all right. Believe you me, they went through the roof. They were ready to have you shot on the spot. I calmed them down a bit and convinced them to let me handle it my way.

"Now, I'm aware you don't own a computer, so it's likely you didn't steal the tests. What I want to know is where you got them from and who else has them."

"I-I can't say."

"Lieutenant, don't be stupid," Alonzo said. "The time to start talking is now. The longer we wait, the worse it's gonna get."

Jason sat with his head in his hands. He had never considered himself a snitch. His stomach knotted up as he contemplated his situation. What could he do? He had wanted to protect his dead friend's name, but not at the expense of his own career, his own life. The sweat began to bead on his forehead and his palms became clammy. He might lose everything he had worked for and possibly go to jail. All for a liar, a cheat, and a thief. Lenny had been a friend, but a true friend would not have put him in a situation like this. But Lenny didn't put him in this mess. Jason had done that on his own, to help his dead friend. Now he would pay for that loyalty. *My dad is gonna flip.* Jason's mind raced. *Would Lenny take the fall for me?* The answer was obvious. He didn't know Lenny Banks as well as he thought he did.

"Okay. The person who stole the tests," Jason paused, as he realized doing the right thing was still hard. "The person who stole the tests was Lenny Banks."

"Lenny Banks? Isn't that the boy—"

"Yes," Jason said, "he's the one who died in the plane crash. I'm not sure how he got the tests. I found them in his desk, much like you found them in mine. You see, Gus McTaggart, our SRO, asked me to clean out Lenny's room yesterday. I boxed everything up, and it's ready to go. Lenny's family will pick it up tomorrow afternoon."

Alonzo looked at him intensely, his brown eyes studying Jason's every move, every word. It made Jason nervous as hell. His story dripped out slowly, out of sequence, with too many holes.

"Anyway I found the envelope in his drawer and the cash fell out all over the floor."

"How much cash?"

"About seven or eight thousand dollars."

"Okay. Go on."

"Well, I was stunned for a moment. I wasn't sure what I was holding until I took a closer look."

"That's when you first saw the tests?"

"Yes."

"So, how or why did they end up in your room?"

"I didn't want anyone to find them. I mean, Christ, Lenny just died. I'm sure his family is a total wreck right now. The last thing they need is to find out their son was a cheat and a thief. I was trying to protect his memory, that's all."

"Okay, where'd the cash come from?"

"I don't know. Lenny gambled a lot. He liked to bet on baseball games. Maybe he hit it big."

"Maybe he was selling the tests to his classmates."

Jason didn't like how this conversation progressed. He started to think he needed a lawyer. He sat in silence.

"Look kid," Alonzo said, "if it's any consolation, I'm starting to believe you. I've checked around. You're not the type who cheats and steals. And you're certainly not the type who carries around eight grand in cash."

Jason looked up at the OSI agent. "What are you saying?"

"I'm saying there may be some truth to what you're telling me. Some truth. There are a few things I need to check out first."

A brief smile came to Jason's face. "You believe me?"

"Somewhat, yes. You see, I've been reading your files and records here for the last hour. I've reviewed your test scores. You min rolled the first two academic tests, the first instrument test, and four out of seven stan tests."

Jason lowered his head with embarrassment.

"I don't think that someone who was stealing tests would cut it that close."

"What are you going to do? What can I do to help you realize I'm innocent?"

"Well, the best thing that you can do is sit tight. You've been pulled out of training as of this afternoon."

"What?" Jason cried. "How the hell can they do that? I'm innocent! They can't kick me out for something I didn't do!"

Alonzo placed his hands up in front of him, "Settle down, kid. Look at it from their perspective. They had a thief, and as far as they're concerned, they caught him. It's only normal that you get pulled out of training. I'll meet with the Wing Commander in the morning and brief him on what I know. I'll recommend a house arrest that will restrict you to base. Look, kid, I know who you are."

Jason's head snapped up. "What do you mean?"

"Your father, Senator Jonathan Bowman, is running for president of the United States next year. If he wins his party's nomination, of course."

Jason's shoulders slumped and his face reflected disappointment. "Who else here knows?" he asked.

"No one else. I figure you have your reasons why you don't want anyone to know who you really are."

"I want to make it through this program on my own. I don't want anyone saying I made it because I'm a senator's son."

"I understand. That's why I haven't brought it up with anyone else. It's also why we need to go through the motions of removing you from the program. We don't want people saying you got preferential treatment because you're a senator's son. In the meantime, I'll be checking the grades of everyone in your class. There might be a link somewhere else. Can you think of anyone who might have been getting tests from Lenny Banks?"

Jason thought for a moment. He suspected Vince, but he wasn't sure. His scores were too perfect for someone who never studied and didn't know the material that well. Lenny and Vince seemed to be always arguing about something. It seemed possible, but Jason had no real proof. It would do no good to accuse him of something he might not have done.

"No. I can't think of anyone right now." Words he had to force himself to say.

CHAPTER 35

September 8, 1995

PALOVICH GREW WEAKER. The loss of blood from the day before weakened him. He needed a doctor, a shower, and a warm bed. For the third night in a row, he had slept on the streets of Moscow waiting for an opportunity to escape. He had been unable to travel much yesterday. The assassins and the Moscow police combed the streets for him.

Shaking the cobwebs from his head, he stood up in the dark alleyway. His joints creaked as he stretched his cramped muscles. As he finished his stretch, his attention turned to a newspaper on the ground. Yesterday's *Pravda* with his picture on the front page. 'KILLER STILL ON THE LOOSE', the headline read. There was a small photo of his wife in the corner of the article. Those sons of bitches. They were blaming him for the death of his wife.

Now he would have to avoid everyone. Complete strangers would be able to point him out to the police. His stomach ached with hunger once again, the food from the marketplace long since gone. Palovich could not risk going back to the marketplace or to an ordinary shop for that matter.

Stumbling through the back streets and alleys, he avoided everyone he saw. In the northern portion of town, the pedestrian traffic picked up significantly for the morning working people. On the far side of the street, he saw two uniformed police officers moving in his direction. The officers stopped to talk to merchants along their path, showing them a picture and asking questions. Palovich studied his surroundings. Next to him, a young man knelt down, changing a tire on his car. When the man went to pull the tire from his trunk, Palovich reached down, snatched up the crowbar, and stuck it under his coat.

Moving along the street, he ducked into an apartment building and raced up three flights of stairs. His legs and back ached with each step. The pain helped him forget his hunger. On the third floor, Palovich listened for any activity, any sounds of life. There were none, and so he pulled the crowbar from beneath his coat and approached the apartment near the stairs. Placing his ear next to the door, he heard no sounds. He knocked lightly, listened, and then knocked again, louder. No one was home. Reaching down and testing the door handle, he found it locked. With the tip of the crowbar wedged near the lock, he gave one good, strong thrust, then another. Snap! The door came free and swung inward.

The early morning rays of the sun broke through the openings in the makeshift curtains hanging from the windows. Walking across the living room, Palovich turned on the light. Cautiously he made his way through the apartment. He did notice a phone next to the kitchenette as he walked through. Approaching the back bedroom, he heard a rasping sound. He sneaked to the doorway, the crowbar tightly gripped in his hand, his pistol still in his pocket. As he reached the doorway, the rasping grew louder as he peered around the corner.

An old woman lay in the bed; her eyes closed, and her breathing heavy. She appeared to be in a deep sleep.

Searching the rest of the apartment, he confirmed that he and the sleeping old woman were alone. Taking off his coat, he stumbled to the toilet to relieve himself. When he finished, he went to the sink. The cold water he threw on his face shocked his body into consciousness. He pulled off his shirts and studied his wound. Caked with dried blood, the flesh surrounding the wound had turned a greenish, blue color. Washing off the dried blood, he saw the infected wound clearly. He'd have to find a doctor soon. First, however, he had to warn the Americans.

Walking back toward the kitchenette, he discovered a half-loaf of bread starting to mold slightly on one end. The hunger pains told him to ignore the mold as he broke a chunk off the loaf. The dry bread absorbed the moisture from his mouth. He drew a glass of water from the sink and downed it at once. He repeated this sequence several times before making his way to the phone and dialing the number.

"American Embassy, information center. This is Debbie. How may I help you?" the woman's voice said.

"John Smith, please," Palovich said. John Smith was one of the code names he used to alert the embassy personnel of an incoming covert call. At that time, that person would activate a two-way scrambler, which allowed them to have a secure phone call for two minutes.

"Just one moment, sir," she said. The process was set in motion. Frank Mese answered the phone three rings later. "Go," Frank said.

"It is Palovich."

"Good God, where are you man?"

"No time for that now. I must relay information regarding Nikolai and his contact in America."

"I'm ready to copy. Go ahead."

Palovich breathed deeply, still light-headed from loss of blood and lack of sleep. "He is going to activate an assassin from Section Nine. The man is located in Oklahoma, in a place called Enid. Your man may be an officer in the US military going by the name of Andrews."

"Enid, Oklahoma. Man named Andrews, possible military, got it. Who is the target?"

"That I do not know. You must follow Nikolai and find this Andrews."

"Great. Where are you? Are you trying to make it here?"

"I was until I saw my face on the front page. I'm sure the embassy is watched."

There was a pause. "You're right," Frank said, "they're watching around the clock. Where are you? We'll come get you."

Palovich started to answer when shuffling in the next room made him stop. He looked up to see the old woman standing in the doorway, her face frozen in horror. She let out a blood-curdling scream that could have belonged to a healthy woman many years her junior. Palovich dropped the receiver and bolted past the old woman for the door. The old woman continued to scream as she let him rush past her out the door.

Racing down the staircase to the streets below, he didn't realize what he had done until he reached the outside of the building. He had left his coat and hat upstairs in his haste to flee the old woman's apartment. The gun! It was still in the coat pocket. His mission was only half over. Now he must escape. The metro. It was the only option right now. The icy chill of the air pierced his sweater and his entire body shivered. Palovich shoved his hands into his pants pockets in an effort to warm them. He could move his bad arm a little, but it still handicapped him. People formed a crowd in the street. Halfway across the street, the morning quiet was shattered by a familiar shriek.

"Stop that man! The one with no coat! He is a thief and rapist!" The old woman screamed from her window. It was obvious who she screamed about. Palovich stood out among the crowd.

Two Moscow policemen on the street corner looked up and moved toward Palovich. One of them talked into his radio. Palovich continued to walk away from the scene, increasing his pace. The old woman continued screaming from her window, pointing in his direction. Palovich saw the two policemen increase their pace as they realized their target was pulling away from them.

Palovich sped up to a light jog. Where could he go? His pursuers were close, and he was unarmed. If he could only find a metro station from here.

The lights and sirens caught his attention first. The police car raced through the street directly toward him, a block away. Looking back, he could see the two police officers in hot pursuit, cautiously working their way through the crowd.

Palovich frantically searched for a way out. Desperation took control of him as he realized the end was near. Something had to happen, and it had to happen quickly, or he was done. Spotting an alley, he darted toward it. The people in the streets cleared the way for the police car spinning its wheels as it rushed through the slushy streets. He reached the alley moments before the police car came to a sliding stop at the entrance. Palovich ran as fast as he could, his breath coming in short gasps.

"Palovich, stop! Surrender! You have nowhere to go!" one of the men shouted from the car.

A shot rang out, a warning shot, perhaps. Palovich didn't turn. He kept running. He approached the end of the alleyway.

Suddenly, a large black sedan pulled in front of him. The door flew open and a large bald man stepped out, his face bearing a devilish grin. Palovich skidded to a stop, almost falling in the filthy slush of the alleyway. The pain of his wound shot through his arm like an ice pick. His eyes met those of the bald man for an instant. Palovich turned to see the two policemen from the car proceeding slowly through the alley, followed by the two on foot who had spotted him initially. He wondered how long he could remain silent under torture. Turning back to the bald one, he saw a pistol pointed directly at his forehead. He began to scream as the bald one squeezed the trigger, the bullet penetrating his skull before his voice ever left his mouth.

CHAPTER 36

September 9, 1995

ALONZO WOKE UP EARLY Saturday morning. He swung his legs off the bed in his billeting room, letting his eyes adjust to the darkness. Standing up slowly, he walked to the window and pulled back the curtain, squinting in the early morning sunlight. The sun peeped over the horizon. The morning light streaked bright red and orange across the sky. He closed the curtain and turned on the television set, not for anything in particular, just background noise.

After a quick cup of coffee, Alonzo put on his navy blue jogging outfit. It had neon reflective green and orange panels sewn into it as a safety feature for late-night and early morning joggers. Alonzo noticed as he put on his Nikes that they were fairly worn. It might be time to buy a new pair. As soon as he dressed, he took a few minutes to stretch his aging muscles. Years ago, he pulled a hamstring and ever since, made sure he stretched thoroughly before working out, especially in the cold weather.

Alonzo finished his jog, showered, and headed to the mess hall for breakfast. He coordinated with Captain Harrison to meet him at nine-thirty to go through Lenny Banks' room again. Alonzo wanted to try to access his computer for information before Lenny's family took everything home that afternoon. He saw the family at the memorial service yesterday and admired their strength and composure in the face of such a loss. He had attended plenty of funerals in his day, two for friends who died in his arms. It was a dangerous business.

Harrison came by Alonzo's room at nine-thirty five. Together, they walked over to the student dorms. Alonzo explained the situation to Harrison twice. He had to calm the over-zealous instructor. Harrison seemed ready for blood when he first found out about the cheating. When they found the tests in Conrad's room, he wanted to move in for the kill. Alonzo held him back and laid out the big picture for him, using caution not to expose the fact that Jason Conrad was the son of Senator Jonathan Bowman.

"So when are his parents supposed to be here to pick up his things?" Harrison said.

"Around one o'clock," Alonzo said.

"That doesn't give us much time. Is the computer still set up?"

"No, Conrad said he boxed it up. It's in its own box, and so is the monitor. Easy to find, he said."

"It's gonna take a little time for me to set it up."

"That's okay. It gives me time to go through some boxes and look for floppies."

"Do we need a warrant for this?"

"No," Alonzo said as they approached the doorway. "These rooms are subject to search at any time. That's why you're allowed your little inspections periodically."

"Yeah, but that's different. We're checking for cleanliness, not theft."

As they reached the door, Harrison fished through his pocket for the key. Unlocking the door, he flipped on the light switch as they walked inside the room.

"Oh, my God," Harrison mumbled.

The two stared in silence at the destruction. It appeared as if a bomb blew up in the room. Every box was opened, torn to shreds. There were clothes everywhere, broken glass, papers tossed all over the floor. The room was literally destroyed. Certainly all of Lenny Banks' belongings were.

"Don't touch anything," Alonzo warned. "They'll need to take prints of this entire room."

"I already touched the light switch."

"Then don't touch anything else." Alonzo scanned the room. "Do you see the computer anywhere?"

"There's the monitor over there," Harrison said, pointing to the couch. "The tower shouldn't be far away."

Alonzo and Harrison searched for a few moments, trying not to move any items that could be used for fingerprints. They found the desktop tower under a pile of clothes. It had been removed from the box and destroyed. Harrison studied the battered terminal. "I think the hard drive is still intact. If I can get back to my office, I can pull it out and upload it into my system."

"Do it," Alonzo replied.

CIA HEADQUARTERS IN LANGLEY, Virginia, was busier than usual, especially for a Saturday. Hundreds of people constantly moved from office to office, from computer terminal to telephone, and from building to building. The secure satellite communications link had dropped off twice before finally getting through the downlink. The communications specialist grew frustrated with the gentleman in Moscow. There were lots of messages from Moscow, and they were always emergencies. He changed his mind when Director Hollings personally came downstairs to read the message with Caldwell. Aaron Caldwell flew in the day before and had been notified immediately after the message was received and the two had come down together. The message had come encrypted, addressed *FYEO Aaron Caldwell*. For Your Eyes Only.

Caldwell and Hollings rushed with the message to the encryption room to have the message decoded. In a matter of minutes, the message was ready.

NIKOLAI ARRIVES MONDAY. ENID, OKLAHOMA.
LOOK FOR A MAN NAMED ANDREWS. POSSIBLE MILITARY.

Hollings spoke first. "I want you to get to Enid tonight. Pack for several days. I'll contact the Oklahoma City office and have a rep meet you at the airport."

"Where are we going to start?" Caldwell said.

Hollings sat at the table in the dark encryption office. "I'll get more people in here. Two groups. We'll trace the background on everyone named Andrews in the Enid area. One group will do the civilians. The other will track the military personnel at Vance Air Force Base. We'll check Tinker, Altus, and Fort… uh, Sill, I think it is, just to be sure. We should have something for you by tomorrow morning."

Caldwell turned to leave when Hollings stopped him. "Aaron," he said.

"Yes, sir?"

"I want to nail this bastard. You know what a sneaky little character Nikolai is, and you know why he's here. This one will be dangerous—don't hesitate to ask for help. We can't afford to make any mistakes. Someone's life may hang in the balance."

"I understand, sir. I won't disappoint you."

ALONZO STARTED TO WALK back to Lenny Banks' room when he noticed Jason in the crowd behind the yellow police tape. He walked over toward Jason and stepped over the police line.

"What's going on?" Jason asked.

"Let's go for a walk," Alonzo said.

Jason and Alonzo walked away from the crowd to the back of the building, by the static display of an old T-34. The plane was in dire need of a new coat of paint; the old silver paint chipping away in large chunks.

"I went to Lenny Banks' room this morning to check out your story," Alonzo said. "When I arrived there with Captain Harrison, we found the room destroyed. Papers, clothes everywhere. Broken glass and furniture. Every box opened, their contents emptied. It's a real mess and will take some time to clean up."

"See, somebody is looking for something," Jason said.

"Maybe. Or maybe someone is trying to hide something."

Jason thought about that comment for a moment. "Wait. Wait a minute. You don't—you don't think I . . ." He was dumbfounded. His story is practically verified; now they're suspecting him of ransacking Lenny's room. Jason felt Vince did it. "This is unbelievable. I mean, this is really too much."

"Slow down there, junior, I didn't say that. Let's wait until they finish going over the crime scene. Once they do and we access the computer, we'll be able to check out your story."

"But this doesn't help me out though, does it?"

"No, kid, it doesn't."

"Have you contacted my father yet?"

"No, not yet. I'd like to get some answers to questions he'll have. My hope is this won't be an issue and will simply go away."

"Thanks, Agent Jacobs," he said, then paused. "I haven't seen or spoken to him since I was a small child."

"I know," Alonzo replied sincerely.

The two walked back toward the crowd. As they approached the parking lot, Jason noticed Vince Andrews walking down the stairs of the identical building on the other side of the lot. Vince spotted him and marched straight toward him. Jason glared at Vince, studying him. Something about him was not right. Did Vince break into the room and destroy it? He must have. Why would anyone else? Maybe Big Joe McCain and his bunch came back, but that was unlikely.

"Hello, Conrad. What's the occasion?" Vince said.

"Somebody broke into Lenny's room and trashed the place," he said.

Vince shook his head unconvincingly. "That's a shame. Hey, I hear on the streets you've gotten yourself into a little trouble."

Jason jerked his head to face Vince. "Where did you hear that?" Alonzo assured him their conversation was confidential, and he had no reason to believe otherwise.

"Oh, I think it was at the gym this morning. It's a small base. People talk."

He's fishing for something; some kind of information. He's not sure if I know about him and Lenny.

"You're right about that," Jason said. "People talk. They talk a lot more than you know."

Vince paused, then grabbed Jason's sleeve and pulled him away from the crowd. "What do you mean by that, Conrad?"

"Nothing. Why do you ask?"

"Don't screw with me Conrad," Vince said. "I'm out of your league."

"I'm sorry, Vince. I thought we were grieving over our dead friend." Jason paused for a moment. "Just what are you talking about?"

"Listen Conrad, whatever you did, maybe I can help."

"You can help?"

"Yeah, whatever you—"

"I didn't do anything Vince. They *know* that. That's what this is all about," Jason said, gesturing toward the police blockade.

"Fine, never mind," Vince said, stalking off toward his truck.

"Hey Vince," Jason yelled after him. "Be careful."

VINCE TURNED TO SEE JASON smiling at him. Vince did not return the smile. Conrad knows. The bastard knows. Maybe not that, but he suspects something. But how? How could he have found out? Vince pondered for a moment about Jason's knowledge of his operation. It wasn't possible for him to know. He might have found out about the tests. That was irrelevant now. Vince looked back to see Jason talking to the large black man he was with earlier. Must be some kind of cop. An investigator, no doubt, but why is he talking to Jason so much? All he did was pack up the room. On the inside of the police barricade, Vince saw Captain Harrison talking to an enlisted airman. Casually, he skirted behind the crowd to reach Harrison.

"Hi, sir, how's it going?" Vince said enthusiastically. He had flown with Captain Harrison on several occasions and knew how to talk to him.

"Hello there, Lieutenant Andrews. What can I do for you?" he said from behind his Ray-Ban sunglasses, a pompous air about him.

"Nothing, sir. Just wondered what you were doing in our neck of the woods on a Saturday."

"Well, Andrews, it seems there is a little excitement going on, and we are trying to straighten this out."

"Why? What's going on?" Vince said with all the curiosity of a schoolboy.

"We are investigating a scandal, potential burglary, and destruction of government property."

"Scandal!" Vince said. "What is it?"

"Quiet. It involves stolen tests, but we've found the culprit, and his ass is mine." Harrison beamed with the pride of a champion. "And don't ask who it is . . . that information is not releasable yet," he offered without being asked.

"So who is doing the investigating?" Vince said, moving in for the kill.

Harrison slowly pulled his sunglasses out of his pocket. "Agent Alonzo Jacobs of the OSI. We cracked the case yesterday, but it's on hold for right now."

Vince wanted to puke. Who was this loser? "I didn't know Vance had OSI officers on base," he said.

"Agent Jacobs is from San Antonio. He's stationed at Randolph. They sent him up here to find our little cheat, and I led him to him."

"There's no agent here. Where is he?" Vince said.

"See that big black fellow over there?" Harrison said, pointing toward the entrance of the dorms. "That's my partner."

"I see," Vince said. Vince wandered off slowly, putting together the pieces of the puzzle— the tests, Jason, and Agent Alonzo Jacobs.

CHAPTER 37

September 10, 1995

Landing firmly on the runway, the 737 taxied clear at Will Rogers World Airport in Oklahoma City. Caldwell's circadian rhythm was out of synch as he'd been jumping time zones and working some long days lately—and today was another one. The aircraft pulled into the terminal and the passengers began to unload. Caldwell scooted off the jet, through the jetway, and into the main terminal. His eyes quickly scanned the crowd as he kept moving past the people waiting for other passengers. It didn't take long for Caldwell to find the smiling face staring straight at him. Caldwell returned the smile and waved.

"Aaron Caldwell, how the hell are you?" Greg Johnson said. The Oklahoma-based CIA case officer stood shorter and stockier than Caldwell, but he didn't carry an ounce of fat. Caldwell grasped Johnson's hand, shaking it firmly.

"Good to see you, Greg. How's the wife and kids?"

"Doing great. The little one has a cold right now, though. It's really a pain in the ass. How was the trip?"

"Long. Too long. Getting stuck in Dallas overnight didn't help either."

"Understood?" Agent Johnson guided Caldwell through the maze of people to the baggage claim area. "You know, I remember the old days," Johnson said. "We'd have a private jet bring you guys in, and we didn't have to put up with this crap."

"Yeah, that was the old days when the Soviets were the only bad guys in town. These days, we got more bad guys and less tools to go after 'em with."

"You can say that again. I went ahead and coordinated with the airline—your bags have already been removed. We'll pick them up at the customer service desk over there," Johnson said, pointing to the desk across the large room.

They waited another ten minutes before Caldwell retrieved his bags. It was all very inconspicuous. The two men looked like anyone else retrieving lost luggage. They left the terminal and climbed into Johnson's Jeep Cherokee. Once on the road, Caldwell turned up the radio in the car.

"So, any developments while I've been on the road?"

Johnson smiled. "I was wondering how long it was going to take you to ask. We've found our man, I think. A lieutenant in pilot training at Vance Air Force Base. Vincent Andrews. He's the only Andrews in a three-hundred-mile radius we definitely can't trace back to a birth date. This guy has moved around quite a bit in the past four years. We can't really trace anything he did before four years ago. We turned up another Vincent Andrews who might have died at a homeless shelter in Los Angeles fifteen years ago."

"Is there a connection?"

"Oh, yes. Same Social Security number."

"That's our man," Caldwell said, staring out the window again.

"So, what's the plan from here?"

Caldwell shifted in his seat. "We know, or at least we are extremely confident, that Nikolai Gregarin is coming to meet with Vince Andrews. What we need to do is find this Andrews and keep him under wraps. Nikolai will be too hard to find coming into the US. Hell, he's probably already here. But Nikolai is always cautious. Andrews has no reason to be cautious. He's been living like an obnoxious American for the past four years. Tomorrow morning, we head out to the base to do some preliminary checking around."

"I just hope we're not too late," Johnson said.

"Don't remind me, Greg. Think positive." Caldwell laid his head against the headrest and dozed off for the hour and a half ride into Enid.

THE TWO SAT IN HARRISON'S OFFICE across the street from the dorms. The day had been long and still they came up empty. Lenny Banks' room had been wiped clean of fingerprints and the hard drive too badly destroyed to find any other evidence.

"Okay, I'll turn this over to my guys, and they can determine whether it's of any value."

Harrison turned away from his computer and faced Alonzo. "He's guilty as hell, you know. Everything points to him. I know he went in there last night, deleted everything, and then wrecked the place. We need to bust this guy now and bust him hard."

Alonzo looked skeptically at Harrison as he studied the bland walls covered with photos of T-37s and jet fighters. "Well, until we have proof Conrad stole the tests, we won't do anything."

Harrison exploded. "Proof! Hell, we found every damn test and a helluva lot of cash in the guy's room. What else do you need?"

"That proves he was in possession of the tests and a lot of money. There is a great deal of circumstantial evidence, yes, but there is no evidence to support his being the thief. You've seen his test scores. It's obvious he hasn't been cheating in this program. Even if those are his copies of the tests, he got them from somebody. And that is the person I want." Alonzo picked up his coat from the chair. "If you'll excuse me, I think I'll go discuss this situation with our suspect."

"Guilty suspect," Harrison said

"Captain, things aren't always what they seem." The OSI agent left the building and walked across the street to Jason's dorm room. Alonzo wished he could tell the young captain Jason Conrad's father was a potential Presidential candidate, but he wasn't sure that would change his mind. The evidence they had fit together too well, and it pointed right at Jason Conrad. He reached the dorm and rapped on the door.

"Agent Jacobs, what brings you here?" he said.

"I wanted to talk to you a bit. Do you mind if I come in?"

It was obvious Jason was cleaning up. There were piles of clean clothes stacked on the bed, dishes stacked next to the sink, and papers piled on his desk. The vacuum cleaner stood propped against the wall, waiting to be used. Jason walked over to Alonzo and handed him the drink.

"What can I do for you this afternoon, Agent Jacobs?"

"Alonzo. Call me Alonzo."

"Okay, Alonzo. What's up?"

Alonzo studied the young man. He didn't seem nervous, but rather curious as to what was going on with the investigation. Jason appeared almost as eager to solve the mystery as he was.

"We've swept the entire room for prints, and it's coming up clean. Whoever did this did a good job of covering his tracks."

"So there's no way of telling who's been in that room?"

"Not exactly. We're currently attempting to access the hard drive on the computer, but I don't know if that will tell us anything."

"So why are you here? To inform me I'm getting kicked out of UPT for something I didn't do? To advise me to seek counsel to defend me for a felony I didn't commit?"

"Calm down now, son. I want you to tell me everything you know. Any little bit of information concerning the tests, Lenny Banks, UPT, whatever. Can you do that?"

"Yeah, but why?"

"Look, I believe you. I don't think you're involved in this, but folks here will expect you to take the fall unless we find out something quick. I don't think bringing your father into this will help out anyone."

Jason nodded his head. He stood up and moved his chair to sit directly across from Alonzo. He rested his forearms on his knees, gazing at the floor in front of him. Jason spent the next few minutes covering how, exactly, he was sent to Lenny's room; and his discovery of the tests and money.

"Lenny gambled . . . a lot. He liked to bet on sports teams—baseball mostly, I think. Anyway, he never really talked about whether he won or lost, but it always seemed as if the teams he liked were losing. If his teams were losing, he would have been deeply in debt. So it appeared to me, he somehow got hold of those tests and sold them."

"Sold them to whom? Right now, you're the prime suspect. Convince me you're not."

Jason stared at Alonzo. He was right—all the evidence pointed to him. Jason took a deep breath and continued.

"I'm not sure, but I think it might be Vince Andrews. He's in our class also."

Alonzo wrote the name on his pad. "Why him?"

"Well, Vince and Lenny go way back. They went to college together, and I guess the story is that Vince made a few phone calls to get in the same UPT class as Lenny. Anyway, Vince has made a hundred percent on every test we've taken so far."

"Is that uncommon?"

"No, it's not. But he never studies. And if you talk to him about the material, he really can't answer the questions. It's obvious his knowledge is limited. Also, he throws around a lot of extra money. He claims to be from a poor family, but he has a brand new truck that cost an easy thirty grand. He owns a ski boat, and he's always buying drinks for people and new stuff for himself. Now there's nothing wrong with that, except it's just a little unusual for a second lieutenant to maintain that kind of lifestyle."

Alonzo nodded. He had checked Jason's background extensively. Jason had no known history of gambling. Despite his parents' divorce at an early age, he grew up basically a good kid. He was given his mother's maiden name. Apparently, his ex-wife took the future Senator Bowman to the cleaners before she split. His grades were not the grades of a student who had copies of the tests beforehand. Jason was barely passing. And then there was the computer issue. Jason didn't have one. How could he have stolen the tests? Alonzo began to believe his story more and more. "Is there anything else you can remember? Anything at all?"

"Well, Vince and Lenny were always fighting. Not physically, but they argued a lot. Lenny always acted as if he had something on Vince, some kind of control over him. I think it was the tests. Lenny was always making comments about Vince's knowledge and Vince would make him shut up. It makes sense."

Alonzo looked at Jason and smiled. "Yes, it sure does."

CHAPTER 38

September 10, 1995

CALDWELL AND GREG JOHNSON checked in at the Holiday Inn on Highway 81, a couple miles from the base. They were lucky to get a room with the upcoming graduation of a class at Vance. The hotel was full of relatives and friends who were in town for the occasion. Both men elected to share a room with two double beds. It was eight p.m. Sunday evening, before they unpacked.

"You hungry?" Johnson said.

"Yeah," Caldwell said, "but I think I'm too tired to go anywhere. Feel like calling for Domino's?"

"Sure. Pepperoni and cheese okay with you?"

Caldwell nodded as he sat at the desk and pulled out his files. One file covered Nikolai Gregarin; the other a detailed listing of known and suspected acts of terrorism committed or supported by Section Nine. He also had a sheet of paper with limited information about Vince Andrews. Caldwell read over the details on Vince twice as Johnson finished ordering the pizza and hung up the telephone.

"Is this all the information you have on the Andrews guy?" Caldwell said.

"Yes," Johnson said, walking across the room to retrieve a large black case he brought in earlier. "About all we could drag out locally in OKC. Driver's record, tax stuff, you know."

"Tomorrow we'll be busy. I'll also need to pick up a car. We'll find out what room this guy Andrews lives in. I want you to tail him. All day. While you're doing that, I'll be on the base digging up what I can on this guy. I'll drop in and report to the wing commander for a courtesy call. He needs to know we'll be investigating one of his people. Hopefully, we get a little cooperation. Hey, when's that pizza going to show up?"

"Thirty minutes or less," Johnson said as he finished hooking up the fax.

"Time," Caldwell said looking at the photograph of Nikolai, "is one thing none of us has enough of."

JASON PACED THE ROOM. Alonzo left his room more than three hours ago, but he was still worried. Convinced Alonzo believed him, Jason focused on convincing the Air Force right now. They had actually removed him from training. After everything he'd done to get here—and as hard as he'd worked to stay here—the Air Force stopped his training for something he didn't do. He was more worried if they found out about his father. Such fodder would have created a media frenzy. It was unfortunate that all the evidence pointed to him. The only thing in his favor was that Alonzo believed his story. However, Alonzo didn't have any evidence supporting his belief—only gut instinct, and that wouldn't stand firmly in a court martial or the court of public opinion. Jason stopped pacing long enough to sit on his couch facing the television. Picking up his portable phone, he dialed Kathy's number. It rang several times before someone picked up.

"Hi, is Kathy there?"

"No, she isn't in right now," a woman said. "Who may I ask is calling?"

"Hello, Mrs. Jones," he said, realizing this was the first time he'd ever talked to her. "This is Jason Conrad. Will she be in later?"

"Oh, Jason, hello. Kathy asked me to give you a message. She's gone back to San Antonio and asked me to give you her number there. Let me see where I put it."

She came back a moment later with the number, which Jason copied on the back of his hand. Jason thanked her and hung up. How could she leave without calling? Jason rubbed his temples slowly. The one part of his life going well and he let it slip away. Jason wondered if his priorities were screwed up, only in the opposite way McTaggart suggested. Life, after all, was simply a series of decisions made while we wait for something else to happen. Frustrated and tired, Jason's stomach growled. He needed to get some dinner. Grabbing his coat, he headed for the door.

Climbing into his Mustang, he pulled out of the parking lot. Once past the main gate, he hung a right turn and headed for Highway 81. As he approached the intersection, Jason noticed the headlights of the truck behind him. They were on bright and were annoying him. The truck pulled in close behind him, slowly moving closer. The first thing that popped into his mind was that he should be under house arrest. While more of an honor system than an actual status, he worried someone might have actually followed him off base.

That thought left him immediately as the truck suddenly swerved into the other lane and pulled up beside the Mustang. Jason slowed as the two vehicles approached the intersection, wondering what the truck was doing. Without warning, the truck swerved to the right, slamming into the Mustang's left front fender, driving Jason toward the shoulder of the road. In a defensive maneuver, Jason took the quick right turnoff onto Highway 81 and escaped the truck.

"Holy crap," Jason said. His heart raced and his mind struggled to understand what just happened. Jason managed to control the Mustang as he headed southbound out of Enid. "What the hell is that crazy son of a bitch doing?" he said as he glanced in his rearview mirror. The bright lights of the large truck made the quick right turn also and follow him southbound.

Tightening his grip on the steering wheel, Jason accelerated steadily. He sped up to sixty miles an hour. The headlights in the mirror stayed with him.

"Who is this guy?"

The truck continued to follow him for two minutes, holding about two car lengths back. Jason slowly increased his speed to seventy as he passed through the small town of Bison. The truck still hung with him. When they passed through Bison, the truck increased its speed. Jason watched in the mirror as it grew closer and closer.

Jason scanned both sides of the road, searching for a way out. The median between the two sides of the highway couldn't be crossed. A small ditch sat in the middle of the highway and on the right side of the road . . . wheat fields. The truck would surely catch him if he went off-road. His best option, he decided, was to stay on the highway and attempt to outrun the truck. Glancing in the mirror again, he realized this might be difficult to do since the truck rode ten feet behind him now at eighty-five miles an hour. Jason pushed the accelerator to the floor and the Mustang slowly crept passed ninety, yet the truck rode close behind him.

The two vehicles raced through the darkness on the deserted strip of highway. Suddenly, the truck turned off its headlights, and for one brief moment, disappeared in the darkness. Glancing in the sideview mirror, Jason could see the truck barreling toward him now, aiming for another strike on his fender. The Mustang shook as the truck slammed into the side fender again, but Jason maintained control, if barely. No sooner had Jason regained control of the Mustang, then the truck slammed into him again.

"Hey," Jason yelled. "What the hell did I do to you?" His thoughts were momentarily disrupted by a loud noise coming from his car, likely the muffler. It must have been knocked loose. Glancing in his rearview mirror, he could see the sparks dancing across the road from underneath his vehicle. He noticed the truck dropping back again slowly to a position two car lengths behind.

Jason never heard the gunshots. The first indication the guy in the truck shot at him was when the round went through his back windshield and buried itself into the dashboard next to him. The back windshield shattered like a spider web, and Jason couldn't see anything behind him. Automatically, he began swerving back and forth across the road in an attempt to keep the person in the truck from getting a good shot at him. He felt a few more dull thuds in the back of his car as the bullets penetrated his classic automobile. Suddenly, the back of his vehicle erupted in flames.

Jason was still swerving the Mustang across the road when he saw the fire and quickly steered the car off the side of the road and into a wheat field. Jason bounced around violently, slamming his head against the steering wheel, then jerking him back into his seat. He no longer controlled the car. It now drove him through the field.

The car slowed rapidly, and Jason managed to gain enough composure to open his door, throwing himself out of the fiery Mustang. He landed on his right side and rolled away, the rear tires of the car barely missing his feet. Jason stopped rolling in time to look toward the path of the burning car and watch his beloved American Classic Mustang explode in the night.

Jason checked himself out quickly. There didn't seem to be any broken bones, although his ribs were sore and blood dripped from his forehead. Instinctively, he crawled deeper into the wheat field, concealing himself. Looking up, he saw the headlights of the truck pull up to the edge of the wheat field. He lay there motionless for several moments, well hidden among the tall grass, fifty yards from his flaming car.

The driver stepped out of the truck. Jason couldn't make out his face and wasn't about to get closer. He could see a pistol in his hand. The figure headed slowly toward the burning car, and then picked up his speed to a jog.

Jason lay motionless, afraid to breathe. His heart pounded so hard that for a moment, he feared his attacker would hear it. He was defenseless. If the assailant saw him, he would die. Keeping his face down, he made feeble attempts to identify his attacker, but that proved unsuccessful. The would-be killer approached the car and walked around to the back end. The flames engulfed the Mustang, preventing the assailant a thorough inspection of his intended victim.

Suddenly, Jason saw the attacker turn and run back toward him. His heart pounded like never before. Had the assassin seen him? The attacker came closer, but Jason refused to move. Was it fear? Or was instinct taking over? The assailant ran past him and jumped into his truck. Jason breathed a sigh of relief, but remained frozen in his hiding place. He heard the truck engine start and watched it back onto the highway, driving off into the darkness.

CHAPTER 39

September 11, 1995

THE FRESH AIR WAS PREVALENT this time of year. Any stench that existed would soon be buried under an icy tomb for the next several months. The snow had fallen early as he predicted, the gloomy winter upon them. Viktor walked through the small field behind his cottage, the fresh snow crunching beneath his boots, the trail back to his cottage visible in the still-white snow. His hands were stuffed deep into his pockets, and a thick fog came from his mouth with each breath. Viktor walked nowhere in particular, but felt troubled, more now than in recent weeks. He could not remember when he had been so disturbed. Perhaps it had been when his wife died.

Stopping short of the tree line, Viktor stared back at the cottage. The dull gray sky showed promise of another snow soon. It was impossible to tell the time of day since there were no shadows cast by the sun. The people would go hungry again, his plan to save them unraveled before it started. News of Palovich's death came as a shock to Viktor. He had handled the news without showing any emotion, a benefit of years of experience in the Soviet system, but inside, the news shook him like an earthquake, shattering years of friendship. His driver, his confidant, his friend . . . was a traitor. He now knew why Nikolai had handled the situation without informing him. Viktor's judgment would have been clouded. He was too close. And now it was done.

Why had Palovich done what he had? Was he angry at Viktor? The government? He had an excellent job. Although being a driver had not been a particularly exciting line of work, Palovich had a certain amount of prestige. It didn't make sense. What is it that drove a man to forsake all those to whom he had been loyal? Viktor stared across the field, his heart heavy, thinking about the future. It long ago became a game for younger men. He no longer had the stomach for it. He hoped the Committee would handle the situation he had created for them. The players were all in place; the process in motion. Nothing he could do now would stop it. In a matter of days, an American senator and potential presidential candidate, would be dead.

AT EIGHT IN THE MORNING, Colonel Benjamin Todd Jensen was ready for the day to end. His job as wing commander of an undergraduate pilot training base was not supposed to be stress free, but it isn't supposed to be this difficult either. He sat behind his desk, leaning back in his chair with his hands in his lap. His eyes peered over the glasses sitting midpoint on the bridge of his nose. He'd had another appointment scheduled this morning, but for some reason his secretary slipped this gentleman in first. The man approached his desk, stopping a good five feet from the edge.

"Good morning, Colonel, my name is Agent Aaron Caldwell, Central Intelligence Agency," he said, flashing his I. D. badge.

Agent Caldwell didn't offer him his hand, Jensen noticed, but neither did he. "CIA? What is it we can do for you? I thought DIA did all the background checks for security clearances."

"Well, sir, I'm not here for that. My partner, Agent Greg Johnson and I, are here working on a case. It is my responsibility to notify you that we will be operating on and around your base. I'm here to ask for your cooperation as much as possible."

Jensen stared at the man coldly as he leaned forward. "I'm sorry—run that by me again. Did I hear you say you were investigating my base?" Jensen said.

"No, sir, we are conducting an investigation on and around Vance Air Force Base. I am here asking for your cooperation when it is needed."

"And just what, sir, is it you are investigating?"

"I am not at liberty to disclose that information, sir."

"But the CIA's job is to deal with intelligence and counterintelligence overseas. This is America. If we have a problem here, the FBI should be handling it. What reason would you have to conduct an investigation on my base?"

"Sir, I'm sorry, but I'm unable to disclose that information. Let me assure you arrangements have been made and the accountability lies with us."

Jensen slammed a fist on his desk. "Damn it! Do you know what kind of week I've had here? I've already had one Class A mishap resulting in a fatality and an aircraft destroyed. I've got the damned OSI investigating a test-cheating scandal. And now the CIA shows up without warning, wanting me to roll out the damn red carpet, but doesn't tell me a damn thing about why they're here. Well, I tell you what, Agent . . ."

"Caldwell."

". . . Caldwell, you can waltz yourself right back to wherever it is you came from until I can find out what it is you are here to investigate. I've seen how you guys operate. I worked with some of you folks during Desert Storm, and I can tell you I wasn't very damned impressed. Do we understand each other now?"

"I think so." Caldwell stood in front of the colonel, silent for a moment. "May I use your telephone?"

Jensen pushed the phone toward Caldwell.

Caldwell picked up the receiver and dialed. After several seconds, someone picked up the phone on the other end and Caldwell spoke softly into the phone. He hung up and stepped back from the desk. "Is there somewhere I can get a cup of coffee while I wait?"

Jensen's face glared a fiery red. "Wait for what? What the hell was that all about? You mark my words, mister—there will be no investigation on my base until I am in-briefed on who is being investigated and why. This is my base, and I will determine who will do what."

"Colonel?"

"What?"

"The coffee?"

Jensen grunted and hit the speakerphone. "Helen."

"Yes, Colonel?"

"Would you be so kind as to get Mr. Caldwell a cup of coffee?"

"Coming right up, sir."

"Have a seat, Mr. Caldwell. I'm sorry. Do you prefer Agent Caldwell or Secret Agent Caldwell?" he said sarcastically. Jensen leaned back in his chair, feeling confident with the way he had handled the situation. He was tired of outsiders coming to his base dictating how to conduct business.

"Mr. Caldwell will do."

Thirty seconds of silence passed before Helen entered with the coffee. Jensen noticed Caldwell stood when Helen entered the room and thanked her for bringing the coffee.

"Okay, Mr. Caldwell, you've got your coffee. Now, since you can't tell me what it is you want to do here, do you suppose you can tell me what your little phone call was about? Do you want to tell me anything before I have you removed from my office and my base?"

"Colonel, you'll get a phone call in about five minutes or less that will tell you everything you need to know. I can sit outside if you'd like, while you wait for that call."

"You can keep your seat. I have a feeling this will be most interesting." Jensen thought he'd effectively taken charge of this situation. He thought it was a good idea for the agent to watch him handle whatever CIA supervisor called to explain why Caldwell was here. Of course, he would cooperate, but Jensen grew tired of these agents popping up out of nowhere. It was time to let them know who was boss. Jensen watched Agent Caldwell sit in his chair, calmly sipping his coffee for several minutes. It began to bother him that Agent Caldwell wasn't intimidated by his authority. Damn spooks. They had always pissed him off. They pissed him off in the desert, and this one pissed him off now.

The ringing phone shattered the silence. It had been six minutes since Caldwell had made his call. Jensen, smiling slyly, looked at Caldwell. *Get ready for the show, boy. I dropped bombs on downtown Baghdad in triple A so thick you could have walked on it. No spook will walk into my office and tell me what to do.* Jensen picked up the receiver after the second ring.

"Colonel Jensen here."

"Ben, this is General Maxwell," the voice over the phone said. General Hiram Maxwell was the four-star general who commanded Air Education and Training Command. Jensen sat at attention in is chair without realizing it.

"Yes, sir, what can I do for you this morning?" he asked, forgetting momentarily about the agent sitting in front of him.

"Look, Ben," said the general in a grave voice, "I don't know what the hell is going on, but the chief of staff just called me about you not cooperating with the CIA on an investigation at your base."

"He did?" His eyes darted quickly to Caldwell, then away again.

"Hell, yes, he did, and every indication is that you are being, in plain English, a pain in the ass."

"But sir—"

"I don't want to hear about it right now. Your orders are to cooperate to the max extent possible."

"Yes, sir."

"If that man asks you to move out of your house, you move."

"Yes, sir."

"Look, Ben. I have absolutely no idea what's going on, but I just had my butt chewed out by the chief because of you. I'll suck it up for now, and we'll sort it out later."

"Yes, sir."

"This one's big, Ben. Don't screw it up, or we'll both be serving Big Macs and fries at McDonald's."

Jensen gulped as the line on the other end went dead. No thanks, no good-byes, no vote of confidence—only the prospect of getting fired if he screwed up this investigation. Jensen stared at his desk for a moment, and then looked at Agent Caldwell. He had expected him to be smiling smugly, but he wasn't. Jensen wondered who the hell this character was and how he had access to the people he did. When he thought about what had just happened, as fast as it did, he decided the general was right. This was big.

"Mr. Caldwell," Jensen said with all seriousness, "what can I do to help you?"

THE EXECUTIVE OFFICER JENSEN assigned to help Caldwell was sharp. In fifteen minutes, he had already retrieved the names and schedules from the database. It was only a matter of time before he found the name Vince Andrews. He gathered all the info on him, placing it in his briefcase. "Do you think you could drive me over to the T-37 squadron?" he asked.

The young executive was a captain named Tyler Daily. "No problem, sir. The colonel's car is downstairs. I'll have you there in minutes." The short, trim exec spoke politely and confidently. Caldwell admired that. The two walked downstairs and climbed into the colonel's dark blue sedan. The two-minute ride made Caldwell feel as if he should have walked, but he tossed the thought aside.

"Here we are, sir," the young exec said. "Is there someplace specific you were looking for?"

"Yes, the commander's office," he replied.

"Through these doors, take an immediate right."

Caldwell shook the young captain's hand. "Thank you, Captain. Your boss could probably use a few more like you." The captain simply nodded. Caldwell exited the car and entered through the double doors, where he was abruptly met by a paunchy lieutenant colonel.

"Mr. Caldwell?" the man asked. Caldwell nodded his head in agreement. "I'm Lieutenant Colonel Baker, squadron commander of the Eighth Flying Training Squadron. Colonel Jensen called and told me you were on your way down. How can I help you?"

Caldwell studied the man carefully. He didn't seem like the typical typecast commander like Colonel Jensen. He was a little overweight with a comical face. "I'd like to review some of your students' files. And I'd like to make sure no one is aware of what I'm doing."

Baker nodded. "Not a problem. Follow me, we'll get you started." They walked into his admin section to the student files. Caldwell noticed Baker never asked who or what he was specifically looking for. He appreciated that. It took several minutes before he found Vince Andrews' file. Removing it, he placed a pink file marker labeled OUT in its place, then slipped the file into his briefcase.

"I'd like to access any information you might have on the computer right now."

"Not a problem." Baker walked across the room to where an older tech sergeant sat at a computer and said something quietly to the man. The sergeant grabbed his hat and left the room. Baker signaled Caldwell as he sat at the computer. Baker had a main menu up with a list of commands showing.

"I think this is the page you want. It contains all the personnel information for everyone in my squadron—instructors and students. It also contains all the information on student performance—daily rides, tests, basic student performance information." Baker stood up and offered Caldwell the chair. "If you need anything else, let me know."

"Thank you," Caldwell said with a smile, "I think this is exactly what I need." He sat at the computer, moving the mouse around, clicking away. The first file he brought up was Baker's. He knew sooner or later he'd need to brief someone on this, and Jensen was such an asshole, he felt more comfortable dealing with Baker. Caldwell felt relieved when he saw Baker had a top-secret clearance. Next, he opened Vince Andrews' personnel file. He scanned it quickly before hitting print. Finally, he brought up Vince's student records and printed those, as well. He placed the pages in his briefcase and stood up from the computer. "Could we go into your office, Colonel?"

"Certainly. This way, Mr. Caldwell." The two walked into Baker's office, and the colonel shut the door behind them. Baker gestured to the soft leather chair positioned in front of his desk. Caldwell sat down as Baker moved over to the coffee pot. "Coffee?" he asked.

"No thanks just had some."

Baker poured himself a cup and took his place behind the desk. "So, Mr.

Caldwell, what can do for you?"

Caldwell took a deep breath. "Do you know why I'm here?"

"I know you are Agent Aaron Caldwell of the Central Intelligence Agency, and I am to assist you in any way possible. It appears you are investigating one of my students."

"I see you possess a top-secret clearance. Where did you get that?"

Baker looked surprised. Perhaps he didn't expect questions about himself. "I'm an old KC-135 guy from way back. Back then, SAC still ran the show, and we all had to get 'em. Nuclear secrets, war plans, standard procedure."

"Colonel, I'm about to brief you on a highly classified situation. This information is on a need-to-know basis. Right now, you are the only person in this wing that has a need to know, and that includes your lovable, wing commander."

Baker laughed, "Oh, you've met Colonel Jensen."

"Yes, and I wasn't very impressed."

"Well, he has a way of affecting people like that."

"You understand that if you are briefed into this, it might cause a conflict between the two of you."

Baker smiled, "Mr. Caldwell, I'm a tanker pilot. My whole career is based on not getting along with fighter pilots. Hell, I've got six months left until I'm eligible to retire anyway. It'll be fun having something to hang over the old buzzard's head."

Caldwell pulled out a non-disclosure statement and gave it to the squadron commander. After he read and signed it, Caldwell walked across the room, locked the door to the office, and turned on the radio sitting on the wooden bookshelf.

Picking up his briefcase, he walked behind Baker's desk and stood next to him. He laid out a stack of blurred photographs and a synopsis of Section Nine. "This is Nikolai Gregarin . . ."

IT TOOK JASON FOUR HOURS to walk back to the base, being careful to stay off the main roads and avoid being seen. He didn't want the driver to circle back around and find him. When he finally arrived home, Jason saw his bruised body and minor cuts from the shattered glass. He cleaned himself up and fell asleep immediately. He awoke seven hours later when the phone rang. It was the Oklahoma State Police informing him about his car.

Jason played the part well, a student not aware his car was gone. He told the trooper he was restricted to base and didn't know how the car ended up there. Someone must have stolen it sometime during the night. Jason spent a minute giving the officer information and discussing his options. They settled on his coming to the station tomorrow to view the vehicle and pick up his paperwork for the insurance claim. A trooper would be dispatched sometime today to take his statement.

He hung up the phone with a slight grin. At least something seemed to go his way. Jason squinted his eyes to check his clock. Ten o'clock. He had a ten-thirty show time and knew he wasn't going to make it. He picked up the phone to get out of it.

"Hello," a voice answered after the first ring.

"Matt, it's Jason."

"What's up, buddy?"

"Hey, I'm feeling like crap today. I need you to tell Gus I'm going DNIF and pass that on to the schedulers." DNIF was the medical acronym for Duties Not Including Flying.

"What's wrong, partner?"

"Uh, just tell 'em I've got the runs and I'll be going to the flight doc for the afternoon sick call to get squared away."

"Okay, buddy, anything else I can do for you?"

"No, that's it for now. Talk to you later." Jason hung up the phone before Matt could acknowledge his goodbye. He rolled over on his back and stared at the ceiling. His side ached, and again he felt for broken ribs. Nothing. Somebody tried to kill him last night, but had only done a halfway decent job of busting him up. It had to be Vince, but he wasn't sure. What angered him more than anything was that his classic '65 Mustang had been destroyed, smoldering in some farmer's field. For the past several weeks, he had felt like a target, as if someone was out to get him. That would end today. He climbed out of bed and headed to the bathroom. Looking at himself in the mirror, he decided he had better clean himself up. It wouldn't be long before the police showed up at the base.

"VINCE ANDREWS?" BAKER ASKED. "Are you sure?"

"That's the best information we have from a reliable source. After a quick, but extensive, background check, we discovered he has no background," Caldwell replied.

"My word, we might have a problem," Baker said, leaning back in his chair, fumbling with his hands.

"What do you mean?"

"Well, I received a phone call last night from Captain Johnson, the 'D' flight commander in charge of Andrews' training. Lieutenant Andrews had a death in the family and needed emergency leave."

"What do you mean by that?" Caldwell asked.

"I mean he's gone. Or at least he should be. We released him for emergency leave as of zero six hundred this morning."

Caldwell's brow furrowed. He walked around and sat in the soft leather chair across from Baker. "Is there anyone who would know Vince Andrews well?"

"Well, the best source would be the SRO, Captain Gus McTaggart. I'm sure he could answer your questions."

"Get him." The SRO would be able to point him in the right direction at least.

"What should I tell him?"

Caldwell hadn't thought about that. "What do you usually tell them?"

"Well, we usually don't have CIA here investigating our students. Would it be satisfactory to say you are here conducting a background check for a security clearance?"

"Colonel, that would be perfect. Just perfect." Caldwell sat alone in the room while the colonel went to find the SRO. The only sound was the radio playing in the background. The room looked like most other Air Force commanders' offices he'd been in—a lot of photos of airplanes and family, plenty of awards, and indications of previous assignments. The plaque with the Japanese flag on it indicated he must have been stationed in Japan at one time.

Lieutenant Colonel Baker returned after three minutes with Captain McTaggart.

Baker spoke first, "Captain, this is Mr. Caldwell. He's here conducting a security background check, and he'd like to ask you a few questions."

"Yes, sir," McTaggart said, shaking Caldwell's hand. "I know the drill."

"Great, Captain, have a seat." Caldwell gestured to the couch against the wall. He turned his leather chair to face him, pleased with the cooperation he was getting at the moment. "What can you tell me about Vince Andrews?"

"Well, other than the fact that he's not here and he left without his orders, not much. He made excellent grades on his tests and flies the jet very well, although sometimes he doesn't perform well under pressure."

"How so?" Caldwell queried.

"Uh . . . well, he struggles during his stand-up emergency procedures. Same for his ground evaluations. It's as if he doesn't understand the material."

"What about his personal life? How well do you know him? Who are his friends? Where does he hang out?"

"I don't really know him that well. He is not a very outgoing individual. He is kind of quiet in a crowd, almost aloof. He usually hung around with Lenny Banks, Jason Conrad, and Matt Carswell."

"Who knew him the best?"

McTaggart took a deep breath and glanced up at the ceiling. "Well, his best friend no doubt was Lenny Banks. He was the guy who died in the plane crash last week."

Caldwell noticed McTaggart's voice trail away. He glanced at Baker and saw him staring solemnly. Banks was still a sore spot.

"I'm not sure what he did in his spare time," McTaggart said, "but the guy who would know him best after Lenny would probably be Jason Conrad."

Caldwell scribbled down the name. "Thank you, Captain, you're excused. Could you send in this Conrad?"

"I'm afraid not, sir. He's not here."

There was a split second pause as Caldwell's jaw dropped. He began to wonder what kind of base they were running here. Sucking in his breath, he asked, "Captain, where can I find Jason Conrad?"

CHAPTER 40

September 12, 1995

HIS SUITCASE BULGED in every direction, the zippers barely closing. The room clutter hinted at a disaster. Piles of clothes and paperwork that had been considered, but not selected, were carelessly thrown across the room. He walked to the closet, pulling his pistol off the shelf. Checking the magazine, he tucked it neatly into his pants. It was time to move out.

Vince always imagined that when he left America it would be under a more controlled circumstance. Instead, he'd pack the things he would need, as well as a few sentimental items. How American. Vince opened the door slowly, peering into the breezeway of the dorm. Empty. Officially, he was on emergency leave. He was supposed to be gone by now. It was almost noon and he needed to get out of there before any of his classmates returned to the dorms for lunch. Walking briskly to his truck, he quickly inspected the front right bumper. Minor damage but nothing that impacted the trucks driving capability. He tossed his bags into the back seat, climbed in the front, and cranked the engine. Scanning the area, he saw none of his classmates or anyone who could identify him.

Pulling out of the parking lot, he drove through the front gate heading for the Ramada Inn. Vince reached the hotel in seven minutes and checked in under the name Jason Conrad. *Conrad, the little bastard.* Vince cursed himself for not getting close enough to verify he was dead.

He walked over to the front desk. The clerk, a skinny woman in her late thirties, gave him a room in the back of the hotel, as requested. Vince drove to the back of the motel and parked. The room had two double beds with earth-tone polyester bedspreads, a dresser, nightstands, and a modest sized closet. The television had no remote control, so Vince opted to leave it off.

He lay on the bed and drifted off to sleep. Nikolai would be calling soon, and he would need the rest for the job ahead of him.

AGENT GREG JOHNSON SAT IN HIS JEEP Cherokee outside the hotel near the suspect's room. Johnson wasn't thrilled at the prospects of sitting and watching the dorms for a kid he wouldn't recognize. Caldwell had the job of doing all the legwork while he sat on his butt all day. Rank had its privileges. He found Vince Andrews' truck still in the parking lot at the dorms. When the tall young man walked out carrying his bags, Johnson got ready to follow him. Greg was puzzled when the truck simply drove into town and stopped at the Ramada Inn. Was this the Vince Andrews they were searching for? The license tag matched, but he still didn't have a physical description. After several minutes of waiting, he went to the front desk.

"Excuse me," he said to the thin woman at the desk. "Can you tell me what room a Mr. Vince Andrews is in?" He gave her his most charming smile as he leaned forward on the desk, propping up his chin with one hand.

She blushed as she flipped through the hotel records. After she went through them once, his smile began to fade. She looked more serious and went back through them again. "I'm sorry, sir," she said after several minutes, "my records don't show a Mr. Vince Andrews registered at this hotel."

Johnson frowned. "Are you sure? He told me he was checking in here this morning."

The thin woman slowly shook her head. "I checked three times. I'm sorry, sir. Perhaps he's staying somewhere else."

"No, he'd be here. Thanks for the help." Johnson turned to walk away, wondering if he'd struck out.

"You might check back later," she hollered after him. "Maybe he's late."

Johnson turned back as he walked toward the glass door. "I might have to do that, ma'am. Thank you."

The blush returned to her face as she smiled. "I'll be here till five. That's when my shift ends."

"You'll be the first one I look for," he said as he walked out the door. Once outside, he pulled the cellular phone out of his pocket and dialed.

"Caldwell here," the voice said.

"Yeah, it's me," Johnson replied. "How's your progress on the case?"

"I'm still working on it. Apparently Andrews called his commander in the middle of the night to take emergency leave. They don't know if he left yet. I'm tracking down one of his buddies as we speak. I want to get a little background on this guy to see if he's really who we want, or some kind of decoy. Nikolai's a sneaky little shit; I wouldn't put it past him."

"Well, just so you know, I sat outside the student dorms this morning watching his truck. Somebody climbed in with their bags, came downtown, and checked into the Ramada. He didn't use the name Vince Andrews, but it could be him."

"I've got his file in my hands now. Did you get a good look at him?"

"Oh, yeah. If you have a photo, I can identify him."

"Great. I'll be done here soon. As soon as I can find this other fellow, I'll meet you there with the photo. Till then, keep an eye on this guy, will ya?"

"You bet." Greg Johnson hung up his phone and stuck it back in his pocket. His stomach growled as he realized he'd not had anything to eat since breakfast seven hours ago. He walked back to his truck and climbed inside. Johnson pulled out a sandwich and a bag of chips. A long, boring day lay ahead.

THE TEMPERATURE DROPPED throughout the day as the wind picked up. The wind chill lowered the temperature significantly. Chilly surges swept across the open field on the base, and Aaron Caldwell began to wish he'd accepted the ride to Jason Conrad's dormitory. Pulling his collar higher around his neck, he quickened his pace. The walk took less than ten minutes, but it seemed more like twenty. He reached Jason's building and found room 107.

Caldwell knocked on the door. A moment later, a ragged young man answered, his wet hair matted against his head. He wore tattered gym shorts and an old football jersey with cutoff sleeves, his face and arms covered with fresh cuts and bruises. The young man squinted as he peered out from the doorway into the light outside.

"Are you Jason Conrad?"

"Yeah. Who are you?"

"My name is Agent Aaron Caldwell," he said flashing his I.D. "I wonder if I could have a word with you."

Jason handled the situation as if it were routine. "Yes, sir, I guess so. Come on in."

Caldwell entered the quarters, following Jason to the couch. Jason moved the loose papers and notebooks spread out on the couch to give his guest a place to sit. Jason plopped down in the chair next to him.

The two sat in silence for a moment. Caldwell could tell Jason was nervous. The student pilot couldn't sit still, constantly tapping his feet on the floor and twirling a pencil with his fingers.

"You get into a fight?" Caldwell asked.

Instinctively, Jason touched the cuts on his face. "No, just fell down the stairs."

Caldwell smiled. "Do you know why I'm here?"

"Look, I've told everyone, I had nothing to do with those tests being stolen. If you check my test scores, it's pretty obvious I haven't been cheating. You can check my bank account and my savings account. Add up my personal assets. I don't have an extravagant lifestyle, and I don't have a lot of money to throw around. I didn't do anything except try to save a friend some embarrassment."

Caldwell looked at Jason, unprepared for the brief monologue, bewildered by its content. "What are you talking about?"

"You . . . you aren't here about the test thing?"

"No, but why don't you tell me about it." Caldwell spent the next several minutes listening to Jason weave his tale about Lenny Banks, Big Joe McCain, stolen tests, and eight thousand dollars cash. Fascinating. Probably more than the average student pilot bargained for during training. Jason finally finished his tale and went to get each of them a Coke. Caldwell opened the cold soda and leaned back on the couch. "So if you weren't involved in this, who do you think Lenny sold these tests to?"

"Vince Andrews, a guy in my class. I wasn't sure at first, but now I am, especially after last night."

"What happened last night?"

"Somebody tried to kill me. I think it was him."

Caldwell leaned forward, interested in the new twist. "How did this happen?"

Jason recapped his story of the night before. He was sure it was Vince Andrews.

Caldwell smiled. They were on the right track. The pieces started to fit together, forming a nice tight puzzle no one knew existed before. "Look, I want you to get dressed. We're going to my place to take care of some business and go through some papers." He noticed Jason not moving.

"Sir, I'm restricted to base. In case you've forgotten, I'm under investigation for computer tampering. If only I had a computer . . ."

Putting his jacket on as he stood, Caldwell pushed his bangs out of his eyes. "You're right. Tell you what," he said, glancing at his watch, "I'll take care of that. I'll be back here at three o'clock to pick you up. We'll grab a bite to eat, and I'll discuss some things with you." Caldwell stood at the door. "Don't talk about this with anyone, understand? If anyone speaks with you, I was never here. In fact, don't answer the door or talk to anyone except me. You may want to pack a bag enough for a couple of days. I'm not sure when you'll be coming back."

"For a background check?"

"This is more than a background check, son. This is national security. And you're coming with me."

IT WAS SIMPLE TO CHANGE the destination from Oklahoma City to Tulsa. The drive from the east took well over two hours. Thirty minutes outside of Tulsa there was nothing to see except the flat land and farms. The sky ahead loomed gray and ominous, indicating snow. The long drive to Enid gave him plenty of time to review his plans. With his hectic schedule, he never had time to sit and think. The drive was serene. He rechecked the map, verifying he stayed on this road all the way to Enid.

When he reached the outskirts of town, he pulled into a truck stop to fill up with gas and grab a quick snack. Glancing at his directions, he saw the Ramada Inn was a few miles away.

Nikolai arrived in a matter of minutes, circling the hotel parking lot. As he rounded the corner in back, he noticed a man in a suit sitting in his truck. Unusual. Perhaps he waited for someone. Nikolai continued his drive around the hotel parking lot and parked on the west side of the hotel. At the front desk, he had the clerk ring Mr. Jason Conrad's room. She handed Nikolai the telephone on the first ring.

"Hello," a man's voice answered.

"It's me."

"Room 134, around back."

Nikolai handed the telephone back to the clerk. Vince's room was in the back of the hotel, as well as the man sitting in the truck. He would be careful. No one should know he's here. No one could have tracked him this far, this long, to the middle of nowhere; he was too careful. He ditched them in Moscow, evaded them in Frankfurt. Surely, there was no way they could have followed him in New York. With his zigzag across the continent, how could they have known he was coming here? Perhaps he was being too suspicious.

Approaching the back of the hotel, he crept like a cat, silently along the walls. He slid the overnight bag from his shoulder and held it firmly in his right hand. As he reached the end of the walkway, he stopped and peered around the corner.

Across the parking lot, he could clearly see the man sitting in his truck, still watching, still waiting.

Nikolai pulled his head back and rested it against the brick wall. Could he be imagining things? He placed the overnight bag back over his shoulder, pulled his shoulders back, and turned his head left, then right. Casually, he rounded the corner and walked to room 134. Reaching into his pocket, he pulled out his car keys and held them in his right hand. The room, sat in the center of the hotel; a location that could be both good and bad. Good to monitor if they were being watched or followed; bad if they needed to escape undetected. Oleg/Vincent, the fool.

Nikolai knocked on the door, which opened right away.

"Don't step outside," Nikolai immediately ordered, smiling and nodding his head. He dropped his keys on the ground. As he bent down to pick them up, he glanced at the truck. Its driver stared intently at him. Nikolai continued and innocently walked inside.

"It is good to see you, Comrade Gregarin—"

"Hush, you fool. You are being watched."

"That cannot be. I've been most careful. No one knows I'm here. And certainly no one suspects who I am."

Nikolai furrowed his brow as he tossed his overnight bag on the spare bed. He walked over to the television, turned up the volume, then walked to the bathroom. The cool water from the sink refreshed him as he washed his face and hands. As he walked out of the bathroom, Vincent handed him fresh bourbon on the rocks.

"Thank you, Vincent," he said, not risking the assassin's Russian name. "I see you've done your homework."

"It is the obligation of every subordinate to be fully aware of his superior's favorite cocktail. I trust you had a pleasant journey?"

"Long, but comfortable. How will you explain your absence at the base?"

"There was a death in the family. I have been granted an emergency leave status for an undetermined period of time. I will call them tomorrow to inform them I shall be back in two weeks. By then, I shall have returned home."

Nikolai smiled, placing his hand on Vince's shoulder. "Yes, you shall return a hero."

CHAPTER 41

September 12, 1995

JASON STARED OUT THE WINDOW of the truck stop café on the outskirts of town. He took a small bite of his cheeseburger, savoring every bite. It was the only thing he'd eaten all day. The French fries were greasy and cold, so he opted not to eat them. He sat alone for the moment; Caldwell stepped to the back of the restaurant to make a phone call. Jason glanced at the clock on the wall: five-thirty.

Caldwell came through the front door of the café and sat at the table. "The food's here already? That's good service."

"Yeah, I guess. Don't eat the fries, though."

Caldwell tasted one. "Yes, I get your point."

Jason took a long sip of Coke. "So what have you been up to?"

"What do you mean?"

"I mean, something's going on that you're not telling me. You come to my room asking questions without ever really asking any. Then you drag me off the base when I'm not allowed to leave and bring me here—"

"Hey, the truck stop was your idea."

"Yeah, I know, but the entire time we're here, you're on the phone. I'm a little curious as to what is going on."

Caldwell nodded as he chewed a mouthful of burger. He put the burger on the plate, wiping his hands with his napkin. "Okay, tell me about Vince Andrews."

Jason shifted in his seat. "Vince makes great grades on the tests, but he doesn't study much or really understand the material," he began. "Apparently, he flies well. He has a 'halo' effect. That means he aces all the tests and he flies good, so the instructors assume he has a firm grasp of the information. Therefore, he usually makes good grades on his daily rides, too."

"Tell me about him personally,"

"I don't really know him that well. He hung out with Lenny Banks all the time. They went to school together. Vince never really talks about his past all that much. I think he has a bad temper."

"Explain."

Jason shifted his position in the booth. "He's kind of like Jekyll and Hyde. One minute he's schmoozin' everyone within eyesight and the next he's blowing his top about something stupid. And he's a fighter. A damn good one. Lenny told me how he got jumped by some guys outside Chicaros once and Vince decked 'em both. I don't know, I guess there's nothing unusual about that."

Caldwell searched through his briefcase, pulling out various files. He slid a piece of paper across the table to Jason.

"Read and sign please," Caldwell said.

Jason reviewed the page. It was a non-disclosure statement saying what they were about to discuss was classified and he could go to jail if he discussed it with someone outside who didn't have a need to know. Jason huffed as he signed the sheet and slid it across the table back to Caldwell. Caldwell tucked the paper in the briefcase and slid one of the files across the table to Jason. Jason opened it up. The file contained a photograph of a well-dressed man walking through a crowd. He didn't recognize the setting, but it looked as if it might be Europe. Jason shrugged his shoulders.

"The man's name is Nikolai Gregarin," he said in a low voice. "He's a part of the KGB, where he heads up a group of highly trained assassins. Through informants, we've been able to establish some methods of their operation. They train their assassins to be moles, to blend into a community in whatever country they're in. The moles might sit dormant for years before being activated to carry out their assigned mission. What we do know is that Nikolai personally assigns each mission. Which brings us to where we are now. Nikolai is in Enid."

"What does that mean?"

"He's here to make contact with his mole. I just got off the phone with my partner whose been staking out the suspect all day. Nikolai showed up at his room over an hour ago. We believe his contact to be the man you call Vince Andrews."

Jason's mouth fell open. He stared blankly at Caldwell. He was confused, nervous, and angry all at the same time. "Are you trying to tell me

Vince Andrews is a Soviet agent?"

"Technically, there are no more Soviets, but yes, there is a Russian agent we believe is Vince Andrews. He is an assassin waiting to meet Nikolai Gregarin for his assignment."

"Wow, this is too much. It's crazy. This is like out of some kind of movie or something."

"I understand your shock, but realize that I need your help. We are running out of time."

"My help? Hell, I'm not sure I believe your story right now. It's too farfetched. A student pilot in UPT is really a Russian assassin. I think you're reaching. You're reaching hard for something that may not be there."

Caldwell reached inside his jacket pocket and pulled out his I.D. "I'm sure you thought I was DIA conducting a routine background check, but I'm not. I'm CIA, and we're not reaching." Jason examined his ID, closely this time. He'd never seen a CIA identification card and badge, but it looked as legitimate as other federal I.D.'s. "Now, I need your help to lure him out and trap him."

"Great, that's all I need. Spend my spare time trapping Russian agents."

"Do you know where his dorm room is?"

"Right across from my place."

Caldwell leaped out of his chair. "Let's go," he said, laying cash on the table. "We may have only a little time."

"A little time for what?" Jason asked as he followed Caldwell through the swinging glass door of the truck stop.

"A little time to look through his place."

"Don't you have to have a warrant?"

"I'm not the police."

Jason contemplated that one for a while as they climbed into Caldwell's car. "It's still illegal, though."

"Don't remind me. It makes me feel guilty," he said.

Jason and Caldwell rode in silence; fifteen minutes later, they pulled into the parking lot at Jason's dorm. They walked until they could see where Vince normally parked.

"Do you see Vince's truck?" Caldwell asked. Jason scanned the parking lot and shook his head, no. "Okay, what's his phone number?" Caldwell pulled out his cellular and dialed as Jason told him the number. It rang four times before an answering machine picked up. Caldwell hung up instead of leaving a message.

"He's not answering. Do you want to accompany me, or do you want to stay here?"

Jason shrugged his shoulders. "I guess I'll go. Maybe I can explain something if you don't understand it."

"Good. Okay, follow me." The two strolled casually across the parking lot to Vince's dorm room. When they reached Vince's room, Caldwell pulled a small leather case out of his coat pocket. He unzipped the case to reveal a number of lock picks. He selected one, along with a tension tool. In a matter of seconds, he opened the door.

Jason hadn't noticed, but at some point Caldwell swapped his lock picks for his pistol. When they entered the room, they did so behind the weapon. "Turn on the lights," Caldwell said.

Jason found the switch and flipped it up, illuminating the room. Vince's room looked like any other student's room: aircraft manuals left on the desk and various study guides laid out carelessly.

"Don't touch anything," Caldwell said. "This room may need to be fingerprinted one day."

"Not a problem," Jason replied. He stood in the center of the room watching Caldwell poke his way around Vince's room. Occasionally, Jason glanced back at the open door, wondering what would happen if Vince came home right now.

Caldwell sifted through the stack of mail on the kitchen counter. "I don't see anything that can really help us right now."

RRRIIINNNGG!

Both men were startled as the telephone rang. Caldwell chuckled at himself for being too focused, unaware of what went on around him. After the fourth ring, the answering machine picked up.

"Hi. This is Vince. I'm not here right now. Leave your name and number and I'll get back to you."

BEEP!

"Hi, Vince, it's Gwendolyn. I just called to see if you got that information on your flight. If not, maybe I can come over and give it to you personally. Call me. 'Bye."

"Who's Gwendolyn?" Caldwell asked over his shoulder.

"She's a girl who's had the hots for Vince for a while now. She works at a travel agency downtown."

"Travel agency?" Caldwell smiled as he moved over to the answering machine. There were five messages on it. One had just been left by Gwendolyn, and one Caldwell had hung up on earlier. That left three.

"Here goes nothing," he said as he punched the small blue button that said

'Play'.

The first two messages were inconsequential. The third message was the familiar voice of Gwendolyn.

"Hi, Vince, it's Gwendolyn. I have you booked on Delta Flight 201 out of OKC tonight. It leaves at ten-twenty p.m. Your reservations in the Davy Crockett Hotel are confirmed. Call me once you arrive in San Antonio if there's a problem. I hope you have questions. Call me."

Caldwell slowly turned toward Jason, his eyes wide and jaw locked. "Paydirt," he exclaimed, raising both hands over his head in triumph.

San Antonio.

DARKNESS FELL OVER THE QUIET TOWN of Enid. Nikolai and Vince spent the better part of the afternoon going over the mission. Vince would leave tomorrow for San Antonio. He would check into the Davy Crockett Motel downtown under the name Henry Wells.

"Then what?" demanded Nikolai

"From there, I will establish my base of operations. Wednesday I will survey the area to finalize weapons selection. The Marriott sits on the Riverwalk in downtown San Antonio. My first choice would be a remote-control bomb. It will be more feasible because of the highly congested area I'll be forced to operate in." He studied the map spread out on the wall as he spoke.

"Thursday, I will investigate the security surrounding Senator Jonathan Bowman. The hotel, Secret Service, limousines, routes of travel, everything. The operation will be finalized that evening. Friday morning America will be short one presidential candidate, and I will be on a Miami flight bound for Argentina."

Nikolai smiled. Oleg had done well. Had the progress reports been false? Was there too much suspicion placed on this young operative? Nikolai pondered these thoughts as he walked to the sink to pour himself a glass of water. Moving across the room, sipping his water, he turned off the lights, walked to the window, and pulled the curtain back slightly. The man in the SUV still sat there. They were being watched. Somehow they had been compromised.

"Vincent, come here," Nikolai said as he let the curtain slide back into place.

"Yes, Comrade Gregarin?"

"A dark-colored SUV sits at the far end of the parking lot. There is a man sitting in the driver's seat. He has been there since I arrived. I believe you have been followed. I would like you to take care of this."

Vince moved up to the window and cautiously peered out. The sliver of an opening was more than enough for him to determine his course of action.

"You may want to prepare to leave," Vince said. "It will be a few minutes before I return."

"Bring him back here," Nikolai said, turning the lights back on.

"What do you plan to do?" Vince grabbed the Smith and Wesson 9mm from a suitcase, checked the magazine, and tucked it in the front of his pants. Picking up the empty plastic ice bucket, he stepped to the door.

"We'll decide that when our guest arrives."

CHAPTER 42

September 12, 1995

BEEEP-BEEEP.

"Hello?" Agent Greg Johnson answered his cellular telephone. He'd been sitting for hours, reading the same magazine four times before darkness stopped him from reading it again.

"Hey, partner, how are you hanging on?"

"Caldwell! Where the hell have you been?"

"Sorry, Greg, I've been busy. I think we've got a real good lead on our boy Andrews. I've got a fella with me that I need to drop off at our place right now. He can't go back home until this is over. I'll be by there in about an hour with a photo of Vince Andrews. If that's the guy in the room, we'll nail him."

"Heck, what are you trying to do to me?"

"Sorry, Greg, this kid is in danger."

"All right, I guess I can hold on for another hour. See you when you get here." Johnson pushed the off button on his cellular phone and set it on the seat next to him. Looking back toward the room, it had been several minutes since his suspect left for ice. Johnson began to get suspicious.

Johnson sat in silence for another ten minutes. Where did Andrews go? Something had to have gone wrong. Nobody goes for ice for fifteen minutes. He contemplated what course of action he should take. "Nuts," he said. "I gotta see what's going on."

He reached for the automatic door lock and pushed the plastic tab forward. All the doors in the Jeep Cherokee unlocked with a dull thud. He grabbed the handle and slowly opened the door.

SLINKING THROUGH THE RUGGED brush next to the hotel, Vince maneuvered himself into position in the empty lot twenty yards directly behind the SUV. He watched silently for several minutes as the man staring at his room talked on a portable telephone. Slowly, he crept toward the target. He gently pressed against the rear of the vehicle. The SUV sat shrouded in darkness, which would serve him well. Vince reached into his belt and pulled out his 9mm automatic, gripped tightly in his right hand.

Vince had been pressed against the rear bumper for a mere two minutes when he heard the locks of the door automatically disengage. He edged himself to the bumper on the driver's side, his breathing steady, his heartbeat unchanged.

He heard the door open all the way as a foot set on the ground.

Like a fog rolling in on the unsuspecting shore, Vince swiftly and silently rounded the corner of the vehicle. Within two seconds, he had the Smith and Wesson 9mm stuck directly in the small of the man's back.

"I'd advise you not to make any sudden movement, friend," Vince said quietly. "Your spinal column will be severed in half if you do."

Vince closed the door of the Cherokee and made a quick search of his prey. He removed the pistol from the man's shoulder holster and stuck it in the back of his pants.

"You've been watching the room all day. Now's your chance to see what it looks like on the inside. Walk over to it and knock on the door."

"Hey, look fella, I don't know what you're talking about," the man said. "You can have all my money. Here, take my wallet," Johnson started to reach behind him, but Vince quickly struck him with the butt of the pistol at the base of his skull. The short, stocky man fell to the ground in pain.

"I give the instructions here," Vince said as the agent climbed to his hands and knees. "You have been found. You are too curious as to who comes in and out of this room. Now it is time for you to find out for yourself. Move!"

The man stood up slowly, rubbing the back of his neck and rolling his head from side to side. He started to look back, but Vince gave him a commanding push toward the hotel room. Understanding the message, the man walked toward the room.

"Knock," Vince ordered when they reached the door.

The man obeyed, rapping twice on the door. Nikolai opened the door slowly, standing inside the dark hotel room, his 9mm fitted with a silencer pointed at the man's chest. The pair entered the room, and Vince closed the door behind them.

"Search him," Nikolai said, still pointing his gun at the man's chest. Vince removed a billfold, two sets of keys, and a money clip from the man's pockets.

"Secure him."

Vince pushed the man into the chair and tied his hands together behind the chair before securing them to the chair itself. Vince tied his ankles to each leg of the chair, then placed several loops of rope around his chest and arms. The man could not move. As soon as he was secure, Nikolai began rummaging through his belongings.

"Well, well, well," Nikolai said, "Agent Greg Johnson, Central Intelligence Agency. I must apologize for not knowing who you are. My personal specialty is the Eastern Hemisphere. No doubt you know who we are."

"It is a routine surveillance of a Russian official on American soil. It's for your own protection," the agent said.

"Don't toy with me, Agent Johnson, I don't have time for it. How many of you are there?"

"Just me."

SMACK! Nikolai backhanded Johnson. His head snapped to the right, blood spewing from his burst lip. "I told you I don't have time for games. Who are you reporting to?"

"Just my boss in Oklahoma Cit—"

SMACK! Nikolai again backhanded him. "Liar! What will it take for you to cooperate with us Comrade Johnson? You have been watching us all afternoon. I want to know why. Who ordered it?"

Before he had a chance to speak, Vince moved over to Johnson and threw a right cross that connected squarely with Johnson's jaw, snapping his head to the side. When his head returned to center, Vince came back with a left. The process continued for several more punches. Johnson tried to anticipate the blows and roll with them, but he had no ability to maneuver. The blood from Johnson's swollen face dripped onto his shirt. His head fell forward, resting limply on his chest like a rag doll.

"It sounds melodramatic, Agent Johnson, but would you care to talk now?" Nikolai asked as he lit up a cigarette.

Johnson struggled to lift his head. His bruised and bloody head was difficult to move. "I got . . . nothing to say . . . that I haven't said . . . already." Blood and saliva dripped from the corner of his mouth onto his pants leg.

"Very well," Nikolai said with a quick glance at his watch. "Perhaps we made a mistake."

Nikolai turned away from the battered agent in the chair and took a long drag on his cigarette. "If we have made such a mistake, I don't think we could justify our actions to our superiors. How could I explain kidnapping an American CIA agent and questioning him under false pretenses?"

Johnson tried to shake his head, but the attempt made him sway. "I don't know."

Nikolai twirled around and stared menacingly at the man, still gripping the 9mm silencer. "I can't," he said as he raised the pistol to the man's forehead and squeezed the trigger.

Johnson's head snapped to the side as his body went limp. Still tied to the chair, his chin rested on his chest. Nikolai walked to the bed and picked up Johnson's wallet, ID badge, and keys. Nikolai placed the wallet in his coat pocket and tossed the hotel key to Vince. "Grab your clothes. We must go now. Before you leave town, check out this man's room. Take care of any problems that might exist." He handed Vince the pistol with the silencer.

Vince tucked it in the front of his pants and quickly grabbed his suitcases. The two Russians, bags in hand, left the room and headed for their vehicles.

"You do understand the importance of not being discovered," Nikolai said to the young assassin. "Our organization is an unknown entity. If you are discovered, it will have implications far beyond your depth of understanding. We will all suffer."

"I understand, sir," Vince replied. In his own mind, he must succeed and return as a hero or spend the rest of his life in a gulag in Siberia . . . if they let him live.

"Good luck Vincent. I hope to see you in two weeks. You will get a hero's welcome upon your return."

Vince simply nodded as he climbed into his truck.

CALDWELL AND JOHNSON SAT in the small hotel room going over some papers. "These are basically forms where you promise not to disclose any information you might have seen or heard involving this operation. Normally, I would have had you sign them first, but this will be okay."

Jason looked at Caldwell uneasily. "Is this going to commit me to some type of job requirement or something?"

"Yeah," Caldwell chuckled, "your ass will belong to the CIA for the next one hundred years." Caldwell walked across the hotel room to the ice chest and pulled out a Coke. "You want one?"

"Sure." Jason finished reading the paperwork and signed both sheets. Caldwell handed him the chilled soda, and Jason drank half of it quickly.

"I'm going to in-brief you on what I believe might be going on. This Friday in San Antonio is the huge NAFTA conference. There will be media coverage everywhere. Mexico's economy is doing extremely poorly. The labor secretary will be at the NAFTA conference instead of the president."

"Why would the Russians want to kill the labor secretary?"

"I don't think they do," Caldwell said walking across the room and picking up the newspaper. He tossed it on the bed in front of Jason.

PRESIDENTIAL HOPEFUL SUPPORTS NAFTA, the headline read. Underneath the headline was a photograph of Senator Jonathan Bowman waving to a crowd.

"You think he's gonna kill the senator?"

"Yes."

"But why? He doesn't have any direct control over foreign policy, does he?"

"Not yet. But he is heavily favored to win the election. It's in Russia's best interest for Senator Bowman to lose the election and keep the current administration in place. Russia's economy is poor and decreasing steadily. The current administration continues to support Russia financially and continues to downsize the US military. We've been watching Russia's domestic issues closely in recent months. Some of the leaders are unhappy with their government. It's suspected that a coup is possible in two years, if not sooner. If the coup is done quickly with minimum bloodshed, there is no doubt that the current administration would simply go along with the new government."

Jason nodded his head. "I get it. If they eliminate Bowman, there's not another candidate strong enough to run successfully to defeat the president."

"Right. I'm sure the Russians are counting on Congress and the American people to 'rally' around the president in this time of 'crisis'. That would keep the new guys in place. That's my theory, anyway. Let's hope I'm close, at least." Caldwell picked up the paper and stared at the picture again. "Look, I know it's been a long day, but it's almost over. I think we have the situation under control. I've notified the feds in OKC, and they should be arriving within two hours. As soon as I get my federal warrant faxed in, I'll head over to the Ramada Inn and join my partner in his surveillance. Hell,

I'm already late and he's not answering his phone. It's probably better if you stay here until we get control of Andrews."

Jason nodded. "He's my dad."

"What?"

"Senator Bowman. He's my father. Little known fact outside a few small circles. He and my mom divorced shortly after I was born. We haven't stayed in contact because my mom wanted it kept out of the press so I wouldn't get hassled over the years."

"We've got to get word to him immediately," Caldwell said.

"I'd like to," Jason said sullenly. "But I've never met the man."

VINCE PULLED INTO THE PARKING LOT of the Holiday Inn on the southern edge of Enid, east of Vance. It wasn't long before he found the room number matching the key in his hand.

Cautiously, Vince crept up to the door, scanning all directions, though primarily focused on the door in front of him. The lights were on in the room. Pressing his ear to the door, he couldn't hear any movement inside

The Russian assassin moved the key toward the lock in the door. The metal key slid silently into the grooves of the lock. Pistol in his right hand, Vince took a deep breath as he grabbed the key and doorknob. In one swift movement, he unlocked the door and flung it open.

The door flew all the way open and Vince entered in a low crouch. Quickly scanning the room, his eyes fell on the lone figure sitting on the far edge of the bed nearest the other wall. The man's eyes widened as he focused on the assassin who now stood before him.

"YOU!"

Vince brought the pistol up and placed the man in his sights, firing off three quick rounds. The muffled shots struck home, and the man twisted and buckled as the bullets hit him.

No sooner had the man's body fell to the floor; a car pulled up and parked next to his truck. "Damn," Vince barked. Tucking the pistol away, Vince closed the door and walked to his truck. He was angry at himself for being careless. Surely, the driver didn't see him. Could he have seen the gun? Vince cursed to himself as he climbed in and cranked the engine. The dirty truck roared to life, and he backed out of the parking space, his eyes locked on the room he just left.

CHAPTER 43

September 12, 1995

THE NOISE SOUNDED unusual; perhaps it came from something playing on the television. Jason turned off the water in the sink as he reached for a towel. "Hey, Agent Caldwell, what are you doing out there?" he yelled from the bathroom as he dried his face.

He finished with the towel, placing it on the rack as he opened the door.

"Oh my God," he exclaimed as he saw Caldwell's motionless body on the floor. Blood pooled on his chest, spilling over his sides. Jason quickly scanned the room. No sign of disturbance. They were alone.

Hearing a car door shut and an engine start outside, he dashed to the door. Flinging it open, a familiar truck raced off . . . driven by Vince Andrews. They were both shocked when they saw each other. Vince smiled, waving his pistol in a salute as the truck speed away. Jason glanced up and down the sidewalk at the hotel.

A family twenty yards away came home from dinner, and another couple two rooms away climbed into their car. That's why Vince kept going. Otherwise, he, too, would be a dead man.

Dashing back inside, he knelt beside Caldwell. "Hey, buddy, can you hear me?" Nothing.

He felt for a pulse and breathed a sigh of relief when he found one. Quickly, he examined the body—three bullet wounds spilled blood everywhere. Caldwell's once white shirt now had a deep scarlet pool. Jason leaped for the phone and dialed nine-one-one.

"Nine-one-one, how can I help you?"

"Yes, a man's been shot."

"Is the man still breathing?"

"Yes, he's still alive, but send someone here fast."

"What is your location?"

"I'm at the Holiday Inn on Van Buren, room 132."

"Stay calm, sir. We'll have someone there soon. What is your name?"

"Jason . . . Jason Conrad."

"Okay, Jason, what kind of wound is it?"

"Uh—I don't know. Bullet wounds. Three of 'em. Two in the chest and one in the stomach."

"Do you hear any gasping noises when he breathes?"

"No. Look, I'm not a doctor. You've got to send someone here right away. The killer is getting away, and I've got to stop him!"

"I thought you said he's alive? Jason, we need you to stay by the—"

Jason hung up the phone as he knelt by Caldwell. Time slipped away. Grabbing a pillow, he stuck it under his feet, treating the wounded CIA man for shock. He folded some towels and pressed them to the wounds.

"Hang tight, Caldwell, help is on the way. I'm gonna borrow your vehicle for a while. I'll get back to you." There was no response from the bleeding figure on the floor. Jason grabbed the car keys and pistol and bolted for the door.

When Jason grabbed the door handle, he realized how bloody his hands were. He climbed into Caldwell's dark sedan, threw the pistol under the seat, and cranked the engine. Picking up a towel from the floorboard, he wiped the blood off his hands. Then he proceeded to wipe the door handle and steering column. Blood was everywhere. He felt nauseas as he noticed the blood covering his pants and shirt. No sooner had he pulled out of the parking lot than he heard the sirens. Once on Van Buren, he headed south, then took a quick right toward Vance. Glancing in his rearview mirror before he turned, he could see lights flashing in the distance behind him.

What was he going to do? For the first time, he realized everything Caldwell told him was true. Vince was a Russian agent. Vince had somehow found out about Caldwell and eliminated him. Now, Jason was involved and Vince knew it. He was probably next on Vince's hit list. Again. A story so farfetched, no one would believe it. Vince Andrews, second lieutenant, U.S. Air Force, was a Russian assassin.

Jason drove to the base, though he wasn't sure why. Clean clothes were a must, no matter what else he did. He made the left to go into the front gate at Vance AFB as panic set in. What if the gate guard stopped him? How would he explain the blood? As he approached the gate, he saw the guard talking on the telephone. Too late to stop and turn around, Jason inched the vehicle toward the gate. The guard stepped out of the small shack and put out his hand for Jason to stop. Only four feet away from him now, the light from the shack illuminated the car.

THE PARAMEDICS ARRIVED SHORTLY after the police. They found Aaron Caldwell's riddled figure sprawled on the floor, bleeding severely, but still breathing. Kim entered first.

"Oh, man," she said to her partner, "it's gonna be a bad one."

"What have we here?" Al asked the sheriff's deputy treating the fallen man. Al scanned the room before kneeling beside the body. Two other officers in the room made sure no one touched anything.

They placed the bloody figure on a stretcher and secured him in the ambulance. Al sat in the back of the ambulance to make sure the I.V. kept running. Kim jumped in the front, and in a matter of seconds, the medical vehicle zipped out of the parking lot, lights flashing and siren blaring, toward St. Mary's Hospital downtown.

"Come on buddy," Al said to the unconscious figure, "hang on. It's only a couple of miles. We'll be there in a few minutes."

Kim continued to weave through traffic, an aggressive driver who stayed just on the safe side of reckless. "How is he, Al?" Kim asked over her shoulder.

"He's still breathing . . . slowly. His heart rate is dropping. Blood pressure is dropping. I think we might lose him. Come on pal, hang on!"

Kim pulled the ambulance into the circular driveway of Saint Mary's Hospital to see the team from the Emergency Room standing by, waiting for them. She brought the ambulance smoothly to a stop, set the parking brake, and leaped out of the front seat. The ER team moved like lightning as soon as the vehicle stopped. By the time Kim reached the back of the vehicle, the patient was being removed. Kim jumped in to ease the strain on the others and help balance the patient. Al monitored the I.V. and the patient's breathing throughout the entire process. The stretcher's retractable legs extended and locked in place when removed from the ambulance. The ER team quickly wheeled Caldwell into the hospital emergency room.

The doctor met them at the door. "Okay, what have we got?"

THE GUARD WAVED JASON THROUGH and focused again on the telephone. Jason's heart skipped a beat. *I'd rather be lucky than good any day.* He pulled into the dorm parking lot. Looking around, he didn't see Vince's truck in the immediate area, but then he really didn't expect to. Jason ran to his room and locked the door behind him. He quickly changed out of the bloody clothes, stepped into the shower for a quick rinse, and put on some clean clothes. He put the bloody clothes in a plastic bag and took them outside to a dumpster.

Jason returned to his room. He paced the room several times. It was clear where Vince learned to fight. He was a trained killer. *If that's the case, why am I going after him? Am I going after him?* He was confused, angry, shocked. *Yes, he's trying to kill my father.*

Stepping out the door, he stood in the dark shadows of the hallway staring at the dorm across the parking lot. He could see Vince's window from here, the lights in his room still out. Several moments passed as he watched and waited. Nothing. He went back in his room and dialed the number again. Still no answer.

The police would be looking for him soon, which meant they would eventually contact the base. The SP's would close the base down and he wouldn't be able to leave. What was he going to do? If Caldwell was right, Vince was headed to San Antonio to assassinate his father. He could call the police; he *should* call the police and let them handle it from here. But he suspected they wouldn't believe him. By the time they decided to check out Jason's story, his father would be dead and Vince would have disappeared.

Maybe he could find a clue or something. If only he could offer evidence to the authorities. He thought it might make up for any trouble he caused with the test fiasco. He was thinking rationally as his thoughts jumped in and out of his head each second.

"Screw it!" he said. He could leave it up to those whose job it was to handle these things, but no one would believe him. By the time Jason convinced them his story was true, Vince would have killed someone else and been long gone. Jason ran to his closet to grab an overnight bag, and then remembered it was still in the trunk of the sedan. He flung the door open and jumped into Caldwell's rented sedan. He drove off base and took a right on Fox Boulevard. When he reached Highway 81, he turned south and headed for Texas and the city of San Antonio.

CHAPTER 44

September 12, 1995

VIKTOR SAT IN HIS OFFICE at the end of the hall on the second floor of the Dacha Complex. Holding his face in his hands, he no longer presented the image of a strong leader who could lead a second Russian Revolution. He had just received word there had been a CIA case officer killed in Enid and another in the hospital. The Americans were on to them and he could do nothing to abort the mission.

Nikolai, had somehow been followed to the United States. The implications were enormous. Section Nine clearly was not as secret as they believed. If word of Section Nine had leaked out, then word of the coup was out as well.

The knock on his door snapped him out of his thoughts, and Viktor turned his head in that direction. "Come in," he gasped. Moving slowly was more out of necessity than desire. He was weak, and for the first time in his life, felt old. The door opened and in popped his old friend Aleksandr.

"Good morning, comrade," Aleksandr said. The general moved in front of Viktor's desk, his hands clasped behind his back.

"What brings you here, old friend?" Viktor asked. It was not that he cared at the moment. Viktor was not interested in socializing.

"I regret that it is business this time. The communications center has detected an increase in communications into the American embassy of three hundred percent within the past six hours. We just received word the American Ambassador will be leaving within thirty minutes to return to the United States at the president's request."

"This is not uncommon, Aleksandr," Viktor said. "We see this behavior periodically. They overreact in some cases. Sometimes they like to test their systems and evacuation plans."

"But they are not testing it this time, are they, Viktor?" Aleksandr said. Aleksandr's cheeks turned a slight pink color as he clenched his fists to suppress his anger. "We are in grave danger, comrade. The committee has gone to great lengths to develop a strategy that would ensure a smooth change of government. How could we have been so foolish as to listen to your plan? Don't you see what you've done? We are doomed. The Americans know what we are doing." He gasped for breath as he berated his old friend. Aleksandr walked around the large oak desk and stuck his finger in Viktor's chest. "You! It was your driver who did this. It was your man in Section Nine who devised such an insane plan as to assassinate Senator Bowman. Viktor, you will be responsible for this." Aleksandr was shaking now. He had never talked to Viktor this way.

Viktor glared at the shaking man in front of him. They were finished before it began. The betrayals were unfolding, with the committee already searching for a scapegoat. Viktor was tired, old, and weak, but he was a fighter. Slowly, he rose to stand eye to eye with his accuser.

"We are responsible for this you, spineless coward," Viktor boomed. "You are all educated, intelligent men who knew the consequences of your actions. If you are looking for someone to toss to the Americans when this is over, fine. Tell them it was me. It does not matter. But don't you try and convince yourself you were not involved. You are. All of you are. You are all cowards!"

Viktor moved from behind his desk, walked to the door of his office, and opened it. "Now leave my office, little man. I see this is how you repay decades of friendship."

Aleksandr lowered his head in shame, realizing perhaps for the first time what he'd done. He moved from behind the desk, then looked toward the door. "Viktor, I—"

"OUT, COWARD!" Viktor boomed. A fire burned in his eyes now. Viktor had reason to be angry. Aleksandr moved briskly out the door without looking into Viktor's eyes. Viktor closed the door behind him, the proud, angry man quickly becoming the sullen figure who had occupied the room just minutes before.

Viktor walked to the window, gazing at the dull gray sky. This was not the ending he had dreamed of for his distinguished career. Where did he go wrong? He missed his Helga deeply. She always kept him focused; pointed him in the right direction. A single tear rolled down his wrinkled face unnoticed.

Shuffling back to his desk, Viktor sat in the large chair behind it.

Reaching into the bottom drawer, he pulled out a wooden box from which he took a shiny pistol. Viktor had taken the pistol from a German officer during the Battle of Stalingrad. He checked the magazine, jammed it into the stock, and inserted a round into the chamber. Placing the barrel to his temple, Viktor pulled the trigger.

CHAPTER 45

September 13, 1995

KATHY SAT ON THE COUCH flipping through *Cosmopolitan*. It was a simple living room in a small house in Southwest San Antonio. Kathy set the magazine on the coffee table and turned on the television for the five o'clock news. She leaned back on the large comfortable couch with her legs tucked under her, one of the fringed throw pillows wrapped in her arms across her chest. Downtown San Antonio was abuzz with national attention from the NAFTA convention taking place this week. Many jobs were created to prepare for the event, and an estimated $2.3 million would be brought into the local economy before the event ever took place. The president would not be making an appearance in San Antonio, but his potential opponent in the upcoming election, Senator Jonathan Bowman, would be. Suddenly a familiar site appeared on the television:

> "In other news, Oklahoma authorities are still searching for this man, Jason Conrad, of Enid, Oklahoma, in connection with the shooting of two men in Enid last night."

Kathy's jaw dropped as Jason's picture appeared in the upper right-hand corner of the screen.

> "Conrad, a lieutenant in the U.S. Air Force stationed at Vance Air Force Base, has been missing since last night. Authorities won't say whether Conrad shot the two men. One is believed to have died. Conrad is currently the only person being sought in the shootings. Officials at Vance Air Force Base in Enid had no comment on the investigation."

"What the . . . Jason?" How could Jason have done such a thing? When she left Enid, nothing appeared wrong. He'd been too focused on pilot training. Maybe he washed out. That might have sent him over the edge.

Kathy bolted up from the couch and went into her bedroom. She grabbed her phone and dialed Jason's number in Enid. It rang eight times with no answer. Obviously if he was sought by the police, the last place he would be was home. Next she called Chicaros. After two attempts, someone picked up at the bar.

"Hello? Hi, it's Kathy. I'm in San Antonio."

"Hi, Kathy, how are you doing? You want to come back to work?"

"No thanks, I'm fine here. Look, I was calling to ask you something. I was sitting here watching the news and I just saw—"

"The story on the Conrad boy."

"Yes, Jason."

"Didn't you go out with him for a while?"

"Yes. We're very good friends, or I guess we were good friends. Do you know anything about what happened?"

"Well, from what I've gathered from the grapevine and my friends in the police department, there were two shootings in town last night. One at the Ramada and the other at the Holiday Inn. At the Ramada, the guy they found dead was in a room registered to your friend. The guy at the Holiday Inn got shot, but is in critical care at Saint Mary's. Jason had been seen hanging out with the guy most of the afternoon."

"Oh my God," Kathy muttered. "It can't be true. He never got in fights . . . I can't believe it."

"Well dear, that's what the current poop is. I guess you should be glad you're not here. It's a real mess right now. In fact, don't be surprised if they come for you eventually, just to ask you questions, of course."

"Thanks for the information. Take care of yourself, I've got to go." Kathy placed the phone on the desk as she stood up. What should she do? How could she have been so wrong? Jason can't be guilty of those crimes, but it looked as though all the evidence pointed to him.

Thirty minutes passed, as she sat there contemplating what course of action she might need to take. The phone in the kitchen rang, shattering the silence.

She entered the kitchen and picked up the telephone. "Hello," she said, running her hand through her hair.

"Kathy, it's Jason. I've got to see you."

Kathy sat in astonishment. She was unsure of everything at this point.

"Conrad, what's going on? I just saw on the news—"

"What did it say?"

"That you might have shot two men and they're looking for you right now."

"Kathy, don't worry, I didn't shoot anybody. I need your help. I'll explain everything to you. Things are a little crazy right now."

"A little crazy is probably an understatement. Your picture is being flashed all over the five o'clock news."

"Oh, Christ," Jason moaned. "Kathy, I need to know, will you help me?"

"I'll talk to you, Jason. Maybe you can explain all this to me. The news is saying you're a killer, but I think I know you better. Where are you?"

"I'm at the Riverwalk right now."

"Okay, I want you to go downtown to Market Square to a restaurant called La Margarita's. Meet me there in one hour. Try to get a table outside."

"Market Square, La Margarita's, one hour, got it. Thanks, Kathy, you don't know how much I—"

CLICK.

Kathy started to grab her purse when the phone rang again.

"Hello," a familiar voice said.

Kathy's face turned grim as she recognized the voice immediately.

"You're a hard woman to track down these days."

JASON GLARED AT THE PHONE and slowly replaced the receiver. He stepped away from the phone booth and into the crowd on the Riverwalk.

The scenic Riverwalk sat in the middle of San Antonio. A small, winding river thirty to forty feet wide meandered through the downtown area. Overlooking the river were numerous restaurants, shops, and hotels. The aroma of authentic Mexican cuisine permeated the air up and down the river, the smell of food enhanced by the variety of flora paralleling the sidewalk. At one end lay the multi-story Rivercenter Mall, which contained an area for live outdoor concerts. A series of escalators encased in glass took people to all levels of the mall and allowed them a view of the stage. Several small gondolas floated along the river, some of which served as floating restaurants. Various outdoor restaurants had several pairs of Mexican men strumming their guitars, serenading the customers. A festive atmosphere permeated throughout the Riverwalk.

Jason walked along the river, back to the multi-level mall and the parking lot next to it. The setting sun struggled to shine through the branches of the many trees overhanging the river. A cool breeze blew between the buildings. He finally reached the T-intersection in the river and turned back toward the Marriott Hotel.

Crossing over a stone bridge, Jason noticed activity on the outskirts of the hotel's property. There were workmen everywhere, hauling lights, lumber, chairs, tables, and everything else one could imagine. As he approached the patio, a man dressed in a suit and wearing sunglasses stepped up to meet him. The man stood taller than Jason and appeared well-built. His crossed arms in the front of his body served a dual purpose: it gave him an ominous appearance, and it hid the bulge under his jacket. Jason also noticed the wire running from his collar to his left ear, no doubt one of the Secret Service advance teams. It would be difficult to reach his father under these circumstances. He'd have to do it the hard way.

CHAPTER 46

September 13, 1995

THE BUS STATION downtown was crowded and the evening bus for Dallas began loading. A large group of elderly tourists dominated the Greyhound. Vagrants trying to stay out of the cool night air occupied several benches in the waiting area. The stench of exhaust fumes filled the room, and sounds from the mass of people, their movements and voices, echoed off the walls. The station itself was filthy, and once the occupants of the Dallas-bound bus boarded, the vagrants clearly stood out.

Vince entered the front door, his eyes scanning the crowd. Wearing the starched button-down shirt and khaki pants he was accustomed to, he didn't blend in too well. Silently, he cursed himself for making such a careless mistake. It wouldn't happen again. He was getting sloppy, careless. Was he nervous, or was he losing his edge for this kind of work?

He pulled the key out of his pocket, rechecking the number. Scanning the area, he saw a series of lockers along the far wall on the left. He meandered through the dissipating crowd until he reached the lockers. Vince searched the locker numbers until he saw number seventy-nine. Slowly, he placed the key in the lock and turned it. Cautiously, he opened the door as he checked for a possible booby-trap. Why be so careful? His people had set this up. He was just being cautious. No more sloppiness. Trust no one. He peered inside and saw there were no wires. Opening the locker, he reached inside to retrieve the blue gym bag. Not bothering to glimpse inside the bag, he closed the door, left the key in the lock, and headed outside to the truck he'd stolen earlier that day.

The ride back to the hotel didn't take as long as it had to get to the station. The evening traffic thinned out. Vince kept the bag in the seat next to him, glancing at it periodically on the ride to the hotel. Parking the truck, Vince grabbed the bag, walked up the stairs to his room, and gently placed the contents of the bag on the bed.

Everything was there, as promised. Eight special tubes of the odorless, powerful plastic explosive Semtex, electronic blasting caps, and twelve feet of antenna wire that would act as a fuse. Perhaps the most brilliant item, the detonator, was a complex array of modern cellular technology with a trigger, built into a cellular telephone that actually worked. The detonator itself, placed above the blasting caps, would be attached to the explosives. The antenna fuse ran from the blasting cap through the detonator and out for several feet as required for best reception. The detonator attached to a cellular phone. When Vince dialed the number, the system armed on the fourth ring. Then, to set off the bomb, all the user had to do was hit re-dial on the cellular phone. On the second ring, BOOM! The delayed rings were installed as a safety device. To either stop the arming or the detonation, the user simply hung up the phone before the designated ring.

Vince pulled out the folder with the plan for the security posted around the hotel. He scanned the plan briefly as he sipped on a soda. This, for the time being, was not his main concern. The second folder he went through was the more important one. The limousines for Senator Bowman were supplied by First Class Limousines of San Antonio. They had the two best limos put aside for the occasion. They were inspected thoroughly earlier in the day and were currently locked up in a garage downtown. Pulling out the schematics on the limousine, Vince calculated how he would implement his weapon.

He would mount the bomb next to the fuel tank. Placement of the antenna from the detonator would be easy. Putting the bomb in place would be the difficult part.

The plans stated that two guards watched the limos constantly, rotating on twelve-hour shifts. Vince smiled when he read that. Twelve hours is far too long for someone to watch anything. Boredom and restlessness eventually lead to sleep and carelessness. He decided the guards would be easy to work around.

LA MARGARITA'S SAT ON THE SIDE of Market Square. Market Square, a small, colorful conglomeration of restaurants and small shops, sat on the edge of the downtown area, but was crowded at the peak dinner hours, despite it being a Tuesday night. Jason managed to get a table for two on the patio outside nestled in the far back corner under the overhang of some trees. He had another fifteen minutes before Kathy arrived, so he ordered a frozen margarita and munched on chips and salsa.

Jason's eyes scanned the crowd, searching for faces he knew. He also looked for faces possibly searching for him. By the time he finished his margarita, he glanced at his watch. Kathy showed ten minutes late. She had never been late before. Now he realized how much he missed her. Kathy was a genuine, honest person who treated him well, and for the most part, he had ignored her. No wonder she lost interest.

He ordered a second margarita. As he sat there feeling sorry for himself, Kathy walked up to the table.

"Kathy," Jason said as he stood up to greet her. He grabbed her in his arms and hugged her.

Kathy smiled as she pushed him away. "I guess you're happy to see me."

"You wouldn't believe."

"I'm a little confused by what's going on." Kathy sat down and an elderly Mexican waiter took her order for a Margarita. They made small talk for several minutes until both of their margaritas arrived.

"Now tell me what happened? Why is everyone looking for you?"

"How long do you want to sit here?"

"Well, I guess 'til I can't drink anymore margaritas."

"Okay, first of all, I didn't kill or shoot anyone," Jason began. "I do, however, know who shot one of those guys."

"Did you see him? The T.V. said one was in your hotel room and the other was with you all day."

"Kathy, when have I ever had time to check into a hotel room in the middle of the day?"

She nodded her head as she sipped her drink. "Good point. Then who is this guy you were with all day?"

"Well, er, he. . , uh . . . he's a CIA agent. Actually, he is what you call a case officer."

"CIA?" she said, an incredulous look on her face.

"Ssshhh, keep your voice down."

"I'm sorry. Okay then, if he's CIA, who shot him? A Russian agent?"

"Yes."

She paused before responding, her eyes searching his face. "You're serious, aren't you?"

"Yes, I am."

"But I thought you said you knew who shot him. Did you mean you saw who it was, or you knew him?"

"Both. And you know him, too."

Kathy leaned forward and placed both hands on the table, her eyes wide. "Oh, God. Don't tell me, I don't want to know . . . no, wait, I have to know. Tell me."

Jason sat back in the metal chair and took a deep breath. "It was Vince."

Connecting the dots, Jason told her how Lenny's death led him to the shocking discovery of the money and tests. He told her how he took them to his room to protect Lenny. He related how Vince had had a minor outburst when he discovered the tests were gone. Then the OSI entered the picture.

Jason disclosed the details of Alonzo Jacobs' search for the thief and told her how he had been removed from flying status. Someone broke into Lenny's room and ransacked it. This happened the day after Jason explained to Vince he had found no test in Lenny's room as he packed it up.

He told Kathy about the mysterious truck that fired at him two nights ago. He was sure Vince ran him off the road into the wheat field. It seemed like weeks ago, he told Kathy, but it was only yesterday that he'd met the CIA officer, Aaron Caldwell. He learned about the assassination attempt on his father, Senator Bowman. He explained all the details of the day, ending with the shooting of Caldwell and Vince driving away.

Kathy sat stoically, observing him closely as he told his story. Jason talked for twenty minutes without stopping, covering every detail, occasionally backtracking to fill in a missing point. He wanted her to believe him. She lightly ran her finger around the edge of her glass, collecting the salt sitting on the rim. "You're not lying to me, are you?" she asked.

"No. My God, do you think I have the imagination required to make up a story like that?"

"No," she said, as she put her drink on the table and looked at him. "So what are you going to do?"

"I'm not sure, but I only have a couple of days to figure it out."

"So you really are convinced Vince is some kind of Russian spy?"

"Well, it sounds odd, but everything I've seen and heard points to him."

"It's odd. Vince didn't seem capable of such . . . scheming. He always reminded me of some dumb jock from high school. All brawn and no brains, the kind women die for."

"Thanks a lot," Jason said.

"Hey, tiger, we had a chance. I threw myself at you and you weren't interested. You were too busy to pay any attention to me."

"I know, I know." He glanced at the other patrons in the restaurant wondering if their lives were as complicated as his was right now. Jason had strong feelings for Kathy, but wasn't sure whether now was the time to bring up the subject.

"Why don't you call your father and tell him what's going on?"

"I wish it were that easy. He and my mother separated when I was two. It must have been ugly because we didn't hear from him much after that, and I haven't seen him since. He remarried and entered the world of politics. We became a footnote in a chapter of his life story. If I had a number, I'd call. Believe me. But even he wouldn't believe it. I haven't talked to him . . . ever."

"What about calling the police?"

"I tried," he said. "They said the Senator doesn't have a son. They think I'm a kook who's trying to kill the Senator."

"Jason, I'm so sor—"

"Would the señor and señorita care for another drink?" the waiter said.

"No thanks," Jason said. "Check, please."

Kathy sat staring at him, a slight smile on her face. The waiter turned his back and started to walk away. Jason leaned forward in his seat, gazing into Kathy's large brown eyes. He wanted to open up his heart to tell her how he truly felt about her. On cue, the waiter arrived back at the table.

"I'll be your cashier for you," he said, setting the check face down on the table. His voice shattered the moment.

Jason looked down, briefly, then at the ill-timed waiter. "Thanks."

He looked back at Kathy, and she giggled. Their brief moment gone. Jason realized that maybe he still had a chance with Kathy. He gazed at her longingly when something caught his attention.

He was being watched. He sensed it.

Jason glanced around the restaurant, searching the faces in the crowd. He saw nothing unusual. Then, as if on cue, one of the guitar players finished a serenade at a nearby table and walked on to another table, Jason saw him.

Across the courtyard of the Market Square, a large fat man, sitting on a bench, reading a newspaper. Only he wasn't reading it, he was looking at it. And he looked at Jason. Back and forth, as if to make something register.

"Jason, what's wrong?" Kathy asked, obviously aware of his quick change of disposition.

"Don't turn around," he said. "There's a guy sitting across the courtyard, looking at a newspaper."

"So, there's no crime in that."

"I'm sure he's watching me. He looks at the paper, then back at me constantly."

"Do you think your picture is in the paper?"

"It could be. Look, you need to get out of here. Get up and walk to the ladies' room. When you get there, go ahead and leave any way you can. Lose yourself in the crowd. As long as I sit here they won't think anything is unusual."

"They?"

"Well, I'm assuming there might be more. Hurry, we've got to get moving. I'll leave five minutes after you. I'll call you in an hour or two."

Kathy stood up slowly, unsure of what was going on around her. "You be careful, Jason. Call me as soon as you get back to where ever it is you're going." She gathered her purse and disappeared around the corner inside the restaurant.

Jason pulled a twenty out of his wallet and set it under the candle in the center of the table. He sat there uncomfortably as if he were waiting for Kathy to return. He scanned the patio, occasionally looking at the fat man. Kathy had been gone maybe two minutes when the fat man's wife showed up in the courtyard with a police officer. The fat man first pointed at the newspaper then in his direction. Damn! They were on to him.

Looking around, Jason realized his options were limited. He slowly rose from the table and walked into the restaurant. He looked around for Kathy, but didn't see her anywhere. Hopefully she made it out of the restaurant. Through a window, he watched the fat man and the police officer, who talked into his radio.

CHAPTER 47

September 13, 1995

H E STOOD AT THE BAR for a moment, fumbling with a box of matches. The bathroom. Maybe there's a window. Jason walked toward the bathroom and slid the matches into his pocket. Glancing out the side window of the restaurant, two more policemen approached the fat man.

Out of sight of all the windows, he dashed into the bathroom. The small facility had two stalls, two urinals, and no window. Damn. He walked out of the bathroom and scanned the restaurant again. Out the front door, sixty feet away, he saw two police officers scanning the restaurant. Apparently they were either waiting for him to leave or coming up with a plan to safely get him with minimum disturbance in the restaurant.

Then it hit him. Jason dashed back into the bathroom and locked the door behind him. Grabbing the trashcan, he dragged it across the ceramic tile floor, pulling off the lid. Inside were some paper towels. He glanced at the ceiling and saw a smoke detector. Filling the trashcan with all the paper towels he could find, Jason pulled the matches out of his pocket and quickly set the trashcan ablaze. He stayed long enough to be sure the fire would not go out, then he unlocked the door and strolled back to the bar. No sooner had he reached the bar then a young Hispanic boy rose from the table where his family ate and walked toward the bathroom.

Smoke bellowed from under the door and Jason wondered why the alarm didn't go off. He glimpsed back toward the courtyard. The two policemen now stood inside the door of the restaurant talking to a man who appeared to be the manager. The police officers eyes continue to scan the restaurant. Apparently, they had lost sight of Jason.

The young boy approached the bathroom as the smoke seeped from under the door. He slowed his approach to the door and reached out for the handle. While watching the smoke billowing around his ankles, he touched the handle of the door and pushed it open.

The fire in the trashcan was fully a blaze. The bright light and brief blast of heat hit the child as he opened the door, scaring him. He let go of the door and ran back to his table, screaming.

People in the restaurant looked in the boy's direction as the boy stopped dead in his tracks, five feet from Jason, screaming.

"Fuego! Fuego! There is a fire in the bathroom!"

Everyone looked at the boy except Jason, who watched the policemen. They were looking at the small boy also. Then they saw him.

The two police officers started walking toward him, their hands on their weapons. Suddenly, a woman screamed.

Jason turned as the woman walked out of the ladies restroom next to the men's bathroom. She stopped, staring at the ground as smoke billowed around her.

"Fire! Fire!" she screamed. At that moment, the fire alarm in the building finally went off. The loud shrill of the alarm pierced the atmosphere of the restaurant. Two seconds later, the water sprinklers overhead came on and pandemonium ensued.

Everyone in the restaurant bolted from their seats and headed for the door. Parents gathered children, husbands grabbed their wives, and all headed for the one exit in the front of the restaurant. Jason saw through the panicked crowd that the two police officers were being pushed back. They lost sight of him again.

He used that opportunity to slip back out onto the patio. The traffic jam at the front door had caused some of the patrons to head for the patio, too. Jason scanned the courtyard outside the restaurant. The policemen all headed for the front door. None were in sight. Neither was the fat man and his wife. Jason hopped over the small fence surrounding the patio and went straight to the alley next to the restaurant, leaving the mass of confusion behind him as he disappeared into the darkness.

KATHY DROVE HER CAR through the crowded downtown streets. She thought about what Jason told her. Obviously Jason had feelings for her, but his actions were a little too strange. He's a suspected killer wanted by the police. He had too many problems for her to become involved with right now.

A loud siren took her attention to the road as several firetrucks, their lights flashing, zoomed by her heading in the other direction. Kathy pulled over to the side of the road until they passed. She pulled back into traffic and entered the interstate. The trip home took twenty minutes, most of which she spent going over her brief conversation with Jason.

Pulling into her driveway, she glanced at her watch. It was nine-fifteen. She climbed out of her car and started walking toward the door. Halfway there, she heard a noise behind her.

"Hi there, stranger."

She turned at the sound of the familiar voice.

"Vince! What are you doing here?"

ALONZO JACOBS SAT IN HIS LIVING ROOM in boxer shorts and T-shirt. Sipping his coffee, he read the article for the third time.

The paper verified the story he'd heard at work earlier in the afternoon: Jason Conrad was wanted for shooting two men, one of whom died. Now, they wanted him for murder. A picture of Jason, in his dress blues, accompanied the story. Alonzo wondered what could have gone wrong. The boy didn't seem unstable. He'd been proven innocent of stealing the tests. Alonzo didn't think he'd been too hard on the boy. Perhaps he had problems that never came up.

The news came on at ten o'clock. Alonzo turned up the volume. He glanced over at his wife, curled up on the couch asleep. The raised volume didn't faze her.

After several news items covering international subjects, the story of Jason and the shootings aired, even before the latest on the NAFTA convention downtown. This story had more detail. It showed the locations of the shootings and released the names of the two men. The media had somehow acquired footage from Jason's UPT class and had pictures of him walking around in his flight suit. They mentioned someone fitting his description might have been seen near Dallas, but the authorities hadn't confirmed that information yet. The newscast ended with photo of Jason flashed upon the screen with a one-eight-hundred number for people to call with any information they might have.

Alonzo copied the telephone number without thinking about it. It might be something he'd need later.

VINCE LEANED AGAINST HER CAR, his hands tucked into his pockets. "I was in town on personal business and I wanted to see you. How have you been?"

Kathy gripped her purse tightly as it hung over her shoulder. "Fine. Fine. I'm a little shocked you're here, that's all. How long have you been in town?"

"A day or two. I'm on emergency leave right now. I'll fly back to Enid this weekend."

"Oh, I see . . ." she said, turning away from him. Her mind raced with the information Jason had given her less than an hour ago.

"Look, I know it's late, but I was wondering if we could get together sometime and go out for a drink. I've missed you. I hope you'll come back to Enid."

She hesitated a moment. She had no real desire to spend time with him, and she knew his offer of going out for a drink really meant let's go to bed. But she was searching for answers.

"Well, what about right now? I'm not working tomorrow. Actually, I don't have a job yet, but I can look for a job in the afternoon. Let's go somewhere and talk."

Vince replied quickly, "Uh, tonight's not good, I've got things to do tonight. I mean, I've got to get to bed because I've got things to do tomorrow. Maybe an early dinner tomorrow?"

"Okay," she replied. Vince waffled for some reason. He seemed uncomfortable. It was as if he were doing something he shouldn't.

"Great, I'll tell you what—I'll call you in the morning."

"No, that won't work. I'll be out job hunting all morning and in the early afternoon. Why don't you give me your address, and I'll meet you at five?"

"Well, uh, can't I meet you at a restaurant? I mean, you don't want to go to my place, do you?"

He had something to hide, all right. He always wanted her to come back to his place. She stepped closer to him, running her finger along the seam of his shirt. "Isn't that the ultimate idea, big guy? I figured I'd cut out some of the hard work for you."

"Who could argue with that? Davy Crockett Hotel, Room 422. I guess I'll see you at five." He leaned over to kiss her. She slowly leaned forward to acknowledge his advances, pulling her head away at the last moment.

"I guess you'll have to wait until tomorrow," she said.

Vince turned and retreated down the driveway. "I guess I will," he said over his shoulder. Kathy watched him walk off into the night.

She walked into her house, setting her purse on the kitchen counter. Instinctively, she reached under the counter and picked up the phone book. Kathy flipped through it until she found the number for the Davy Crockett Hotel. She dialed the seven digit number. The phone answered on the third ring.

"Davy Crockett Hotel," a man's voice answered.

"Yes, could you ring Vince Andrews' room?"

"One moment, please."

Kathy stood in the quiet kitchen of her house waiting for the man to come back on the line.

"I'm sorry, we don't have a guest registered under that name."

"What?"

"I said we have no guests under the name Andrews or Vince."

"Then could you tell me if Room 422 is occupied?"

"Let's see . . . uh, yes, ma'am, it is."

"Then who is it registered to?"

"I'm sorry, ma'am. I can't give out that information."

Damn. "Thank you, I must be mistaken." She hung up the telephone and stood alone in the kitchen. There was a puzzle here, and the pieces didn't fit.

Kathy crossed into the living room and sat on the couch. The television sprang to life as she clicked on the remote. She curled up, held the pillow tight against her chest, and stared blankly at the TV. Kathy sat in the darkness except for the light from the television. She resumed staring at the screen. What was she going to do?

RRRIINNG!

The telephone broke her concentration, and she grabbed it as it began the second ring.

"Hello," she said.

"Kathy? It's me."

"I thought it might be you," recognizing Jason's voice. "What's going on?"

"I wanted to make sure you made it home okay. I was worried about you."

"You were worried about me? Jason, you're the one with the police after him. Are you sure you shouldn't just turn yourself in?"

"No way. There is an assassin on the loose in San Antonio, and I'm the only one who can stop him in time. I have to determine when and where he is going to strike."

Kathy listened to this man's words. He was determined. Or crazy. She could tell it didn't really matter whether she believed his story or not. *He* believed it. Her first assessment of Jason those many weeks ago when she first met him in Enid was correct. He was a good-hearted man who could be trusted. Now, he was a man who was in trouble and needed her help.

"Jason, Vince came by to see me tonight."

"What?"

"He was here waiting when I drove home from the restaurant."

"What did he want?"

"Dinner. Tomorrow."

"Are you going?"

"Yes," she answered. There was a long pause on the other end of the phone. "Jason I have no feelings for Vince."

"You don't?"

"No."

"Then why dinner?"

"Because I want to believe you. Because I want to help you. Maybe I can find out something that will help you."

"Kathy, I can't allow that. He's too dangerous," Jason said.

"What do you mean you can't allow it? I don't recall checking in with you to verify my schedule for anything."

"I'm sorry, I didn't mean for it to sound like that. I don't want you to get involved. This can get dangerous. Maybe dinner could be trouble, maybe not. I don't know."

"Look here, Jason Conrad, if I want to place myself in danger, I'll do it. And I don't need you or anyone else giving me permission."

"Kathy, I—"

"Conversation over, Conrad. Call me tomorrow."

CLICK!

CHAPTER 48

September 13, 1995

IT HAD BEEN A LONG NIGHT for Vince. First, he studied the guards' routine for three hours at the limousine service depot. The men stationed to guard the limousine service were apathetic at best. The Secret Service agent responsible for coordinating, briefing, and implementing the limousine security program had left for the evening. The men sat watching TV most of the night. Occasionally, they played cards. Every hour on the hour, one of them walked around the garage and checked the locks on the doors and windows. They checked the doors and windows of the limos as well. Not an impressive display of security, but for Vince's purpose, it was perfect. Tomorrow night he would observe them again, later in the evening.

The neighborhood was quiet as he drove along the street. The occasional street lamp cast an eerie glow as the light fell on the ground. Vince drove slowly, reading each address as he passed. Turning down the radio volume, Vince slowed the stolen truck to ten miles per hour. He was getting close. He was sure of that. Two houses later, he saw it: 1844 Mulberry Drive. Vince drove the truck a hundred more yards and pulled over against the curb, killing his headlights.

He reached into the gym bag sitting in the passenger seat next to him and pulled out the small block of Semtex bound in duct tape, a detonator plugged firmly into the middle of the explosive. The timing device secured to the detonator had a set of wires running into one end of the explosive. The entire setup only weighed a few ounces, but it would be adequate.

Vince opened the door of his truck and slid out into the dark street. The street lamps every fifty yards or so on alternating sides of the street provided minimal lighting. Stealth would not be a problem tonight, his black pants and shirt blending into the night. Vince slipped along the sidewalk, maneuvering as necessary to avoid any light that might shine on him. His black sneakers silently flew over the grass and concrete. The neighborhood looked deserted except for an occasional cat running across the street.

Two vehicles sat in the driveway. One, a fairly new Isuzu Trooper; the other, the Buick Vince had seen his 'target' climb into in Enid. The sedan blocked the Isuzu in the driveway, indicating it would leave first in the morning. He had made a call earlier in the day to the target's office to get a rough estimate of when to set the timer. He paused in the dark shadows as he lifted the bomb closer to his eyes. He flipped the switch on the side of the timer. Four red digits appeared, their glow not enough to illuminate his hands. Setting the timer for six hours, he engaged the switch. The luminous red numbers clicked away silently in the darkness as he moved toward the dark sedan.

Vince had no problem getting to the vehicle undetected. He gripped the small bomb tightly in his right hand and laid on his back next to the rear right tire. Pushing himself halfway under the vehicle, he secured the bomb to the underside of the sedan next to the gas tank. In a matter of seconds, he slid out from under the car.

Ninety seconds later, he climbed in his truck and drove back to his hotel. It was now one thirty-five in the morning. Vince knew the importance of clearing any trace of his covert activities in the US. Anyone who might be able to identify him had to be eliminated. Conrad might be a problem still, but someone accused of killing CIA agents won't be believed, no matter what he said. The corners of his mouth curved upward. Everything was coming together nicely, his work for tonight complete.

THE COOL BREEZE WHIPPED along the sidewalk; kicking up pieces of old newspaper and dead leaves lying on the ground. The wind ripped right through the tiny windbreaker she wore over her tight black T-shirt and blue jeans. Kathy stood across the street from the entrance to the Davy Crockett Hotel wondering what she should do next. She had called Vince's room three times since she had talked to Jason. Vince never answered.

At a quarter of two in the morning, surely her phone calls would have awakened him by now. Vince wasn't home. He couldn't be.

She inserted another quarter into the telephone and dialed Jason's number. After two rings the hotel clerk picked up the phone and put her through to Jason's room. He answered after the first ring.

"Hello."

"Jason, it's me."

"What time is it?" the groggy voice asked over the phone.

"It's almost two a.m."

"Wow, I must have dozed off."

Kathy stood in the booth unsure of what to say next. She wasn't sure why she called. "Look, I don't want you to worry. I'm at Vince's hotel right now. He's at the Davy Crockett, room four twenty-two."

"You're what? Get out of there! Are you nuts? I'm telling you, Kathy, this guy is dangerous!"

"I know what you think, but the truth is I'm worried about you. If what you've told me is true, call the police and let them handle it. You won't have to be involved anymore."

"That sounds great, Kathy, but you don't need to do this."

"I know I don't need to, but I want to."

"It's too dangerous."

"I'll be okay. Look, he's not home right now. I'll just sneak into his room and see what's there."

"He's not there?"

"No. I've called several times in the last fifteen minutes. No one has answered."

"Kathy, please don't do this."

"Jason, I'll be okay. He's not around. I'll be in and out in no time. I've got to go." She shouldn't have worried Jason like that. There would be no problem—she was sure of it. But it gave her comfort that someone at least knew where she was. Taking a deep breath, she started walking across the street.

The Davy Crockett was an older hotel, built in the early days prior to San Antonio's rise as a major metropolitan city. Kathy didn't focus her attention on the old building as she crossed the street and entered the lobby. Clean for an old hotel, it had a sense of Old World charm about it. Looking across the lobby, she saw the elevator. She smiled as she passed the desk clerk who sat idly behind the desk, his nose buried in a book. Kathy walked up to the elevator and stepped inside. The elevator climbed at a snail's pace.

The elevator came to a stop and the doors opened, revealing a long, well-lit hallway. She crept along the hallway, following the room numbers until she found room 422.

Reaching into her purse, she pulled out a credit card. She worked the card between the doorframe and the door. It was a matter of seconds until she worked the lock back into the handle. Silently, she pushed the door open.

"Hello?" she said into the room. No one answered. She pulled out her keys and turned on the small flashlight attached to her key ring, closing the door behind her. The double bed in the center of the room lay empty. She found the light switch on the wall and flipped it on. A suitcase sat on a chest of drawers on the far side of the room, the television perched on a nightstand in front of the bed next to a small desk with a lamp.

Kathy walked to the desk and started rummaging through the drawer. Nothing of significance lay inside. Closing the drawer, she noticed a briefcase against the wall under the window. She grabbed it from the floor and carried it over to the bed. It was heavy. There was definitely something inside.

She set the case on the desk, laid her keys next to it, and pressed the small buttons on either side. Simultaneously, both latches clicked up. She cautiously lifted the lid. Inside lay a variety of items which proved her instincts were correct. Stacked neatly in the top of the briefcase were several folders, each filled with a number of papers. Underneath those was a string of what looked like clay wrapped in plastic, several small boxes, and a cellular telephone. Explosives.

Jason would be surprised how right he is. Kathy grabbed the stack of folders and opened the one on top. The first thing she saw as she opened the folder was a full-color brochure for First Class Limousines of San Antonio. She pulled the brochure out and opened it up and saw the address had been circled. Other pages in the folder were detailed schematics of a limousine from some kind of maintenance manual.

In the next folder was a list of locations and times with a number by each of the locations. Top of the list, First Class Limousines, followed by the Marriott. There were only two spaces under the Limo shop's heading, both ranging from seven to seven with a number four by them. Under the Marriott, however, there were many locations. Hallway, lobby, stairs, patio, garage, roof, crowd, each with different times and numbers. *Can this be security team members?* Kathy wondered.

The third folder had a photograph on top of a sheet of paper. It was a picture she recognized immediately. She had seen the elderly gentleman in the neatly pressed suit on television and in the newspapers. It was Jason's father, Senator Bowman. Behind the photo she found a sheet of paper with data about the senator. Following the data page, the senator's schedule while in San Antonio.

The realization of what she had discovered gripped her like a vise. *I'll be damned, Vince Andrews, a Russian assassin—and the son of his target knows it.* Angered, she sat on the bed, looking through the notebooks repeatedly. Kathy never heard the door open silently behind her.

HE WAS TIRED AFTER SUCH A LONG night of surveillance and thought he would sleep late in the morning. Vince rode the slow elevator to his room and looked forward to a good night's sleep. The elevator stopped abruptly with a loud TING, and Vince stepped out. Perhaps it was instinct, Vince wasn't sure, but he sensed something wrong when he reached his room. Silently, he slipped the key into the lock and turned the handle. The fact that the light in his room was on confirmed his suspicions. Slowly, he opened the door. It took a split second for him to analyze and react to the situation. Vince leaped across the room at the figure by the desk as he pulled his pistol from his coat pocket.

MAYBE IT WAS THE SOUND, maybe it was the movement from somewhere behind her. Something in the room changed, setting off an alarm within her. She slammed the notebooks shut, throwing them back into the briefcase. In her haste to cover her spying, she knocked the briefcase and her keys to the floor. As she bent over to retrieve her keys, she turned around to see a large figure descend upon her.

Kathy opened her mouth to scream, but before a sound escaped, the figure's arm came swooping down in an arc, smashing into her skull. Vince's face was the last thing she saw before darkness enveloped her.

CHAPTER 49

September 14, 1995

I T HAD BEEN ONE OF THOSE mornings. The alarm clock went off with minimal results. On top of that, there seemed to be a hot water shortage in the shower again. All in all, it had been a rough day already for Alonzo Jacobs, and it wasn't even eight a.m. He stood in front of the mirror with thoughts of the day that lay ahead, his shirt unbuttoned and his face half covered with shaving cream. He knew he'd be late for work if he didn't start cutting corners. Decisions had to be made.

"What would you like for breakfast?" his wife asked, poking her head into the bathroom. She seemed to enjoy it when he slowly started his day like this. Perhaps it might remind him that he was old enough to retire.

"I think I'll skip breakfast this morning, honey. I'll swing by the donut shop and pick up something."

"The donut shop! You'll pick up another inch around that waistline."

"Another inch? What are you talking about, woman?" he laughed as he continued shaving. "I'll get a muffin. That's healthy."

"A muffin. Oh, yeah, that's healthy. And for dinner, just to make sure you get your vegetables, order a pizza with green peppers. Alonzo the Muffin Man."

"But, baby . . ."

"Uh-uuhh, I don't won't to hear it Muffin Man. You'd better hurry up or you'll be late for work. Even worse, they might run out of muffins at the store."

Alonzo watched her in the mirror behind him. He knew he was truly lucky to have a woman like her. She'd enjoy not having to make anything for him this morning anyway. She was never much of a breakfast person, but had always gotten up and prepared breakfast for him. Over the years, and after two children, she'd gotten quite good at it, too.

A few more strokes and he finished shaving. He washed his face, and she handed him a towel. She stood there, shaking her head and smiling.

"You'd better hurry, Muffin Man. It's almost seven-thirty, and you have an eight o'clock meeting."

"Thanks, baby." He kissed her on the lips as he passed her on his way out of the bathroom. Buttoning up his shirt, he slipped into his shoes and looked around the room for his tie. He couldn't find it. Great. That's all he needed.

"Baby, you seen my tie?"

She approached him seductively and slowly pulled the tie out of the pocket of her robe. "You mean this tie? I found it lying on the bed. You know, the bed I plan to fall asleep in after you leave. I figured I could probably charge you for it."

He cocked his head to one side. "Oh, woman, what you got up your sleeve?"

"Oh, I got nothing up my sleeve. In fact," she said, reaching to her waist and untying her robe, "I got nothing anywhere." The robe fell open and she slid it back off her shoulders, standing naked before him.

"Da-amn."

"And if you want this tie, you gonna have to kiss me a lot better than that kiss you just laid on me."

She pulled closer to him and wrapped the tie around his neck. She gave him a long, soft kiss. When the kiss ended, she pulled away slowly. "There, baby, have a nice day at work."

Alonzo, his eyes still closed, suddenly broke out of his trance. "You did it to me again. Damn! Only when I'm late. Never on the weekend. Never when I've got two or three hours of nothing to do." He began tying his tie feverishly as he moved toward her.

She bent down and grabbed her robe, laughing the whole time. "Oohh, Muffin Man can't play. He gots ta go ta work and make the big dollas." She slipped the robe back on as he continued working on the tie. She flashed him one last time as he finished the knot. "Alonzo, you better think about one thing—girlfriend here ain't gonna look like this forever. One of these days, you best just call in sick." She turned and sprinted out of the room.

"I will baby. I love you."

"I love you, too."

Alonzo raced out the door and went straight to the car. He turned the ignition at seven-twenty two and the car roared to life. Putting the dark sedan into reverse, he backed out of the driveway and zipped down the street, out of the neighborhood.

He had to slow his speed twice for school zones, but in no time, he was speeding toward the donut shop. He made it in less than ten minutes. The parking lot only had two other cars in it, and he could see through the large plate glass window that no customers stood in line. This was good. He could get in and get out in minimum time. It looked like he would be late anyway.

"Good morning, Alonzo," the small man behind the counter said as the agent walked in the door. "What will it be for you this morning?"

"Hello, Charlie. I'll take a couple of bran muffins and a large coffee. And I'm in a hurry."

"Debbie, get me a large coffee," Charlie yelled over his shoulder. "Yeah, I notice you're in here a little later than normal. Don't speed to work, though. It's dangerous."

"Yeah, tell me about it." Alonzo walked over to the paper machine and bought a newspaper while Charlie wrapped his muffins. He saw Debbie place his coffee on the counter next to the muffins. Alonzo paid quickly and walked out the door.

He checked his watch. Seven thirty-four. He definitely would be late, so he did not need to hurry. Once you're late, you're late. Twenty feet out the front door, he finally took a sip of coffee as he approached his car. Alonzo's face contorted as he turned his head and spit the coffee on the ground.

"Uugh, this is awful," he said. "Cold, sweet, and weak." He turned to walk back into the donut shop. Five feet from the front door, the explosion ripped through the morning calm.

It wasn't so much the force of the blast that sent him to the pavement, but the heavy vibration associated with the loud noise all too familiar. Shards of glass flew through the air and penetrated his back and legs as he fell. He hit the oily ground on his chest, knocking the breath out of him. He turned in the direction of the blast just in time to see the rear end of his car settle back to the ground, engulfed in flames.

Alonzo's vision grew blurry and the pain in his body overwhelmed him. He couldn't move to get up, as his vision narrowed into unconsciousness.

HE HAD STAYED UP LATE awaiting her call and finally fell asleep sometime about four or five o'clock in the morning. Perhaps the sun shining through the curtains woke him up, or maybe his subconscious working overtime. At any rate, he awoke thinking about Kathy, the woman he loved.

Jason still wore the wrinkled, dirty clothes he'd had on the previous night. His skin felt sticky. He needed a shower. He had a dry mouth and the pressure in his lower abdomen let him know that he needed to go to the bathroom.

A quick glance at the clock on the nightstand, and he rolled his eyes. Nine-fifteen. Just about five hours of sleep. Another five would have been nice. Jason swung his feet off the bed onto the floor. Methodically, he made his march to the bathroom to relieve himself. Returning to the bed, he began to stretch his sore muscles as he removed his clothes.

When he undressed, he headed for the shower. He waited outside the shower to avoid the shock of the ice cold water. When the hot water started, he made a few minor adjustments to control the temperature, then stepped in.

The warm water felt good against his skin, peeling away the layers of perspiration and filth. As he started to lather up, the fresh smell of the soap pierced his nostrils, and he began his slow return to the "land of the living". The shower was a quick one, but it gave him time to formulate his strategy for the day.

Stepping out of the shower, he toweled off and moved to the sink. Wiping the steam from the mirror, he stared through the condensation at the three-day growth of hair on his face. He'd let it stay. Maybe it would help disguise him.

What about Kathy? Jason wondered if she was okay. She never did call back. For all he knew, she could be shacked up with Vince after a glorious night of sex. He quickly tossed that image out of his mind. It wasn't healthy, and he knew it wasn't true. Vince was a killer, and the potential for her being in danger was great.

Jason dressed, then sat on the bed and picked up the phone. He dialed Kathy's number and waited with anticipation for someone to answer. His heart raced with each ring, hoping Kathy would pick up, praying she got home safely last night.

After eight rings, he determined she wasn't there and hung up the phone. Jason's mind wandered, imagining what might have happened to her. Where could she be? Logic dictated he start searching at her last known location.

Grabbing the phone book, he flipped the pages until he reached the hotel section. His eyes raced through the pages until they landed on the Davy Crockett Hotel. He picked up the phone and dialed the number.

"Davy Crockett Hotel, may I help you."

"Yes, could you ring room four twenty-two please?"

"Just one moment."

Jason heard a few clicks and the phone started ringing again. He was unsure of what to do or say if Vince picked up the phone. The phone continued to ring.

"I'm sorry, sir," the desk clerk cut in, "there doesn't seem to be anyone there. Would you like to leave a message?"

"No," Jason replied, relieved that Vince didn't answer but terrified of Kathy's predicament. "Do you know whether the guest checked out of the hotel or not?"

"I'm showing him to be registered until next Tuesday."

"Okay, thank you." Next Tuesday. He knew Vince would be gone long before that.

CHAPTER 50

September 14, 1995

NANCY WILLIAMS STOOD ALONE in the hospital room watching the still patient lay helpless on the bed. She had spent all of her spare time in here since the gunshot victim was brought to the hospital three days ago.

At age thirty-five, she looked thirty and was still in good shape. Nancy's strawberry blond hair and piercing blue eyes got her noticed everywhere she went, particularly at work. There had not been a doctor at the hospital who hadn't made a pass at her, even the married ones.

Nancy knew the other nurses talked about her behind her back. Perhaps it was their insecurities or their petty jealousy. She was not sure, nor did she care. Nancy was a good nurse. She had a life outside the hospital. She didn't have to create a soap opera around the workplace to have a reason for living.

She held Aaron Caldwell's chart loosely in her hands and reviewed it again. It was a miracle he was still alive. The doctors said that he should have died from his wounds, and there was still a very real possibility he might. Caldwell had faded in and out of consciousness the day before and was beginning to show signs of hope. Some color had returned to his face, and he had some slight movement in his hands and feet. Still, the doctors were unsure.

Nancy brushed the bangs back from his face and gently wiped it with a towel. She was one of three nurses who were assigned an eight-hour watch with the patient. The hospital had ordered that he be under constant surveillance at all times. Aaron Caldwell was obviously someone important. The hospital administrators were nervous about everything involving his recovery. Not only that, but at least three uniformed guards stood by the door at all times, with two more at each exit and the elevators. Rumors ran rampant around the hospital that several other new employees in the hospital were actually undercover guards. A few reporters tried to enter the ward, only to be turned away by the police. Quite a bit of excitement for sleepy Enid, Oklahoma.

Checking the I.V. and the other life-support equipment, Nancy felt confident that the patient would recover in time. But this morning, there would be no change.

JASON PULLED INTO A TRUCK STOP along the interstate on the way into town. He bought a newspaper in the machine outside the door and returned to his car. The story of the Enid shootings hadn't been on the news for the past two evenings. Jason kept a close watch on both CNN and the local channels. The story, it seemed, started to drift away.

He leafed through the newspaper in the confines of Caldwell's rent-a-car. There was no story about the fire at La Margarita's either. More importantly, there was no picture of him anywhere. The last thing he needed was to draw attention to himself.

His stomach growled, and Jason realized he hadn't eaten all morning. He looked toward the truck stop and the convenience store inside. He'd have to take a chance sooner or later. Leaving the security of the car once again, he entered the convenience store. The small bell rattled and clanged as he entered, telling everyone that he was here. It made him nervous. He didn't realize that no one paid attention to him as he entered.

Jason grabbed several fresh pastries and a large cup of coffee. It had been days since he'd had anything to eat that hadn't come out of a machine or a drive-thru. On the way up to the register, he walked past the cheap souvenir section found in every convenience store in every city. It contained the usual squirt guns, plastic cars, and puzzles. Out of the corner of his eye, something caught his attention.

A rack of baseball caps with a false ponytail sewn onto the back of them sat invitingly on the counter. Jason scanned the rack until he found one that resembled the light brown color of his hair. He took it to the register along with his food. He paid for his items, then returned quickly to the security of his car. Once inside, he put the cap on his head and adjusted the mirror so that he could inspect his new disguise. Not bad, he thought. He adjusted the cap slightly to give the ponytail a more natural look sitting on the back of his head. The ponytail, combined with the three-day growth of whiskers, made for an effective disguise. He certainly didn't look like a military officer.

Within thirty minutes, he stood outside the Davy Crockett, unsure what to do next. He paced back and forth around the phone booth on the far side of the street, wondering if Kathy had called him from here. He knew he had to do something, but what? If Kathy was in danger, time was running out.

Jason took a deep breath and let it out slowly. Despite the cool temperatures, he began to sweat. He was worried, nervous, anxious, scared. All of the emotions a young man feels when the fate of the woman he loves is in question.

Gathering his courage, he made his way across the street toward the hotel. He walked to the glass doors and opened them. His eyes searched the faces of each person in the lobby. No Kathy. Vince was nowhere to be found either. He continued walking to the elevator. The doors opened as soon as he pushed the button.

Climbing to the fourth floor, the elevator stopped smoothly with a light ping. The doors opened onto a long hallway leading away from him. Jason stepped out of the elevator and proceeded down the hallway. Four twenty-two was at the other end of the hallway. Jason realized that it was a long way back to the elevator if he needed an escape.

As he got closer, he spotted an exit sign leading to the stairs in the shadows at the other end of the hall. That gave him some comfort. Jason reached Vince's room quickly and stood off to the side. Cautiously, he approached the door, placing his ear against it. Light shined from underneath the door, telling him the lights were on, but that was all. He ran his hands over the door, then knocked lightly. He jumped to the side in a defensive posture. Seconds that seemed like minutes passed and no one answered the door. Jason approached the door again. This time, with more confidence, he knocked loudly. Again, he braced himself on the defensive.

"Are you okay?" a woman's voice asked.

Jason didn't move. Slowly his eyes closed, then opened and stared straight ahead for a good second or two before looking at the woman. She was an older woman, barely five feet tall, wearing the dusty gray service dress and worn-out black shoes of a hotel maid.

He relaxed his stance and tried to stretch the soreness from his neck. "Yes, I'm fine. Thanks for asking. I'm just trying to get into my room. I gave my girlfriend my key, and she's not answering the door." His voice was soft and didn't echo through the hallway.

"Oh, don't worry, I've got a key right here. Don't tell the hotel manager, though. He might think I was letting just anybody into our guests' rooms. He wouldn't understand that a nice young man was locked out with no key."

Jason beamed ad stepped back. The elderly housecleaner put her key in the lock. She gave the key a slight twist before Jason heard a click.

"There you go, young man," she said cheerfully, her good deed done.

"Thank you," Jason whispered in reply as he reached for the handle. He was unsure of what lay on the other side of the door. Kathy might be dead, or she might be entwined naked in the arms of a killer. He shook the visions from his mind and tried to focus. She was missing; she was in danger; and was the only one who could help.

Again, taking a deep breath, Jason Conrad grasped the handle of the door firmly, flung it open, and charged inside.

CHAPTER 51

September 14, 1995

LONE IN THE ROOM, Jason looked around quickly as he shut the door behind him. Whoever checked in to this room was no longer here. Had Kathy been here? There must be a sign somewhere.

Jason scanned the small room. In the bathroom, a small bottle of shampoo sat in the tub and a used double-edge razor blade lay in the trash. Walking back into the bedroom, he saw a suitcase on the dresser, packed but unzipped. Jason grabbed the trashcan from under the desk and sorted through the food wrappers, Coke cans, and apple cores. At the bottom of the can, Jason noticed ashes from papers that had been destroyed.

He emptied the contents of the can on the floor, and the ashes hit the floor or floated up into the air. There was no way he could tell why the paper had been burned, but it did give him reassurance this was the right room. Who else but a Russian agent would need to destroy papers in a hotel room?

Jason sat at the desk and stared around the room. Except for the packed suitcase on the dresser, items in the trash, and those left in the bathroom, the room was empty. He stared at the bed as an uneasy feeling overcame him. He hadn't checked under the sheets.

The thought ripped his guts out, but he had to check. Jason rose and walked to the bed. He grabbed the bedspread in his left hand and ripped it from the bed, throwing it behind him on the floor. Nothing was visible in the bed, and he cursed himself for letting his imagination work on him like that.

He studied his reflection in the mirror hanging over the desk. He saw the scraggly growth on his face and the artificial ponytail hanging from under the baseball cap. His clothes hadn't been washed in days, and his eyes were red from lack of sleep. Jason Conrad began to resemble a bum in the truest sense of the word.

Walking closer to the mirror, he reached out to touch it. Out of the corner of his eye he saw it. The reflection feint, but significant in the dark shadow under the bed. Jason wheeled around and stared directly at it. He dove to the floor and grabbed the shiny object.

Jason recognized them right away.

Kathy's keys. Jason recognized this set of keys because he knew this key chain. He gave it to her. The small circle and horse's head even glistened in the dull light of the hotel room.

She had been here, but now she was gone. And she left without her keys, which meant she was in trouble. Jason knew as he ran out of the room that he had only one choice.

THE STENCH WAS NOT UNBEARABLE, but it was annoying. The particular smell wasn't familiar, but it did help her focus. She realized now she must concentrate on the smell. It reminded her of the odor one might find near a dumpster behind a restaurant. When she tried to lift her head, it was too heavy.

Kathy Delgato sat in darkness, unable to open her eyes, her head throbbing. The dampness of the room made her skin feel sticky. The only sound she could hear over her breathing was the dripping water that seemed only a few feet away. Although her arms and legs did not hurt, they also felt too heavy to move. At some point, she realized that she was tied to a chair, and her desire to move faded as she drifted back into darkness.

Fading in and out of consciousness several times, she had no idea how long she had been there or what time it was. For that matter, she wasn't sure of the day.

Slowly, she tried to recall what happened. As the cobwebs cleared, she gently raised her head. Kathy winced with pain as she cocked it to the left. The pain propelled her into reality. She opened her eyes to find only a small beam of light threading its way across the small, cramped room she now occupied. She was dizzy and felt as if she would vomit.

Jason was in town. He tried to warn her . . . warn her about . . . about Vince. Jason was in trouble, but he'd come to warn her about Vince. She didn't believe Jason, so she went to talk to Vince. What did he say? Vince didn't say anything . . . she never talked to him. She got into his room . . .

Kathy saw the source of the dripping water now. There was a metal pipe protruding from the wall. It had a light but steady trickle dripping from it. She could tell that the pencil beam of light came from above and behind her. She couldn't move, her hands and legs, bound to the chair. That was okay for now. She didn't really want to move.

She had made it to Vince's room, hadn't she? It was like a dream, as if it happened a long time ago. She fought against the pain in her head. She had been alone in his room. She searched through his things . . . things that were in the room. Nervousness crept over her—a nervousness that transformed into fear.

Jason told her Vince was a killer. She had been in Vince's room and found items that proved Jason was right . . .

Now she was here.

Kathy held her head up steadily, looking around the room. Careful not to move her head too far to the left because it hurt too much, she attempted to adjust her eyes to the surroundings. Maybe it was the minimal lighting, or the grogginess stemming from her throbbing head, but things were still a bit blurry.

She tugged at the bindings. They were tied securely, but she could move a little.

Had Vince put her in this predicament? If so, where was he? Was he going to kill her? Her mind raced with questions as she returned to a higher state of consciousness. As she realized her situation, her heart beat faster and her breath came in gasps. It was the first time she'd been in a situation like this. How was she going to get out of here?

THE HOSPITAL WAS CROWDED. Alonzo tried to avoid hospitals as much as possible, but this had not been his day. He lay on his stomach on the sterile white cot in the doctor's examination room. The doctor spent the last fifteen minutes pulling tiny pieces of metal and glass from Alonzo's back and legs. The police officers standing in the room were making jokes about not getting any in his rear end. Strangely, Alonzo found himself able to laugh about it while at the same time enraged that someone tried to kill him.

His office had tried contacting his wife all morning but she hadn't answered the phone. Concerned, they sent two agents to his house but there was no sign of her. Alonzo told them she had planned to be gone most of the day.

When the doctor pulled the last piece of shrapnel out of Alonzo's back and cleaned the wounds, Alonzo got dressed. He got a ride home with one of the investigators. It was almost eleven-thirty in the morning. The lunch crowd began to hit the streets.

"So, can you think of anything else that might help us?" asked Bill Owens, the investigator driving the car. Bill was in his early fifties and was a very intelligent man. He had a little trouble moving around in the gym these days but his mind was still sharp.

"No, Bill, I can't. I haven't had any death threats, no obscene phone calls. I don't think I pissed anyone off in the office. I just can't figure it out. Why me?"

"Have you been working on anything big lately?"

"Not really. I was working on a test-cheating thing at a pilot training base, but that was in Oklahoma and didn't pan out."

"What do you mean?"

"The tests were stolen by computer. The guy they tried to finger was innocent. He didn't have the hardware or the knowledge on how to steal the information. The guy who did steal the tests was accidentally killed in a plane crash a couple of days before I got there."

"So what was he doing with the tests? Was he selling them?"

"We're not sure. The suspect didn't have the test scores that reflected having copies of the tests. He was barely staying in the program. He did mention one of the other students who might be getting copies of the tests, but I didn't have time to question him. I just had time to clear the suspect of not having stolen the tests. Then I was called back here for on-call back-up support to the Secret Service for the conference tomorrow."

"You must've had all kinds of fun up there in Oklahoma. Wasn't there some big killing by an Air Force guy up there a few days ago? They're still looking for the guy, I think."

Alonzo lowered his chin onto his chest and shook his head. He'd seen the reports. Maybe people aren't always what they appear. He felt strongly that he'd been right about Jason. Was he a killer? Alonzo might never know. They rode in silence for the next few minutes. The next thing Alonzo knew, they pulled into his neighborhood. Alonzo gave Bill the directions to his house, and in a couple of minutes they drove into his driveway. He thanked the investigator for the ride and assured him that he would keep him posted on the progress of his wounds.

Alonzo entered the house. He wondered if his wife knew what happened. She wouldn't take this news well. He emptied his pockets on the kitchen counter and grabbed a soda out of the refrigerator. It didn't take long for him to finish his drink as he walked toward the living room.

Alonzo turned on the television for background noise and lay on his stomach on the couch. Within fifteen minutes, the pain meds had him fast asleep.

JASON STOOD ON A STREET CORNER in downtown San Antonio across from a newsstand. He'd been waiting for the last five minutes to use the telephone. An older woman had been using the phone ever since Jason arrived. He grew impatient and looked hopefully up and down the street for another telephone booth. There were none in sight.

After three more minutes, she finished and Jason bolted for the phone. Pulling the phone number out of his pocket, he dialed and waited.

"OSI, this is Judy. May I help you?" the voice on the other end said.

"I'm looking for Agent Jacobs. Is he in?"

"Agent Jacobs is gone for the day. May I take a message?"

"Gone? He can't be," Jason bit his lip, unsure of what to do next. "I've got to see him. It's an emergency."

"May I ask who is calling? Who is this?"

Jason stood there for a second before he hung up the phone. The one person on the side of the law he felt he could trust wasn't there. Where could he be? If not in the office, he could be almost anywhere. The secretary said he was gone for the day. Maybe he was at home. It was certainly worth a shot.

Depositing another quarter in the machine, he dialed 411 for information. There was only one Alonzo Jacobs in San Antonio. Realizing he had no pencil or pen to write down the number, Jason listened to the number twice, and then hung up and dialed it.

The phone was answered on the fourth ring.

"Yeah," a groggy voice said.

"Hello, I'm looking for Alonzo Jacobs."

"Speaking."

"Sir, it's Jason Conrad. I need to speak to you."

"What?" Alonzo said. "Where are you? What time is it? Hang on."

Jason was surprised by his reaction. But why should Alonzo be any different from anyone else? Right now, everyone wanted to know the location of Jason Conrad.

"Where are you, Jason? You've got to turn yourself in. My God, son, it's all over the news. What the hell happened?"

"Hey, I didn't shoot those guys. I've got more important things to worry about right now."

"More impor—are you crazy? Jason, you've got—"

"Listen to me, damn it! I didn't do that. If you don't believe me, contact the CIA and ask for an Agent Aaron Caldwell. He was the man who got shot and lived. He'll tell you what happened. All I have time to tell you is I didn't do it."

"Jason, why are you calling me?"

"I need your help. You're the only other person in San Antonio I know. Hell, you're one of the few people I can trust for that matter."

"You're in San Antonio?"

"Yes."

"Where? Tell me, and I'll get there right away."

"Not yet. I need you to promise me that you'll come alone and you won't try to turn me in."

"Jason, I can't do that."

"You've got to, for Christ's sake! I don't have anyone else to turn to."

"What the hell is so damned important that you'd risk running from the law?"

"Kathy's been kidnapped. She's in deep trouble, and I've got to find her fast."

"The girlfriend from Enid? Good God. How—"

"That's all I can tell you over the phone. I need you to trust me. We may have only one day left."

"Jesus, kid. This is too . . . too strange. I don't know why I tend to have some kind of immune system that causes me to believe you."

"If you don't believe me, just call the CIA and ask for Caldwell."

"Okay, I'm gonna do that for my own satisfaction. Where can I reach you?"

"Nice try, sir. I'll call you back in an hour."

"An hour's not much time to track down this information."

"That's because I don't have much time."

KATHY HAD BEEN AWAKE for least thirty minutes. She had drifted in and out of consciousness, but she now sat fully awake. The familiar sliver of sunlight let her know it was daytime. It was a little different this time, perhaps based on the position of the sun or an overcast sky. The sunlight shot over her shoulder onto the wall across the room in front of her.

Kathy surveyed her surroundings. She could see only what stood in front of her. There was a door on her far right, but she could not tell whether it was the only door into the room. The walls were old and worn and the water pooled in several spots. A stench of mildew and mustiness filled the air despite the cooler temperature.

The chair she was tied to felt heavy, but she detected a slight wobble when she leaned to either side because of loose nails. Kathy made several attempts to rock it back and forth with no success. Her hands, arms, legs, and feet were all bound to the chair. Her head still bothered her if she moved too much, especially to the left. She had no way of investigating the pain.

She sat in silence, scared, confused, worried, and angry about her predicament. What did Vince plan to do with her? Would he let her go? Use her as a hostage? He was planning something—something different, something dangerous. What was it? It would happen soon, she remembered. It was here in town. Kathy struggled to remember as the scene played back in her mind like a movie reel: breaking into Vince's room, finding the briefcase, all the unusual items, the diagrams, and the folder . . . the folder on Senator Jonathan Bowman.

Kathy remained lost in her thoughts until she heard footsteps outside of the room. Her eyes, widening with terror, focused on the dark outline of the door across from her. She knew it was Vince. Only in the far reaches of her mind lay a slight glimmer of hope it would be someone else. The footsteps grew louder, then came to a stop. She heard the click of the door handle and instinctively dropped her head to her chest to appear unconscious.

The door opened slowly and then closed behind whoever entered the room. She knew it was no rescuer.

"Are you awake, my little wench?" Vince said coldly as he walked toward her. "You wouldn't sit there and pretend to be unconscious, would you?"

Kathy sat motionless, unsure of what to do. She tried to breathe easily, but the pain in her head kept her from it. Within seconds, she sensed Vince standing over her. Without warning, he grabbed the hair on the back of her head and jerked her head up to look at her face. The pain shot all the way through her spine.

"You had to be a nosy bitch, didn't you?" he barked at her as their eyes met. Vince reached into his pocket and pulled out a switchblade. He held it in front of Kathy's face and hit the release. The blade snapped into place with a sharp click.

Kathy's eyes followed the movement of the blade with extreme interest as Vince moved it in front of her. The grip on her hair was maddening, as if he were about to pull a handful from her head. She winced with pain as the tugging increased. He brought the blade toward her neck.

"What the hell did you think you were doing in that room, girl? Were you searching for something specific or did you just stumble onto something you shouldn't have?" He eased his grip on her hair.

"I . . . I was just w-waiting for you," she sobbed. She did her best to appear frightened, hoping it would buy her time. "I didn't know where you were and was . . . waiting for you."

Vince released his grip and stood in front of her, the knife still held tightly in his right hand. "That's an interesting story. I certainly hope you can come up with something better than that." He paced back and forth across the dark room. The pencil beam of light streaked across his black trench coat. "The question I must answer now is, 'What do I do with you?' You are an unexpected addition to the equation. I could kill you, but that seems like such a waste."

"You bastard! Vince, what are you talking about? You can't kill me! You don't know what will happen! Vince, please let me go."

"I guess I could just leave you here, and in time, maybe someone will find you before you starve to death or die of dehydration." He rubbed his chin as if in thought. "No, that would be cruel. There's too much of a chance for you to escape. My people simply would not understand that. No, my dear Kathy, you must die. But I promise to make it swift and complete."

"Vince, NO!" she screamed as the anger welled up inside her. She struggled against her bindings, but they kept her secured to the chair.

"Stop screaming, damn it. I've got to think," he said against the background of her sobbing and pleading. "Tell you what. You sit tight. I'll be back later. I don't have a lot of time to mess with you. Tomorrow's my big day." Vince closed the switchblade and placed it back in his pocket. Pulling a rag out, he fastened it tightly around her mouth and left her once again in darkness.

CHAPTER 52

September 14, 1995

THE CLOCK ON THE WALL indicated it had been an hour and fifteen minutes since he'd talked to Jason. Alonzo Jacobs had been on the phone talking to his contacts in the CIA and in Enid. Unfortunately, the one person who could verify Jason's story remained unconscious.

What should he do? The CIA had done a good job keeping the fact that Caldwell was still unconscious out of the papers. Once again, Alonzo found himself relying on his instincts about young Jason Conrad. Could Jason have known that Caldwell was unconscious? It's possible, but not likely. The kid was worried. That was obvious. Alonzo had never met Kathy, but he remembered Jason talking about her.

The phone rang and Alonzo reached for it gingerly, his back still in pain, He picked up on the second ring. "Hello," he blurted.

"Alonzo?"

"Yes, Jason it's me. Where are you?"

"I'm at a phone booth right now. I'll be leaving in just a minute, so don't bother tracing the call."

"I'm not tracing the call. How you doing, kid? Any word on Kathy?"

"No, but I know she's in trouble. She's disappeared."

"You got any idea what might have happened to her?"

"That's what I want to talk to you about. Do you know the Naked Iguana restaurant on the Riverwalk?"

"Yes, I've eaten there before."

"Good, meet me there in one hour. Alone please, or I won't show."

"Jason, I give you my word I'll be alone. You trust me, don't you?"

"I called you, didn't I? Right now you're about the only person I can trust. Hey, I gotta go. One hour. See ya."

The phone buzzed a steady dial tone in Alonzo's ear as Jason hung up. Alonzo put down the receiver and checked his watch. It was two forty-five. It would take him almost thirty minutes to reach downtown from his home. Alonzo limped into the kitchen and grabbed his 9mm from its shoulder harness draped across the back of a chair. He was still too sore to strap a harness across his back. For the first time in years, he tucked a holster into his waist, covered it with his windbreaker, and walked out the door.

JASON CONRAD HUNG UP THE PAYPHONE at the convenience store and jumped in his car. He had just rounded the corner when he saw Alonzo Jacobs leave his house and climb into a car different from the one he drove in Enid. Jason had studied the route to the Riverwalk enough so that he could follow Alonzo without getting too close. He knew of no other way to be sure Alonzo came alone.

Alonzo pulled out of his driveway and zipped up the street. Jason eased out into traffic about fifty yards behind him. He kept that distance between them until they reached the interstate, then he closed in. It really didn't matter if Alonzo saw him. It was more important that Jason knew Alonzo came alone. So far, Alonzo appeared to be a man of his word.

THE YOUNG ORDERLY STOPPED by the nurses' station to talk to Nancy Williams during his afternoon rounds. Nancy had grown accustomed to his flirtations and accepted them as a daily ritual. It made her feel good that a man fifteen years her junior found her attractive. They talked for several minutes before Nancy started her rounds. She nodded toward the two uniformed police officers who stood by the elevator. They checked the identification of everyone who entered the hospital floor.

Nancy continued down the hallway checking on various patients. All of them seemed to be doing fine, unaware of the flurry of activity that took place in the hallway. Her final stop was her favorite. She spoke briefly to the three guards who stood outside the door before she entered the room. Nancy quietly opened the door and slipped inside.

Aaron Caldwell lay unconscious on the sterile hospital bed in the quiet room. As soon as his vital signs stabilized, they removed the twenty-four-hour watch over him. Nancy reviewed his chart to make sure everything remained in order, and then walked into the bathroom. Taking a towel off the rack, she soaked it in cold water, wrung it out, and returned to the patient's bedside.

Such handsome features, she thought as she wiped his face. She wondered what kind of occupation warranted this type of attention. So many guards and so many phone calls from around the country, even a few from outside the country. He had to be a good man. The guards were more concerned about keeping people out of his room than him possibly escaping. Everyone wanted the patient to get better. Who was Aaron Caldwell, and why was he so important?

THE CHILL IN THE DAMP ROOM started to take its toll. Kathy, tied to the chair, shivered constantly, and her head throbbed. She found that she could move her head around slowly without too much pain. Kathy sat in the dark room, her eyes having adjusted, surveying her surroundings. The dirty floors were barren, save for the trash scattered throughout the room. Light reflected off the small puddles of water pooled in the corners. There was only one door into the room, but there were a series of swing windows behind her. One of the windows was the source of the thin beam of light, which barely showed now, indicating it was the evening.

Kathy had spent the last hour rocking herself against the chair. She started it just to help the circulation in her legs, then realized the more she did it, the more the framework of the chair became more unstable. The ropes that tied her to the chair were tied too expertly for her to loosen them by rocking. If she broke the chair apart, she just might escape.

She continued rocking for another thirty minutes, until she heard the footsteps. She thought of yelling if she got the gag off, but quickly decided against it. If it were Vince, he just might go over the edge and kill her. Jason was right—she should have believed him. If only he were close by now.

The footsteps got louder and seemed to stop right outside the door. Kathy again dropped her chin to her chest in order to appear unconscious. Suddenly the door slammed open. Her heart racing, Kathy couldn't keep her head down. She lifted her head to stare her tormenter in the face. Vince stood in front of her, a blank look in his eyes, and a shotgun in his hands.

THE BANQUET ROOM HAD BEEN converted into a makeshift headquarters for the Secret Service. They rapidly approached the seven p.m. shift change and the group meeting that followed. Agents Ervin Calloway and Dexter Douglas sat at the table furthest from the entrance to the room. On the table in front of them, they had laid out their high-powered Heckler & Koch PSG1sniper rifles complete with the Hensoldt ZF6x42PSG1 scope with an illuminated reticle. They checked each rifle, compared the sight line, and verified the action and the trigger release. Everything was checked and rechecked.

Ervin glanced at his watch. No sooner had the digits switched over to indicate seven o'clock than the shift supervisor gathered everyone around his table. There were thirty security personnel working the convention. All of them would be plainclothesmen and placed in various positions around the Marriott. Ervin and Dexter were different. They were the snipers. They would be positioned on rooftops across the street from the Marriott, each accompanied by two uniformed police officers. There usually wasn't a need for such tactics but the Secret Service had continued to implement them on a regular basis. Better to have them and not need them than to need them and not have them.

"Okay, ladies and gentlemen, this is the current intel we have," the supervisor began. "The schedule is ops normal for tomorrow. The senator will be attending the brunch here tomorrow morning at nine a.m. Following his speech, he'll have approximately thirty minutes of handshaking and photographs. We will escort the senator out of the building at eleven-thirty. He'll enter the limousine and be escorted to San Antonio International Airport, where he will fly back to Washington for a three p.m. press conference. Are there any questions on the schedule?"

No one spoke up. It was nice to have a schedule with stability, Ervin thought. Usually, these things were a goat rope. Senator Bowman seemed to be a very sensible man, though. He knew what he had to do and how to do it. Ervin thought Bowman would make a good president.

"Ervin," the supervisor barked, "do you and Dex have your spots surveyed yet?"

"Yes, sir, we both have the sites surveyed. Each is a rooftop, mine at six stories, Dexter's at eight. Each of us is thirty degrees off the entrance, offering intermixing crossfire across the entire entrance area. We both have a clean shot at the entire street. We can each cover the perpendicular street where we are located a full hundred and eighty degrees."

"Great. Have you met up with your locals who'll be accompanying you?"

"Affirmative, sir," Ervin said. "They accompanied each of us to our specific locations. They were very helpful in locating emergency exits and spotting potential danger areas. Basically, they dig us."

Ervin's comment brought a few laughs around the room. "Okay, hotshot, nice job. Now everybody listen up. There are no known legitimate threats out there at this time. We did get a call from an individual claiming to be Senator Bowman's son. Says someone is trying to kill the senator. We've written him off as a kook." The supervisor walked over to the table and picked up a stack of papers and began passing them out. "The FBI, however, did pass on a warning concerning this gentleman."

Ervin studied the young man's photograph on the paper. They were about the same age.

"He apparently shot two of our friends from the CIA up in Oklahoma earlier in the week. It is believed he might be in the San Antonio area, based on some money machine transactions three days ago. As of now, there is no suspicion that he might attempt anything against the senator. However, the FBI considers him extremely dangerous."

As he studied Jason Conrad's eyes in the photograph, Ervin tried to picture in his mind what the young man actually would look like. "Sir?" Ervin queried. "What are our orders if we locate the suspect?"

The supervisor took a deep breath and looked at all of the men, then directly at Ervin. "Shoot to kill."

A faint smile formed on Ervin's lips.

CHAPTER 53

September 14, 1995

SHE SHIFTED HER WEIGHT in the chair, struggling for some sign that would help her out of this situation.

"What do you want from me?" Kathy asked, searching his eyes for answers.

"What I want is irrelevant. It is what I must do that matters." Vince stood five feet in front of her, the shotgun leveled at her chest.

She studied his body language. It was tough to estimate how much time she had left.

"Vince . . . I-I thought I meant something to you. Why are you doing this to me?"

She saw the doubt in his eyes. He meant for her to die, but she felt confident she could buy herself more time. The more time she had, the greater her chances for escape.

"Why did you have to be so nosy?" he screeched. His eyes were red and swollen, his breathing heavy. "There are things that you have no reason to know about. But you had to stick your whiney little nose into my business and see for yourself. You don't know what you're dealing with Kathy. It's bigger than you. It's bigger than me. That's why I have to kill you. No one can find out what you know."

"But Vince, I don't know anything. I don't know what you're talking about," she cried. She was getting concerned now. Vince was acting irrational and distant. His mannerisms were totally out of character. He was unstable, and that was not a good sign for her.

"You went into my room. You read the senator's schedule. You saw the diagrams of the limousine. You saw the explosives. Perhaps you didn't realize at the time what all those things mean. But after tomorrow, you would have pieced them together. You would have led them to me. It would be only a matter of time until they realized that I am not who they thought I was. And when that happened, my people would kill me."

"Vince, please don't kill me," she sobbed. "I thought we meant something to each other."

"Meant something to each other? Fool. Although I hate to kill a woman as beautiful as you. Believe me, if there were a way, I'd bring you back with me. It's just not possible." Vince raised the shotgun to his shoulder.

"Vince, don't . . . please . . . I love you." It was a last-minute gamble. If it didn't work, she had perhaps one more chance.

Vince started to lower the weapon, then quickly brought it back up again. "Don't say that! Just shut up!" He shook his head violently and his eyes opened wide, blinking several times.

"Vince, please, you can't do this." It was working, she thought. This guy is really confused. Kathy knew he would kill her unless she did something fast. *Maybe,* she thought, *maybe I've found his soft spot.*

Vince still stood in front of her, staring at the floor off to the side. It wasn't as if he was thinking. It appeared more as if he were in a trance. He looked haggard and unkempt. His dark eyes were bloodshot, sunken, with bags under them, his hair uncombed. This time he lowered the weapon completely.

"You're right, Kathy, I can't kill you. Congratulations, you're a first. But I can't let you live either."

Kathy stammered, confused, "What do you m-mean? It will be okay, Vince. I won't tell anyone . . . I promise. Please, Vince, just untie me . . ." She was running out of options. *But there was always . . . no, I can't go there.*

"No, I can't. But I can't kill you either." Vince laid the shotgun on the floor and walked around behind Kathy. She could hear him moving things around on a table and the sound of a jar opening. Straining, she tried to turn her head, but it was no use. She couldn't see what he was doing.

In a matter of seconds, Vince stood behind her. Vince reached around, grabbed her face, and covered it with a thick towel. Kathy had only seconds to notice the familiar odor before she submerged into darkness once again.

THE RIVERWALK WAS CROWDED on Thursday night. The fair weather and cool temperatures brought out the locals and tourists alike. Alonzo strolled casually from the covered parking area through the multi-level mall and finally outside by the water. Jason followed him not far behind. It was obvious so far that Alonzo had kept his word by meeting him alone.

Jason stayed at least fifty feet behind him along the way. They rounded the corner at the Marriott, and Jason paused and studied the back patio. Outside were the men in the ill-fitting suits who no doubt had some sort of small automatic weapons underneath their coats. What was he going to do about his father, the senator? Where was Vince going to strike? Hopefully, Alonzo had the answers.

Alonzo walked along the stretch of land by the river on which there were no restaurants. Jason continued to follow Alonzo, but a little further back. When Alonzo reached the next intersection, he turned right and was out of sight. Jason didn't increase his pace. He walked with his hands in his pockets, looking at the ground, trying not to draw attention to himself. His fake ponytail flailed in the breeze.

When he reached the corner, he could see Alonzo again. Jason watched him cross the footbridge to the other side of the river and walk toward the Naked Iguana. Jason continued to conceal himself in the crowd. The ponytail made his neck itch, and he adjusted it slightly.

Alonzo sat at an outside table now, casually surveying his surroundings. Jason watched him for several minutes. He appeared to be alone. Not that Jason could be totally sure. But he'd seen all the movies. That's the way it was done, right? Jason left the seclusion of the crowd and walked across the footbridge. Alonzo looked at the menu and didn't notice the scraggly young man approach his table. "Agent Jacobs," he said casually.

Alonzo's head snapped up from the menu, causing Jason to stop in his tracks. "Jason . . . Jason?" Alonzo queried, looking at him cautiously. "Good God, son, I hardly recognized you. If I hadn't recognized the eyes, I wouldn't have believed it was you. Have a seat, son."

Jason sat down slowly, unsure if he would be jumped by the police in some form of trap.

"Relax, relax. You said to come alone, and I give you my word, we are alone. Don't insult me by implying that if I wanted to take you in by myself I couldn't do it." The black man's face broke into a big smile.

"Now tell me, boy, what the hell is going on?"

"Kathy Delgato, my girlfriend from Enid, is missing. She went to check something out two nights ago and didn't come back."

"I don't understand. What was she doing here, and where did she go?"

"She's from San Antonio. I talked to her when I first got to town to warn her, but she went to his place to see for herself. She never came back. Which probably means there's going to be more cops looking for me."

"Jason, you're not giving me complete information. Who did she go see and why?"

"Vince Andrews."

"The fellow in your class you thought might be getting the tests?"

"Yes. He's a Russian spy."

"What?"

"That's where the CIA guys come in. They were tracking some guy named Nikolai for months. I guess he's Vince's boss. The CIA followed Nikolai to Enid, where he made contact with Vince. I guess it was perceived that I knew Vince better than anyone else. Caldwell, he's the CIA guy I told you to call, came and found me.

"Somehow, Nikolai and Vince discovered the CIA was on their trail. While I was at Caldwell's hotel room, Vince came to the door and shot him. I was in the bathroom at the time so he didn't know I was there until he drove away in his truck.

"I called 911, then bolted back to the base to find him. He wasn't there," Jason said as he adjusted his cap. "Caldwell and I had found out earlier he was going to San Antonio, and Caldwell linked it to the NAFTA meeting."

"Why didn't you stay at Caldwell's room until the police showed up?"

"I don't know. Too much adrenaline, I guess. I thought he was already dead. The realization that everything Caldwell had told me was true . . . I was angry. I wanted to strangle this bastard who pretended to be a friend."

"So what's the purpose of his being here?"

"That's where I know I'm right. Before Caldwell was shot, he briefed me on Nikolai and Vince. These guys are assassins. Vince is some kind of mole they've activated to take out Senator Bowman. That's why he's here, to kill my father."

Alonzo stared at Jason, his mouth partly open. It was momentary, but long enough to show Jason that he was shocked. "Where does the girl fit into all of this?"

"When I got into town I called her and told her Vince might try and contact her . . ."

"Wait—why would Vince contact Kathy?"

"Well . . . that's a whole different story. Basically, when we were all happy and normal in Enid, he was making the moves—"

"Okay, I get the picture. Continue."

"Well, Kathy doesn't know who to believe. She sees on the news that I'm supposed to be a killer on the run. Then I tell her Vince is a Russian spy. She gets confused and decides she's going to figure all this out for herself by going to his hotel and looking for clues. She never came back."

Alonzo nodded his head. "That would appear suspicious all right. I tell you Jason, that's a hell of a story. I almost believe you. I want to believe you. Your Agent Caldwell is still unconscious up in Enid. I'd like to try and call up there again and try and get in touch with someone. Just to give you some credibility."

Jason slammed his fists on the table, knocking over his water glass. "Damn it, Alonzo we don't have time for this. We've got to start looking now."

Alonzo glanced from side to side. Jason's actions drew a few looks from the people around them, but nothing too obvious. The waiter slowly approached the table. "Check, please," Alonzo asked. The waiter dropped off the check, and Alonzo laid three dollars on the table to pay for his tea. Jason and Alonzo stood and walked out of the restaurant, back toward the mall.

"Your car or mine?" Jason asked

"I'm not sure I even want to hang around with you, kid. Bad things seem to happen to people who do. I've already had somebody try to blow me up this morning."

"What?"

"Yeah, somebody planted a bomb with a timer in my car. It was a small one, but lethal. I was lucky enough to be outside at the time."

"I think we'll take my car.'"

"Okay," Alonzo said smiling.

The two continued along the Riverwalk until they reached the Mall entrance and went up the escalator to the parking lot. They climbed in Jason's car and pulled out of the garage.

"I want to show you what I know so far," Jason told Alonzo as they entered traffic. "The hotel where Vince is staying is right over here a couple of blocks. The Davy Crockett."

Jason drove cautiously as they snaked through the traffic toward the Davy Crockett. The further away from the Riverwalk area they drove, the more the traffic thinned out. As they turned onto the hotel's street, traffic was almost non-existent. They passed in front of the hotel and went a block beyond before Jason made a U-turn on the empty street and came back on the opposite side. Jason parked the car on the side of the hotel.

"What are you doing?" Alonzo asked.

Jason continued to stare at the hotel. "I thought we might just sit here a minute. Maybe he'll show up."

"I got a better chance of winning the lottery than for Vince Andrews to show up while we sit here." Alonzo pulled out his cellular phone and started to dial. "Damn, the battery must be dead. I thought I recharged this thing." He gawked at the phone as if it were a foreign object he didn't understand.

"Who are you trying to call?" Jason asked, looking away from the hotel for the first time. His hands still gripped the steering wheel as if he had somewhere to go.

"I need to call my wife and let her know what I'm doing. I don't want her to worry. Then I want to call Enid and see if I can get in touch with this Caldwell or anyone who might back up your story."

Releasing his grip on the steering wheel, Jason pointed forward. "There's a phone booth right there on the corner if you really need to call."

Alonzo looked through the front window. He saw the phone booth about two hundred feet away. "Thanks, kid," he said as he opened the door. "I'll be back as soon as I can."

Jason shielded his eyes from the interior light when the door opened. Alonzo closed the door and Jason watched him walk toward the phone on the dark empty street.

ALONZO REACHED THE PHONE, which stood directly in front of the hotel entrance. Pulling a quarter out of his pocket, he dropped it into the slot and started to dial. The phone rang once before his wife picked up and started asking him a hundred questions. He calmed her down and explained what happened earlier in the day. She was glad he was okay, but couldn't understand why he was working again hours after someone tried to blow him up. He couldn't explain it to her over the phone, he said, but he'd tell her when he got home. Oh, and he needed her to pick up her car at the Riverwalk parking garage.

When his wife hung up, he dialed the number for the CIA chief at the hospital in Enid. A nurse answered the phone. "I'm trying to find out the status of Aaron Caldwell. My name is Agent Alonzo Jacobs, and I'm with the OSI in San Antonio."

"Just one minute please," the nurse said as she put him on hold. Alonzo glanced back toward Jason in the car when a reflection in the booth caught his attention. He wheeled around to see a truck coming down the street a block away. The truck wasn't driving too fast or too slow. Alonzo didn't think much of it and continued to scan his surroundings.

In a matter of seconds, the truck pulled up to the loading zone in front of the hotel. Alonzo turned and focused on the truck. He couldn't see the driver until he opened his door and stepped out. Alonzo hung up the phone and stepped out of the booth to get a clearer look. The man fit the description of Vince Andrews.

The sound of Jason's car starting up caused him to look away momentarily. *No, kid, not now.* When he turned back toward the man, he, too, was looking at the sedan down the street. Then he looked directly at Alonzo as if he'd noticed he was there for the first time. Their eyes locked for what seemed to be several minutes. Actually, it was about two seconds.

Suddenly, the man's right hand reached under his coat and whipped out a pistol. He started firing at Alonzo, who had nowhere to hide.

CHAPTER 54

September 14, 1995

THE FIRST TWO SHOTS whizzed by Alonzo's head, smashing into the wall behind him. The third shot was wilder and hit the sidewalk several feet to his left. By the time Alonzo could dive and roll behind a cement and wooden bench, the shooter was leaping into his truck and cranking the ignition. Instinctively, Alonzo snatched his 9mm from his holster. In one quick movement he managed to squeeze off two shots at the truck as it peeled away from the curb, its tires spinning in trails of smoke.

Instantly, Jason pulled the sedan forward to a position between Alonzo and his would-be killer. Alonzo jumped in before the car came to a complete stop. "Follow that son of a bitch," he screamed. Jason floored the gas pedal and whipped the car around, heading in the opposite direction, following the taillights of the truck up the dark street.

"He's heading for the interstate. Stay with him. Is that Andrews?" Alonzo asked.

"Yeah. I got 'em."

"That was a gutsy move, kid. Thanks."

"Yeah, just be sure to tell the jury for me, okay?"

The truck slowed as it started to round the corner toward the interstate. Jason pushed harder on the accelerator, closing the gap between them.

"Easy, kid, that turn's coming quick," Alonzo said as he started to buckle his seatbelt.

"Don't worry," Jason replied, concentrating on driving. "Hang on."

Approaching the corner, Jason applied the brakes. As he started to make the turn, he hammered down on the gas again, accelerating through the turn.

"Where's he taking us?"

"He's probably gonna get on the interstate," Alonzo replied. "It's that huge overpass a quarter mile out front."

"Got it, and he's going left," Jason said as he watched the truck's progress.

Jason followed him up the steep incline of the entry ramp. The underpowered sedan had a slight surge before it shifted and caught in a lower gear. Vince was pulling away at a steady pace. The sedan entered the interstate and moved into the flow. Traffic was light but steady. Vince was still in sight. The truck zigzagged between cars as Vince attempted to blend in with the traffic.

They were about one hundred yards behind him now and slowly gaining. Jason gripped the steering wheel as if he were holding on for his life. His breathing was heavy and labored. He loosened his grip by wiggling his fingers and took a couple of deep breaths. He had to stay in control.

Alonzo had his pistol out of its holster. He ejected the magazine and noted the rounds. He carefully checked to make sure the other two magazines were full. Jason paid little attention to what Alonzo was doing. He saw the truck was holding its position ahead at seventy-five miles per hour.

Slowly they started gaining ground on Vince. They were heading due south toward Mexico. "How far to the border?" he asked.

"Too far. He won't go there," Alonzo said. "He knows he'll get stopped at the border."

"So do you believe me now?" Jason asked, his voice sounding unsure.

"Kid, right now you could tell me just about anything and I'd believe you."

VINCE CHECKED HIS FUEL GAUGE—he was down to a quarter of a tank. This chase couldn't go on forever. He knew they were behind him, he just wasn't sure how far. The last thing he needed tonight was this damn interference. He was behind schedule already. He'd wasted too much time on Kathy. Conrad, he should have killed him long ago. Vince's eyes searched forward among the dancing taillights for an exit. It was time to end this chase.

Less than a quarter mile away was an off-ramp. It was too dark to tell where the road led, but at this point it didn't matter. Vince whipped the truck from the far left lane across the two adjacent lanes and onto the off-ramp into the darkness below the exit ramp.

"THERE HE GOES, KID," Alonzo said. "Get over, you're clear over here."

Jason looked over his right shoulder as he pushed the accelerator to the floor. The car scooted across the three lanes and lined up on the off-ramp that the truck had taken only moments earlier. The exit led to a dark street and Vince continued to the right, past a Texaco station, which appeared to be the only open building on the street.

"He's getting nervous," Alonzo said. "That was a big mistake. For all he knew, we could have lost him. Now, he's just highlighted himself again. He's going right."

"What part of town are we in?" Jason said, wiping the sweat from his brow as he followed the distant truck. The sedan plunged down the off-ramp, leaving the solitude of the elevated interstate to race through the unsuspecting neighborhood.

Alonzo looked around. "I'm not sure, but I think if he would have taken a left when he got off the ramp, it would have taken him back to town."

"Where does it go to the right?"

"Into the desert."

VINCE SAW THE SEDAN turn onto the street with a slight fishtail before it straightened out in pursuit. "Damn," he exclaimed, "Jason Conrad, I should have killed you when I had the chance," he screamed out of frustration as he peered over the steering wheel.

The truck zoomed through the dimly lit street, causing old newspapers and trash on the side of the road to fly through the air in its wake. Vince searched desperately for a way out. There were nothing but small houses and buildings on either side.

He silently cursed himself for becoming sloppy during this operation. There were too many factors which went wrong that shouldn't have. Next time it would be different. Only he knew there would be no next time. This was his one chance, his sole purpose for existing for the last six years. He either went back a hero or got sent to the gulag.

The buildings were thinning out. The gauge on the gas tank said a little more than an eighth of a tank. Something had to happen fast. The headlights were still shining brightly in his rearview mirror, probably a hundred yards or so behind him.

He could try to shoot his way out, but there was no knowing what kind of weapons they had or how many of them were chasing him. No, that would be a last resort. There had to be something . . .

He saw it in the distance. A sign for a side road to the Desert Springs. Vince slowed the truck, made the turn onto the dirt road, and quickly put the truck into four-wheel drive. The car followed him as expected. Vince led them down the road for about two miles, then made a quick left turn onto the hard clay that surrounded the dirt road. Vince waited a few seconds, then checked his mirror again. They were still following him. He eased off the accelerator and put his lights on high beam as he led them deeper into the blackness of the desert night.

JASON MANEUVERED THE SEDAN along the dirt road without much difficulty. When he left that for the hard clay, the car answered with a resounding thud of the front axle hitting a rock.

"This doesn't look good," Alonzo said. "He's got us in his element."

The car pushed sluggishly through the rough terrain, bouncing them around in the front seat.

"The ground seems okay for now. We're not in any soft stuff."

Alonzo strained to see the two faint taillights in the distance through the dust-filled darkness. They were starting to move up and down and side to side. "The terrain is starting to get rougher ahead," he said.

"How can you tell?" Jason shot back. He was working twice as hard to keep the car from running into the small rocks and trees that obstructed their path everywhere.

"He's bouncing around too much . . . too much dust to see," Alonzo said as he tightened his grip on the dashboard.

"He doesn't know where he's going. He's just trying to—"

BAM! The car came to a sudden stop and the two pursuers' seatbelts dug into their waists and chests, holding them in place. The airbags in front of them inflated, instantly stopping any chance of forward progress, nearly smothering them. Jason gasped for air as the shock of the airbag knocked the wind out of him.

The two sat motionless for a minute, still dazed from the impact. Alonzo spoke first, "Are you okay?"

"Yeah, I think so."

"Turn off the headlights. We don't want him to know we're stuck."

Alonzo reached into his pocket, pulled out his pocketknife, and pierced the bag. The bag made a dull hiss as it deflated. He reached over and punctured Jason's bag as well.

Jason reached around the deflating air bag and flipped off the headlights. His eyes scanned outside the car, searching for Vince. It didn't take long for him to spot the headlights about a mile away heading back toward the road. For the second time in a week, Vince Andrews had left him stranded in the middle of nowhere. "Damn! He threw out the bait and reeled us in. I should have seen that coming," Jason said.

"I think you did. It was just a little too late."

They watched the truck bob and weave in the distance until it passed behind them, then they got out of the car. Jason pulled out the small Mini-Mag flashlight he uses as a key ring and shined it on the car.

"It's totaled," Alonzo said, walking around the car. It was a mess. The front end sat in a two feet deep depression and had rammed into the rocks that were on the far side, blowing the tire on the driver's side. "Do you have a spare tire?"

"Yeah, but it's not a real tire. It's one of those tiny ones they use these days to get you to the nearest mechanic. It'll never get us out of here. Even if we had a real one, I don't think we could jack up the car. Plus, I think the axel is bent. We're gonna need a tow truck to pull the thing out of this hole."

"I figure it's probably four, maybe five miles to that last stretch of houses with the Texaco, right?"

"Yeah, that sounds about right."

"There's got to be a phone there. We'll get a ride back into town. What do you say we start walking?"

"Might as well," Jason said. "It's not like we have much of a choice."

IT HAD BEEN FIVE MINUTES since he'd last seen their headlights in the desert. Vince drove along the deserted streets toward the interstate, praying the Texaco station was still open. His gas gauge sat on empty now, and he wasn't sure how accurate it was.

As he rounded the corner, he let out a sigh of relief. The gas station was in sight and the lights were still on. He pulled the dusty truck up to the pump and stepped out. It took several minutes to fill the empty fuel tank.

The drive back to his hotel seemed to be a long one. He knew he had to move. Somehow, he had been compromised. It couldn't have been Kathy. She'd spoken to no one. How could he have been discovered? Conrad, the bastard. He'd been in the hotel room with the second CIA man. What was he told? How much did they know? They knew where he was staying— could there be more of them? Maybe he didn't tell anyone else.

Vince parked down the street from the Davy Crockett and entered the back door. He cautiously surveyed his surroundings, alert for any unusual signs that might indicate trouble. His silent footsteps fell one after the other, propelling him closer to the stairwell. He crept up the stairs until he reached the fourth floor. Cracking the door ever so slightly, he peered into the hallway. Empty.

Sliding into the hallway, Vince went to his room, unlocked the door, and ducked inside. It took him less than a minute to zip up his suitcase and retrieve his plane tickets from the safe. He slipped back into the hallway and back down the stairs. There was no reason to check out. In twenty hours, he'd be on his way to South America.

CHAPTER 55

September 15, 1995

MARTHA SCHNEIDER ENJOYED working the graveyard shift at Saint Mary's. The portly, graying woman had done so for the last twenty-three years. She worked the shift partly because of the pay, but mostly to stay away from her husband. He didn't hit her now as he did in the old days, but she had grown accustomed to their life apart and saw no real reason to change it. Martha knew that there was never much happening in the Intensive Care Unit in the middle of the night. Most of her nights were spent reading romance novels.

This night was different. Martha had gradually gotten used to the other police officers who had been hanging around the hospital guarding their special patient, whoever he was.

At three in the morning. Martha slowly got herself together to make her rounds. She placed her romance novel on the desk and stood up. She stretched her arms above her head, and her plump, five-foot six-inch figure jiggled, reminding her of the choice of ice cream over exercise for the last two decades. Gathering her clipboard, she stepped out of the sanctity of her quiet little office and into the darkened hallway.

At the end of the hallway, she could see two of the three police officers guarding their guest. That had been their procedure for the past few days. Two guards at the door at all times, the third was the errand boy. Martha glanced at her watch. Only four more hours to go. That time would probably be shortened, too, if Nancy Williams came in early again. She had done so every day since the patient had checked into the hospital. Martha didn't care. She was saving an hour every day in work because Nancy was showing up early and staying late.

She stopped in the first room and checked the patient there, an older man who had been hit by a car yesterday. He was in stable condition, and it appeared he would be okay. The man had only been bumped by the car, but it had been enough to put him in ICU for a couple of days. The doctors wanted to run complete diagnostic tests on his internal organs before they released him, just to make sure he was all right.

Martha walked back into the hallway and was about to enter the second room when she heard a loud crash at the end of the hallway. By the time she turned, the two guards had drawn their pistols and were barging into the patient's room. Martha stood frozen in the middle of the hallway. What could be going on in there? Gunfights in hospitals only happened in the movies and in Houston.

Before she could move, one of the guards was in the hallway. "Nurse! Nurse! Get down here fast!" the man ordered.

Martha's mouth opened and her head cocked to one side. What would they need a nurse for with their guns drawn? Then her instincts kicked in. She moved toward the room slightly, paused, and then started running. As she approached the room, the guard was putting his pistol back into his holster and smiling. "Hurry," he motioned for her, "he's waking up. He's waking up!"

THE FIRST RAYS OF THE MORNING sun filtered through the room. She woke up an hour ago, and for the first time could see her grave situation. Kathy Delgato stared intently at the shotgun, only four feet away, pointed directly at her chest. It was securely fastened with duct tape and twine to the column in the middle of the room. A string ran from the trigger to the doorknob on the door across from her. A simple set-up, Vince must have been in a hurry. Kathy realized if someone found this room, she'd be blown away when they opened the door.

This of course was assuming she didn't starve to death first. It seemed as if it had been several days since she last ate. Vince had given her bottled water when he'd come before, but she was sure those times were gone. Her mouth was dry, and she bit down on her gag. She wondered if she would ever get another drink of water.

Wrestling with the ropes that bound her to the chair, she tried to increase the circulation to her hands. They were numb, and she feared the worst. She continued flexing her fingers for the next two minutes. When she was sure there was some form of blood flow, she took a deep breath and began working on the chair. It seemed an impossible task, but she was confident if she could break the chair apart, she could escape these bonds and Vince's death trap.

The morning dampness hung in the air, and she started to feel the winter chill. Kathy thought about how she could escape to avoid thinking about how hungry, cold, and sore she was. Slowly and steadily, she continued to rock back and forth. She felt the chair move with her, the joints holding the chair together starting to give. She continued the process for another ten minutes, and it seemed that with every repetition, the chair gave a little more. Kathy worked feverishly all morning, then she suddenly stopped. In the hallway; voices. She started to holler out through the gag, then her eyes focused on the inanimate sentry pointed at her chest. To alert someone would bring them to the door, and when they opened the door, she would be dead.

Kathy sat in silence and listened carefully for any clue as to who they were or what they were doing. The only thing she was sure of was the voices were getting closer and louder. It wasn't until the voices stopped outside the door and she saw the handle start to rotate, that she realized what fear truly was.

Vigorously she struggled against the ropes, rocking back and forth. After what seemed like an eternity, the legs of the chair on the right side lifted off the ground with her momentum. Kathy's eyes remained fixed on the door throughout her struggle. No sooner had she began her fall than the door flung open and the string attached to the trigger on the shotgun pulled backwards.

The roar of the shotgun exploded through the empty room and echoed in the hallway. The buckshot from the shotgun sprayed the wall behind her, just missing her leg on the way to the floor.

Hitting the ground hard, the chair back broke on impact. Her left shoulder slammed into the slimy stench on the surface of the floor. The pain shot through her body, and she cried out loud through the rag fastened around her mouth.

Kathy lay there in the cool dampness for several minutes until the pain subsided. Whoever opened the door had been scared off by the shotgun. She was still alone in the room.

First, she managed to free her right arm, although the wooden chair's arm was still fastened to her wrist. Reaching over, she untied her left hand. With that done, she removed the rope from her right hand. Kathy rubbed her wrists, even though the rope burns cutting into her wrists stung. She then pulled the gag from her mouth. When she bent over at the waist to untie her feet, a previously unknown pain shot through her back and neck. Fighting to overcome the agony, she continued to work on the ropes.

Within ten minutes, she was free from the chair.

As she stood, her body ached from the extended period she had been tied to the chair. Slowly the blood circulated through her body. A sharp pain struck her midsection, which she recognized as her bladder. *Oh, God, I've got to pee.* Bent over like an old woman, she limped out of her prison toward the city streets.

CALDWELL SAT IN HIS HOSPITAL bed, drinking juice on his own for the first time in days. He scanned the unfamiliar room, then leaned back in his bed. His memory didn't function well; he vaguely remembered how he got here, but he wasn't sure why. He remembered he was in Enid looking for someone, but that was about it. It didn't faze Caldwell too much. He was sure that once his people debriefed him, things would start to fall into place. Right now he was concerned with the fact that his painkillers were starting to wear off. Things were still a blur, but he felt like he was getting better. Several different attendants and nurses had been removing the life-support equipment; now, he lay in his bed as any other patient, although he still found it difficult to move.

Caldwell finished his juice and placed the small paper cup on the metal tray that extended over his bed. He had no desire for food, but his mouth was still very dry. Caldwell clicked on the television and switched over to CNN. He caught the tail end of the coverage on Senator Bowman at the NAFTA convention and the president's response for not attending. He stared at the television for the next few minutes until the door to his room opened.

In walked the lovely nurse he remembered seeing when he was fading in and out of consciousness. "Hi, how are you?" he said.

She smiled brightly at him. "That's my line, Mister Caldwell. You've been giving us quite a scare the past few days." She walked to the bed and moved the tray to the side. The lovely nurse pulled out a thermometer and thrust it into his mouth, then proceeded to press her hand against his forehead and cheek. Picking up his wrist, she checked his pulse. He noticed that her skin was soft, but her grip firm.

Caldwell glanced at her nametag. N. Williams. "What's the 'N' stand for?"

"Excuse me?"

"I'm assuming the 'N' doesn't stand for 'Nurse Williams?'"

"Oh," she said, blushing, "I'm sorry. Nancy Williams."

"Hello, Nancy Williams. I'm Aaron Caldwell. Nice to meet you."

"Hello, Mr. Caldwell."

"Aaron, please."

"Hello, Aaron. You seem to be an important man these days. A lot of your friends are hanging around the hospital."

"Can't imagine why. Nancy, I was wondering if you could . . ." he winced with pain as he shifted his body on the bed, "if you could get me some drugs to start with. And then maybe track me down a newspaper?"

Approaching the bed, she adjusted his pillow, then made a quick check of his bandages. "Sure, I'll have to check your charts to see when your last dose of medicine was, but I'm sure we can find you something. A newspaper will be no problem. Anything else?"

"No, just come back," he said with a smile.

Nancy walked out the door, Caldwell's eyes following her all the way. A man goes for years hoping to wake up and see something like first thing in the morning. She was gone for a few minutes before she returned, her bright smile still present. Handing him the newspaper, she walked to the end of his bed and picked up his chart.

"Are you the one who saved me?" he asked.

Her face turned crimson, "No, not really. I have made it a point to make sure that you've been well taken care of since you decided to check in."

"My guardian angel."

"Hardly. That's what I'd call those guys waiting by the doors. By the way, you'll be able to have another painkiller in thirty minutes."

"Thanks." Caldwell grinned as best he could and flipped through the local paper. He had only gotten to the fifth page when it hit him. There was the picture, the official military photograph with the name underneath. Caldwell read the headline. "No, no, this is not right."

Nancy put down the chart she was reviewing. "What's wrong?"

"This article—have you seen it?"

She took the paper and read the headline where he was pointing.

KILLER STILL AT LARGE

Local Police Still Searching for Missing Student Pilot Suspected of Murder

"Yes, I've seen this story. This is the young man they say shot you and your friend. We were fortunate you made it. You have some nasty wounds."

"My partner is dead?"

"Yes, I'm afraid so. I'm sorry you have to learn about it this way." Her voice was soft and comforting as she placed her hand on his forearm.

Caldwell seemed lost in his thoughts for a moment. "It's starting to come back to me now. Where are the people I work with? Can you find them?"

"I can try. It's still early."

"Find them now," Caldwell said. "I remember what happened."

"You remember?"

"Yes, now get them here fast. Because if they don't, some innocent kid is gonna get blown away by some trigger-happy cop."

CHAPTER 56

September 15, 1995

THE CHAIR WAS COMFORTABLE enough. It was large and soft with a leather covering that smelled like a new chair. Alonzo Jacobs awoke in the chair just as he'd fallen asleep, still in his dirty clothes, his blistered heels now bleeding on the leather.

It had been a deep, solid sleep, though he was still sore from the walk in the desert and the bomb blast that embedded his body with glass. Leaning forward, he glanced at his watch. Nine-fifteen. He looked over at the couch and saw Jason lying sprawled out, still unconscious. The baseball cap with the ponytail lay on the floor at the foot of the couch, next to Jason's dusty hiking boots.

Alonzo lifted himself out of the chair like an invalid climbing from a wheelchair and pointed himself toward the kitchen. As his mind came into focus, he realized his wife was up, fixing breakfast. The bittersweet aroma of fresh coffee pierced his nostrils first, followed immediately by the sound of bacon sizzling in the hot frying pan. Reaching the doorway, he saw his wife standing over the stove, placing bacon into the hot pan.

She squinted at him with a sly grin, "Good morning, Muffin Man. Are you okay?" There was a hint of uneasiness in her voice.

"Yes," he replied, "I'm fine." She had a lot to be concerned about. First, the explosion yesterday morning, then his escapades last night. She hated it when he brought his work home.

"Who did you call this morning?"

"Bill Owens. I needed to tell the office about an attack on Senator Bowman. No one was in the office."

"Is there someone else you can call," she said.

"Yeah, I just need to find the number."

"Do you want to talk about it?"

"No, not now. We'll talk later."

"I picked up the car."

Alonzo looked at her blankly, then smiled. "Thank you."

Carol reached into the hot grease with a fork, pulled the cooked bacon out, and placed it on a stack of paper towels. The towels, leaving crisp bacon smoking on top, quickly absorbed the excess grease.

"Who's your friend?"

Alonzo poured himself a cup of coffee and took a big sip. "Jason Conrad. He's the boy from Enid I was telling you about the other day."

The fork fell out of her hand and clattered on the kitchen floor. "The one that's wanted for murder?"

"Yeah," Alonzo said, taking another sip of coffee, "that's him."

"Shouldn't we call the police or something?"

"Baby, I am the 'or something' part."

She drove her fist into his chest. She wasn't smiling. "What is he doing here, damn it?"

"He's looking for a girl who is missing. And tracking down an old . . . an old acquaintance."

"But he's a killer, and he's sleeping on my couch!"

"Jason Conrad didn't kill anyone."

She stood, arms folded across her chest, her head cocked to one side. "Have you bothered to tell the police yet? Or the media? Everyone else thinks the man is a killer except you, so you bring him home to sleep on my couch?"

"Yeah, thanks, baby. I knew you'd understand," he mumbled as he walked out of the kitchen and headed upstairs. He took a quick shower and bandaged his blistered feet, then examined his wounds from the explosion. He'd been wounded more in the last twenty-four hours than in all his tours in the Army.

Heading back downstairs, he saw Jason still asleep on the couch and Carol still working away in the kitchen. He noticed her glimpsing at the strange figure on the couch every time she passed by the doorway. He'd wake him up in a little while. The kid needed rest. It was a stroke of luck that Jason had found the scrap of paper on the ground verifying his— actually the CIA's—assumption of the target. Alonzo grabbed a cup of coffee and headed back to his chair. As soon as Jason woke up, Alonzo would make the call to warn the feds. He sat down in the leather chair and picked up the morning paper. The front page was filled with stories of

Senator Bowman and the NAFTA conference. Alonzo read the stories with a new interest, knowing they would have to arrive there soon. He saw in one of the articles that the senator had a one o'clock flight to catch. That didn't make sense. If he was having a luncheon . . .

"Oh, no!" he shrieked.

Carol came bursting into the room, "What's wrong, honey?"

"I've made a big mistake, hon. I think we'll take breakfast to go." He leaped to the couch and shook the young sleeping figure. "Jason . . . Jason, wake up."

Slowly the figure came to life. "What's going on? What time is it?" he asked.

"It's ten-fifteen. We've made a big mistake. The senator isn't having a luncheon today."

"He's not?"

"No . . . it's a breakfast. And he's supposed to leave the hotel at eleven o'clock. His plane leaves town at one."

"Holy. . ! I hope we're not too late." Jason stood and stretched. "We've got to get down there."

"Yeah, right. Honey, we've got to go! I'll be back."

"I know," she said as she handed each of them a breakfast sandwich and a Coke. "You'll be back when you're done. Nice to meet you, Mister Conrad."

Jason nodded and waved as he walked through the door.

Alonzo kissed her on the cheek and headed out the door. "Damn," he said outside, realizing he no longer had a car. Looking across the lawn, he saw his wife's Isuzu parked in the driveway. Alonzo checked his pockets, fumbled around for a few seconds, then turned back to the house to see his wife standing in the doorway shaking her head. He walked briskly toward her, and as if she were reading his mind, she reached into her pocket, pulled out her car keys, and handed them to him. "Try to bring this one home."

"Thanks, baby," he said. "Jason, let's go." Still half asleep yet chewing enthusiastically on the sandwich, Jason staggered toward the Isuzu. In moments, the two were inside, driving downtown.

THE BATHROOM WAS EMPTY, thank God. Kathy had locked the door behind her as she entered. She was disgusted by what she saw in the mirror. Her face, peppered with cuts and bruises, had patches of dried blood caked on the side of her cheeks. Her short, bouncy locks were dirty and matted and lay flat against her head. It was hopeless for now; she would have to fix it later. After relieving herself, she proceeded to wash the last few days of filth from her face and arms.

Kathy left the bathroom and entered the main hallway of the Mexican restaurant which was getting ready to open for lunch. One of the waitresses jumped and dropped the tray of glasses she was carrying when Kathy walked past her. No one had seen this ragged young woman enter the restaurant, but they all saw her leave.

Back on the streets, she headed toward a bridge that had steps that led to the Riverwalk. As she got closer, she noticed the streets getting more crowded. This was a big event for San Antonio and the nation. The vast amount of media coverage brought extra people to the downtown area, each trying to get a better glimpse of the event.

Glancing at her watch, she saw it was now ten forty-five. Fifteen minutes was all she had to make it to the hotel before the senator left. Based on what she saw in Vince's hotel room, he was going to blow up the senator's limo once he climbed inside. She knew she couldn't stop him herself—she was too tired and dehydrated. All she could do was find someone from security and notify them.

The limousine would be parked out front for the senator's departure. Kathy decided to stay at street level instead of taking the stairs down to the Riverwalk. The streets would be faster. She glanced at her watch again, then peered through the skyline that lay in front of her. Between two dust-colored buildings with long, flat windows, towering above the surrounding buildings, Kathy could see the Marriott.

She increased her pace as she silently calculated the time it would take her to reach the hotel. As she started to juggle the numbers in her head, she increased her pace to a jog, and then a full sprint.

ALONZO LOOKED AT HIS dead cell phone. He forgot to call Bill Owens before he left.

"Problem?" Jason said.

"We need to warn the police. I meant to call my office again, but my battery is still dead."

"How much longer?" Jason asked.

"We're almost there," Alonzo replied. "Here's the exit now." Alonzo steered the car off the exit ramp, drove straight for several hundred yards, and came to a stop. He stared at the line of cars in front of him. Traffic was at a complete standstill. "Oh, crap."

"What are we going to do?"

"Not a whole lot we can do."

"How much farther to the hotel?"

Alonzo pointed through the windshield to the towering building a half mile away. "There, right over there."

"What the hell are we waiting for?" Jason asked as he jumped out of the vehicle. "Let's get moving."

"But kid—"

It was too late—Jason was on his way. Alonzo pulled the Isuzu Trooper over to the side of the road and in moments was following Jason toward the mass of people gathered outside the hotel.

By the time they reached the edge of the crowd, it was almost five 'til eleven. They franticly pushed through the crowd, fighting for each step.

"Jason," Alonzo called to his younger partner over the noise of the crowd. "What are we looking for?"

"I don't know. Vince, I guess." Jason paused and turned to Alonzo. "He could be anywhere. How can we find him?"

Alonzo's eyes searched the area. "There," he said, pointing off to the side. "Head to that platform in front of the news camera. From there we should be able to see the whole crowd."

The two men pushed their way through the crowd, closer to the platform, as time ticked away.

CHAPTER 57

September 15, 1995

O F THE THOUSANDS of people lining the streets of downtown San Antonio, the crowd at the entrance to the Marriott was the most enthusiastic. The mass of people before him ebbed and swayed like a great ocean. Vince sat on the outskirts, a mere hundred feet from the limousine. He had calculated it was the closest he could get and not suffer any effects from the explosion, though it was still close enough to ensure the signal would be undisturbed. He glanced at his watch—ten fifty-eight. The senator would be leaving the building any minute now. He had a tight schedule, and the senator was always on time.

Vince reached into his pocket and pulled out the cellular phone. He gently caressed it, fully aware of its power to change history. Sliding the phone back into his pocket, his squinty eyes surveyed the crowd again. Secret Service agents stood in front of the wooden barriers separating the public from the hotel driveway. No doubt there were several undercover police officers among the crowd. He'd have to keep an eye out for them.

Meticulously, he mentally retraced his escape route after the explosion. The plan was to let the senator get in the car and roll a few feet, then BOOM! In the ensuing confusion, Vince would slip into the lobby of the hotel, down to the Riverwalk, follow it to the Alamo exit, and pick up a cab to the airport. That would be far enough away from the hotel to avoid any roadblocks nearby. The flight to Miami left in two hours. It should be no problem to get on his plane, and then on to South America. Next week, he would arrive in Mother Russia, a hero of the Republic, the catalyst for a new Russia.

Vince wondered what it would be like living in his homeland after so many years in the United States. He admitted to himself that he had become spoiled since living here—the women, the money, the television, the food, and the cars. The women would be the hardest adjustment. Going back to Russia would hurt, he decided, but going back a hero would ease the pain.

These thoughts caused him to think of Kathy again, and he felt a sharp pain in his stomach. He was sure he could love her to some degree, of what little he knew of love. If only it were possible for her to return with him. Surely, it was possible, but with her disposition, it just was not probable. She was a proud and determined woman who was not about to let a man get the best of her.

The roar of the crowd brought him back to reality. Vince looked toward the entrance to see one of the hotel employees walking out the front door. People in the crowd were laughing at themselves for mistaking the bellman for the senator. One by one, they started calling out the senator's name until the multiple calls evolved into a unified chant of, "We want Bowman! We want Bowman!"

It was getting close now, and Vince reached into his pocket and pulled out his cellular phone again. Flipping open the casing, he extended the antenna. His fingers gently ran over the keypad as he stared at this deliverer of destruction. Slowly, he punched the seven-digit number into the phone and lifted it to his ear.

There were four rings, followed by four clicks, arming the bomb. The receiver sitting next to the fuel tank had a small red light confirming it had been armed. All he needed to do was press the redial. Vince lowered the antenna on the phone. It operated as a safety switch. At this range, it prevented him from inadvertently setting off the bomb. But when the senator climbed into the limo, Vince would raise the antenna, press redial, and make history.

SHE WAS WEAK, but had managed to push her way to the front of the crowd. Once people had gotten a good look at her, they made sure her path was clear. Kathy looked like a bag lady; and she smelled like one, too. Soiled clothes, uncombed hair, days since her last shower . . . people gave her space. It helped her progress to the front.

Her heart raced and her breathing came in gasps as she stared at the limousine, fully aware of the potential of the bomb inside the vehicle. She noticed the noise of the crowd pick up as an employee walked out the front door. The crowd surged as the volume of cheers increased. The noise was deafening until the crowd realized this was a false alarm. In less than a minute, they chanted again, "We want Bowman! We want Bowman!"

She looked around, scratching her head, and analyzing her options. She was here, the bomb was here, and the senator would be here soon. Certainly, she wouldn't be able to find Vince and get him arrested—her luck just wasn't that good. Then it came to her. Why not just tell the police? It made sense. There was no way they would find the bomb in time, but they might find Vince before he left the downtown area.

As she searched, she saw a police officer a mere twenty feet away to the left of her. She yelled at him, but he couldn't hear her over the chanting crowd. The yelling accomplished nothing, she realized. Kathy moved from her position a few feet back into the crowd and started clawing her way toward the cop. A little boy shrieked as she walked in front of him, startled by her ragged appearance.

Pushing between two overweight men, she reappeared at the front of the crowd again. Kathy was standing against the barrier in front of the police officer a mere ten feet away. He was tall, probably six-three, and close to two-hundred-and-fifty pounds. He was a local San Antonio officer, hired to augment the Secret Service agents floating around the hotel. The cop stared at the crowd from behind his reflective sunglasses, concealing the direction of his gaze.

She waved to him to get his attention. It was at least twenty seconds before he noticed her. He glared at her for a moment, smiled, and waved back, then continued to scan the crowd. Kathy shook her head. "I can't believe this asshole . . . what an ego!"

Kathy jumped up and down, waving her arms, yelling, "Hey, you! Cop! Hello, come over here!" It was only a matter of seconds before she got his attention again as she continued to frantically wave him over to her. He stood there, his hands on his hips, staring at her from behind the mirrored glasses. Finally, he started toward her.

"What's the problem, miss?" he said, analyzing her, wondering why she looked the way she did.

"The senator can't leave," she said. She placed her fingers over her mouth as she thought that was a dumb thing to say.

"Well, I'm afraid he has to, sweetheart," the cop said as he turned to walk away.

Kathy, realizing her only chance to save the senator was ignoring her, yelled at him, "Hey you, asshole, I'm not through talking to you yet." That got his attention as he stopped, turned, and looked right at her.

He walked back to her. "Miss, am I going to have trouble out of you this morning? Because if I am, I certainly can put you in jail. That would make my day much easier."

"You don't understand," she screamed above the noise of the crowd, waving her arms as she did so. "The senator is in danger."

JASON AND ALONZO STOOD on the platform with three other people, all protesters to this display of support for Senator Bowman. Each held up a sign calling Jonathan Bowman a pig, a crook, and a puppet of the New World Order. The fact that they were insulting the crowd didn't help matters. The protesters periodically got pelted with things. Jason and Alonzo did their best to avoid becoming targets, keeping one eye on the crowd and one eye out for Vince.

"Do you see anything?" Alonzo asked, yelling into Jason's ear over the noise of the crowd.

"Not yet. I'm not even sure what we're looking for."

"It's getting close. I'm going to grab one of those Secret Service guys and tell them to hold up the senator. We know something is going down— we just don't know how." Alonzo scanned the surrounding buildings as he spoke, noting the various sharpshooters and policemen surrounding the area.

"That's a good idea," Jason said, scanning the crowd. "I'll keep looking for Vince from here." His scan continued across the mass of people until it fell upon a large police officer across the plaza talking to a woman frantically waving her arms. "Kathy?"

He searched in the direction of his partner. "Alonzo . . . Alonzzooo!" he yelled. The OSI man stopped and looked in Jason's direction. Jason waved him back as Alonzo pushed his way past a few spectators to reach him.

"What's up?"

"It's Kathy. She's over there by the limousine talking to the big cop," Jason said over the noise of the crowd.

"The one with short dark hair in the black T-shirt?"

"Yeah," Jason nodded with a big smile on his face.

"Okay, stay here. I'll go get her and warn the cop. You keep looking for Vince."

Jason nodded. "Gotcha."

Climbing back onto the platform, Jason resumed his search as Alonzo snaked through the crowd toward the limousine.

THERE WAS A SLIGHT BREEZE blowing at the sixth-floor level,

enough to warrant wearing a windbreaker. The cool, moist air finally gave in as a light rain began to fall from the heavy gray clouds hanging overhead. Agent Ervin Calloway sat in his perch peering through binoculars at the crowd below. Flanking him, two local San Antonio police officers who also observed the crowd.

"That's sure one hell of an enthusiastic bunch down there," one of the cops said.

"It sure is," replied his partner. "I'm glad we're up here instead of down there on crowd control."

Ervin said nothing as the two carried on their conversation. Continuing his scan of the crowd, he attempted to ignore the small talk. Periodically, he pulled away from his binoculars to give his eyes a break and stretch his neck, then go right back to his observation.

"Hey, you still got a picture of that Conrad kid?" one of the cops asked the other. Suddenly they had Ervin's attention.

"Yeah," his partner replied.

"Let me see it." The two exchanged the photograph. There was a moment of silence as they studied the picture. "Holy sweet mother of Jesus, that's him!"

"Where is he?"

"He's the guy standing on that platform, by the news camera, about a hundred, maybe a hundred fifty feet from the front of the crowd. Wearing blue jeans and a blue jean jacket. He's looking around, like he's searching for someone."

Ervin swapped the binoculars for his rifle, then scanned the crowd to find the location through the scope. It was mere seconds before he found him. "Let me see that picture," Ervin said. He was sure that it was Conrad, but he wanted to cover every base before he took him out. Certainly, there would be questions afterward. He studied the picture and looked back through the scope at the unsuspecting figure below. "That's our man." Ervin keyed his radio transmitter. "Dex, I've got the Conrad suspect in my sights. I'm requesting a confirmation."

A squeaky voice came back over the radio, "Roger, give me a location."

Ervin directed him where to look and gave him the description.

In a matter of seconds, Dexter was back on the radio. "Roger. That's our man. I don't have a clear shot. How's yours?"

"Good," Ervin said, his aim rock steady on the suspect.

"Copy. If he makes any aggressive move, take him out."

The San Antonio cops were talking excitedly over their radios, spreading

334 Michael Byars Lewis

the word that Conrad was at the hotel. Ervin withdrew himself from the conversations taking place over the radio. He took a deep breath and exhaled slowly, perspiration forming on the side of his head and dripping slowly down his cheek. Lining up the crosshairs on Conrad's head, Ervin slid his finger from the side of the rifle onto the trigger. Ervin replied over the open mic, "I've got him right where I want him."

"WHAT DO YOU MEAN the senator is in danger?" the police officer asked looming over Kathy's petite, filthy frame.

"Someone is trying to kill him," she shouted over the noise of the crowd.

Now the officer was starting to pay attention to what she had to say. He leaned closer to her. "What did you just say?"

"Someone is trying to kill the senator!"

"Who is? How? Where did you come across this information?"

"His name is Vince Andrews, but that's not his real name. He's a Russian spy. I saw his plans . . ."

"A Russian spy? So the Russians are going to kill Senator Bowman?" he replied. "And just who else is in on it? Elvis and Jimmy Hoffa?"

The fact that he didn't believe her aggravated Kathy. As the cop started to walk away, he shook his head at the crazy girl he'd just met. "Hey, you asshole! Are you going to listen to me or not? Call somebody on your damn radio and stop him!" The cop stopped dead in his tracks and looked back at her.

By this time, the people surrounding Kathy had diverted their attention from the senator to her and the cop. Realizing this, the cop returned to Kathy. "Miss, I'm going to have to ask you to settle down, or I'll have you escorted from the area."

The roar of the crowd was getting louder. The senator and his entourage stood at the entrance of the hotel just inside the glass.

"Look, you asshole! There is a bomb in that limousine, and as soon as the senator gets in, he's gonna get blown to hell and back."

Teeth clenched and jaw tightened, the big cop grabbed her arm. "All right, that's enough. You're going in." He reached down with his free hand and pulled out his radio.

Spectators cheered louder as Senator Bowman exited the hotel and walked toward the limousine, waving to the crowd, and shaking hands along the way.

"Base, this is Unit 16. Potential threat in custody, requesting back-up."

Realizing she had no choice, Kathy grabbed the cop's pistol from his holster. She released the safety on the weapon and pointed it toward the long black limo less than thirty feet away.

"Gun! Gun!" someone in the crowd shouted as Kathy squeezed off three rounds at the limousine.

CHAPTER 58

September 15, 1995

ALONZO CONTINUED to force his way through the crowd. His back and legs burned as the perspiration continued to agitate his tiny wounds speckled about these areas. The cop talking to Kathy should be able to get on his radio and stop the senator. Just a little bit further. He was ten feet away when he heard the shots. His eyes scanned the area quickly until they settled on Kathy. She had the gun! The three shots brought a momentary silence over the crowd as they hit the side of the limousine.

Then all hell broke loose.

Cheers turned to screams as everyone scurried away from the front of the hotel. The senator's handlers took him to the ground, searching for the shooter.

The large cop wheeled around and pulled the pistol out of Kathy's hands. He backhanded her across the cheek with the hand holding the pistol. Collapsing on impact, the cop grabbed her and held her against his chest so she couldn't move.

Alonzo fought the crowd to get to Kathy, but it was like swimming upstream in a raging river. "No!" he shrieked as the cop struck Kathy, his cries drowned out by the screaming crowd.

VINCE HEARD THE SHOTS and looked first toward the disturbance, then at the senator, who was thirty feet from the limousine. Damn! What the hell is going on? He knew he only had one option now. Reaching into his pocket, he grabbed the cellular phone as the senator's handlers lifted him from the ground and started to take him back inside. In a split second, Vince decided that he should attempt it. They were still close enough that the bomb blast might kill him. His thumb slid down the keys and pressed the re-dial button. There was a slight delay, then . . .

KA-BOOM!

The once shiny black limousine erupted in a volcano of fire and steel, lifting it off the ground slightly before bouncing back to the pavement, the entire back end missing. The fireball rolled upward and outward toward the crowd. The force of the blast knocked those closest to the limo to the ground, shards of fiery shrapnel and glass flying in all direction, striking many of the spectators.

Vince stared with anticipation as the senator and his small group again went to the ground.

KATHY STRUGGLED WITH THE LARGE COP, unable to move and hoping to avoid being struck a second time. She knew she was in trouble now and could only hope she stopped the senator from entering the limousine. And she hoped no one would kill her.

The noise of the blast rapidly ripped through her ears. The large cop who stood between her and the limo came crashing down on top of her. She screamed as the hulking figure pushed her to the ground. She landed on top of someone else as the heavy cop slammed her to the ground, once again sending her into darkness . . .

JASON IMMEDIATELY FELL to the ground as the explosion tore through the crowd. He was nearly a hundred feet away and could hear pieces of the automobile landing around him.

Lifting his head, he surveyed the crowd as they scattered like ants to get away from the hotel. He stood up, checked himself for wounds, and looked toward the burning car. Everyone was running or helping someone who was injured. Everyone, but one. Perhaps it was the lack of movement that caught his attention. Jason focused on the familiar figure. Not fifty feet away, standing amid the chaos, looking toward the hotel entrance, was Vince Andrews.

"HE'S DOWN, HE'S DOWN," screamed one of the cops on the roof as the force of the blast took the senator and his entourage to the ground.

"Wow!" Ervin shrieked. He had been distracted when the initial three shots went out, dropping Jason out of the sights of his rifle. When the explosion went off, all he could do was stare. He'd never seen a vehicle destroyed like that. He used his scope to quickly scan the crowd. There were several people close to the vehicle who were killed, with dozens more wounded. Blood covered those closest to the limo, many of whom were trampled by those trying to run away.

The three men atop the sixth-floor roof stared in disbelief at the disaster unfolding below. "Hey, they're moving," Ervin said. He placed his hand to his earpiece as he continued watching the escort team.

"That's a roger," Dexter barked over the radio. "I've got a good angle over here. The senator appears to be alive. I've lost your mark, though. He's disappeared in the crowd."

"Yeah, I've lost him, too."

"I'm not so sure he's what we need to worry about, though," Dexter said.

"Yeah, well, he's gone now," Ervin acknowledged. As much as he hated it, he knew Dexter was right. He was the wrong target. His John Wilkes Booth. His Lee Harvey Oswald. His opportunity of a lifetime. Gone.

"GET OUT OF THE WAY," the Secret Service agent yelled as blood streamed from his forehead. He held the senator's arm firmly with his left hand, his SIG Sauer P226 chambered in .357 magnum in his right. The agent had caught a piece of the blast that grazed his forehead. Fortunately, the senator and the three other Secret Service agents with him were untouched.

The small group raced into the lobby of the hotel, one clearing a path, two holding the senator on each side, and the fourth bringing up the rear. It was a scenario these men had rehearsed many times, yet it was the first time any had performed these actions for real.

It took them less than forty-five seconds from the initial gunshot to move the senator inside the hotel and across the lobby into a service stairwell. The group flew down a set of stairs, then turned right, moving rapidly through a long hallway. The lone figure with a gun at the end of the hallway they recognized as one of their own. Had they not, the point man would have shot him immediately.

The new figure slung open a door at the end of the hallway, and the group raced through a small alley and into the next building. Racing down another flight of stairs and through another set of doors, all guarded by security team members, the group entered an underground parking garage. It was a matter of seconds before they climbed into the waiting limousine.

As soon as the last of the group entered the limo and closed the door, the driver floored the accelerator and the limousine raced out of the garage and into the streets. The police escort had this portion of the street blocked off and four motorcycle cops escorted the limo to the interstate as it headed for the airport.

JASON LOOKED BRIEFLY in Kathy's direction, but she was nowhere to be seen in the ensuing madness surrounding the burning limousine. He glanced back to where his father had come out, but he and all the Secret Service agents were gone.

"Andrews, I'll kill you," he said under his breath as he looked back at Vince. He'd cut the distance between them in half when Vince turned and saw him approaching.

Their eyes locked. Jason saw the hatred in Vince's eyes. A violent swell built in Vince's face, and his body tensed in anger. Almost as quickly as the anger had developed, Jason could see reality set in. Vince Andrews turned and ran.

Jason continued to push through the crowd, keeping Vince in sight. The chaos of the crowd was maddening. People dispersed in all directions, the wailing sirens of the police cars augmenting their screams. Smoke and the smell of burning gasoline filled the air. Jason jumped up periodically to see Vince over the crowd. His quarry was moving toward the Riverwalk at the same pace as Jason, the crowd slowing them down.

Jason needed to catch Vince before he made it to the Riverwalk. With the number of shops and restaurants there, it would be an impossible maze. He could lose Vince and never find him.

"COMING THROUGH—move, damn it!" Vince shouted as he pushed and clawed his way through the crowd. This was a disaster of the worst kind. His operation crumbled from under him. There was no real backup plan because he was operating alone. This wasn't supposed to happen. A myriad of different scenarios raced through his mind as he subconsciously forced his way to the Riverwalk. Why had he killed the two agents in Enid? If he had killed them, why hadn't he killed Conrad, as well? How had Conrad found him? Why had he become involved with Kathy? Why hadn't he killed her? How had Jason and Kathy found their way here at this particular time?

Vince knew his fantasy of returning to Mother Russia a hero was rapidly dwindling. If he survived, the second-guessing of all his actions would continue while he rotted away in a gulag somewhere in Siberia. If he survived.

The seriousness of his predicament overwhelmed him. He was an assassin in a foreign land. He had been discovered and was on the run. In a matter of time, every law enforcement official within five hundred miles would descend upon San Antonio and the surrounding areas. Texans were too proud and noble to stand for a second political assassination in the Lone Star State.

Escape, he realized, might be impossible. He hadn't given it much thought before today. How foolish he was to take Nikolai at his word regarding the mission. It had sounded so easy. Had Nikolai really thought that Vince could kill the senator, walk to a cab, and ride to the airport? Vince cursed himself for his carelessness.

Reaching the stairwell to the Riverwalk, Vince noticed that the crowd had slowly dissipated. He glanced over his shoulder to see if Conrad was still following him. No sign of him yet . . .

"Buddy, go down the stairs or get out of the way!" Vince turned to see a man and his wife frantically trying to get around him. He let them pass and scanned the crowd for a moment more.

What was he doing? He should be fleeing the scene. It wasn't going to get any easier than it was right now. The longer he waited, the more security forces would arrive. And then it came to him.

The little bastard had been a thorn in his side for months in one way or another. Jason was close behind now, and Vince didn't want to lose him. He wanted closure.

Vince looked briefly down the staircase and saw two uniformed police officers running up the stairs. He stepped back to let them pass. As they paused, the second cop stopped and did a double-take at Vince. Then, he continued running toward the hotel and the destroyed limousine.

That was more than enough for Vince. Not having seen Conrad, he raced down the stairs toward the Riverwalk. The crowd continued to thin out, but those who remained were still confused and darting about frantically. Vince raced toward the cement footbridge that led to the other side of the river.

When he reached the bridge, Vince slowed his pace and began to ascend the steps. He pushed his way past the man and his wife he'd seen earlier.

"Hey, fella! Watch it!" the man exclaimed. He was still trying to calm his hysterical wife.

"Out of the way, asshole," Vince said. He was about to push the two of them to the side when he noticed the man looking behind him, his eyes wide with terror.

Vince paused and looked over his shoulder to see Jason Conrad, not four feet away, running right at him.

CHAPTER 59

September 15, 1995

ALONZO PICKED HIMSELF off the ground shortly after the blast. The sound had been deafening and his ears were ringing. His body still hurt from the wounds he'd gotten from the donut shop explosion. He was getting too old for this.

He'd only been a few yards from where Kathy stood before the limousine exploded. Pushing past the few people who remained between him and the police barricade, Alonzo stood in horror.

The entire rear section of the limousine separated from the rest of the automobile. In fact, it was gone. There were burning pieces spread over a hundred-foot radius. It looked as if those people in the first two rows had been hurt by the blast. Unfortunately, that was exactly where Kathy had been standing. The force of the blast was directed up and to the left, toward the crowd away from the hotel. Wounded bystanders lay sprawled out on the sidewalk, screaming in agony. The total number of dead would not be determined for some time.

It only took a moment for Alonzo to locate the large police officer Kathy had been talking to prior to the blast, the back of his body peppered with small fragments of metal from the blast. The large cop had a huge gash at the base of his skull. He had been hit by a fairly significant piece of metal. Blood poured from the wound and pooled on the muddy ground. The body appeared to be lying on top of a small, petite female.

Alonzo detected no pulse from the cop. Rolling him over, he saw the tattered young girl squished underneath. Placing his hand gently on the side of her neck, he felt a pulse. Alonzo checked her quickly and found no major injuries—just a few cuts and bruises.

Suddenly, the girl coughed violently as her body fought for oxygen.

Kathy opened her eyes and tried to sit up.

"Easy girl," Alonzo said softly, "you've been hurt."

"Huh? What happened?" she asked, rubbing the back of her head.

"There was an explosion. You were knocked down. You had the wind knocked out of you. How do you feel?"

Kathy propped herself up on her elbows and took a deep breath. After a moment, she sat up and did a quick self-inspection of her limbs. "I seem to be okay," she said, looking at the body of the police officer she had been arguing with when the bomb exploded. "I'm definitely doing better than him."

Alonzo helped her to her feet as people slowly wandered back into the area, helping the wounded. In the distance, the wail of sirens could be heard as emergency rescue personnel and more police officers arrived on the scene. The news camera team that had been near the platform earlier was busy rushing around the bombed vehicle. They were intent on giving the entire country a live broadcast of the latest tragedy in America.

"My name is Alonzo Jacobs. I'm an agent with the Office of Special—"

"Hey—you're Jason's friend."

"Yes, I am."

"Where is he?" she asked, more worried about Jason than her own wounds.

"He's gone after Vince Andrews."

"Vince? He's still here?" Her face turned crimson and her mouth tightened. "Vince is behind all this you know."

"Yes, I know. Jason was right, I'm just sorry it took me so long to believe him."

"Where did they go? We've got to help him. Vince is dangerous."

"I know. Jason was looking for Vince before the blast," Alonzo said, gesturing toward the platform where they had stood only moments before. The skies overhead were a dark gray and the wind was cool and moist. Two starkly contrasting figures made their way through the crowd toward the side of the hotel. The initial shock of the event appeared to be wearing off. More law enforcement officials and rescue personnel arrived, and the shrill sirens filled the air as Kathy sat on a bench near a staircase leading to the Riverwalk.

BAM!

Both of their heads jerked toward the sound, toward the Riverwalk.

"That was a gunshot," Kathy said.

"I think we've found them."

"Let's go." Kathy bolted off the bench and headed down the stairwell before Alonzo could say anything. All he could do was follow as a light rain began to fall.

VINCE HAD ENOUGH REACTION time to pull out his pistol before Jason reached him. As Jason plowed into him, Vince fired a shot before the force of the impact slammed him into the rail, his ribs absorbing most of the impact. The shot went wide. Vince lost his grip on the gun and dropped it into the dark river water.

Jason grabbed the Russian by the collar. He drew his fist to swing at Vince. Vince rolled his head to the right just before Jason's fist impacted, easing the blow. Grabbing the other side of Vince's collar with his free hand, Jason jerked him closer. "You son of a bitch! I know who you are!" he said. Jason felt Vince go limp as he held on to him. "I trusted you, and you're a damn spy. A killer!"

Jason looked around for a police officer. There were none in sight due to the explosion. A small group of people stood nearby watching the struggle, ignoring the need for shelter from the increasing rain.

Jason, too late, realized that Vince tensed his muscles. It only took a second for Vince to shift his body.

Stepping to his left, Vince threw his right arm over Jason's arms, which still had him in a tight grasp. Continuing to move left, he stabilized his footing, bringing Jason closer and off- balance.

Jason had no time to react. "What—" was all that came out before Vince's right elbow came back, smashing him in the forehead. The pain spread throughout his head like a bolt of lightning, but he held on.

Vince's elbow recoiled for two more quick shots. Somewhere between the second and third hit, Jason loosened his grip. He fell to his knees as the crowd, watching the struggle roared, their approval. Wasting no time, Vince turned and ran down the stairs to the sidewalk that meandered along the river.

His head throbbing with pain, Jason grabbed the rail on the footbridge and pulled himself to his feet. Placing his hand to his forehead, he saw there was no blood. Another two inches lower and the blows would have broken his nose for sure. Taking a few deep breaths, Jason watched Vince jog down the sidewalk and into the crowd.

VINCE RUBBED HIS JAW he slowed to a walk. Even though he rolled with the punch, it was a fairly solid shot. His ribs were also hurting from the impact into the bridge rail. Vince reached the T-intersection of the river and had no choice but to go to the right. The crowd was getting denser. It appeared most of the people were oblivious to the actions that had taken place only minutes before.

As soon as he reached the first restaurant, the movement of the crowd came to a virtual standstill. The mass of people were funneling into the narrow sidewalk, umbrellas popping up everywhere. Breathing heavily, Vince silently cursed himself for losing his gun. He had been sloppy. He knew he couldn't afford to be sloppy any more.

Moving off the sidewalk toward the river, Vince attempted to circumvent the crowd. He felt a hand grab his shoulder. He turned right into Jason's fist as it hit him squarely in the nose.

"Not so fast, asshole," Jason gasped.

The force of the blow knocked Vince off-balance on the slippery rocks by the edge of the river. He started teetering backward, grabbing Jason's arm at the last second.

Awkwardly, the two men fell sideways into the shallow river.

The water was only three feet deep, but it was enough to cushion their fall. Vince wasted no time grabbing Jason from behind, squeezing the young American's chest tightly, using every ounce of strength to force the air out of his opponent's lungs.

It was only a few seconds before Jason stopped struggling. Vince, also, was getting short of air. Repositioning his hands around Jason's neck, Vince attempted to stand.

Vince thrust his head above the surface. His lungs burned as the cool oxygen filled the empty void in his chest. Attempting to keep Jason underwater, Vince shifted his stance. When he put his right foot down, it landed on a smooth surface covered with the gooey sludge that permeated the bottom of the river. As he put weight on his foot, it began to slide . . .

Vince's feet quickly flew out from under him as he fell on his back into the water. The pressure gone, Jason pushed himself away and up to the surface. Vince kept his eyes on Jason, who wheeled around to face him. He was oblivious to the cheering crowd, hatred burning in his eyes. Vince struggled to his feet. The two men circled each other, anticipating the other's next strike.

"Give it up, Conrad. You're going to die."

Jason shook his head, gasping for air. "No way, pal. You're a long way from home, and your friends are running out fast."

"I promise you, if I die, I'm taking you with me."

"Not today," Jason said as Vince lunged forward with a right cross. Barely reacting in time, Jason threw up his left arm to deflect the blow and step inside to deliver two quick blows to Vince's rib cage. Vince doubled over in pain, his side still sore from the collision on the bridge. Jason followed his jabs with an uppercut to Vince's jaw. But Vince shifted slightly to the side and grabbed Jason's arm. That move caused a loud cheer from the spectators under the shelters. They assumed that they were watching a barroom brawl that found its way outside. No one knew the impact these two people had on international relations and the future stability of the world.

Wincing in pain, Jason attempted to escape Vince's grip but could not get free. Without warning, Vince delivered two quick karate chops to the base of Jason's neck. Down he went.

Vince wasted no time heading for the cement river bank. It would only be a matter of time before the police arrived. He waded through the water toward the sidewalk, watching the people pointing, laughing, or shaking their heads.

The crowd was loud, and Vince hadn't heard Jason charging through the water behind him.

Jason grabbed Vince in a chokehold, his right forearm tightly pressed against his neck. Once again, the two fell beneath the surface of the cold water as the darkness and silence of the river enveloped them.

CHAPTER 60

September 15, 1995

KATHY AND ALONZO moved steadily along the Riverwalk, oblivious to the rain that pelted them. As the two approached the bridge, they noticed a large group of people gathered by the river. They darted through the dwindling crowd on the sidewalk to reach the group. Their heads bobbed from side to side to avoid the open umbrellas.

"What's this crowd watching?" Alonzo asked.

"It's got to be them," Kathy said. "The crowd is cheering something. It's got to be a fight."

"People stand around and cheer a fight?"

"Hey, it's San Antonio. You're on the Riverwalk."

"Right." Alonzo grabbed her arm above the elbow as they pushed their way through the crowd. Alonzo noticed that some people were still running from the chaos near the hotel while others seemed unaware that anything had happened.

"How are you feeling?"

"I'm okay, I think," she said. "I probably look worse than I feel. I'm just very sore, my head hurts, and as soon as we slow down, I'm sure I'll be hungry."

Alonzo nodded. Kathy had been through hell and was holding up better than most men would have under similar circumstances. Alonzo strained his neck to see above the crowd as they approached the river. "Can you see anything?"

"No, but everyone's looking toward the water."

JASON RELEASED HIS GRIP on Vince as he pushed himself off the bottom of the river. His lungs were on fire as he broke the surface of the shallow water. He wasn't able to take in the fresh oxygen as fast as his lungs demanded it. Standing tall, he placed his hands behind his head in an attempt to help his breathing.

Two seconds later, Vince shot above the surface directly in front of Jason. He drew his fist back and delivered a fierce blow to Jason's stomach.

Jason doubled over, his hands clutching his midsection.

Vince brought his fist up in an uppercut that landed squarely on Jason's exposed jaw.

SMACK!

Jason's head jerked back as he fell back into the river on his butt. He wouldn't be going anywhere for a while.

Vince stood there, glaring at him for a moment, catching his breath. Satisfied that Jason had been stopped, Vince headed back to the sidewalk. Oblivious to the cheers of the crowd, he climbed out of the river and into the mass of people.

While Jason sat motionless in the river, Vince, his face a bloody mess, disappeared into the crowd.

"DAMN, IT'S HIM," ALONZO EXCLAIMED. "Keep an eye on Vince." Alonzo jumped off the ledge and waded toward Jason, who sat twenty yards away.

"Hurry, it looks like he's going under," Kathy said, momentarily ignoring Vince to keep an eye on Jason. No sooner had she finished her warning than Jason fell onto his back. For the third time, he was submerged below the river's surface.

Alonzo picked up his pace, almost running in the shallow water. He reached Jason in seconds. Grabbing Jason by the jacket, he pulled him up and out of the water. Jason coughed and gasped for air. Blood and water spewed out of his mouth.

"You okay, kid?" Alonzo asked.

Jason blinked and looked at Alonzo. A faint smile crossed his battered face. "What took you so long?"

"You know, I'm getting tired of saving your butt," Alonzo said, smiling at him.

"That's good," he mumbled, "I'm tired of needing it saved."

Alonzo helped him to his feet, leading the young man to the sidewalk. Kathy moved through the mass of people to meet them.

"Jason, are you okay?" she asked.

He looked at her weary-eyed. Kathy was as much a mess as he was, if not more, but her eyes glistened at him, telling him she cared.

"I think the question is, are you?"

Kathy nodded. "Yes, I'm fine," she said, grabbing his hand. "Vince is headed that way. We've got to go." She let go of him and darted into the crowd.

Jason and Alonzo glanced at each other, then followed Kathy through the crowd.

VINCE PUSHED HIS WAY through the mass of people. Other than a few strange looks or laughs for being soaking wet, Vince went unnoticed. Most of the people along the Riverwalk had managed to stay dry during the deluge and simply assumed his inability to stay dry was related to the rain. Two drunks looked at him and laughed. Vince cast them a scornful look and walked on. He had no time for them.

Vince saw a set of glass doors that led to a large foyer and charged through them. He passed a few stores before exiting through another set of glass doors. Up another set of stairs and Vince found himself on the street again, standing in front of the Alamo. Traffic was at a standstill, marred by honking horns, wailing sirens, and people cursing at each other. Down the street to his left, an ambulance struggled to get through the bumper-to-bumper traffic.

His mind racing, it took Vince only a moment to realize his bomb caused this. Glancing up and down the sidewalk, he saw policemen at each intersection setting up roadblocks. It was best to avoid them now, as he wasn't sure how much information they had on him. Going back the way he'd come here was not an option.

His only alternative lay in front of him: The Alamo.

THE BEDRAGGLED GROUP OF THREE pushed through the crowd, Kathy in the lead. They reached an area where they had to make a choice: either continue along the river or pass through the glass doors leading to the Alamo Plaza. The three of them stood silently under an awning, searching in all directions.

"Hey," a drunk called out to them, "are you guys looking for that guy who's all wet and bleeding?"

"Yeah, how did you know?" Jason asked, blood dripping down his forehead.

"You're kidding, right?" the fat one said. His partner laughed at the comment.

"Cut the crap, beer boy. Where did he go?" Kathy demanded.

The fat one looked at her, then at the gun on Alonzo's hip. "That way," he pointed to the glass doors. "He headed for the street."

Jason was the first to move this time as the three darted through the foyer and up the stairs. The tiny Alamo Mission was across the street less than a hundred yards away.

"Damn, where is he?" Alonzo exclaimed. He was frustrated. Alonzo seemed to be one step behind ever since he became involved in this thing. It bothered him.

The three stood on the sidewalk looking for Vince. It was easier on the Riverwalk—their focus was more channeled. But here in the open, it might prove impossible to find him.

Jason wiped the blood from his mouth with his sleeve. He quickly scanned the area as he'd been taught in the airplane. Look in a quadrant for a few seconds, then look somewhere else. Look there for a few seconds, then look somewhere else. When you've looked everywhere, go back to the spots where you've already looked.

He looked for about ten seconds when he saw the familiar figure, hobbling toward the entrance of the old mission. "There he is," Jason said, "heading for the door."

The three ran, searching for a way to weave between the cars blocking the street. Frustrated, Jason jumped on top of the hood of a nearby car and began jumping from car to car.

"Hey, you asshole, get off my car!" someone shouted at him. Horns blared as everyone stuck in traffic joined in the chorus to break up the monotony. Jason jumped off the last car onto the sidewalk on the other side of the street, landing in a crouched position.

"Oh, crap," he said as he saw Vince looking directly at him a mere hundred and fifty feet away.

VINCE RAN INSIDE THE ENTRANCE of The Alamo, slamming the door behind him. Ignoring the tourists around him in the dark mission, he frantically searched for a way out. The main chapel was crowded, probably because of the rain.

Pushing through the crowd, Vince knocked an old man down as he ran. He dashed through a door that led him into the gift shop. As he entered, all heads turned toward him. Vince's soaking wet clothes smeared with blood was a scary sight.

A small Japanese man moved through the crowd and took a quick photo of Vince standing in the doorway. Vince lashed out and grabbed the man by the shirt. He quickly delivered a right cross to the man's jaw.

The Japanese photographer fell back, unconscious before he hit the ground.

"All right, young fella, that's about enough of that."

Vince turned around to see a security guard approaching him. He was slightly overweight and well into his fifties. Vince's eyes immediately fell on the .38 caliber revolver pointed at his chest.

The guard had no nervousness in his voice. His hands did not shake.

Vince figured he was a retired police officer. He was a threat.

Slowly raising his hands, Vince let out a big sigh, shaking his head. When the guard moved closer, Vince's shoulders dropped and his body relaxed. As the guard moved within arm's reach, Vince lashed out and clasped both of his hands on the pistol. The guard squeezed off one round that went wild into the far wall. Twisting the guard's wrists toward him, the guard's grip loosened. Vince had the gun in less than two seconds. He leveled the pistol directly at the guard's chest.

"WHICH WAY DID HE GO?" Kathy asked Jason as she and Alonzo joined him in the main chapel of the Alamo.

"I'm not sure," he said, looking at the woman helping the old man to his feet. "He's been here. I heard a gunshot just before I came inside. I'll look out back. You two look in here." He did not wait for confirmation as he bolted out the exit that led into the courtyard.

"I guess we'll look in here," Kathy said to Alonzo.

"Let's try this door," he said, pointing to the one on the left.

"Sounds good to me."

BLAM!

They glanced at each other and ran to the doorway.

Reaching the entrance to the gift shop, Alonzo could see Vince standing over the man he'd just shot. Alonzo wasted no time in charging Vince from behind.

The OSI agent's large frame smacked solidly into the Russian assassin's back, and the two fell forward, smashing into the glass display case. Shards of glass and antique pistols fell from the case as the two men crashed to the floor.

Alonzo landed squarely on Vince's chest, knocking the wind out of him. Blood oozed from the small wounds caused by the broken bits of glass from the case.

Vince lost his grip on the pistol, which went flying across the room.

The tourists and employees bolted out the exits as fast as they could.

Kathy, moving unnoticed among the fleeing patrons, crossed the room and retrieved the guard's pistol from underneath another display case.

Grabbing an antique flintlock pistol, Vince whacked the large black man across the back of the head with the butt of the pistol. Alonzo fell to the floor, and Vince saw he was down but not dead.

Struggling to his feet, Vince moved to the side door. People rapidly moved out of his path. Once in the courtyard, Vince saw the gathering people staring at him. They had nowhere else to go. He stared at their faces as the rain pummeled them all. They were scared and angry. He decided this was not a good position to be in.

Heading back into the main chapel, Vince walked toward the front door that had brought him into this maze of violence. Entering the room, Vince saw that it was empty except for one man.

Jason Conrad.

The rage and hatred swelled within him as his fists clenched at his sides. Jason represented everything that had gone wrong in this operation and Vince Andrew/Oleg Stolovich wanted revenge.

"Enough of this," Vince said. "I am probably finished. But I tell you, old friend, you are about to die here and now."

Jason took a deep breath, his breathing labored. "You know, you . . . are starting . . . to sound like . . . a broken record."

"I'm going to kill you, Conrad."

Putting his hands on his hips, Jason grinned. "Look, asshole, you've tried to kill me—what? Five, six times now? In my country, that makes you a pretty bad killer." Jason's breathing came in large gasps. He was pissing off Vince, which was good. Vince never made good decisions when he was pissed. "If you ever make it back to Russia, do you think you'll even have a job? I mean, your performance report is gonna suck."

Vince charged Jason, who braced for impact. Knocking away his hands, Vince grabbed Jason by the jacket lapels and slung him into the wall. Jason hit hard, his head smacking against the edge of a picture frame. His legs buckled and his knees hit the concrete floor.

Vince walked to a glass display case containing a large knife. Smashing the case with his elbow, he retrieved the knife from the case and moved toward Jason.

Jason was in obvious pain. *This will be a quick kill,* Vince thought. But he'd make him suffer first.

Grasping Jason's hair with his free hand, Vince backhanded Jason in the face with the butt of the knife.

Jason's head jerked violently to one side and hung limp, blood dripping to the wet floor.

Vince slowly and methodically placed the knife against Jason's throat, picturing the best way to carve his victim.

BLAM!

Vince felt a stinging sensation in his right arm as the force knocked him forward. The knife dropped from his fingers as Vince fell to the floor.

Jason slumped over, battered but breathing.

Vince rolled around on the floor in agony. His left hand clasped the wound in his right arm. He rolled over to look at the shooter. "You," he mumbled. "You should be dead."

Kathy stared at Vince through the sights of the guard's revolver as she moved within ten feet of him, the barrel was pointed directly at his forehead.

"It's like Jason said—you're just not very good at killing lately."

Vince slowly rose and backed up until he was against the wall. He continued edging along the stone until he reached the doorway. Kathy followed him, making sure she kept a safe distance with each step. He was hurt, but he was a trained killer.

Backing out of the doorway, Vince re-entered the courtyard. The people outside moved away from him quickly. A woman screamed when Kathy walked outside pointing the gun at Vince.

Vince stood trapped. He was exhausted. His legs felt like jelly and his arm was numb.

The rain continued to fall. The blood dripping from his arm mixed with the water on the ground.

"Kathy," he pleaded, "I I love you . . ."

"Can it, you bastard!" Her jaw tightened as she adjusted her grip on the pistol.

"But Kathy, I need help. It's not what you think . . . I'm hurt real bad."

Kathy started to lower the gun. Could she be wrong? She struggled with her emotions for a moment.

"Kathy, I—" he stopped what he was about to say as their eyes met. His eyes were searching hers for some evidence of compassion, but all he saw was determination. He would not get away this time. He spied the gun in her hand, watching her thumb reach down and cock the hammer. He looked back at her and grinned. An evil grin.

"Dah sveedahnee yee," she said. Goodbye. Her eyes narrowed and her finger tightened as she pulled the trigger.

EPILOGUE

December 14, 1996

JASON GRINNED AFTER TAXIING his T-38 onto the taxiway. Life sure was full of surprises. It was a little over a year ago that he was struggling as a student pilot in the T-37. There were moments he didn't think he was going to make it through the program. Perhaps it was his unknown association with Lenny's test cheating scandal or Vince's dual identity as a Russian assassin that saved him in pilot training. Ironic how those two events propelled him into the national spotlight and helped him save his father's life.

Senator Jonathan Bowman dropped out of the presidential race shortly after the incident. He took the time to get to know his son, who he'd not seen nor heard from since he was an infant.

The Air Force, with encouragement from the CIA and the Senate Armed Services Committee, gave Jason a few months to recover from his adventure before returning to pilot training. This had been a blessing, and he returned with a vengeance. While his T-37 performance was average, Jason excelled in the T-38—it finally all clicked. His scores and daily performance led to him graduating in the number four slot in his new class, and he was happy to return as a T-38 Instructor Pilot.

Pulling into the hammerhead, Jason lowered his canopy. He thought about Kathy and what she meant to him. She saved his life at The Alamo. He was sure she was the one who pulled the trigger, killing Vince. Kathy disappeared that day. When the police went to Kathy's parent's house, it was empty except for the furniture. She disappeared along with her parents and the Joneses in Enid. At one point, he thought he loved her, but he realized a relationship was the last thing he needed right now. Right now, the only thing he loved was this jet.

Cleared for takeoff, Jason eased the T-38 out onto the runway, lined up on the centerline, and stepped on the brakes. He slowly pushed the throttles up and checked his engine instruments. Convinced they were good, he released his brakes and pushed the throttles over the hump into afterburner. The two J-85 jet engines felt like a kick in the pants as he accelerated down the runway. Jason hollered with joy as he rotated the jet and climbed away from earth. This truly was the most fun you could have with your clothes on.

THE ROOM WAS SULLEN AND DARK, but the man behind the desk was beaming from ear to ear. He looked around the room at the important people, lined around all four walls, who came for this special occasion. He stood up from behind the wooden desk and walked around to the front. A lone officer stood in front of the desk, barely breathing.

Nikolai Gregarin spoke, "My comrades, it is with great pleasure that we honor one of our greatest today. It has been over a year since the failed attempt on Senator Bowman, but the overall objective was a success. He dropped out of the race, a race that the incumbent went on to win. And that my friends, was the ultimate objective.

"It saddens my heart that during this operation we lost one of our own, Oleg Stolovich. But with every loss is a rebirth. And one of our best has returned to Mother Russia a hero. It is with great pleasure that I award the Order of Glory, First Class, for service to the Homeland in the Armed Forces of Russia, for exemplary service in the armed forces, both during a war although it be a cold one, and during peacetime, to Lieutenant Irena Vodianova."

Nikolai leaned forward and pinned the medal on the beautiful young officer's blouse pocket flap, paying no concern of touching her breast. He placed both hands on her shoulders and gazed in her eyes. "Welcome home, Irena. You've had a long, hard journey. It took almost this long to get you home, but I think you will find it was worth the wait. Kathy Delgato is dead . . . long live Captain Irena Vodianova!"

"Long live *Captain* Irena Vodianova!" the crowd roared.

"Thank you, Comrade Gregarin," said the woman who had once been known as Kathy Delgato. Nikolai noticed the soft but confident voice and the enticing fragrance of her perfume. It was a soft, rosy smell that had an edge to it, like her voice.

THE END

Follow Jason Conrad's

adventures in

VEIL OF DECEPTION

1

April 14, 2001

SHERRI DAVIS APPROACHED THE ENTRYWAY, already regretting her decision. After filling out paperwork and release forms for thirty minutes, she hid behind the filthy curtain covering the doorway, the knot in her belly growing tighter. She pulled a small section of the worn fabric to the side. Colored lights blinked rapidly, and several spotlights locked on the mirrored ball above the stage, creating hundreds of dancing reflections around the large room.

"It doesn't hurt, ya know," a voice said over the loud music.

Turning her head, Sherri spied a girl in her late teens standing next to her.

"You look nervous. It's your first time, isn't it?"

"Yes," Sherri said, releasing the curtain. In the dark hallway, Sherri could barely make out the girl's features, though her heavy eyelashes and straight black hair were clearly prominent. It was the young girl whose locker was next to hers.

"It's not like sex. Doesn't hurt the first time."

Sherri nodded. "Got any advice?"

"Have fun sweetie, that's my advice. Go out there and relax. You'll do fine."

"Relax. Right."

"Honey, once those assholes hand you a twenty to sit on their lap, you'll relax," the girl said. "Now get on out there and bring home the bacon," the girl said as she patted her on the rear. Sherri noticed the pat was a little too soft and lingered a little too long before the girl retreated toward the stage.

Sherri sighed heavily, her hands pressing the pleats of her skirt. She cupped her breasts for a quick adjustment and pulled her shoulders back. The transition from the dark hallway was dramatic. Mist spewed from the smoke machine, burning her eyes, and her ears pulsed as the deep bass vibrated through the speakers. Her steps were short and deliberate, as if she had a choice in these five-inch stiletto heels. She meandered between the tables, dodging a waitress carrying a tray full of beers.

The girl who spoke to her, nineteen at most, took the stage like a veteran and danced around the pole while a variety of clientele watched her every move. The music made her head hurt. Sherri scanned the crowd. Unable to see the two men she was looking for, she worried she might be wasting her time.

"Hey, baby," an overweight, bald drunk said as he reached out and tried to grab her arm.

"Not tonight, sweetie," Sherri replied, pulling away.

While she looked the part—plaid miniskirt and a white button-down tied in front of her push-up bra—she wasn't acting the part. She sensed her awkward movements through the bar. Relax.

Standing by the DJ booth, she tapped her foot to the music and rhythmically swayed her body. Sherri closed her eyes and started a slow, seductive dance. Her hips swayed like sea oats blowing in the ocean breeze. It didn't take long before she noticed the men nearby stared at her instead of the stage, waving twenty dollar bills at her. Feeling more confident, she moved around the bar again. She had to work fast. Her stage debut was in half an hour.

After a couple minutes meandering through the crowded bar and refusing three more requests for lap dances, she saw the first subject. He had come out of the men's room and returned to a table located away from the stage.

His name was Ahmed Alnami, a Saudi Arabian living in and moving around the United States. Now he was in Pensacola, sitting at a table with his partner, Saeed Alghamdi, who was getting a lap dance from one of the girls. Alnami sat at the table where he took a long swig of his beer and flashed his partner a smile. Weren't these two supposed to be devout Muslims? Why were they here?

Sherri approached the table. She leaned toward Alnami, her breasts at eye level, right in front of him. He stared in her eyes, looking fearful. Not the fear of danger. The innocent fear, like a teenage boy about to lose his virginity. "Hey, big boy," she said, "are you lonely?" Alnami continued to stare, clearly unsure what to do.

Sherri smiled and pointed at her eyes. "Honey, you need to change your focus from here, to here," she said as she moved her hands to her breasts. Alnami's face beamed.

"Yes, please to sit," he said in broken English. Sherri sat on his lap. Her breasts were at his eye level. No wonder he was smiling—a blond Amazon had landed in his lap. She reached over and ran her hand through his hair. It was oily and hadn't been washed for a while. Wiping her hand on the back of his shirt, she cringed, yet forced a weak smile. Alnami lunged his face forward and buried it in her breasts. Sherri pushed him back. She wanted to punch him, but that would undo all she'd accomplished.

"Settle down, big boy, we need to get to know each other first."

"This is what I want," he said, pointing at his partner, whose lap dancer was grinding aggressively into him.

"Oh, you'll get that and more," she replied. "We've got to do some talking first."

"What is this talking?" he said in a louder voice. He pulled out a roll of bills. The smile faded and his eyes bulged. "I want boobies. I want the grind-a-grind." The teenage innocence disappeared, and the self-absorbed arrogance of the immature adult surfaced. He started to push her off his lap. Sensing she was losing her opportunity, she grabbed his head and shoved his face back into her breasts.

"Better?" She pulled his face from her bosom, and the smile had returned.

"Yes please."

"Now, before I give you the grind-a-grind, we've got to get to know each other. What's your name?"

"Ahm—" He paused. "Keevin. My name is Keevin."

"Kevin? Okay, Kevin will work for now. My name is Bambi. What do you do, Kevin?"

"I do fine. Thank you, Bom-bi."

Sherri cringed. This was painful. "What's your job?"

"Oh, I train to be pilot."

Interesting. She shifted herself on his lap and ran the fingers of her left hand along the buttons of his shirt. "Are you out at the Navy base?"

He said nothing and his eyes remained focused on her breasts.

"How long are you in town?"

"Two more weeks."

Sherri thought for a moment. The two Saudis had already been in Pensacola for two weeks. Obviously, they weren't students, and they weren't flying with the Navy, but they were there to fly something.

"You must be really smart," she said. "Not everybody gets to fly airplanes."

"I am one of Allah's warriors," Alnami said, his voice rising. "Allahu Akbar."

Sherri studied Alnami. "What is Allah having you do?" She bit her lower lip, realizing she might have pushed the conversation too far, too fast.

His eyes moved from her breasts back to her eyes. His nostrils flared as he bared his yellowing teeth. "No more talk of this," Alnami shouted. "I want grind-a-grind from you." He pulled a fifty out of his pocket and waved it at her. Sherri sighed, realizing she would not get any more information unless she took it to the next level. That was not going to happen. She took the bill and stuck it in her bra.

She rose from his lap and posed in front of him, hands on her hips. He's done talking. It's time to get out of here. She slowly swayed back and forth, running her hands along the sides of her hips up to her breasts. The dancing must have been good, because she noticed his partner staring at her while still getting his lap dance.

Sherri leaned forward, nearly rubbing her breasts from his knees to his head, her body barely missing contact with his. She said in his ear, "How about you and me leave this place?"

Alnami's smile grew bigger. "Yes, please."

Pushing herself away from him, she moved behind his chair and ran hands down the front of his chest. "Okay, I've got to go clock out and change clothes. I'll be back here in fifteen minutes. Don't move."

"I not move. Don't change your clothes. You sexy momma."

Sherri forced a weak smile. "Okay, baby. Whatever you want."

She left the table and headed to the dressing room. Closing the door behind her, she shielded her eyes from the steady light. As her eyes adjusted, she went to her locker and gathered her things. Standing in front of the mirror, she pulled off the blond wig, and her deep red hair fell to her shoulders. Pulling out a brush, she touched it up from where the wig had pressed it down or tangled it. She slipped her tan overcoat over her shoulders and retrieved her clothes from her locker. A few of the other girls watched her.

"Sorry, ladies, I'm not cut out for this," she said. She turned and walked out the back door of the strip club.

The light by the back door was burned out. She clutched her purse tightly and gripped the can of mace in her coat pocket as she approached her rental car, a shiny new red Toyota Celica. She grabbed her keys and cell phone from her purse and climbed in. Kicking off the stiletto heels, she cranked the engine and pulled on to Highway 98, dialing on her cell phone as she drove.

The phone answered on the first ring. "Did you get it?"

"No, I didn't get that far. Alnami was getting a little too friendly."

"I told you this might happen. Did you find out anything?"

"They're here two more weeks, and they'll be flying next week, but I don't know what and I don't know why. Sorry, it's the best I was willing to do under the circumstances."

"Okay," the voice replied. "Get back here tomorrow. I've got something else for you."

"Like what?"

"Our informant in New York wants to meet with you ASAP."

"All right," Sherri said begrudgingly. "I'll see you tomorrow." As she hung up the phone, the car lurched forward. The phone slipped from her fingers, falling to the floorboard as her body slammed into her seat belt. She glanced in the rearview mirror as a car slid back and accelerated toward her again.

"What the hell?"

She put both hands on the wheel and her foot pressed the accelerator as the car made contact with the red Celica a second time. As she reached the Pensacola Bay Bridge, the vehicle tried to spin her car by striking the left rear fender. She accelerated again, making the assailant miss his mark.

The mystery car pulled behind her, two car lengths back. Every time she passed a vehicle, the car followed her.

Who the hell was attacking her? Could it be Alnami? No, she hadn't been gone long enough. He would still be waiting for her inside the strip club, probably constructing ridiculous fantasies in his head.

It was a dark, starless night, and the rise in the bridge was a half mile away. This hump in the bridge allowed larger boats to enter and exit Pensacola Bay from the Gulf. Once on the other side, she would be in civilization again.

Vinyl and glass shards flew everywhere inside the vehicle as bullets pierced the back window of her car and hit the passenger side of the dashboard. She screamed and let go of the steering wheel, her foot coming off the gas for an instant.

Her eyes darted back and forth as her car veered toward the rail to her right. Grabbing the steering wheel, she pressed the accelerator once again as she jerked her car away from the side rail.

"Oh, God," she said, "why the hell are they shooting at me?"

She swerved to put another car between them, then pushed the accelerator to the floor. The innocent car she just passed bumped into the guardrail, sending sparks flying. It spun around as the assailant hit the car from the rear, then continued on. The dark sedan accelerated and closed the distance between them.

Another burst of machine-gun fire. Sherri screamed as the bullets struck the rear of her vehicle. At the bottom of the hump, she checked her rearview mirror. Shattered glass and bullet holes in the rear window were all she could see. Based on the lights in the distance, she estimated she'd reach the end of the bridge in less than a minute.

With a quarter mile until the end of the bridge, the car shuddered. Sherri's gaze shifted to the front of her car, and her shoulders slumped. She beat her fist against the steering wheel as smoke rose from under the hood and the car started decelerating.

The speedometer read 80 mph at this point, but the car no longer responded to her foot pressing the accelerator. She pushed it all the way to the floor, but nothing. In her side mirror, she noticed the assailant closing in behind her. The car had closed within three car lengths when another round of bullets hit her vehicle.

Her heart pounded as she reached the end of the bridge and the Celica slowed through 55 mph.

"Shit . . . If I break down on this bridge, I'm done," she said as she pumped the accelerator. "Who the hell are these guys?"

The Celica slowed to 25 mph now, and other cars quickly caught and passed her.

Glancing in the mirror, she saw the dark-colored sedan make a U-turn at the end of the bridge and head toward Pensacola.

In front of her, red-and-blue lights danced on top of a parked car. Sherri had driven into a speed trap. Her assailants turned and ran.

"Yeah," she said. "Take that, asshole. You'd better run."

A faint nervous smile eased across her face as she glided the unpowered vehicle into the right lane and onto the side of the road. The car came to a stop, and as soon as she put it in park, her body began to shake as the adrenaline faded. Leaning forward on the steering wheel, she began to sob. She had almost been killed. A myriad of thoughts raced through her head as the police car pulled in behind her. The officer tapped on the window with his flashlight. She lowered the window and covered her eyes as he pointed the light in her face.

"Driver's license and registration," he said.

"No problem." She dug in her purse for her driver's license. When she reached into the glove box for the rental agreement, she glanced in the passenger's side mirror and saw the dark outline of the officer's partner approaching the other side of her vehicle. Why didn't he say something about the smoke coming from under the hood? Or the blown-out back window?

She stopped digging and glanced back at the officer who spoke to her. Is he wearing jeans? With a quick glance back to the passenger-side mirror, she saw his partner approaching the vehicle was wearing—shorts? Wait, how could this guy not have noticed the bullet holes?

"Hey, what agency are you guys with?" she said as she turned back to the cop. Before she could react, he jammed a long stick through the window and pressed it into her neck. The electric shock was fast and intense, then—blackness.

2

April 15, 2001

A SMALL SLIVER of glistening sunlight cut through the dark hotel room, illuminating its small interior. Dust particles danced through the piercing beam like fireflies on a clear summer night. The light pried into his consciousness while the grinding gears of a construction vehicle outside ripped it open.

Jason Conrad buried his face in a pillow and moaned as his head felt ready to explode. He recognized this place, barely. The hangover reminded him that his recent lifestyle choices had their consequences.

It didn't take long for his body to tell him he needed to relieve himself. He swung his feet off the bed and glanced next to him, rubbing the sides of his throbbing temples with his fingertips. The blonde lay nude on top of the sheets. She had every appearance of being attractive from here. He struggled to remember her face. He definitely could not remember her name.

Jason tiptoed to the bathroom, as much to protect his pounding head as not to wake the blonde. After relieving himself, he washed his hands and face and brushed his teeth. When he left the bathroom, she was sitting up in the bed, watching him. *She is pretty. Now, what is her name again?*

"Good morning, sexy," she said. She sounded much more awake than he did.

"Hi," Jason said. She was too bubbly for early morning.

"I can't believe you're up," she said in a strong Texas drawl.

"Yeah."

"Am I still beautiful?"

Jason grinned. "Absolutely."

"You're quiet this morning. You wouldn't stop talking last night."

Vague memories of the night before pushed themselves into his consciousness. He crawled back into the bed, and she leaned over and kissed him.

"Oh, you brushed your teeth. I'll be right back," she said, climbing out of bed.

Jason studied her figure. She had all the right equipment. He could see why he would have been talkative. Now he wished he didn't drink as much. This was a night he would have liked to remember.

Yesterday started off well. As flight lead of a four-ship of T-38s, they'd done a flyover for a Texas Rangers game. It was a great TDY, or temporary duty, to Dallas, with per diem. The flyover during the national anthem at the Ballpark in Arlington was uneventful, and they landed at Naval Air Station Fort Worth, formerly known Carswell Air Force Base, right afterward.

A limousine provided by one of the Rangers' owners, picked them up outside Base Operations. It contained a cooler full of beer and a tray of cheese and crackers to tide them over until they arrived at the stadium in Arlington.

It was a tight fit with eight sweaty, cocky T-38 instructors, but they didn't care. They were amazed at the red carpet treatment and relished every minute of it. The pilots were treated like rock stars in the owners' VIP suite, with all the food and alcohol they wanted. After the game, the limo drove them to the West End in Dallas. Jason and his buddies found themselves in Gators, a piano bar/restaurant with dueling white grand pianos and a rowdy crowd. He remembered meeting her at Gators. *What is her name?*

Jason rolled over on his back and stared at the ceiling. The nameless faces of his women over the years skipped through his thoughts. He felt empty. Like every other one-night stand, *she* crept back into his head. What happened to the one who'd slipped away six years ago?

Whatever happened to Kathy Delgato?

The door to the bathroom opened, and the blonde traipsed back into the room. She took the time to brush her hair and put on lipstick. Posing at the end of the bed, she riveted her eyes at him wantonly.

"Oh, good, you're still awake." She traipsed around the bed to the window and opened the curtain, standing nude in front of the window.

"I can't help it," she said with a wry smile. "I'm an exhibitionist."

"Clearly."

"What time do you fly back?" She posed seductively in front of the window.

Jason glanced at the clock. Red digital numbers displayed eight thirty-three. The pilots planned to leave the hotel at noon. "I need to be at the base at eleven," he lied.

"Oh," she said, sauntering toward him.

"Do I..." He paused. "Do I need to get you a ride home?" He couldn't remember how they made it back to the hotel.

"No silly. I drove us, remember?"

No, and I can't remember your name either, so please don't ask.

"Well," he said, glancing at the clock, "we have some time."

The blonde smiled and crawled back onto the bed. He stopped hating himself as she wrapped her arms around him. Even drunk, he had done very well.

SHERRI SHIVERED from the cool breeze as she lay on her back. Fading in and out of consciousness, she tossed her head from side to side. Various colors edged their way into her brain. She writhed in place, and the ground shifted slightly. Her muscles ached, but the sun on her face was irritating. When she tried to open her eyes, her hand shielded them from the brightness. The smell of saltwater filled her nostrils as waves crashed onto the shore.

She was at the beach.

The sun glared as she struggled again to open her eyes. The sky was a bright blue, and seagulls called out to her as they bobbed and weaved ten feet overhead, floating rather than flying.

Her body ached. Rolling her head to the right, she saw nothing but white sand and sea oats. To the left was more of the same, but with a stinging sensation as she turned her head. Sherri managed to roll to her left side and prop herself up on her elbow. Her joints were stiff and her skin covered with goose bumps. Her head hurt as she tried to figure out how she ended up here, wherever here turned out to be.

Shifting her weight, she managed to sit up on her knees and check herself out. Nothing was broken, and she didn't notice any injuries other than the neck pain, stiff joints, and sore muscles. She still wore the schoolgirl outfit from the night before. Checking her bra and panties, she found everything in place and Alnami's fifty-dollar bill still tucked in her bra.

What the hell happened? Someone chased her on the bridge and shot up her car, but she managed to escape. The cop. He did something to her. When she touched the left side of her neck, the pain shot through her body again. The cop shocked her with something. Only he wasn't a cop.

They had to be working together. She was an easy target and nobody is that bad of a shot to miss her for that long. Whoever it was, they were sending a message. The thoughts hurt her head as she shielded her eyes from the sun, which was inching its way above the horizon.

Sherri rose to her feet. She had no shoes. Rolling off the white stockings, she tossed them in the sand and untied her white shirt to cover her belly. She buttoned her shirt and felt a little more comfortable. She slowly brushed the sand off her thighs, waist, and arms. Placing her hands in her deep red hair, she desperately tried to shake out the sand. It would take days, she determined, if not weeks, to get all of the sand out. She searched her immediate area: no purse, no phone, and no car keys.

When she started on this story, Sherri never thought she would experience something like this. She always enjoyed the sense of accomplishment from hard work. As an investigative reporter, she put herself in many compromising situations, but this had been the worst. Being shot at wasn't something new, but being shot at with automatic weapons was a twist. Even in Sarajevo, she hadn't faced such firepower. There she'd been dodging sniper fire.

Sherri's head ached; she was dehydrated. She scanned the beach. The closest people were an elderly couple using metal detectors a hundred yards to the east. To the west, more people in the distance, the silhouettes of condos and hotels, and the familiar water tower of Pensacola Beach. It was about three miles away. Leaving the solitude of the sea oats and sand dunes of this isolated portion of the beach, she trudged toward the water, then west, toward civilization.

3

April 15, 2001

JASON DRESSED IN JEANS and a T-shirt, then slid on his flight boots. Stirring a cup of coffee, he sat in the recliner, smiling, watching the striking blonde get dressed. It didn't take her long. She wore a blue jean miniskirt and a white lace bra. When she saw him examining her, she smiled. He could not, for the life of him, remember her name.

"Why are you looking at me like that?" she said, brushing her hair.

"How old are you?"

"You're not supposed to ask a girl that question."

"Oh, no, don't get me wrong. You don't look old. I just want to make sure I didn't spend the night with a teenager," Jason said. "Let me see your driver's license." It was a tactic he'd used before, a quick way to find out a name.

"I left it in my car. I didn't want you to rob me when I finished having my way with you," she said, putting the brush back in her purse.

"Oh," was all Jason could say.

She stopped in the bathroom doorway, half-dressed, frowning at him. Her head tilted to the side. Jason knew he was in trouble.

"What's my name?"

Damn.

Jason squinted at her inquisitively. It was the best he could do in his present physical condition.

"What kind of question is that?" he said, shrugging his shoulders.

"A legitimate one. What's my name?" Her Texas accent was more prominent now. She said she was born and raised in Garland. That one detail didn't bring back her name.

"What do you mean, what's your name? Of course I remember your name. I can't believe you'd ask me that question."

"Okay, then, what is it?"

"Well, what's my name?" Deflecting was the only strategy he could come up with at the moment.

"Oliver."

Jason grinned. "Oliver what?"

"Klosi—something. Hell, I don't know," she said, her voice getting louder. "I couldn't pronounce it. You said last night it was Russian."

Jason chuckled. He'd forgotten they were wearing their "Friday morale" nametags. His bore the name "Oliver Klosov" which, after a few beers, translated to "All of her clothes off." He was pleased he'd managed to stick with his story while drinking so much.

"Well, see, you don't remember my name," Jason said.

"Bullshit. Oliver, what's my name?"

He could see her body tense. Jason had every intention of being apologetic. There was no way out of this one.

"I'm sorry. Candy?"

"Candy?"

"Cindy?"

"Are you kidding me?" she screamed. "You son of a bitch. You had sex with me all last night *and* this morning, and you don't know my name?" She grabbed his shave kit from the bathroom and threw it at him. He caught the bag, but the contents fell on the floor. She started throwing everything she could at him. He was able to dodge it all, or deflect it.

"Look, I'm sorry. I had a lot to drink. You *know* that. You brought me home."

She started crying as she buttoned her shirt. "Why do I always find the assholes? I thought you were nice. You talked to me nice, you treated me nice. You said I was beautiful—"

"You *are* beautiful. And I'm nice. I'm sorry—"

"You're not nice or sorry—you're an asshole."

"I'm not an asshole," he said. "I'm a jet pilot." It was a stupid one-liner from an old joke, but hey, he was hung over.

She grabbed her sandals and headed for the door.

Jason jumped up to follow her. He hadn't meant to hurt her feelings, but it was a little too late.

She marched to the elevator, rode down to the lobby, and headed out the front door. Jason followed her all the way, trying to apologize, but she ignored him. When they reached the parking lot, she stopped. Two guys were leaning on her BMW.

"Carly, what the hell are you doing at this hotel?" the shorter one said, stepping away from her car. "And who's this asshole?"

Carly, that's it. He chose to disregard the asshole comment under the circumstances.

"Why the hell are you followin' me, Billy Ray?" she yelled. Jason watched her disposition change once again as the crying stopped immediately. Jason had pissed her off, but this guy? He lit her fuse.

"You're my girl, Carly," Billy Ray said, as he started to bow up to Jason. He was shorter, but stockier. Not muscular, but a lot of attitude. The sidekick, however, might be someone to worry about. He stood a rather wiry six-four.

"Billy Ray," she said, "we broke up three weeks ago. You've got to quit followin' me." Jason noticed her accent came out naturally when she fought with this Billy Ray.

"But Carly, you're my girl."

"I ain't your girl, Billy Ray. You can't tell me who I can have sex with and who I can't."

Oh shit, here we go.

Billy Ray's eyes grew wide, and his nostrils flared like a bull in the ring. Jason turned to leave. He knew where this was going, and the outcome wouldn't be good.

"Where're you going, asshole? I ain't through with you yet," Billy Ray said. The tall guy moved around in front of him, blocking his path. Jason turned ninety degrees to the right and backed up two steps, positioning the two in front of him.

"Look, fellas, I don't want any trouble. I was just walking Carly to her car," he said, glancing at Carly.

"Oh, great," she yelled. "*Now* you wanna act like you remember my name."

Damn.

Billy Ray glared at her before slowly turning his head back to Jason, his eyes wild and his face contorted. "You screwed my girl, and you didn't even know her name?"

"Look, fellas—"

"And he's a helluva better lay than you, Billy Ray," she yelled. Jason knew she was trying to piss off her ex-boyfriend to get him to start a fight.

It worked.

Billy Ray lunged at Jason and threw a wide roundhouse at his head. Jason deflected it, using Billy Ray's momentum to push him against the car next to him. He immediately turned to focus on the tall guy.

The giant was slow and tried to grab Jason in a bear hug from the front. Mistake. Jason hit him with the heel of his flat palm just below the sternum, and he stumbled backward. Billy Ray turned and charged again. Jason grabbed his wrist and pushed it toward his forearm, and Billy Ray yelped with pain. Jason pushed him on the ground, but now the tall guy grabbed him from behind, lifting him off the ground. His arms were pinned against his body. Billy Ray leaped from the ground and swung wildly to punch him in the stomach. It was a sloppy punch, but he was a captive target. The tall guy grew tired of holding him up and lowered him to the ground.

As Jason's feet touched, Billy Ray moved in closer. Jason lifted his feet off the ground and started to slide out of the tall guy's grasp until he squeezed him again. It was enough, though. Jason kicked his left leg out, slamming his foot into the inside of Billy Ray's right knee. Billy Ray screamed in pain and fell to the ground. The tall guy squeezed him harder and Jason brought both feet underneath him.

Lifting his right leg, he scraped the side of his boot against the tall guy's right shin and slammed his heel into the top of the tall guy's foot. The tall guy yelped and released him. Jason spun around and delivered several quick blows to the tall guy's stomach and a quick right cross to his chin, and the tall guy fell to the ground.

He turned to deliver a quick blow to Billy Ray's left eye as he tried to stand. Billy Ray went back to the asphalt, unconscious.

Jason gasped for breath. Sweat dripped from his forehead, and his heart pounded against his chest. He felt like he was going to vomit. Instinctively, he scanned the area for other threats. Seeing none, he glanced back at the cowboys lying on the asphalt and bent over at the waist, his hands on his knees.

"Oliver," he heard Carly say.

Dammit. He needed to stop pursuing women easily impressed by a flight suit. He glanced at Carly for the first time since the altercation began. She gazed at him like a high-school crush as she stepped over and placed a piece of paper in his T-shirt pocket.

"Call me," she said, kissing him on the cheek.

Jason stared at her and grimaced. He knew it was time to get out of there. Cursing himself, he marched back into the hotel.

4

April 18, 2001

THE T-38 BARRELED THROUGH THE SKY, five hundred feet off the ground at three hundred knots, the morning sun glistening off its canopy. Daylight had pushed its way above the horizon well over two hours ago, making the sky over western Oklahoma clear for miles, though the temperatures still reflected the cold front that had pushed through the Midwest. The jet experienced occasional light turbulence as the morning sun heated the ground, and the two occupants bounced in their seats.

Jason sat in the back seat of the Northrop T-38 Talon. The T-38 had been designed as a trainer for the 1960s Century Series fighters. The T-38 was such a successful design that it had remained the US Air Force's advanced supersonic jet trainer ever since.

The tandem-seat aircraft was sexy. It had the appearance and flight characteristics of a fighter jet, and while the T-38 was a great jet, it had its flaws. The biggest challenge students faced was landing the jet. The small wings required a faster takeoff and landing speed, and that detail often undid many students. They simply could not adapt to the speed needed to think and work in the T-38.

Jason had been an instructor pilot in the aircraft for the last four years. He was what the Air Force called a FAIP (fape), a first assignment instructor pilot. After graduating from pilot training, he went directly to instructor school to return to Vance AFB as an IP.

Teaching someone to fly a supersonic jet was the best way to make a living, period. It was a job he relished, but being required to do it in Enid, Oklahoma, as a bachelor, was a difficult task. He spent as much time out of town as he could, flying student or instructor cross-country sorties. Unfortunately, these trips sometimes ended up like his Dallas trip a few days ago—one-night stands he couldn't undo.

His mind wandered as he considered what his commander asked him over a month ago. "You'll be up for an assignment soon. What do you want to do with your career?" Jason was aware the Air Force was ready for him to move. He needed direction in his life. He'd shown up as a student with no desire to meet a woman, and then *she* stumbled into his life. As quickly as she fell into his life, she fell out of it. Jason had kept Kathy out of his thoughts for most of his time at Vance. But today, for some reason, the vision of her pushed in like a fullback on the one-yard line. Perhaps it was the incident with Carly. Perhaps it was loneliness creeping up on him.

"Okay, sir. I'm coming up on the next turn point in thirty seconds, according to my timing. Fuel checks, altitude, and time are good. Next heading is three-two-zero for three minutes and fifteen seconds. Sir, working big to small, I see the two rivers I want to turn between. Now I'm looking for a farmhouse to the south and the grain silo about a mile north. There's the silo. Confirm?"

"Check, that's the silo," Jason responded to his student in the front seat, snapping out of his daydream. Jason did not need to reference his chart for the turn points. He'd flown this route a hundred times over the years. He'd memorized all the turn points, which was good since it gave him the opportunity to keep his eyes outside the aircraft. Jason cross-checked the stopwatch strapped to his knee board to the time calculated on the chart and nodded silently in the back. His student's times were good.

"There's the farmhouse. Turn point is in twenty seconds. The cows are starting to run away from us."

"Check, Stanley, but those aren't cows, they're horses. The cows don't move—they're used to us. The horses don't like the noise or the speed." Jason glanced at his instrument panel to cross-check his fuel and the Heading Situation Indicator (HSI). Stanley wasn't actually the student's name. It was a generic name all instructors used to identify students: Stanley Student. Jason wasn't sure how it evolved, but it was time-tested and applied to all students, including females.

"Stand by turn," the student said. "Turning in three, two, one, turn now . . . new heading is three-two-zero for three minutes and fifteen seconds." The student rolled the sleek jet into a sixty-degree bank turn and pulled the aircraft to three-and-a-half G's. Their g-suits quickly inflated with air, putting immediate pressure on their legs and abdomens, preventing blood from pooling in their lower extremities. The jet started to lose altitude as the nose tracked below the horizon.

"Climb," Jason said. The command coincided with the student reaching the required heading, rolling out, and raising the nose of the jet. The student rolled the T-38 wings level, and the g-suits deflated. "Remember, just like in the traffic pattern, when you bank this aircraft, you've got to move more than the ailerons. You've got to add a little power and change the pitch."

"Roger," the student replied.

They continued on course for several minutes. Jason kept his own cross-check going, clock to map to ground, bringing his instruments into cross-check periodically. They bounced around more violently as the turbulence increased. He could tell the student had not strapped in well by the way his helmet bounced around.

"Stanley, do you remember in the brief when we talked about low-level turbulence?"

"Uh . . . yeah. Would you mind taking the jet for a moment?"

"I have the aircraft," Jason said, taking control of the jet.

"Roger, you have the aircraft."

Three seconds later the student chimed in, "Okay, sir, I'm back. I have the aircraft," the student said, shaking the stick.

"Roger, you have the aircraft."

"Ten seconds to the next turn point, but I'm not sure where it's at."

"What are you looking for?"

"Uh, it's supposed to be a windmill."

"Do you see it? It's one of the old western-style ones like you see in the movies—not like those wind-power windmills." Jason cross-checked his timing with his chart. His eyes darted from his chart to his instruments, particularly his altimeter, and back to his chart.

"Uhm . . . which one?"

He glimpsed over the shoulder of the student. Five windmills on the right and two on the left. "Huh, that's different," he said. "I guess they put those up recently. There was only one here the last time I flew this route. Turn on time. Turn now."

The student banked the T-38 in a nice, level turn and rolled out on his heading. The jet leveled off, and the student went back to work with his timing and navigation. The two flew in silence for the next four minutes, enjoying the ride. Jason wanted to see how the student would fly with no instruction, and the kid was doing well.

"Fifteen seconds to the next turn point," the student said. "I'm looking for the T-intersection going from north to south. No visual yet, so we'll be turning on timing."

"Checks."

"Three, two, one, turning. Heading one-one-five. There's the turn point to the east. We're a quarter mile off course, sir."

The turn was thirty degrees to the left. Jason cleared in front of the jet for the turn, as he knew from experience that most students glued their head inside the aircraft to the Attitude Direction Indicator (ADI) and the altimeter. Quickly, Jason checked where the student was looking, and his suspicion was correct. Jason was about to speak up when he noticed a black flash in front of the jet.

Uh-oh. Birds. Jason felt the impacts on the side of the jet. He didn't wait for the student in the front seat to react. "I HAVE THE AIRCRAFT!" He grabbed the stick and rolled the aircraft's wings level. He immediately raised the nose of the jet to climb away from the ground. "You okay up there?"

"Yeah, that spooked me," the student said.

"Attention all aircraft, Colt Seven-Two is departing IR-145 at turn point three. Passing through three thousand three hundred," Jason broadcast on the common radio frequency for the low-level route. They were too low and too far away from Vance AFB's approach control to make radio contact with them.

The aircraft shuddered as both J-85 axial flow engines flamed out. Cross-checking his engine instruments, the tachometers, EGTs, and fuel flow indicators were all rolling back, confirming his dual engine failure. The Master Caution light came on immediately. Glancing at the Caution Light panel, he saw the left Fuel Pressure light illuminate instantly, followed by the right Fuel Pressure light. He cross-checked his airspeed, now decreasing through 250 knots indicated airspeed (KIAS). He raised the nose twenty degrees while simultaneously moving both throttles over the hump.

The "Boldface" emergency action procedure for emergency air start is THROTTLE/THROTTLES - MAX. Both throttles slammed into the afterburner range—nothing. He moved the throttles back and over the hump once again.

Still no ignition.

The Left and Right Generator lights illuminated on the Caution Light panel, followed by the Utility and Flight Hydraulics.

"Mayday, Mayday, Mayday . . . Colt Seven-Two on IR-145. Dual engine failure at turn point three." The jet passed through 6,000 feet at one hundred eighty knots. "Okay, Stanley, I'll try to start these one more time, otherwise we'll have to take the silk elevator to the ground." There was no response from the student. "You still with me up there?"

"Yes, sir. Please start it."

Jason moved the throttles into the afterburner range for the third time with the same result.

"Mayday, Mayday, Mayday . . . Colt Seven-Two, T-38, two souls on board, seventy miles southwest of Vance. Engine failure times two. Crew is ejecting at 7,000 feet."

Jason checked his airspeed indicator one last time. "Okay, Stanley, airspeed's passing through one hundred twenty knots. BAILOUT, BAILOUT, BAILOUT!"

The student left the jet after the first command to leave the aircraft. The eerie silence shattered by the deafening wind blast as the front canopy left the jet. Jason reached for his handgrips and braced his body for the ejection. Placing his knees together, he pulled his feet back, pushed his back straight against his seat, pulled his elbows in, and held his chin down toward his chest. When he pulled the handgrips up, the aft canopy blew off the top of the jet. Everything not welded to the jet left the interior space of the cockpit: checklists, charts, and knee boards all sucked out by the wind.

Less than a second after the canopy left the aircraft, the rocket in his seat exploded and he felt a slight pinch in his neck. The wind blast ripped at his head and body as his seat shot up the rails and pushed him out into the cold blue sky.

We hope you enjoyed this preview of

VEIL OF DECEPTION

From SATCOM Publishing!

About the Author

Award-Winning author Michael Byars Lewis, is a former AC-130U Spooky Gunship Evaluator Pilot with 18 years in Air Force Special Operations Command. A 25-year Air Force pilot, he has flown special operations combat missions in Bosnia, Iraq, and Afghanistan. He served as an Expeditionary Squadron Commander for AC-130U combat operations in Iraq and spent his final assignment on active duty instructing and mentoring the next generation of gunship pilots at the Air Force Special Operations Air Warfare Center's schoolhouse for flight instruction, the 19th Special Operations Squadron. Michael is currently a pilot for a major U.S. airline.

Active in his community, Michael has mentored college students on leadership development and team-building and is a facilitator for an international leadership training program. He has teamed with the Air Commando Foundation which supports Air Commando's and their families unmet needs during critical times.

While his adventures have led to travels all around the world, Michael lives in Florida with his wife Kim and their two children, Lydia and Derek.

Follow Michael Byars Lewis:

www.facebook.com/mblauthor
www.michaelbyarslewis.com
Twitter @mblauthor

Contact Michael Byars Lewis:

michael@michaelbyarslewis.com

Also from SATCOM Publishing

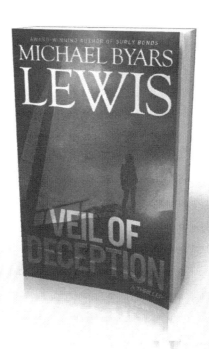

Available online in paperback and ebook from these fine retailers!

39033757R00246

Made in the USA
San Bernardino, CA
18 September 2016